10 Things
I Hate About
Mistletoe

10 Things
I Hate About
Mistletoe

Codi Hall

Podium

To all the fans who begged for more Mistletoe. I gotchu!

Cover design by Wendi Chen

Mistletoe image designed by Freepik (www.freepik.com)

ISBN: 978-1-0394-7819-0

Published in 2024 by Podium Publishing
www.podiumaudio.com

Podium

10 Things
I Hate About
Mistletoe

Chapter One

Delilah Gill took the last turn into Evergreen Circle like she was rounding the final lap on a NASCAR track, and her Subaru fishtailed briefly before she could straighten it back out. She parallel parked in front of her best friend's house, shoving the gearshift into park harder than necessary, frustration pulsating through her body like a detonated bomb ready to explode. Delilah took a deep, trembling breath as she surveyed the quiet neighborhood. In a week, it would be lit with Christmas lights and displays, with lines of cars and people coming from around the state to see the jolly sight. She loved this small town but could definitely do without the traffic.

All part of Mistletoe's charm.

On this chilly November morning, no creature was stirring as Delilah exited her car and marched carefully up the driveway to the walkway, avoiding any patches glistening with ice. Holly must not be up yet since she hadn't salted her sidewalks, and Delilah wasn't looking to add a slip and fall to her day. That would be the frosting on her already sad cake. Idaho was predicted to have a wet, cold winter this year, and Delilah was not ready for the severe windchills. She pulled her purple scarf over the lower half of her face when it started to tingle like a thousand tiny needles simultaneously pricking her skin.

When she reached Holly's red front door, she didn't knock. Holly's boyfriend, Declan, was out of town until the next day, so Delilah had been having coffee with Holly all week, and today, she desperately needed it. Delilah used her leopard-spotted key on the door, pushing in the heavy wood plank with a creak. The house was quiet except for the tinkling of a bell as Declan's cat, Leo, came trotting down the hallway to greet her. The orange cat's big belly swayed back and forth as he moved; his sweet, chirping meow making her smile.

"Good morning, Leo." She dropped down on her haunches to pet the fur ball behind his ears.

"Should we get some coffee?" she said, standing back up and brushing the rogue cat hair from her leggings.

"Delilah!" Holly hollered from down the hall.

"Yeah, sorry," she said, making her way toward the kitchen, "I know it's early, but I need to—Yip!" Delilah yelped when she spotted her best friend on the counter, a kitchen towel clutched against her chest. Her legs were crossed, shielding Delilah's gaze from her other naked parts, and Delilah slapped her hands over her mouth in horror. "Why is your bare ass perched on the counter?" she yelled.

Delilah spotted the top of Declan Gallagher's dark head peeking around the island before he responded, "Because we were in the middle of something."

"Sorry!" Delilah turned her back on the scene, déjà vu washing over her as this wasn't the first time she'd walked in on her best friend and Declan in a compromising position. "I thought you were out of town!"

"I forgot to text you; he got back this morning. It was a bit . . . spontaneous."

Delilah could hear the laughter in Holly's voice and groaned. "I am trying to be mature about this, bestie. Walking in on Declan cooking sans clothes in your kitchen is one thing, but interrupting your naked Olympics is another story! This is almost as bad as the time I played third wheel to you and Jake Masters at homecoming when he tried to feel you up and grabbed my breast instead."

"Delilah?" Declan said.

"Yes?"

"Do you think the two of you could rehash this later when Holly and I aren't so nude?"

Delilah smothered a giggle and stepped toward the hallway. While she loved teasing Holly's boyfriend, even she could take a hint.

"Alright, I will drag myself out of here and let the two of you continue your escapades. Holly, can you call me later? I need to talk."

"Yes, I'll call you in ten—" she let out a squeal, and Delilah tried not to imagine what Declan had done to emit such a sound from her, before Holly amended, "I mean, later."

Delilah practically jumped over Leo to get out the front door before she heard something she couldn't unhear. The cold blasted against her face, instantly numbing her nose. She carefully made her way down the sidewalk and driveway to her car, her gloominess returning without the prospect of coffee and a chat with Holly. She'd have to settle for a mocha from Kiss My Donut as a consolation.

Today is just not my day.

"Hi, Ms. Gill!"

Delilah looked up when she heard her name, recognizing J. J. Cox walking past the entrance to Evergreen Circle. The seventh grader was bundled up in a blue puffer jacket and gray beanie, strands of blond hair poking out from beneath his hat.

"What are you doing up so early? It's Saturday!"

"Heading to Chris's to play Fortnite."

"No cap?" she teased, earning a groan from the kid.

"You're so cringe."

She loved being a substitute teacher at the middle school. High schoolers were too ready for adulthood, and while elementary school kids were adorable, it was like herding cats most days. Seventh and eighth graders were the sweet spot, although the pay in Idaho was insanely low in education. At least what she earned from subbing paid her rent.

"Have a great Thanksgiving break. Don't forget to finish your poem for Mrs. Paulsen's class!"

JJ shot her a sheepish grin, spinning around so he was walking backward. "I'll get it done, Ms. Gill. I swear."

"Uh-huh." Delilah opened her car door, giving him a little wave. "Be good."

"See ya." He turned back around and took off, disappearing out of sight.

Delilah climbed into her car and took a deep breath, her troubles still weighing on her mind. The polite rejection letter from Skylark Publishing yesterday was branded into her brain, bringing the total to four publishers who wanted nothing to do with her paranormal romance series. Her agent had taken her books out on submission before Halloween, but there were no takers.

She started the car and pulled onto the road, taking a left at the stop sign into downtown Mistletoe. Delilah wanted to hold out hope that the last publisher they subbed to would come back with an offer, but if there hadn't been a blip of interest from the others, why would this one be any different?

Although substitute teaching and submitting freelance articles paid her bills, Delilah had wanted to write epic world-building romances with dark, brooding heroes and strong, independent heroines since middle school. She'd finished her first series at nineteen but tucked those manuscripts away on a thumb drive. She'd written six more books after that, but it wasn't until she'd finished this last series that she'd drummed up the nerve to query several agents and had two interested in her. She'd gone with Beth because she was young and hungry, just like Delilah. When Delilah had asked her agent about her previous manuscripts, she'd said they didn't have a strong enough hook.

Her stomach twisted into knots, realizing that this could be her first and only chance to achieve her dream, and it wasn't looking good.

She pulled into the parking lot off the side road next to Kiss My Donut, grumbling internally about all the cars taking up the prime parking spots. Delilah whipped the Subaru into the first space she found, wrinkling her nose when she realized she'd taken the slot in front of Adventures in Mistletoe. The store was still dark, which eased some of her anxiety, because that meant the owners weren't in yet. Although bumping into Pike Sutton, with his cute dimples and sparkling blue eyes, wouldn't be the end of the world, sharing the same space with his business partner would be the cherry on top of today's crap sundae.

Pike had been the subject of her fantasies since she was a moody twelve-year-old wearing too much eyeliner. Back in the day, when others would tease him for his red hair or short stature, he took the flaws others saw and owned them, embracing his uniqueness like she had with hers. They were kindred spirits. There was four years between them, which wasn't a lot as adults, but between middle school and high school, Pike had never looked at her as anything more than his friend's little sister's best friend.

Delilah laughed out loud. What a complicated way of putting it.

Maybe if they'd been thrown together at some point in their adult lives and he'd gotten to know her one-on-one, he might have seen her differently. Unfortunately, it wasn't Pike's name she'd pulled last year during their friends' combined bachelor/bachelorette weekend. Instead, she'd been paired with Anthony, who was everything she'd learned to despise. A gorgeous jock who looked through women like her, or worse, mocked them for their flaws. At least, that was what she'd assumed, since the man had never said more than two words to her before that weekend.

It had taken less than half an hour of working together during the scavenger hunt to realize Delilah may have misjudged him. Anthony had jumped in alongside her, competitive and funny, and incredibly sweet, which was something she hadn't expected from him. He had a keen mind for riddles and a vocabulary that rivaled her own. Not to mention he was strong. When she'd slipped on a patch of ice, he'd caught her before she hit the ground.

"I got you," Anthony said, wrapping his strong arms around her.

Delilah ignored the shiver that raced down her spine at the memory of those hard bands of muscly sinew imprinting on her body. Delilah knew her reaction to Anthony was ridiculous, but throughout that night, she'd foolishly compared him to the book boyfriends she'd obsessed over since she'd picked up her first romance novel. Her real-life experiences with men had been eclectic, but none had measured up to the possessive heroes she'd read about in books. Did she realistically want a dragon lord who would throw her over his shoulder and keep her locked away so no one else could look at her? No, but Anthony taking her hand to help her down the bus's stairs when they'd arrived at the rental house that night made Delilah's core burn brighter than any spicy scene she'd ever read.

Looking back, Delilah had no idea what she'd expected to happen when she suggested they swipe a bottle of Fireball from the liquor tote and go to her room. But if she'd known how the evening would end, Delilah would have skipped it and stayed downstairs·with the group. Saved herself a spoonful of humiliation.

The events of that night played through her mind like a bad movie, and once it started, she couldn't stop the memories from surfacing.

Sitting on the floor with her back against the bed, Delilah giggled as she refilled her shot glass and some liquid sloshed over the side.

"Oh, shit, party foul!" Delilah downed the shot and passed the bottle and glass to Anthony before she grabbed the nearest item, which happened to be her sweatshirt, to soak up the alcohol from the floor.

"You need to keep your hand steady. Like this," he said, holding the bottle at an angle as he filled his glass. Not a drop was spilled. "Perfect!"

"Braggart," Delilah muttered, leaning her head back as the liquor spread warmth from the center of her body outward. "I think we should pause the drinking, or you may be holding my hair back later."

Anthony took off his hat, ran a hand over his short, dark hair. "I don't have that problem. I could chug rotgut and get up the next day with a smile on my face."

Delilah wrinkled her nose. "Why would you ever drink anything called rotgut?"

"Because I was underage and it was free?"

Delilah giggled. How had she never realized that Anthony was so funny? Or was that the whiskey talking?

"Why haven't we ever hung out like this?" she asked.

"We've never been paired for a combined bachelor slash bachelorette scavenger hunt before," he said, grinning. "Say that three times fast."

Delilah gave it a try but fumbled on the first line. She fell against Anthony's shoulder, which was shaking with laughter. He had a nice laugh, all deep and rumbly, and it did things to her nethers.

Nethers? She nearly snorted. She really was drunk.

"Seriously, though," she said, when their mirth subsided. "I thought you were just a broseph jock."

"I'm not?" He gasped in mock outrage. "I was planning on having that tattooed on my ass."

"I would pay to watch that." Her face flushed when she caught his grin, realizing it sounded like she wanted to see his bare butt. "No, I mean—"

"Delilah I-don't-know-your-middle-name Gill. If you want me to take my pants off—"

Delilah covered his mouth with her hand. "Stop! Don't ruin my opinion of you now."

He mumbled against her palm, his lips brushing her skin, tickling the sensitive flesh, and she pulled it back. "What?"

"What is your opinion of me?"

Man, that smile should be bottled and sold as lethal. "You're funny and considerate. You had several key moments of chivalry today."

"I try to keep them limited, otherwise word will get around. I know how you ladies like to gossip."

"Hey, we don't gossip! We inform at length." She smiled, the aftereffects of the Fireball making her feel lighter.

Anthony chuckled, turning toward her. "You weren't who I thought either."

"Do tell."

"For one thing, I assumed you were shy."

"Ha, you're funny." Delilah was a lot of things but shy was not one of them. Although she didn't always say everything that popped into her mind either.

"I try," he said with a grin. "With all the sarcastic shirts you wear, I assumed you'd be snarkier."

"Stick around. It will come."

"Oh, yeah?"

Delilah wasn't sure if it was his smile or the Fireball going to her head, but she slid her hand along his neck to cradle the back of his head and pulled him toward her. When she kissed his full lips, Anthony froze against her, and she could have dissolved into the floor in embarrassment.

She started to pull away, only he'd chased her lips with his. Anthony kissed her back, sweeping his tongue into her mouth, and Delilah melted against him, heat rushing through her veins like warm honey.

Delilah stopped walking suddenly, squeezing her eyes shut against the memory.

No, we are not doing that today.

She'd been an idiot who should have followed her instincts about him and kept her distance. If the universe had any mercy, Delilah would never see Anthony again, but in a town like Mistletoe, that wasn't likely to happen, especially when her best friend's business was right next door to his. Delilah spent too much time visiting Holly at A Shop for All Seasons, her year-round holiday store, to let Anthony Russo scare her off.

All in all, it hadn't been that bad. The few times they'd crossed paths, they'd greeted each other and kept their distance. Apparently, he'd wanted to engage with her as much as she wanted to exchange pleasantries with him.

Delilah passed the shop windows, decorated for the upcoming Thanksgiving holiday with falling leaves, beloved cartoon characters, and even a few gnome scenes. Mistletoe took every holiday seriously, not just Christmas, and prizes were awarded to the business that put on the best display. Kiss My Donut's frosted windows portrayed an orange coffee cup with a pumpkin on the sleeve, clasped in the hand of a smiling woman in a brown sweater. Her painted companion wore a green sweater, and he seemed to be gazing at her adoringly, dipping a sprinkled donut into her lidless cup of coffee.

Delilah snorted. As much as she loved romance novels, finding diverse heroines in books and movies who weren't perfectly proportionate was a difficult quest. Although plus-size women as heroines were more acceptable now than when she was an impressionable thirteen-year-old, the majority of marketing, especially with romantic elements, featured thin women only. Didn't they think ordinary people fell in love, too?

Delilah stood in front of the painted window, puzzling over it. Why did the world want to portray love as this picture-perfect scenario? Every romantic movie was set somewhere gorgeous, with enough messy drama to heighten the stakes, and the subjects were stereotypically white, hetero couples with sculpted bodies. Only those movies didn't represent the real thing, especially since 60 percent of the U.S. was plus size.

Dang, Delilah, you really are in a mood today! Go inside, get a latte, and maybe go back to bed. Or write out your aggressions. Either way, you need a happy today.

Delilah grumbled under her breath as she opened the door and stepped inside, the hissing of the espresso machine and multiple conversations surrounding her. As she took her place in line, Delilah's gaze immediately locked on to a shock of styled red hair and a matching, trimmed beard. The man standing three people in front of her with broad shoulders and a crisp, pressed collared shirt peeking out above a blue sweater was Pike Sutton, and if this was a Hollywood rom-com, he would have been cast as the comic relief sidekick. He never suffered from a lack of female company in real life, yet the world didn't consider him leading man material.

Not like Anthony, who happened to be standing next to him. All she could see was his broad back and the skin of his neck above his jacket collar. His head was missing its usual ball cap, showing off his short dark hair that looked like he'd just run his fingers through it. It may have been eleven months, but Delilah remembered how soft it had been as she'd tangled her fingers in the strands, their mouths colliding—

Stop thinking about it.

Delilah did her best, but it was hard when every other kiss she'd experienced before Anthony had been mediocre. Just because Anthony Russo couldn't appreciate her plus-size shape didn't mean other men hadn't considered her the perfect leading lady. Unfortunately, none of them had lived up to her sexual fantasies, and they didn't make it past the first encounter. Delilah had made a vow after her last few sweet but unimpressive sexual partners: If she was going to up her body count, they'd better know how to make her skin burn with the lightest of touches.

"Delilah!"

She swung around at the sound of her name and saw Merry Griffin waving at her from the edge of the café. Delilah waved back, and Merry got up, leaving her stuff at the table to cross the café toward her.

Delilah noticed Pike had turned around now, and when she caught his gaze, he smiled and waved, those adorable dimples making her stomach flip. She gave him a little salute and wanted to kick herself. Why did Pike's notice always discombobulate her? Any time he paid the least bit of attention to her, Delilah would end up scrambling her words or making some boneheaded gesture like a freaking salute.

Dork.

To Delilah's relief, Anthony continued facing forward. At least he didn't see her idiotic response, although Pike might relay it, and they could have a good laugh at her expense later.

"Hi, sorry to catch you like this," Merry said, rubbing her pregnant belly. "I've been meaning to call you, but the pregnancy brain is strong with this one."

Merry was her best friend's older sister, and in their adult years they had become closer. Merry was sweet, funny, and juggled many hats in Mistletoe, putting a lot of energy into the holiday activities.

Better her than me, Delilah thought, spotting a sprig of mistletoe someone had already pinned above the exit. She'd have to be careful not to get caught under there.

"Oh, you didn't have to get up," Delilah said, greeting Merry with a warm hug. "I would have come over after I ordered."

"I know," Merry said, hugging her back, before releasing her. "But I'll be in a meeting by then with Pike and Anthony, so this works out better."

"Okay then. What did you want to talk to me about?" Delilah asked.

"Would you be interested in helping Holly and I put together the holiday bachelor auction?" Merry asked quickly, as if afraid Delilah would scream "no" and race out the door in panic.

"Uh, when is it?"

Merry smiled, probably happy she hadn't gotten rejected right off the bat. "We're holding it after the Parade of Lights at the community center. We'll be combining bachelors with a service from local businesses, and we need a tiebreaker because you know my sister and I. We can't always agree gracefully. You in?"

Merry's pleading look was Delilah's undoing and she gave in without a fight. She loved the Winters and had a hard time telling any of them no, especially when she'd been a witness to disagreements between Holly and Merry and they definitely needed a buffer.

"Sure, Merry," Delilah said. "I'm always happy to help out."

"Great!" Merry clapped her hands together. "You can be the notetaker since you have better handwriting than either of us."

"Sounds like a plan."

Merry reached out and took Delilah's hands in both of hers. "As my wordsmith, would you be willing to draft some flyers, letters, press releases, and invitations for the event?"

Delilah thought about her lack of publishing prospects combined with her week off from subbing due to the Thanksgiving holiday and forced a smile. "I've got all the time in the world this week."

"You are the absolute best, Delilah! We're going to get together on Wednesday. Does that work?"

"Sure. I don't head to my parents' until Thanksgiving morning."

"You're awesome. This is going to be so much fun and, hopefully, we can turn it into a new Mistletoe tradition." Delilah opened her mouth to respond, but Merry barely stopped to take a breath before she continued, "Okay, I'm going back to my table, but I'll put you and Holly in a group text so we can finalize the meetup time and place." Merry hugged her swiftly, her hard round belly pressing into Delilah like a volleyball, and pulled back with a pat to Delilah's arm. "We'll talk soon."

"Bye," Delilah got out before Merry headed back to her table with a waddle in her gait. Holly's sister had always been a blond bundle of energy, but had pregnancy given her *more* energy? Or maybe it was the excitement of gathering up Mistletoe's finest men and parading them around for charity that had her buzzing around like a pollen-crazed bee?

Delilah fought a grin, her mind already racing with titles for the event. Merry Man Candy? Mistletoe Men on a Mission?

She'd keep workshopping, but suddenly, her crap day was taking a turn. Maybe making a list of the eligible men in Mistletoe would remind her of someone she'd been overlooking. After her vibrator died last month, Delilah realized she hadn't had sex for over a year and it had been lackluster at best. At the very least, it would be nice to find a friend-with-benefits situation. Something to alleviate her stress.

Otherwise, she was going to have to hop online and find a new handheld buddy, because her fingers were not getting the job done.

"I can help the next in line," Teagan Hulse, the girl behind the register, called out.

Delilah stepped up. "Hey, Teagan, could I get a large vanilla latte with an extra shot?"

"Sure thing, Delilah." The tall, willowy teen's fingers flew over the computer keys and she pressed a final button with a smile. "You're all set."

"How much do I owe you?" she asked.

"Oh, there's a pay-it-forward going, so your coffee is covered."

"That's nice. Here." Delilah handed her a ten. "We'll keep it going."

"Fantastic. That will be ready at the end of the bar for you."

Delilah crossed to the pickup window, standing out of the way.

"Pike and Anthony!" the barista called, setting two white cups with black lids on the counter.

Delilah refused to look, but out of the corner of her eye, she could tell it was Anthony picking up the drinks by the height difference as he passed by her to retrieve the coffees from the counter. When he turned around, instead of heading to the left toward his table, Anthony made a beeline toward her and stopped. Her first instinct was to ignore him until he went away, but Delilah realized that might draw more attention and she finally looked up. His wide grin flashed white on his tan face, the green of his eyes bright and beautiful.

Damn it, why did I look at him? It was like staring into an eclipse without special glasses and now her wits were addled.

Her heartbeat quickened when he raised his chin, nodding at her.

"I like your shirt."

Delilah glanced down at her I Heart Boobies T-shirt before scowling at him.

"It's for breast cancer awareness."

"It's okay if you like boobies." He winked. "I do, too."

The few people closest to them laughed and Delilah's face warmed, realizing they'd overheard his asinine comments. Before she could devise a scathing retort, he'd already turned and headed to the table where Pike and Merry were sitting.

May you sit wrong on one of your testicles, Anthony Russo.

Chapter Two

Anthony could feel the heat of Delilah's gaze as he carried the coffees to the table and wished he could turn around to witness the full effect of her irritation. After that night at the rental house, she deserved his every needle and poke. He wasn't one to hold a grudge, but he also didn't appreciate being used.

He'd tried to let it go at first. After all, they'd both had a few shots, and he'd wanted to chalk it up to Delilah not being able to hold her liquor, but the more Anthony thought about it after the fact, the more hurt he'd been. Anthony channeled that hurt into avoiding and ignoring her when they ran into each other, but that was juvenile, especially since Mistletoe was too small to hide from anyone. Besides, if talking to him made her uncomfortable, that sucked for her. It was one thing to bring up the torch you were carrying for someone else, but to kiss the socks off the best friend of the man you're pining for?

That was a low he'd never imagined she was capable of.

Anthony had been over that night numerous times, coming at it from every angle, and the only thing that made sense was that Delilah had wanted it to get back to Pike that she'd made out with Anthony. Unfortunately for her, there was no way he'd give her that satisfaction. He'd take that secret to his fucking grave with a smile.

If only Anthony didn't relive their brief moment together every time he saw that lush, sexy mouth of hers.

As the barista called her name and Delilah stepped forward to retrieve her coffee, smiling, he remembered the jolt of awareness when they'd been sitting on the floor next to each other the night of the scavenger hunt. The way she'd looked at him with that beautiful, bright smile right before she'd kissed him. Her actions had taken him by surprise, but when she'd tried to pull away, he couldn't let her go. Flashing back to their kiss, he lost himself in the memory, wishing he could regret it.

Delilah opened her lips, and he thrust his tongue inside, tasting Fireball and something sweeter underneath. Anthony deepened the kiss, heat gripping him as he guided her onto his lap with his hands on her hips. She straddled him, the softness between her thighs settling over his straining cock, and his fingers flexed instinctively. When she rocked against him with a little moan, it was the best and worst sensation, and he whispered her name, releasing her hips to tangle his fingers in her hair.

Delilah's hands slipped under his shirt, resting against his stomach, fingertips tracing the ridges of his abs, painfully close to the button of his jeans.

"Anyone seen Anthony?" Pike yelled from downstairs. "Yo, Anthony! Come on, man, get your ass down here!"

Delilah broke the kiss, her breaths coming in rapid gasps. "Pike's looking for you."

It was on the tip of his tongue to tell her he didn't give a fuck, but staring into her dreamy blue eyes, he remembered something she'd said earlier in the evening when they'd got to talking about relationships. "I'm sure you know I've had a crush on Pike forever, but he doesn't know I exist. It's pretty sad, really."

It wasn't a secret; the Winters siblings and all their friends knew about Delilah's longtime infatuation with Pike. And when she'd mentioned it offhandedly at the beginning of the night, it hadn't fazed him.

Hearing her say another man's name with the heat of her pussy burning a hole in the front of his jeans? It was like sticking his dick in a bucket of ice.

Anthony lifted her off of him and climbed to his feet. "We better go join him. Wouldn't want him to see us together, right?"

"Hello, Earth to Anthony!" Pike's irritation broke into his deep thoughts and Anthony realized he'd walked across the coffee shop in a daze and sat down next to Pike without saying a word. Both Merry and Pike were staring at him in confusion, and he wondered how long he'd been lost in his night with Delilah.

"Hey, sorry."

"What is with you today?" Pike asked.

"Nothing," he muttered. "What did I miss?"

Pike picked up his cup of coffee, wagging his eyebrows. "I said thanks for the coffee, snookums."

"Don't call me that, bro," Anthony said, giving the smaller man a friendly nudge with his shoulder.

"Easy there, you almost made me spill." Pike set his cup down, checking the front of his sweater for droplets.

"That's why you shouldn't be an idiot."

"Stop denying our love," Pike said, making kissing noises. "You know you're my boo for life."

While Anthony wouldn't have used that word to describe their connection, there was no denying his friendship with Pike and their other close friends, Nick and Noel Winters, were the lengthiest relationships he'd ever had. Other people might think that was a strange accomplishment, but for Anthony, it meant a lot. They were the family Anthony made, better than the one he'd been born into.

"Are you two done stroking each other's emotional penises, or can we get started?" Merry asked.

Anthony cocked a brow her. "Really? Emotional penises?"

Merry just smirked in return. Even though she was a woman of twenty-eight now, Anthony still remembered her following along behind them when they were kids, her front teeth missing and sticks and leaves tangled in her hair. Now Merry sat poised across from him, blond hair piled on top of her head, with a sizeable open binder on the tabletop in front of her, looking like a type A angel and not the obnoxious little sister of his other best friend.

"Merry, I'm offended," Pike said, holding one hand over his chest. "A woman in your delicate condition talking that way."

"Pretty sure that's how she got into that condition, bro."

"Ant!" Merry laughed.

"Don't Ant me. There's no denying it, love. The proof is in the puddin'."

Before Merry married Clark Griffin last year, she was just the middle child of the Winters clan and had given Pike and Anthony as much crap as she did her older brother, Nick, growing up. It was nice that nothing had changed besides her marital status.

Merry coughed, smothering her remaining laughter, and putting on a serious face. "Moving on to business. I asked you here because I have officially taken on the responsibility of organizing the Mistletoe Christmas festivities, and as new business owners, I want to invite you to participate."

"Hell, yeah, we're in," Pike said, without even looking at Anthony to confirm. "Thanks, Merry."

"No thanks needed," she said, writing rapidly in her binder. "Additionally, I want to add a few events to the schedule, and I need your help. As our outdoor sports experts, would you be willing to organize a winter obstacle course for people to compete in? Participants will find sponsors, and then they must complete a series of tasks. It will take place the Saturday before Christmas."

Four weeks to plan a major event and participate in several others while trying to run a business?

"That sounds like a huge undertaking—" Anthony said.

"You've come to the right men for the job!" Pike shot Anthony a look, and Anthony pressed his lips together, frustration rippling up his throat, but he held his protests at bay.

Merry frowned. "Anthony? You were saying."

Anthony caught Pike's pleading look and relented. "We could develop various ideas, depending on the budget," Anthony said, grimacing when he heard Pike's relieved sigh.

Merry brightened. "Great! I'll see what items I can get donated to help offset costs. Please send me a list of ideas by Friday so I can start putting things in motion."

"We will," Pike said.

Anthony tried to bite back his irritation at Pike's eagerness. This business was his dream, too, but the last thing Anthony wanted was to overcommit them for a bunch of events they couldn't follow through with. "One thing, Merry! I'd like to focus on one event. We're a new business, and I'd hate to stretch ourselves so thin that we disappoint you by doing a subpar job."

Anthony ignored the heat of Pike's stare. When they'd agreed to go into business together, they'd decided that Anthony would handle the marketing and financial side of things, especially since that's what he'd received his degree in. Pike would handle most of the guided tours and lessons. It worked out well for them, except when Pike got excited and didn't take the time to consider all the angles.

Thinking about the dozen or so events that occurred every holiday season in Mistletoe, Anthony could feel the walls closing in. The Festival of Trees was one of Mistletoe's most significant charity events. While Anthony had helped set up the event in the past, he knew the tree and decoration costs would be several hundred, depending on where they ordered their supplies. People voted and bid on their favorite trees; all the money went toward extracurricular programs this year for the school district. On top of that, the Parade of Lights would require hours to design a float, money for supplies . . .

Anthony could see the costs adding up in his head and a cold sweat broke out along his skin. They were too new to be shelling out thousands of dollars in a few weeks.

"Okay, so how about this?" Merry said, setting her pen down on top of her open binder. "Adventures in Mistletoe will be the official sponsor of the Mistletoe Winter Games and we'll forget the Parade of Lights this year. However, if you want to participate in the Festival of Trees, you buy the tree and the supplies and one of the volunteers will set it up for the event. It's for charity after all."

Anthony couldn't argue with that, especially if they didn't have to waste a Saturday decorating. "Sounds fair."

"Fabulous. Thanks, guys," Merry said, picking up her pen again and clicking the end. "You are doing me a huge favor and the last thing I want is to put a strain on you."

"We'll be fine, Merry," Pike said, slapping Anthony on his shoulder. "With this guy as the brains of the operation and my can-do attitude, we can handle anything."

Merry laughed, while a pounding had started at Anthony's temples. With their already scheduled appointments on the books, not to mention the day-to-day of running the store when it was just the two of them, how would they develop an event, a tree, and balance everything else without losing their minds?

"Let's see. We talked about the trees—" She handed Anthony a business packet with information regarding the event and crossed it off her list. "I almost forgot the Christmas concert raffle! Donation forms . . ." She thrust another one at them and looked up with an apologetic smile. "That one is optional, of course, but it's great publicity."

"Is a gift certificate for free snowboarding lessons alright?" Anthony asked, realizing how exasperated he sounded.

"Yes, that would be perfect!" Merry reached across the table and grabbed both of their hands. "Sorry to dump all this on you guys, but once Thanksgiving hits, time flies by fast."

"We understand," Anthony said.

"I can go back to the office and print two certificates for the Christmas concert raffle and the winter games prizes and drop those to you this afternoon," Pike added, bouncing in his seat like a restrained Goldendoodle.

"I'll be here for another couple of hours meeting with people and then I'll be heading home, so just text me. I could also swing by when I leave here. Up to you."

Anthony tried not to think about how much they charged for those lessons, reminding himself it was for charity and that at least it wasn't coming directly out of their pockets. They'd barely gotten Adventures in Mistletoe up and running nine months ago, and, although they'd done well, Anthony knew most businesses failed in their first five years. Giving away their time for free and taking focus away from their business was counterproductive.

Then again, being a part of the Mistletoe Christmas festivities was getting their name out to locals and the tourists who vacationed there. The publicity and word of mouth might offset the cost.

"You can pick it up. Save me a trip back in here. The last thing I need is to be tempted by one of their Red Bull drinks and end up having the jitters this afternoon," Pike said, pushing his chair back, and Anthony followed his lead, but Merry held up her hand.

"Last thing before you go, I promise."

Anthony was halfway out of his seat and settled back in as Merry continued, "Holly and I are planning a Christmas bachelor auction, and we would like both of you to volunteer."

"Are you talking about dressing us up in penguin suits and parading us around like slabs of meat?" Anthony asked incredulously.

Pike laughed. "You know I'm in."

"I knew you'd be the easy one to convince," Merry said, fixing her gaze on Anthony. "Anthony, on the other hand . . . "

Anthony leaned back in his chair with his hands up. "Believe me, you don't want me involved."

"Sure I do." Merry picked up her coffee mug with both hands, grinning over the top of it. "You're a cinnamon roll."

A bark of surprised laughter escaped him. "A what?"

"Soft and sweet inside. Believe me, you're a total catch. Spending the day with your handsome face, learning how to snowmobile or ski?" Merry rubbed her hands. "I smell big money."

Anthony chuckled at the same time Pike burst out laughing.

"I should be offended." Pike pouted. "You're not trying very hard to woo me."

Merry clasped her hands together and begged mockingly, "Please, Pike, would you be a dear and join our bachelor auction?"

"You don't have to butter me up, Merry," Pike said, dancing in his chair. "I love being up on stage."

"Just make sure you keep all your clothes on," she teased.

"My days as a stripper are over. Unless Adventures in Mistletoe goes under, all bets are off."

"Heaven help us," Merry muttered.

"Hey, now, Merry, don't razz him too much. My boy keeps it tight," Anthony joked.

Pike fluttered his lashes. "Thanks for noticing, Snoo—oof!"

A swift elbow to the stomach cut Pike off and made Anthony less tempted to strangle him for creating more stress and financial burden for their freshman business.

"Ant?" Merry clasped her hands in front of her. "You wouldn't make a pregnant woman beg, would you?"

"You don't play fair." When she stuck her lip out in a pout, Anthony threw up his hand. "Fine, I'll do it."

"Thank God! My bachelor pool is running low with Clark and Nick off the market."

It made sense, as most young people graduated high school and put Mistletoe in their rearview, whether for college or some other opportunity. The chances of them coming back were slim, too, especially without family still living in town. Most of the people who stayed behind got married before the age of thirty. Mistletoe wasn't exactly a hot spot of activity for single people.

Despite his average height and red hair, Pike was funny with a larger-than-life personality, and women tripped over one another to be near him, which made Pike perfect for the event. Anthony had spent his life being more comfortable in the background than the center of attention, preferring team sports to school plays, and didn't relish parading across the stage for the female population to scrutinize.

Merry flipped through the binder to the beginning and pulled out a piece of paper from the front pocket. "Here is the calendar schedule with the rehearsal and event dates."

"Rehearsal? We're not doing a choreographed dance like a Miss America Pageant, are we?" Anthony asked, taking the paper from her.

"No, but we want to interview you for the program, highlight your best skills and qualities. Plus, I don't want you tripping over one another and creating a domino effect that results in injuries."

Pike leaned over Anthony's shoulder, looking at the paper with him. "This is doable," Pike said.

Anthony was not as enthusiastic, but he remained silent.

"I can email or text you the to-do list tonight for the winter games, whichever you prefer."

"Email is fine," Pike said, pulling out his wallet and handing her their business card.

"Look at you, being all professional. I'm so proud." Merry pulled out her phone from her purse and studied the screen. "My next appointment will be here in five minutes, so if there's nothing else, I'll see you both for Thanksgiving?"

"I'll be there," Pike said. "My parents decided to visit my sister in Montana instead of feeding me, so I feel vulnerable and abandoned. Maybe you could pass that along to Sally?"

Merry's eyes narrowed. "Sally is dating a doctor and has no interest in the man who told her she should look into a nose job!"

Anthony covered his mouth with his hand, smothering his laughter. He'd heard about Pike sticking his foot in his mouth with Sally, Pike's ex-girlfriend and Merry's best friend, more times than he could count and it never stopped being funny.

"That is not what I said!" Pike protested. " I told her she should see if she had a deviated septum because she snored like a trucker. I like her nose!"

"The doctor likes everything about her," Merry said, setting her mug down with a clatter, "including her snoring."

Pike opened his mouth like he was going to defend himself more, but Anthony clapped a hand on his shoulder and said, "Pike, this is your chance to back out slowly before she hurts you."

"Good advice," Merry said dryly.

"Alright, fine." Pike pushed back his chair and stood, adding, "Let your mom know I'm bringing a side dish."

Merry groaned. "Not the Brussels sprouts thing!"

"What?" Pike gasped, placing a hand over his heart. "Everyone said it was delicious!"

"They were being nice, man. Nobody likes Brussels sprouts." Anthony picked up his coffee cup in one hand and wrapped his other arm around Pike's neck. "He'll bring mac and cheese. Grab your coffee, bro."

"Unhand me, cur!" Pike bellowed in a stage whisper, drawing the attention of half the room.

"We're leaving here before you start talking about kale chips," Anthony whispered back, waiting for Pike to grab his coffee with a grumble. "Thanks again, Merry."

"No problem." Merry stood up, stretching out her back. "Thank you for stepping up. I can't wait to see what you guys come up with."

"We'll be in touch." He dragged Pike toward the exit, ignoring his protesting friend. When they got outside, he released Pike and continued walking to work, grunting when he felt a sharp kick to his thigh. "Your pants are too tight to kick me in the ass, huh?"

"Fuck you. I can't believe you hate my Brussels sprouts." Pike said, pouting. "That hurts my feels."

"They're fine, but not something you *want* to eat, man."

Pike sniffed dramatically. "I like them."

"Good for you, but you should go with the majority on this one."

"You suck."

"Maybe," Anthony said, reaching into his pocket for his keys, "but better you know now than when they're spitting your dish out in a napkin."

"Speaking of a dish . . . " Pike took a sip of his coffee with a grunt. "What did you say to Delilah Gill?"

"When? Today?"

"Yeah, when you went to grab our coffees. She looked ready to twist your head off." Pike chuckled, waving at a car driving by. "I'm used to that reaction from women, but you?"

Anthony hadn't told Pike about the kiss with Delilah because he'd thought that's what her goal was, but also because, as hurt as he'd been, he didn't want anyone to think badly of Delilah. Despite how the night ended, he'd liked the woman he'd gotten to know that night.

"I simply wished her a good morning. Nothing out of the ordinary."

"Why do I want to call bullshit?" Pike asked.

"You know what?" Anthony snapped his fingers. "I told her I liked her breast cancer awareness shirt."

Pike pursed his lip thoughtfully. "There is something afoot. Are you into her?"

"No, man." It wasn't a lie. While there might have been a moment during their kiss when he'd been tempted to lose himself in her softness, Anthony was thankful he'd come to his senses.

With her snarky T-shirts and magnetic tops for her glasses that seemed to match everything she wore, they were polar opposites. Yet, even with everything that happened, wearing that I Heart Boobies shirt had made him smile.

"You should think more about hitting the bar to meet women," Pike blurted.

"That came out of left field."

"I'm serious, bro. We go to Brews and Chews a couple times a week, and you just sit there nursing a beer."

"You date enough for the both of us."

"Because I'm looking for something real."

"You think you'll find your dream girl in a bar?"

"Why not? Nick and Noel kissed for the first time at Brews and Chews. Clark realized his online date was Merry."

"I seem to remember you telling Nick a few years ago there was plenty of fish in the sea or some shit like that."

Pike shook his head. "That was before I realized I was staring down the barrel of thirty-two, and other fishermen are getting their hooks in the best catches."

Pike didn't talk about the girl who'd burned him the year before Nick returned from the military or his unrequited feelings for Noel often, but when he did, it was always some weird food metaphor.

"There's no reason to rush into something because you're afraid of being alone," Anthony said.

"That's not my problem. In every relationship I've ever had, I've always cared more. Becky. Noel. Even Sally, although her dumping me may have been my fault."

Something about talking to Pike about Nick's wife made him twitch. If he found someone who made him want to settle down, Anthony wouldn't want another man carrying a torch for her.

"Nick is gonna beat your ass if you don't stop pining for Noel."

"I'm not pining. I'm stating facts." Pike sighed loudly and leaned against the front of Adventures in Mistletoe while Anthony unlocked the door. "Maybe I pick emotionally unavailable women because then it's not a reflection on me that they can't love me back."

They stepped through the door, and Anthony shut it, locking it behind them. "Sally was emotionally unavailable?"

Pike made a face. "Sally was always looking for something better. I think she only stuck around because of my oral skills."

Anthony grabbed a pen off the counter and threw it at Pike. "Shut the fuck up, man. I don't want to hear that."

Pike laughed maniacally. "You're such a prude."

"No, I don't want to hear about your cunnilingus talent."

"I love you, man. You always use big words when you're uncomfortable." Pike set his coffee on the counter. "I'm going to take a piss before I head out to meet the Martin party. Any chance they have a single daughter over twenty-one?"

"They're all in their fifties. It's a bird-watching hike."

"Hmmm, gmilf. That could work."

"You're a sick man! Do not hit on our customers," Anthony hollered as Pike headed for the back.

"I can't shut this down, bro!" Pike yelled back, laughing.

Chapter Three

Delilah spent the day curled up on the couch with her corgi mix, Leia, watching *Shadow and Bone* and scrolling through vibrators on her phone. Although she loved the show, not even the evil sexiness of Ben Barnes could banish the dark cloud of depression that hovered over her.

Leigh Bardugo is so lucky, Delilah thought. She'd created these amazing worlds that people loved, that were so exciting she'd been picked up by a major streaming service. Delilah would never write anything clever or intriguing enough to get published, let alone have her book turned into a hit show or a blockbuster movie. She was a sad sack of sand, dull and irritating.

Delilah paused on an interesting toy that looked like a unicorn with a very long tongue and added it to her cart. At least if she was going to be a whiny loser, she could have satisfying orgasms.

Her doorbell rang, and Leia bounded from the couch, her furry butt wobbling back and forth as she ran for the front door. Delilah huffed off the couch and shuffled to the front of her two-bedroom home, slipping her phone into her pocket. She'd have to finish her order later.

Delilah checked the clock on the microwave and saw it was after six in the evening. Not really caring who it was, she answered the door in her *Star Wars* Life Day snuggy to find her best friend standing on her porch with a bottle of peach wine and a bag of chocolate.

"I brought the best medicine to cure any awful day," Holly said with a wide grin.

Delilah stared at the label of her favorite wine, which featured a country girl in cutoff shorts holding two large peaches in front of her chest, and sighed. "Not even boob wine and Dove can banish my melancholy."

"Oh, come on." Holly stepped past her, heading toward the kitchen with Leia dogging her heels. "Tell me what happened."

"It doesn't even matter," Delilah said, laying her forehead across the cool countertop in her kitchen. "I suck at life."

"Stop avoiding my question and explain yourself so that I can help you come up with a solution."

Delilah rested her cheek on the surface to scowl at Holly. "You can't fix this."

"Please, I should legally change my name to Ms. Fixit. Now spill."

She straightened up, rubbing her hands over her damp eyes. "I got another rejection letter for my book proposal."

"And?" Holly tossed the chocolate onto the counter and opened the top drawer in Delilah's kitchen with an arched brow. "That just means they weren't a good fit and couldn't appreciate your genius. Next."

"I walked in on my bestie and her boyfriend getting it on."

Holly giggled. "It was funny but not your fault."

"I know, but even if Declan is out of town, I should probably still call or text before I come over."

Holly rubbed her chin as if deep in thought before wagging her finger at Delilah, speaking in what Delilah could only imagine was an impression of Robert De Niro. "You. You. This is why I keep you around. You're so smart."

"Shut up," Delilah said, fighting a smile as she straightened up. "That shouldn't count as your fix since I'm the one who suggested it."

"Fair enough." Holly held out the golden bottle of wine with a grin. "I feel like we need to open up this bottle of thinking juice for the rest of it."

"Drinking is probably counterproductive to rational thought."

"Tell that to Hemingway. He was sotted most of his life and wrote the most beautiful books."

"Maybe that's what I'm missing," Delilah said, tapping her finger to the side of her head as if she'd just come up with a brilliant idea. "A touch of alcoholism."

"Let's not go drowning our sorrows just yet." Holly pulled out the corkscrew and slammed the drawer shut. "What came after the rejection?"

Delilah sighed. "I bumped into Pike and Anthony at Kiss My Donut this morning."

"Why is that a bad thing?" Holly asked.

"Anthony talked to me."

"No," Holly gasped sarcastically, popping the cork out of the bottle. "The nerve of that jerk."

"I'm serious. He said he liked my shirt."

"Which shirt?" Holly asked, turning her back on Delilah to grab two glasses from the cupboard.

"My I Heart Boobies shirt. He looked at it and said he liked boobies, too!"

Holly tried to keep a straight face. "That's probably true."

Delilah glared at her. "Not funny."

"Why does he bother you so much?" Holly filled each glass half full and recorked the bottle. "Is this about the party last year?"

While she loved Holly, Delilah hadn't told her everything that had gone down with Anthony for many reasons, but mostly because she was embarrassed. She'd gone upstairs with Anthony and a liquor bottle because he'd been nice to her. Saying the words out loud made her feel a little desperate but that was not the case.

"It bothers me because I thought he might like me," Delilah said softly, tucking a hair behind her ear. "So I invited him upstairs to my room."

"You told me that part," Holly said, handing a glass to Delilah. "But I suspect there's more."

"We had a few shots of Fireball and then . . . I kissed him."

Holly's jaw dropped open. "You kissed Anthony last December and didn't tell me?"

"Because it wasn't a big deal! It meant nothing!"

Holly gave her a skeptical look over the rim of her wineglass. "If it meant nothing, why are you holding a grudge?"

"I kissed him, and he whispered my name—"

"Still not following."

"And immediately bailed." Delilah snapped her fingers. "Like he was picturing someone else while kissing me and realized his mistake when he opened his eyes."

"Are you sure that's what happened?" Holly asked. "I've known Anthony forever, and he isn't a jerk."

Delilah sighed. "It doesn't matter. You're right, though. I should stop holding a grudge. Honestly, I should thank him. That kiss proved that I am missing something in my life."

"Whiskey-fueled make-out sessions with strange men?" Holly joked.

"Close, but nope." Delilah took a sip, humming as the sweet wine swept over her tongue and down her throat. "I am missing passion with a man who knows how to kiss. You know what I attract? Men who think the clitoris doesn't exist."

Holly choked on her wine, coughing laughter erupting from her. "Um, didn't they take health class?"

"Their parents probably opted them out of it to protect their precious sons from learning how to pleasure a woman!" Delilah yelled the last part, her chest rising and falling rapidly. She was sick of disappointing sex and something had to change.

Holly put her hand on Delilah's shoulder, her eyebrow arched. "Do we need to make a calming circle?"

"With just the two of us, it would be more like a square, but no, I'm good. Got all that pent-up rage expelled from my body, and now it is time to act." Delilah removed her glasses and tossed them onto the counter. "I am going to find a man whose kisses makes the ground shake beneath my feet."

"Not without your glasses, dork." Holly picked up the black frames and handed them to her.

"It was a metaphor. The girl removes her glasses in the movie, and the audience realizes she has always been gorgeous." Holly opened her mouth and Delilah held her hand up, placing her glasses onto her face. "Don't say I'm beautiful because I know that. However, I am not giving off the vibe that attracts men who are fantastic in bed! I know I'm a rock star in the sack. I could become a plus-size stripper as a side hustle and bring men to their knees before me."

"Really?" Holly hopped up on the counter without spilling her wine and waved a hand at her. "I gotta see this. Dance for me. Time to collect those dollar bills."

Delilah bit back a smile as she set her wineglass down and dropped her snuggy on the floor, revealing gray lounge pants and blue tank top. "Give me a beat!"

Holly laughed but pulled her phone out of her pocket, tapping the screen. While Britney Spears crooned "I'm a Slave 4 U," Delilah took several steps forward, shaking her hips and shimmying. When she reached the cupboard, Delilah held on to the knob and spun out as she opened it before dropping into a squat and hopping across the floor.

Holly bent over the counter screaming with laughter, and Delilah lost her balance when Leia jumped on her, knocking her into the cabinets. Delilah rolled on the floor, avoiding Leia's darting tongue.

"See! I got this!"

"If I had a fistful of dollar bills, they would be yours!" Holly said, clapping.

"Leia, I'm fine. Off, love." The tan and white dog sat back, her bat ears perked. Delilah climbed to her feet less than gracefully and hobbled to where she'd set her wineglass. She picked it up, wincing at the sharp pain in her derriere. "I think I pulled something in my butt."

"Uh oh! Is it a career-ending injury?" Holly asked between laughter.

"I'm afraid so."

"I don't think you need to change your appearance to find a man with bedroom skills," Holly said, downing the rest of her wine. "I also remember saying something about not needing a man to make me happy."

Delilah chuckled. "Uh-huh. Should I mention that philosophy to Declan?"

"I was already happy," Holly said, grinning cheekily. "He's just a bonus prize."

"Like the ring at the bottom of the cereal box?" Delilah teased.

"Exactly." Holly set her glass down before jumping off the counter. "Now, for our manhunt. Sometimes, the quiet ones surprise you." Holly tapped a finger to her chin before she snapped her fingers with a, "Ha! What about that science teacher at the middle school you dated earlier this year?"

Delilah winced. "Tom is nice, but . . . " She searched for another way to describe him, only what popped out was "bland."

Holly grimaced. "Bland is not good." She turned to face Delilah once more, gripping the side of the counter behind her. "What about Fletcher Nielsen? He is back in town, and you always thought he was cute."

"Holly," Delilah said with a heavy sigh. "I appreciate you advocating for me not to change, but what if I want to?"

Holly crossed the room and hugged her. "Whatever makes you happy makes me happy. I don't want you ever to think you aren't good enough for love just how you are."

"I know that, bestie." Delilah wasn't surprised Holly had reservations about Delilah changing who she was.

Holly had been there in middle school when Delilah saved up her money and bought a pair of the distressed skinny jeans everyone was wearing. They'd dug into her stomach when she sat down, and after a long day of suffering for fashion, one of the popular girls had dropped a nasty note onto her desk, with multiple handwriting. It turned out to be a group note, with dozens of people talking trash about her. They'd spent the day making fun of how she looked, and it had taken everything in her to hold back the tears.

It wasn't until Delilah pulled off the jeans that night and saw how her thighs had been rubbed raw from chafing that she let the tears fall.

She'd faked a stomach ache the next day, and her mom let her stay home, curled up in bed watching *Drop Dead Diva*. When she tried to fake sick again the following morning, her mom shook her head and told Delilah to shower. Instead of taking her to school, they'd headed to Boise for the weekend. They'd gone to dinner, and after some gentle prodding, Delilah broke down and told her what had happened.

"Lilah, honey, do you like those girls?" her mother asked.

"No, they're mean."

"Then why do you care what they think of you? You are smart. You are funny. You are kind. You are beautiful inside and out. Fuck those kids."

"Mom!" Delilah's horrified cry at her mother's cursing dissolved into laughter. Her mom joined her and the two of them had an amazing time.

She'd returned from that weekend with some new clothes and, although she wasn't bulletproof yet, a thicker skin.

However, she wasn't twelve years old anymore, and her mother was right. If someone didn't like the way she looked, they could fuck right off.

Holly pulled back with a sniffle and poured more wine into her glass. "Alright, then, let's do this. Come on, universe! My friend needs a handsome, funny, intelligent guy to sweep her off her feet!"

"Which might be a tough find in good old Mistletoe."

"Oh, no," Holly said firmly. "I will support you in finding your bliss unless it means you are leaving me, and the only time I get to see you is over FaceTime."

"I'm not saying I want to leave, but you have to admit, Mistletoe has a lot going against it."

"Such as?" Holly asked.

Delilah started ticking things off on her fingers. "It's cold for nine months out of the year."

"That gives us all an excuse to cuddle and take more vitamin D," Holly said with a salacious grin and an eyebrow waggle.

"The traffic during peak tourist season is ridiculous."

"Please," Holly scoffed, "don't make me laugh. Ten cars backed up on one road in the evening does not traffic make."

"It does when you just want to get home," Delilah fired back. "To be honest, the only thing I like about Mistletoe is a handful of people. I'm not outdoorsy, so no recreational stuff appeals to me. I think the holiday events are over the top—"

"How dare you?" Holly interjected with a scowl.

"It's true! And it takes packages two or more days longer to get here."

"That's just Idaho in general," Holly protested. When Delilah gave her an "oh, really" look, Holly sighed. "Fine. I'll admit, Mistletoe isn't for everyone, but you're selling this place short. I've heard the way you talk about the kids you sub for."

"I can substitute anywhere for a lot more money."

"Go on then, flee," Holly said, waving her hands and pointing. "Go on, get! I'll be better off without you."

While Holly's tone sounded lighthearted and teasing, Delilah heard the slight tremor and set her wineglass down. She circled the counter and hugged Holly tight. "Stop trying to White Fang me. We both saw that episode of *New Girl* one too many times."

Holly laughed, returning her hug. "So, when do we start this search for the great, rare sex-god?"

"I'm thinking tonight."

"Oh, dang," Holly said, frowning. "We can't go shopping tonight. By the time we got to Twin, all the stores would be closed."

"That's okay; I have something in my closet that might do the trick."

Holly followed Delilah into her bedroom, and when she pulled out the hanger with the sparkling blue dress, Holly nodded. "That will freaking do."

Chapter Four

M*aybe this was a bad idea.*

The thought popped into Anthony's head as he sat with his friends at Brews and Chews Bar and Grill, listening to the loud music and the hum of conversations around him. Anthony had been looking forward to hitting the bar with the boys tonight, but his mood tanked the minute he crossed the threshold and spotted the large sprig of mistletoe hanging over the door. Pike's rant yesterday about getting older and their shrinking group of single friends hadn't been far from his mind. Now, the matchmaking plant of the holiday season was staring him in the face, reminding him that of all his friends, he was the only one who hadn't ever come close to a long-term relationship.

His relationship status wasn't from lack of interest, but he had no interest in bullshit games. Anthony tried dating apps, but every woman he'd gone out with had lied about something on her profile. Usually, he could spot the lie after a date or two, but the last woman he'd dated over the summer almost had him fooled. It wasn't until he'd surprised her with a weekend getaway and she'd realized they were going camping over Couch Summit that she admitted her idea of camping was a twenty thousand dollar camper with all the bells and whistles.

He'd flipped the truck around in the next turnout and taken her home. At a young age, he learned that lies were like poison; no matter how small, they led to more significant issues and, ultimately, ended in chaos. If a woman couldn't be honest about her interests, what else would she lie about?

Brews and Chews Bar and Grill was packed to the gills like every other Saturday night, with a live band playing a rowdy rendition of *Hard Workin' Man*. Men and women were already on the dance floor, circling each other like they were practicing a mating dance. A table of women smiled at their group as they passed by, but the only one who acknowledged them was Pike.

"Looking lovely tonight, ladies."

A couple of them giggled, and Anthony shook his head, knowing Pike would eventually make his way over there and try to drag Anthony along. While he wasn't opposed to connecting with someone, he wasn't looking for a one-night stand or a casual fling, the usual goal of people meeting in bars.

They'd scored a table by the hallway that led to the back exit to the patio and spontaneous bursts of cold air rushed down his spine every time someone stepped outside to smoke. Pike was at the bar with Nick, getting drinks while Anthony listened to Declan talk about his recent trip to visit his parents in Arizona.

"Dad's doing great. I was worried that the change in scenery might mess him up but heading south for the winter agrees with him. My mom says his doctor is surprised; he'd expected his dementia to progress faster than it has. She is convinced it's all the supplements she's been feeding him and that they've cut out processed food, but who knows?"

"Some things can't be explained," Clark said. "Merry thinks the power of positive thinking can overcome anything."

"Is that a Winters thing?" Declan asked, grinning conspiratorially. "Holly is the same way."

Clark and Declan had been indoctrinated into their friend group via their relationships with Nick's sisters. Anthony liked the two men regardless of how they came to be there. Clark was the Winters Family Tree Farm's foreman, and Declan had been pursuing his art and selling items online. It was thanks to Declan that Pike and Anthony were able to open up Adventures in Mistletoe at all. If he hadn't closed down his family's hardware store when his dad retired and sold the building, they would still be waiting for a space to open up in town.

However, he was tired of hearing about their women and opted to change the subject. "Where's your brother tonight, Clark?"

"At the tattoo shop until eleven. He might swing by after, but he wasn't sure if he'd have company later."

Declan chuckled. "Did Merry ask him to do the bachelor auction yet?"

And they were back to talking about women. Worse, one of the many events he needed to talk to Pike about. He'd started going through everything Merry asked them to contribute and participate in during lulls in the day, and they would be over a grand in the hole if Pike had his way. Some of the buy links to intricate ornaments his partner had sent him were almost fifty bucks a piece! On top of that, parading men on stage like cattle for the town to bid? It was a wasted day when he could take people out on the mountain for money instead of spending an awkward evening with the highest bidder.

"She did ask him, and Sam told her no, but then Holly got after him." Clark grinned when Declan shot him a dark look. "Hey, don't get pissed at me. I can't help that my brother has a soft spot for your girl."

Anthony tuned out the band at the mention of Holly's name, which turned his thoughts back to Delilah. While he'd been irritated with her and himself after their kiss last December, he appreciated her authenticity. She didn't care about putting on a bunch of makeup to lure a man in under the illusion of perfection or conforming to the world's idea of how women should dress and act to attract a man. Being partnered with her on the scavenger hunt had been natural, and he'd let his guard down, forgetting she wasn't emotionally available when she'd kissed him. He'd wanted to do more than kissing and petting, dying to strip her down and bury himself in her soft heat.

Only the aftermath flashed through his brain; he'd stopped it before it went too far. Even if she hadn't been hung up on Pike for half her life, she was best friends with Nick's little sister. Mistletoe was small enough without dipping into their friend group, and by extension, making future events awkward and uncomfortable. All they'd done was kiss, and she wouldn't even say hello when she saw him—this morning had been the most words she'd uttered to him in almost a year.

"I'm telling you, Sam will get punched in the soft spot if he doesn't get a girlfriend soon," Declan grumbled. "Between the shop, Sam, and Delilah, I gotta make an appointment to get Holly alone."

"Ooof, word of advice from an old married man," Clark said, grinning. "Never say anything negative about their best friend. It's the fastest way to end up on the couch."

Declan sighed. "I like Delilah, but I want to have coffee with my girlfriend without her showing up." Declan rubbed his hands over his face. "Shit, I sound like an asshole."

"You sound human," Anthony said, joining in the conversation. "Believe me, I like my space, and if someone kept popping up and invading it without an invitation, I'd be over it, too."

"What I need is for Delilah and your brother"—Declan punctuated the words with a scathing look shot Clark's way—"to find people to occupy them."

"It will take a miracle to get Sam to settle down," Clark said.

"What about you, Anthony?" Declan asked.

"I'm not interested in Sam." Anthony smirked. "Thanks, though."

Clark laughed while Declan threw a straw wrapper at him. "I mean, are you dating anyone special?"

"Not at the moment."

"Perfect. Wanna take Delilah out?"

Anthony froze. "No, man, I'm not going to take Delilah off your hands like I'm a fucking babysitter."

"Whoa," Clark said, holding his hands in a time-out. "Calm down there, sparky."

"No, he's right," Declan said, holding his hand out for Anthony to shake. "I'm sorry, man. That was a douche thing to suggest."

Anthony took it with a sheepish grin. "Nah, that came out harsher than I meant. I'm in a shit mood."

Declan nodded. "I get that. Hell, I wanted to spend time with Holly tonight, but because Delilah needed to talk, she went straight over there after work. Here I am, drinking with you instead of spending the evening with my girlfriend."

Pike and Nick came back to the table, Nick with several bottles of beer in his hands while Pike held a tray of shots.

"Who's ready for a dirty pilgrim?" Pike asked, grinning.

"I hope that's a drink, not something else," Anthony said.

Pike huffed. "Mock me if you will, but you'll love this." He placed a shot in front of each of them before knocking back the last one. "Mmm, so good." Pike set the shot glass down with a hard thump. "What are we talking about?"

"Declan's trying to hire Anthony to occupy Delilah Gill's time," Clark said.

"Oh, yeah?" Pike glanced at Anthony. "And what did he say?"

"Turned me down flat." Declan took a beer from the tray, ignoring the shot.

"Probably because she's not his type," Nick said, sitting across from Anthony.

"I never said she wasn't my type," Anthony said, his voice tight, frustration snaking through him. "I'm just not going to pursue a woman under false pretenses."

"Which makes you an honorable man." Nick held out the bottleneck of his beer, and Anthony clinked it with his.

"Thank you."

"I'll take the bullet," Pike blurted.

"What?" Anthony and Nick chorused.

"What? Tell me that woman isn't *my* type," Pike said, staring at something over Anthony's shoulder. The entire table turned to look, and Anthony's stomach bottomed out as he got a look at Delilah sans glasses in a shimmering blue halter dress that dipped into a low V partially covered by a hint of fabric that did nothing to hide her ample cleavage. The dress flared out at the waist into an A-line, swishing around her legs as she walked past with Holly leading the way. Both women had their hair down. Delilah's dark curls bouncing against her back, and Holly's red waves were pulled forward, hanging over the front of her tight black dress.

"Hol?" Declan called. "What are you doing here?"

Holly put her finger up to her lips. "Shhh, just pretend I'm not here. It's guys' night. I'll see you in a couple of hours."

"How am I supposed to do that when you look like that!" Declan spluttered.

Holly blew him a kiss and kept walking. Delilah's blue eyes glanced toward the table briefly, but they didn't linger long enough to meet Anthony's. He'd never seen her in a dress like that.

Declan swung his wide-eyed gaze around the table. "What the fuck just happened?"

"I don't know, but Pikey likey."

Anthony resisted the urge to punch Pike in his leering mouth. While he loved the man beside him, his blatant perusal of Delilah's assets made his blood boil. "How can you go zero to douche in ten seconds flat?"

"I'm just appreciating what she's putting out there."

The table groaned in unison, except Anthony, who scowled at him. "It's just a dress, man. She's the same woman."

"That dress, my friend, signals that she is looking for attention from the right man."

Nick laughed. "Interesting theory."

"I don't think I've ever seen Delilah in anything other than pants," Pike said, his voice heavy with wonder.

Anthony's gaze inadvertently strayed to Delilah, perched on a bar stool beside Holly. She held a glass of blue liquid and sipped from the straw, her eyes wandering over the room. He didn't break eye contact when their eyes met, even when he raised his beer to take a drink. He noticed her cheeks flush before she spun away and said something to Holly.

Nick set his beer down and leaned toward Pike, lowering his voice. "You do realize if you fuck around and break Delilah's heart, Holly will rip your nuts off and shove them up your ass?"

Pike pulled at the collar of his plaid shirt like it was choking him. "I'm not afraid of your sister, bro. Besides, my intentions are honorable . . . ish."

"Of the two Winters' sisters, Holly should scare you," Declan said dryly. "And I can say that 'cause I love her."

"Regardless of how scary Holly is, I am willing to face her wrath to possess such an exquisite creature. "

Anthony's jaw clenched. "She'll be back in those graphic tees tomorrow."

"It's like I was telling you earlier, bro," Pike said, adjusting his bow tie. "Our dating pool is getting thinner and it's obvious we've all been sleeping on Delilah Gill. I'm getting in the water before someone else does."

Pike took off before anyone could respond, heading straight for Delilah and Holly.

"What in the hell was in that shot?" Anthony asked.

Nick laughed. "Love potion?"

Declan picked up the last shot on the tray, licking his lips before he said, "I guess some men need a wake-up call to recognize what's right in front of them."

"She doesn't look that different," Anthony muttered.

"Why does it bother you?" Clark asked, studying him.

Because she was the same woman Pike had ignored for fourteen years. Once he realized that, he'd get bored, and Delilah would get hurt.

Besides, he'd just referred to being with her as taking a bullet, and that
didn't sit well with Anthony.

Anthony spotted Pike trudging his way back to the table and plop-
ping back in a chair.

"Struck out?" Declan chuckled.

"Didn't even get close to her before the hordes descended."

Anthony realized he was smiling over his friend's failure and fixed
his face before anyone noticed.

"Son of a bitch," Nick said. "Look who's at the front of the crowd?"

Every man at the table followed Nick's line of vision, and Anthony
spotted the large, dark-haired man leaning on the bar next to Delilah.
When she tipped her head back and laughed, Anthony's hand clamped
around his beer bottle painfully.

"Hey, man," Pike asked, pointing, "Isn't that your brother?"

Chapter Five

"Y ou want another, beautiful?"

Whether it was the two glasses of wine at her house or the blue drink she'd slurped down upon arrival, Delilah regretted not pacing herself as the room swayed like the deck of a ship when she shook her head.

"I think I'll stick with water for now."

"Coming up." Grant held a hand up to get the bartender's attention, and Delilah caught Holly's gleeful expression. When they'd sat down, several men approached them, offering to buy their drinks. Although Holly politely informed them she was taken, Grant had focused all his attention on Delilah. He was a big man in his thirties with dark hair and hazel eyes. His cheeks and chin were covered in a dark shadow of whiskers, and his boyish smile was vaguely familiar, making Delilah relax the minute he'd flashed it at her.

"So, Grant," Holly asked, swirling her straw in her empty glass, making the ice hit the sides with a *clink*. "What do you do for work?"

"I'm a truck driver. I took a little detour on my way to Boise and thought I'd grab a drink." His gaze swept over Delilah, lingering on her mouth. "Sure am glad I did."

Her cheeks warmed at his apparent interest, and when Ricki, the bartender, came over with her water, she took it with a trembling hand. She'd never gone home with someone she didn't know. Every man she'd ever hooked up with had been an acquaintance at least. She knew nothing about this man except he was a truck driver passing through.

You wanted to attract the attention of a sex-god, and this guy is giving off those vibes in spades.

"Where do you call home?" Delilah asked, wanting to know more about him.

"If you're asking about a city, Boise would be it, but I'm all over the place. My truck has everything I need." He dropped his mouth close to her ear and murmured, "Well, almost."

The warmth of his breath on her skin made her shiver and she tried to come up with something flirty to say, but was completely at a loss. The man was smooth as pudding.

"Delilah, are you good if I check in on Declan?" Holly asked.

Delilah cleared her throat and waved her best friend off. "Yeah, sure."

"Thanks." Holly hopped off the stool and entered the crowd where her boyfriend sat with her brother, Nick, his friends, and her sister's husband, Clark. She'd noticed Pike hovering around earlier, but he'd gone back to the table.

"Is Declan her boyfriend?" Grant asked, looking over to the table.

"Yeah, he's sitting over there with the group of guys—"

"Holy fucking shit!" Grant crowed, jumping to his feet. "Is that my baby brother?"

Delilah watched Grant push his way through the crowd with her mouth hanging open as Anthony stood up. Grant was a few inches shorter but lifted Anthony off his feet in a bear hug.

His brother?

Delilah got down from the stool, unable to believe her rotten luck. How could the one guy she'd seriously considered taking home be related to *him*?

The universe had a perverse sense of humor.

Grant stepped back from the embrace when Delilah approached, his gaze traveling over Anthony in awe. "Man, how are you doing? I tried calling, but it said the number wasn't in service."

Anthony's small smile didn't reach his eyes. "I changed it about five years ago when I switched services."

"Why didn't you tell me at Mom's funeral?" Grant asked.

"Probably because there wasn't time to catch up after everything."

"We don't need to rehash that!" Grant slapped Anthony's arm. "Let me buy you a drink, and we can catch up."

Anthony's gaze flicked to Delilah. "Seemed like you were in the middle of something."

"Oh, shit, Delilah!" Grant shot her a sheepish grin. "You don't mind if we put a pin in this so I can catch up with my brother, right?"

"Not at all," she said.

"Thanks, honey. I knew you were a good sport." He wrapped an arm around Anthony's shoulder, leading him toward the bar. Delilah sat down in the empty seat, frustration rippling through her. Holly was settled onto Declan's lap, giving her a sympathetic look.

"Want a drink, Delilah?" Pike asked, sliding a golden shot her way. "It was meant for Anthony, but it's yours if you want it."

He stole my potential sex partner, so why not?

"Thanks," Delilah said, tossing back the shot. The sweet, tart taste of apples and cinnamon teased her tongue before the warm liquid slid down her throat. "What was it?" she asked Pike.

"Warm apple pie shot."

Delilah laughed as she set the glass down. "I'd take another of those."

"I thought you were going to slow down," Holly asked, frowning.

"I changed my mind." Delilah got to her feet but Pike shook his head, waving her down.

"I'll get it in exchange for one dance."

It took her a moment to realize she hadn't misheard him and a thrill of excitement raced through her. Pike was interested in dancing with her?

Since when? the snarky voice in her head asked, but she ignored it. She'd been waiting on this moment for over a decade and she didn't care why he was asking her to dance . . . she was just happy he was.

"Sure, Pike."

Delilah watched him walk away, but her gaze strayed from his retreating form to Anthony's profile. He hadn't seemed as happy to see his brother as Grant was to spend time with him.

Delilah leaned over to whisper loudly at Nick. "How have I never heard of Anthony's brother?"

Nick shrugged. "When his parents split, Anthony was ten. Grant is six years older and went to live with their dad when he moved to Boise. Anthony stayed with his mom. He's got four older brothers, but the rest were already out of the house."

"I think it's weird he didn't want to say hi when he recognized his brother," Clark said.

Delilah watched Grant and Anthony, noting the similarities between them. While Anthony was taller and Grant was broader, they had the same thick dark hair and jawline. If Anthony bothered to smile, Delilah could confirm her suspicion that they shared the same smile, which was why Grant seemed so familiar.

Of all the men who could have caught her attention, it had to be Anthony's brother.

"Here's your warm apple pie," Pike said, holding out the shot glass with a dollop of whipped cream on top.

Delilah took the shot from Pike with a smile, knocking it back. Warmth spread through her, settling in her stomach. So far, the night had been relatively disappointing, but she was determined to salvage it.

The lead singer of the band belted out the first few lines of "Brand New Man" by Brooks & Dunn, and Delilah stood. "Pike?"

"Yeah?" he asked.

"You feel like dancing yet?"

His face lit up, and a flush of confidence rushed through her. "Sure, I was going to ask, but wanted to let you enjoy your drink."

"I'm good," she said, pushing in her chair. "I wasn't sure if you were waiting on a slow song because you were a turn and shuffle kind of guy."

"Nah, that's Anthony." Delilah resisted the urge to look at Anthony and his brother, who had seemed to forget all about his interest in her not a half an hour ago.

"I got moves that will make you dizzy." Pike held out his hand, and Delilah took it, her palm settling against his. It was warm and smooth, which was odd. She'd thought it would be rough and calloused from all his years working road construction and his love of outdoor activities.

"Your hands are softer than mine," Delilah said.

"Thank my expensive hand cream. Although, I'm probably losing manly points telling you that."

Delilah laughed. "I didn't know there was a point system, so you're good."

She followed him through the crowd and onto the dance floor, where he gracefully spun her into his arms. "Thank God for that. Can't let my competition get one up on me."

"What competition?" Delilah laughed.

"You must not be paying attention. Every guy in here nearly broke his neck when you walked through that door."

Delilah blushed. "You exaggerate. Holly was with me—"

"Every man in here knows Holly is taken and not one of them wants to tangle with Declan. It's you in that dress that has us all bewitched."

Delilah didn't know why his comment rubbed her wrong, like

she wasn't attractive without the dress, but her expression must have revealed her irritation, because he asked, "Did I say something wrong?"

Why are you being so sensitive? He's trying to be charming and you're taking it out of context.

"Of course not. I was just thinking you're a great dancer," she said, looping one of her arms around his neck. Her three-inch heels closed some distance between their heights, and she came up just past his chin.

"I took lessons as a kid until I got into high school." He held on to her other hand, leading her around the dance floor in a swift two-step, his strong arm pressed into the small of her back. "I was afraid of giving people another reason to give me shit, but it gave me an advantage at school dances."

"I bet," Delilah chuckled. "My date to senior prom could only shuffle back and forth, but I appreciated the effort."

"I tried to help Nick and Anthony, but they'll never reach my skill level."

She rolled her eyes in response to his boast. "Stated like a true narcissist."

"Come on, have you ever seen Anthony dance?" Pike laughed, putting a sway into his hips as he spun her out and back in. "Twerking is his go-to move, and the man doesn't have an ass."

Delilah almost argued that he did, but that would mean admitting she'd checked it out. "I'll take your word for it."

Silence settled between them as they took another turn around the dance floor. When they passed by the table, Delilah saw that Anthony and Grant were caught up in an intense-looking conversation and she wondered what they were talking about.

"I like your dress," Pike said, breaking the quiet.

"Thanks. It's been hanging in my closet waiting for a special occasion, so I made one."

"What are you celebrating?" he asked.

"Going after what I want." Anthony's back was to her, but she could see Grant's expression locked in a scowl. Anthony walked away from his brother, heading toward the outdoor patio. Grant took a deep gulp from his glass, and Delilah thought he would follow his brother, but he went out the front door instead.

"What is it that you want?" Pike asked.

"I'm sorry?" She asked, jerking her attention back to Pike. "What did you say?"

"You said you were going after what you want. What is that?"

"I'm . . . " Delilah wasn't going to tell Pike she was on the hunt for a sex-god. He might take it as a come-on, and she was uncertain why he'd asked her to dance out of the blue. "I'm still figuring it out, but I'll know when I find it."

The song ended, and Delilah followed Pike back to the table.

"What are we talking about?" Pike asked, grinning as he held a chair for Delilah. She took a seat and Pike settled in next to her.

"The Broncos," Nick said.

Pike dived into an animated conversation about football with his friends, and Delilah caught the wide-eyed look Holly gave her. She probably expected Delilah to be jumping for joy, but she couldn't stop checking the patio doors for Anthony to return. Whatever happened with Grant, he'd obviously been upset, yet none of his friends had gone outside to check on him.

Delilah stood up, but Pike reached up to touch her arm before she could take a step. "Hey, where you going?"

"I don't usually announce it," she said, biting back a harsher response. "But the bathroom."

"Sorry," he chuckled. "Hurry back."

Delilah experienced an unexpected rush of irritation at those two little words, followed by intense confusion. She should be excited by Pike's sudden attention, yet his familiarity rubbed her wrong. He'd always been friendly to her but never flirty.

What are you complaining about? You wore the dress for exactly this reason. To get the right kind of attention.

Yet, it was one thing to catch the eye of a total stranger, but for Pike to suddenly trip over himself to get her a drink?

It didn't seem real.

Delilah bypassed the bathroom and stepped through the back door. Out on the patio, a rush of cold air over her bare skin left prickles of gooseflesh in its wake. She searched the dim area for Anthony and found him at the edge with his back to her, staring at the trees behind the bar. Delilah crossed the cement slab and stepped up beside him.

"Hey."

He jumped, turning to face her with a wary expression. "What are you doing out here?"

"I saw you and Grant talking, and it looked intense. When I saw you both head in opposite directions, I came out to check on you."

"I'm fine."

His clipped response should have been her clue to go back inside and leave him be, but she turned to the side, leaning her hip against the iron fence that enclosed the outdoor area. "I know family can suck sometimes—" she said, searching for something more to make him feel better, but he cut in harshly.

"Are you not getting enough attention from every other man inside?"

Delilah reeled back like he'd slapped her. "What?"

"You following me out here. Is it a game because I'm not drooling after you?"

Delilah's eyes burned, but she wouldn't cry in front of him. "Fuck you."

She spun away from him but didn't go back inside, heading instead for the side gate. Flipping up the latch, she closed it with a slam. Delilah heard him call her name, but she was not slowing down for him. Her only thought was escape.

Without warning, a large hand grasped her arm and spun her around. She lost her balance and found herself pressed into a hard male chest. She thought it was Anthony and placed both hands flat against his front, shoving back, but he didn't release her. The smell of alcohol and smoke hit her nostrils and Delilah wrinkled her nose in disgust.

Not Anthony.

"Where you running to?" The slurred question came from a voice she didn't recognize, and she looked up into half-closed eyes staring down at her in the dim lights of the parking lot.

"Back off," she snapped, fear seizing her chest. She's never been accosted like this before, and as she turned to search the parking lot, there wasn't a single body beside the two of them.

"I just wanted to tell you how"—he made some kind of gurgling sound—"pretty you are."

Delilah's voice trembled as she shoved him again. "Get the fuck off me!"

The man heaved a stream of vomit over her chest and down the front of her body. Delilah cried out in horror as the warm, noxious ooze settled into the cups of her bra, saturating the soft fabric of the dress to her body. The sound of dripping preceded the sensation onto the tops of her feet and she stared down at the mess in horror.

"Oh, no," the man mumbled. "I ruined your dress."

Delilah almost laughed aloud as she thought, *The dress can be cleaned but this night is flipping shot. Thanks.*

Chapter Six

Way to go, asshole.

Anthony gripped the fence, watching Delilah slam out of the side gate and disappear. He called out to her, but she ignored him.

He couldn't blame her. She'd come outside to check on him, and he'd lashed out at her because he was pissed off at his family. It wasn't Delilah's fault his brother's appearance brought up shit he'd rather forget about. Being the youngest of five brothers, he'd idolized them, especially Grant, who was the closest to him in age. But the way they'd bailed on his mom to live with their dad had destroyed his admiration for his brothers significantly when he grew up enough to understand why.

Except for his brother Bradley, the rest of the Russo boys were trash.

Anthony pushed off the fence to follow Delilah because she deserved better. He didn't treat women like garbage, and he needed her to know that.

When he rounded the corner, Delilah was standing over a man curled in the fetal position, and his stomach dropped out. He burst into a run, eating up the gravel in his work boots, and skidded to a halt at her side.

"Are you hurt?"

"No," she sobbed, waving a hand. "He puked on me."

"What?" The sour smell of vomit hit Anthony at the same time the man on the ground burped.

"I was going to sit in my car, and he grabbed me. I thought he was letting me go, but then he projectile vomited all over me. It's sticky and stinky, and there are clumps—"

Anthony gagged, and Delilah's eyes widened, taking a step away from him. "Are you a sympathy puker?"

"No, but you're being super descriptive, and the—smell—isn't helping."

"Are you kidding me right now?" Delilah said shrilly. "I am coated in someone else's stomach contents, trying not to freak out, so if you can't handle it, then go away."

"I can handle it." He nodded toward the parking lot behind her. "I've got a gym bag in the back of my truck with my workout clothes. You can change into them and use my gym towels to clean yourself up, at least."

"I'm not going to fit into your clothes," she murmured.

Anthony almost scoffed, but he caught the crumpled expression on her face. "If not, I've got a blanket."

"I don't want your help," she grumbled. "If you'll go get Holly, I can just leave."

"If I go get Holly, she needs to drive you home in her car, right?"

Delilah shook her head. "No, my car."

"Even worse. Wouldn't you rather stink up my truck than your car? I deserve it for being such a dick."

Delilah sniffled. "You do."

"That's the spirit," Anthony laughed.

"My phone and purse are in the car, and Holly has my keys," Delilah said, arm held out stiffly at her sides as if she was afraid to touch herself.

Anthony reached out and patted her shoulder briefly. "I'll run in and grab them while you get cleaned up. Come on."

"What about him?" she asked, pointing to the prone man at her feet.

Anthony leaned over and reached under the man's arms, dragging him back to prop him against the building. "I'll let Paulie know he's out here." He cupped Delilah's elbow, surprised she didn't jerk away as he led her to the second row where his truck was parked.

"Alright—" He clicked the fob and opened the back door, hauling out the gym bag, the blanket, and a trash bag from the door. "Change out of those clothes and get inside. I'll warm it up."

"Why are you being nice to me?" she asked.

Anthony chuckled. "Don't I seem like a nice guy?"

"Not in my experience."

"Fair enough," he said soberly. "You may not believe it, but I'm not known for taking out my bad temper on people. I apologize for doing it to you."

Delilah didn't meet his eyes when she nodded, turning her back on him. "Will you please unzip me? I'd rather not pull it over my head and get chunks in my hair."

He swallowed back the urge to gag at the imagery and did as she asked, dragging the metal tab down until it stopped above the curve of her ass. Anthony saw the flash of lacy underwear and dropped the zipper like it burned him.

"I'll go get the stuff from Holly," he said, rubbing his singed fingers against the front of his jacket.

"Thanks." He took a step back, turning to leave, but she called out, "Wait, Anthony?"

He twisted around and met her gaze. "Yeah?"

"Please don't tell anyone except Holly what happened," Delilah whispered with wide, shimmering eyes.

Anthony almost reached out to hug her, but stopped, remembering his behavior and the vomit. "I won't."

Anthony turned when she started sliding the straps of the dress down her arms, and went around to the driver's side to start the truck. He turned the heater on high and hopped down, addressing her through the open back door. "There's a towel in the bag if you want to wipe up any excess. Just put your dress and the towel in the trash bag."

"My shoes, too," she said. "It dripped all over them."

"On that note, I'm out." Anthony thought he heard Delilah laugh as he walked away, heading for the front of Brews and Chews, where Paulie was watching the door.

"Anthony, I thought you were already inside," the burly bouncer greeted him.

"I was, but there was an incident off the patio. There's a drunk guy on the side of the building puking."

Paulie grimaced. "Fucking idiots. No one knows how to hold their liquor."

"Sorry to be the bearer of bad news."

Paulie hollered for someone to cover the door as Anthony stepped inside and made a beeline for the table, only to make a sharp turn when he spotted Holly coming in from the patio. They met in the hallway outside the bathroom and before he could get a word out, Holly asked, "Have you seen Delilah?"

"Yeah, she had an accident." At Holly's horrified expression, Anthony added, "She's not hurt, but she needs to leave. I came in to get her purse to give her a ride home."

"Why?" she asked, giving him a quizzical expression. "I drove her car."

"She doesn't want to ride in the car in her condition," he explained, trying to move things along so he could get back to Delilah.

"What happened to her?" Holly asked.

"A drunk guy puked on her."

Holly covered her mouth with her hand, her voice coming out muffled. "Oh my God! Gross!"

"Yeah, which is why she doesn't want to ride in her car."

"And you don't mind her getting it all over yours?" Holly asked.

"Yes, but I gave her some stuff to clean up with and a change of clothes and came to find you." Anthony lowered his voice when a couple passed by on their way out to the patio. "She doesn't want anyone to know what happened."

She nodded. "I'll get the stuff and drive her car home."

"Won't Declan have questions?" Anthony asked.

"He'll be fine," Holly said casually, waving her hand. "Give me a few minutes to say goodbye."

"Sounds good."

He hung back by the bar and watched Holly talk to Declan, who started getting up but sat down when she touched his shoulder. Once she disappeared out the door, Anthony headed over to say his goodbyes to the others around the table.

"I'm taking off. See you guys later." He noticed the additional empty seat and scanned the room. "Hey, where's Pike?"

"He went out front looking for Delilah about five minutes ago," Nick said.

Shit. What the hell was Pike going to think if he found Delilah in Anthony's truck, wearing his clothes or worse . . . naked under a blanket? "I better go find him," Anthony said hurriedly. "Enjoy the rest of your night."

He rushed out the door, passed Paulie and the other bouncer, and nearly collided with Holly. He managed to catch her by the shoulders before she fell backward.

"Sorry," Anthony said, releasing her. "Pike is out here looking for Delilah. I doubt she wants him to find her."

"You're probably be right," she said, holding up what he assumed were Delilah's keys. "I'll take off, so if you see Pike, tell him I had to get Delilah home because she didn't feel good."

"I will," Anthony said.

"Thanks."

Anthony watched her get into the car and back out before he jogged across the parking lot, stalling when he heard Pike calling his name. Pike was coming around from the other side of the building from the patio, frowning. "What are you doing?"

"I'm heading home," Anthony said. "The guys said you were out here, so I came to let you know Nick will give you a ride home."

"That's fine, you were in a sour mood anyway," Pike said, searching the parking lot. "Have you seen Delilah?"

Anthony wasn't thrilled with his friend's description of Anthony's behavior and gritted out, "Holly took her home. She wasn't feeling well."

Pike's frown deepened. "I just saw Holly ten minutes ago. She was looking for her, too."

"I guess she found her."

Pike's shoulders dropped with obvious disappointment. "I'll have to get her number later, then." Pike's demeanor switched up and he eyeballed Anthony with intensity. "Are you okay? Grant left, and you disappeared."

"I'm fine," Anthony said, shrugging. "After bumping into my brother, I'm just not in the mood to hang."

"I get that, but I can come with you if you need—"

"No!" he said, coming off more rushed then he meant to be. He took a slow, even breath and smiled. "I'll be fine. I'm just going to read a book and go to bed."

Pike watched him for several ticks silently, "You're acting twitchy."

Shit, he thought he was doing a better job of hiding it.

"What?" Anthony asked. "Why would you say that?"

"You're shifting your feet like you can't wait to bolt," Pike said, pointing at the ground.

"I told you. I want to go home and relax. It's been a long week," Anthony said, impatiently glancing toward his truck.

"Fine, go." Pike shook his head. "I'll see you tomorrow morning, bro."

"See you."

Pike gave him a disgruntled look and headed back into the bar. The minute he disappeared, Anthony booked it for his truck. The dark tint obscured the view inside, but when he opened the door, he found Delilah wrapped in his blanket.

"Clothes didn't work?" Anthony would never say it out loud but he had been looking forward to seeing her wearing his T-shirt and sweats.

"I didn't even try. I didn't want to get your clothes all nasty." She held up the edge of the blanket without exposing anything important. "This will be easy enough to wash."

"Holly came by with your stuff?" he asked.

Delilah pointed to her little purse. "She did and only snickered a small amount."

Anthony grinned. "It could be a funny story you tell your children someday."

"No, I don't think it's appropriate to tell my children about the time a drunk guy told me I was pretty and puked all over me."

Anthony laughed, putting the truck in reverse. "On a happy note, the smell isn't bad."

"Open the trash bag in the back seat and say that again."

"I don't think I will." He pulled the lever down to drive and headed toward the exit. The nighttime scenery whizzed by as he pulled out of the parking lot, along the main road; the silence thick and heavy in the dark cab.

Searching for a segue to jump-start the conversation, he finally asked, "Do you think we could forget about my blowup on the patio?"

Anthony saw her turn his way out of the corner of his eye. "You offered to let me wear your clothes, knowing I was covered in vomit. I think I can let it go." She cleared her throat, and he glanced her way briefly, "If I can ask you something personal?"

"Uncomfortable personal?" he asked.

"It depends on how close you keep things to the vest."

A few seconds ticked by as he considered and eventually shrugged. "Shoot."

"Why didn't your brother have your new number?"

Anthony grimaced. Of course, she would latch on to the awkward encounter with his brother and wonder about his fucked up family situation. He didn't hang with anyone outside his friend group, and they all knew why he didn't talk to his father and brothers.

He almost didn't answer, but Anthony decided he had nothing to hide. "I guess because I didn't think to reach out and let him know."

"I have additional questions now," Delilah said, chuckling, "but I'll let it go because you clearly don't want to get into it."

"I don't discuss my relationship with my brothers with anyone," Anthony said, his tone harsher than he meant it to.

"You have brothers, plural?" she asked.

"I have four. All older." Anthony's fists clenched the steering wheel until they throbbed. "I was a surprise when Grant was six. Before that, my parents thought they were done."

"They must have been excited," she said, hesitantly.

"My mom was. My brothers were, too, until they got older and lost interest in me."

"I'm sorry." Delilah's tone was soft, heavy with empathy, and he shifted in the cushioned driver's seat. The last thing he wanted was for Delilah pitying him.

"What about your siblings?" he asked.

"I'm an only child."

Anthony chuckled. "That's what I felt like after my parents' divorce. Grant chose to move with our dad to Boise, and I stayed here with our mom. The only one of my siblings to visit was my brother Bradley."

"Where does he live?" Delilah asked.

"Northern Idaho."

"What about your mom?"

A lump climbed up Anthony's throat, making it hard to swallow. "She passed last spring."

"I'm so sorry."

"It's life. I had almost thirty years with her, which is more than some kids get." Anthony cleared his throat. "What about your parents?"

"They moved to Boise while I was in college. They thought I would want to live in the city after graduation and were shocked when I came back here."

Anthony made a left, slowing down through the heart of town. "Why did you?"

"Holly, mostly. I have trouble making friends because I have trust issues with most people."

He didn't tell her he felt the same way about his friends. When his dad left, his mom broke down, and he had no idea how to comfort her. He'd spent a lot of time at Pike's and Nick's houses until she'd finally stopped crying at the drop of the hat.

"Where am I going?" he asked, realizing he'd never asked her address.

"The duplexes on Spruce. Number 404. You'll make a right up ahead, and they'll be on the left."

"Got it. Do you rent or own?"

"I rent. What about you?"

"I live in a camper trailer." He was used to horrified silence from women and wasn't surprised when Delilah didn't respond immediately.

"In an RV park?" she asked, finally.

There was no judgment or disgust in her tone or expression when he glanced her way, just the high-pitched lilt of curiosity.

"No, I bought a few acres past the Winters' Christmas tree farm when I was nineteen." Anthony turned on his blinker and took the right like she'd said. "I saved up to put in a well, septic, and electricity and bought a cheap trailer to fix up. I've been saving for ten years to build my dream house. I'm really close, too."

Now was the time when most people had an opinion on his choices. *"Wow, you've been saving for ten years and still live in a trailer?"* Or his favorite, *"You should have just bought a home already built. It would have been cheaper."* It didn't do him any good to argue because people didn't understand. This was going to be his forever home and he wasn't going to settle for less than what he wanted.

Exactly how he felt when it came to romance. The woman he finally fell in love with was going to make him feel so intensely for her, there would be no question that he loved her.

The house was something he could control, while love was a little more unpredictable.

Anthony braced himself, ready to fire back with a snarktastic comment to whatever condescending opinion she had.

"I think that's astounding," she said, reaching out to touch his shoulder briefly. "Doing something like that takes a lot of patience and sacrifice. I like to spend my money, which is why my dad is always going off on me about emergency funds and unexpected expenses."

Warmth rushed through him and he relaxed, glancing away from the road to smile at her. "Would I get smacked if I said I agreed with your dad?"

Anthony caught the roll of her eyes in the street light. "No, but that's only because I'd flash you in the process. Can't punish and reward you at the same time."

Her tone was lighthearted and playful, but his imagination ran wild thinking about what was going on under the blanket. He'd have to be oblivious not to notice how big her tits were and while he'd tried not to, he'd pictured what they looked like a time or two. His cock strained against the confines of his jeans as he pictured large, rosy nipples and areolas contrasting against her creamy skin. He made a jerky left turn on Spruce, trying to remember what they'd been talking about before.

Delilah cleared her throat. "Sorry, I shouldn't have said that."

"No, you're fine. I was just thinking"—*Don't say about her breasts!*— "I was luckier than a lot of young people. I was paid well in a job that I jumped right into after high school. I was able to get grants for college and pay out of pocket for what was left, so I have no debt. I spent some of the money I earned getting Adventures in Mistletoe off the ground, but I was able to sell my mom's house for a nice profit, making up the difference. I miss my mom, but she always said that house was a constant reminder of my dad. She'd have moved if she could have been able to afford it."

He hung a left into her driveway and put the truck into park, leaving it on so the heater could run. "Looks like Holly dropped off the car and went home."

"I told her I'd be fine." Delilah opened up the door, the dome light catching her smile. "Thank you for your help and seeing me home."

Anthony reached across and gripped her hand when she started to get out. "What are you doing?"

"Getting the bag from the back and going inside."

Anthony scowled. "You've got no shoes on, and it's freezing."

"It's not far—"

"I don't give a shit if it is one foot or ten. Do not get out of this truck."

He opened the driver's side door and shut it on her protests. He rounded the back of the vehicle and grabbed the trash bag from the back seat with her dress and shoes. He dropped it unceremoniously into her lap, and when the blanket slipped down slightly, revealing the top of her bare breast, he cleared his throat. "Pull the blanket around you tighter."

"What are you going to—" He slipped his arm behind her back and under her knees, lifting her from the seat. "Anthony!" she squealed.

He tapped the door with his hip, closing it. "Can you get the keys to your front door out?"

"You don't need to carry me! I can walk."

"I already told you I'm not letting you walk on the cold ground in your bare feet," he said, his voice breathless and a little high, "so stop arguing and get those keys ready to open the door."

Delilah leaned her head back, studying his face so intently he almost squirmed. "Are you holding your breath because I stink?"

Anthony's lips twitched, suppressing a laugh. "A little bit."

Delilah buried her face in his chest, her breath escaping in a groaning laugh. "This is so embarrassing."

"It could be worse. You could have puked on yourself." He paused on her front step, inches from the handle. "Open that storm door, would you?"

"This is ridiculous," Delilah muttered, doing what he asked. Once she had access to the front door, she stuck her key in and unlocked it. "Look at that! You can put me down."

"Turn the knob."

She did, and when the door swung in, he dropped her gently inside her home. A series of high-pitched barks erupted behind her and Delilah turned, speaking calmy. "It's okay, Leia. I'll let you out in a minute."

Anthony couldn't tell where the dog was in the dark house, but it's bark was yappy. "What kind of dog?"

"A corgi mix."

"One of those fuzzy things with short legs?" He laughed.

"She is not a thing!"

"If you say so." Anthony grinned at her outrage and shoved his hands in his pockets. In spite of the sour, subtle smell of the drunk's vomit, Anthony still wanted to reach for her and pull her in for a tight, warm hug. He'd loved the feel of her in his arms and wanted to experience it again.

Rather than come off like a creeper though, he simply said, "I recommend a hot shower and that you deep soak that dress. The shoes might be a lost cause. They're impractical anyway."

"Oh, you think so, Mr. Know It All?" She shot back with only mild irritation, and he was relieved that she really seemed to have forgiven him for his earlier behavior.

"I do, and since you said yourself I know everything, you should probably listen." He twisted and removed her keys from the door, holding them out to her. "Don't forget these. Good night."

"Good night," she whispered.

Anthony closed the storm door and headed back down the walkway to his truck. He suddenly heard the creak of the metal open again and the pitter-patter of bare feet on cement behind him. Anthony stopped and turned around with an exasperated, "Damn it, Delilah, get back ins—"

His words got cut off when Delilah launched herself against him, and he caught her, wrapping his arms around her blanket-clad body.

"I wanted to hug you but remembered I was naked under here."

Anthony groaned and lifted her off her feet, the heat of her body burning through the blanket. He carried her back to the front door while she laughed and wriggled in his arms.

"Good god, woman, are you trying to kill me? Stop wiggling like that before I drop you."

Delilah giggled and twisted the knob of the storm door when they reached it. Although Anthony set her down inside with a scowl, his lips twitched. "Do I have to tell you to stay?"

She held on to the blanket with one hand and smacked him with the other. "I'm not a dog, you jerk!"

"Ow! I'm sorry," he said, laughing before he leaned closer, sniffing loudly. "Seriously, go shower. You stink."

Anthony shut the door on her loud, "Hey!"

Chapter Seven

Delilah pulled Anthony's blanket from the laundry and carried it into the kitchen to fold. The school was closed because of Thanksgiving this week, so there were no jobs to take. She needed to get onto the freelance website and find some writing jobs, so she'd have money coming in. She'd applied for a few open positions at various online publications but understood how competitive they were. Everyone wanted to be able to write from home, and while she'd made decent money writing for hire, submitting editorials and research articles didn't bring her joy.

Her phone rang in the distance, and she dropped the blanket, running down the hallway with Leia barking excitedly on her heels. Delilah spotted her phone on her bed and dived across it, scrambling to answer when she saw her agent's name flashing across the screen. Leia bounded up and proceeded to pounce on her back, mistaking her panic for play.

"Hi, Beth," she answered breathlessly, ducking her head to avoid Leia's darting tongue. "Stop it."

"Delilah?" Beth said. "Is this a bad time?"

"No, I was just in the other room." She sat up, pushing Leia off the bed. The dog sat back on her haunches and looked up at Delilah, her ears pinned back. Delilah mouthed, *I'm sorry*, as if the dog could understand her, before addressing Beth. "How are you?"

"Oh, getting ready to drive south for the holiday. How about you?" she asked.

"Doing laundry at the moment."

"The never-ending battle." Beth cleared her throat, the small, short cough a common tell Delilah had learned for when her agent had bad news. "I wanted to talk to you about your manuscript. I got an email from Rebecca Stone of Orion Publishing, and she doesn't think it'll be a good fit."

Delilah's heart sank, and she flopped onto her back on the mattress. "That's it, right? We're dead in the water."

"With this series, but the good news is, she loves your voice," Beth said cheerfully. "If you're free, she'd like to hop on the phone with you next week and discuss some potential story ideas?"

Delilah wanted to squeal with joy but swallowed it back, keeping her voice even and calm. "That works for me."

"Great! I'll email you both and make official introductions, and we can set something up."

"What about my series?" Delilah asked.

"That's up to you," Beth said, her tone neutral. Considerably different from the excitement she'd conveyed when Delilah first pitched it. "You can self-pub it. It's a great idea, and the writing is on point; otherwise, I wouldn't have taken it out. Some things are hard to sell to trade publishers, but that doesn't mean they don't have an audience."

Delilah thought about the two series on her computer, numbering nine books total. Without someone to read them, they were worthless. While Delilah knew very little about self-publishing, she'd read enough articles to know it was expensive up front. She was barely getting by now; how could she afford a bunch of out-of-pocket expenses?

Still, it wasn't Beth's fault no one had fallen in love with her series, so she tried to mask her disappointment with pleasantness. "Thank you for trying, anyway."

"We will find you a writing home, I promise. More to come. Bye, sweets!" Beth called out, her words running together in one run-on goodbye.

"Bye." Delilah ended the call and stared up at the ceiling. An editor at a major publishing house wanted to work with her. Even if there wasn't anything concrete, she felt like celebrating.

She sat up and checked the time on her phone. Holly would be at A Shop for All Seasons by now. Delilah could drop Anthony's blanket off at his store, then go next door to Kiss My Donut to grab two mochas and deliver the news to Holly at the year-round holiday shop. That way, she wouldn't be tempted to linger with Anthony and make an ass out of herself again, the way she had Saturday night. When she replayed running back outside and jumping into his arms like a love-struck idiot, she wanted to crawl under her comforter and never emerge again.

Delilah could blame it on being drunk, but that only made it more embarrassing. Despite her initial protests, Anthony picking her up and carrying her easily to the front door was the biggest turn-on she didn't know she wanted. After cleaning up in the shower, Delilah couldn't stop reliving Anthony's strong arms around her or how his pinewood-scented cologne distracted her from the mess she'd been underneath the blanket. She'd pulled her seafoam green "assistant" out of the drawer and imagined Anthony carrying her all the way inside and into her bedroom, where he'd put her in the shower and helped her clean up.

While the reality of scrubbing vomit from her body hadn't been remotely sexy, in her head, it was erotic as hell.

Delilah sat up, catching Leia's eye as the dog was wiggling on the floor by her feet. "Do you want to go for a ride and visit Aunt Holly?"

Leia bounded to her feet at the word "ride" and disappeared down the hallway before Delilah could even get off the bed. She followed her bouncing dog. Delilah grabbed the blanket from the table, disappointed that it no longer had the lingering scent of Anthony on the soft fabric. She helped Leia into her harness and snapped her leash onto the metal loop on the back before heading out. She admonished her dog for pulling ahead, and Leia did a neat circle back to her side.

While it would have been a short walk into town, the temperature had dropped ten degrees since yesterday, and Delilah didn't feel like going inside for her heavy coat. Her Easily Distracted sweatshirt was warm enough for short bursts of outside activities. She'd put on her tennis shoes because she had every intention to stop by the gym and sign up. Part of her journey to change would include some form of physical activity in a climate-controlled environment with access to watch a hit show to distract her from the pain.

Once Delilah had Leia settled in the passenger seat, she circled around the front to the driver's side to start the car. She turned the heater up, but the first few minutes of air were frigid, so she turned it back down. Having lived in Idaho her entire life, she should know to warm up her car before she got in it, but she'd rather sit in a cold car than make two possible trips along the walkway where she could easily hit a patch of ice and slip, cracking her head against the ground.

While she waited for her car to warm up, she pulled out her phone and scrolled through TikTok. She followed a few prominent fantasy romance authors, but most of her For You page was delicious recipes and hot men cosplay dancing. It was a weird obsession, but she couldn't look away.

She clicked her notifications, and the first one that caught her eye was that Pike had followed her. She hadn't posted videos yet, except a few of Leia, but he'd liked all of them. She clicked on his profile and checked out his pinned video.

Pike and Anthony sat on the couch playing a video game, throwing shade at each other. Pike suddenly screamed, and Anthony tossed his controller on the couch. The camera moved with them, and Nick's voice came through from behind the camera, "I think you hurt his feelings, bro."

"Aw, don't be mad, baby!" Pike laughed, jumping across Anthony's lap. The bigger man stood up and curled Pike in his arms several times.

"You might have killed me in the game," Anthony growled, lifting Pike in his arms, "but I could break you in half."

"I don't know whether to feel turned on or emasculated," Pike said, making kissing noises at Anthony.

"Get the fuck out of here," Anthony said, tossing Pike onto the couch, all of them laughing. Delilah paused the video, staring at Anthony's smile, and her heart accelerated.

How had this happened? A year ago, she'd have been losing her mind over Pike following her on social media, and instead, she was scrolling through his videos and ogling his friend.

What was wrong with her? Anthony Russo was not into her. The only kiss between them had been a drunk one-off that he had cut short, clearly because he wasn't interested in hooking up with her. His actions on Saturday, except biting her head off, had been those of a concerned acquaintance and not a protective potential love interest. She needed to get her head examined because something was malfunctioning up there.

Delilah set her phone in the cup holder and addressed Leia. "Tell me the truth. Do you think Mommy is crazy?"

Leia wiggled adorably, but her ears flattened against her head, and her eyes darted away almost guiltily as if to say *"I probably shouldn't answer that but yes."*

"I appreciate your honesty."

Delilah put the car into reverse and backed out of the driveway, heading toward the main street. The house on the corner sported a giant blow-up turkey on the lawn, which was at odds with the house directly across from it that had a massive Santa. A sign staked in Santa's yard was directed at the turkey's owners.

No one cares!

She craned her neck as she pulled up to the stop sign, and sure enough, there was a sign she hadn't noticed before. *It's too early for Christmas!*

While Delilah agreed with Mr. Turkey, she would never tell Holly that. Her best friend lived and breathed Christmas, and although she supported her in all things, Delilah thought people took it too far. All those videos that would start popping up on social media of teens asking for expensive gifts or Christmas trees with fifty thousand presents underneath? No wonder kids were so entitled today; society taught them to consume, consume, consume!

Bitter, party of one!

Delilah pulled into the first parking spot she found, arguing silently with the little voice in her head. Her parents hadn't wanted her to be a spoiled brat and had kept Christmas simple. Maybe that was why she didn't understand going overboard.

Delilah grabbed the blanket she'd tossed in the back and got out of the car, rounding the hood to gather Leia. They'd parked across the street from Adventures in Mistletoe, and Delilah checked both ways before she and Leia jogged across.

"Delilah Gill, don't make me write you a ticket for jaywalking!"

Delilah waved at Officer Wren Little, who had spotted her from down the street and was now on the other side.

"There was no one coming," Delilah said.

"It doesn't matter; crosswalks are there for a reason!"

"I'll remember that next time," Delilah said, escaping with Leia inside Adventures in Mistletoe. The last thing she wanted was Officer Wren to find said crosswalk and come to her side of the street just to lecture her more.

Anthony looked up when she shut the door, smiling. "Hey, you."

"Hi." She held up the blanket with one hand. "All clean."

"Thanks," he said, coming around the counter. When he spotted Leia, he stopped, squatting down. "Were you the one barking like crazy the other night?"

Leia wiggled and pulled, trying to get closer, and Delilah took a few steps forward so he could pet her. Leia put her paw on his knee, leaning into his hand.

"You're a cute little fluff, aren't you?" Anthony said.

"She thinks so," Delilah said, holding his blanket out to him. He took it as he climbed to his feet and set it on the counter.

Anthony smiled at Delilah, even as he addressed the two of them like Leia understood him. "Are you two just delivering the blanket, or do you have something fun planned?"

Dang, why is he so flipping cute? "We're going to stop next door and say hi to Holly, and then we'll most likely go home. What about you?"

"I am taking a couple up the mountain on four-wheelers today."

"That sounds like . . . something."

He chuckled. "I know you don't like outdoor activities."

"Especially not in the cold," Delilah said, shuddering just thinking about it.

"That's why we bundle up and keep blankets in the car for emergencies."

"Like when girls need to strip down and wear one home?" Delilah laughed.

Anthony winked at her. "What other emergencies are there?"

Delilah suddenly sobered. "Thank you for not telling anyone what happened. I was embarrassed."

"You didn't have any reason to be. It could have happened to anyone."

"Yeah, but it didn't." Delilah sighed. "When I was younger, people laughed at me all the time. I was the best punchline around. I don't want to go back to that."

Delilah didn't know why she'd told him that and avoided looking at his face because if she caught him watching her with anything resembling pity, she would expire on the spot.

"Nobody thinks of you as a punchline." Anthony took a step closer, his hand settling under her chin, and she let him lift her gaze to meet his. "From the minute you walked through those doors on Saturday night, you had everyone's attention in the room because you were mesmerizing."

Including yours?

She didn't dare to ask, though.

"I've been curious about it," he said, dropping his hand from her face. The warmth of his touch lingered for several moments as she tried to concentrate on what he was asking, but those moss-green eyes were incredibly distracting.

"What?"

"Why did you get all done up on Saturday night? Were you looking to take someone home?"

God, he was so close. Those full lips hovering, and she wondered what he'd taste like today.

"I—yes. I wanted . . . that." *Real smooth, Delilah.*

"Anyone?"

"Um . . . " *Oh God, don't say it!* "I was looking for someone good in bed."

Anthony's eyebrows shot up. "Really? How would you know before you took them home whether they are or aren't?"

"I wouldn't know for sure, but there are certain characteristics of a"—*Not sex-god*—"sexually proficient being."

He burst out laughing, and her cheeks burned.

"Why is it funny?" Delilah asked defensively. "Because a fat girl can't possibly want good sex? She should just take what she gets and be grateful anyone wants her at all?"

"What?" Anthony's jaw dropped open. "Delilah, that's not what I meant!"

She'd already spun around to rush out the door, but Pike was coming through when he spotted her, a broad smile spread across his face. "Hey! Is it weird if I say I've been looking for you?"

"Hi. No, I mean, depends," she said, fighting to rein in her emotions. "I don't owe you money, do I?"

"Funny!" Pike said, unknowingly blocking her escape. "But no, I wanted to check in and see how you were feeling."

"Feeling . . . Oh, after the other night. You know, drank too much. Needed to sleep it off."

"If you're fully recovered, maybe we could have coffee sometime?" Pike asked, stepping closer to the counter. "Either before or after work?"

"Um—" Delilah couldn't believe that after years of wanting Pike, of worshipping him, that she was at a loss now that everything she'd ever dreamed of was within her grasp. "I mean, we—"

"I'm going to take off," Anthony said behind her, making Delilah lose her train of thought again.

"Alright, man." Pike patted him on the back as he walked by, and only Delilah could see when Anthony paused at the door his expression thunderous as it shifted from Pike's back to her face before it dissolved into an evil grin.

"By the way, thanks for bringing my blanket back, Delilah."

Her mouth dropped, and Pike turned around, watching Anthony walk past the window and disappear.

Pike faced forward, his forehead furrowed. "Why did you have his blanket?"

Chapter Eight

Anthony heaved the bar above his head in angry, rapid thrusts while Nick spotted him from above. It was Monday after work and once he'd gotten back from taking the Andersons out, he'd still been wired about the misunderstanding with Delilah and Pike's obliviousness.

"Hey, Hulk, why don't you take it easy?" Nick said, his hand hovering under the bar. "I'm afraid you're going to tear something."

"I'm fine," Anthony grunted, setting the weight bar back into the J hooks, his muscles burning at the overuse. He needed to let off some steam, or he would seek out the source of his frustration.

Because a fat girl can't possibly want good sex?

Anthony sat up, desperately wanting to hit something. Why had Pike walked in right then like an eager puppy, drooling all over her before they finished their conversation? She stood there and encouraged Pike like Anthony hadn't been the one making sure she got cleaned up and home safe on Saturday night. Making plans to date his best friend, who hadn't even noticed her before Saturday while he'd—

Kissed her? Rejected her? Ignored her?

"Hey, man," Nick said, jarring him out of his thoughts with a hand on Anthony's shoulder. "I don't want to come off like a nag, but you aren't acting like yourself."

"I'm in a mood, man, alright?" Anthony said roughly, climbing to his feet.

"No, I got that. I'm trying to suss out why."

Anthony made his way toward the locker room without responding. While working out together was usually chill, Anthony wished he'd come alone. Nick was like a dog with a bone and wouldn't let up until he told him.

Which he didn't plan on doing. If he was going to talk to anyone, it would be Delilah about what she'd accused him of.

Anthony wasn't naive. He knew some men cared about a woman's weight. Hell, it was everywhere. Movies. TV. Books. The damn tabloids at the grocery store commenting on a celebrity's weight, usually a woman, and the next magazine would be advertising some miracle diet. He wasn't obtuse to these things because his mom had pointed them out to him, especially after his dad left.

"This world sure gets off on telling us how we should look, right?"

The reality was Delilah had lumped him in with all those assholes. Assholes like his dad and brothers.

Thinking about them brought up a new irritation he'd been trying to forget. Grant showing up in town hadn't been to catch up. He'd been on a mission from their dad to invite Anthony to Thanksgiving with his father and his wife. Anthony hadn't talked to the man since his mother's funeral, when his dad acted like he cared, and then his dad had the balls to ask him what Anthony would do with *his* house.

Not his mom's house. Not Anthony's house. *His.*

Nick and Pike had jumped in to pull Anthony off his dad. Grant had his father in a bear hug, hauling him out of the wake. His other brothers had tried talking to him after that, but he didn't want to hear from any of them. Since the divorce, he could count how often his siblings had visited on both hands. With the exception of Bradley, the rest of them could fuck off.

Which brought him back to Delilah. She'd assumed he thought she was less than because of her size, and nothing could be further from the truth.

He hadn't gotten a chance to tell her that before Pike showed up and apology-blocked him.

Anthony shouldn't be such a dick to Pike. The guy had no clue as to what he'd walked in on, and even if Pike had known, it would have been weird to ask him to leave Anthony alone with the woman he was interested in.

"Is Pike being a pain in the ass?" Nick asked, breaking into his thoughts.

Anthony opened his locker with a laugh, grabbing his towel. "Pike is always a pain in the ass." He wiped the scratchy cloth over his sweaty face and tossed it back inside. "But no. I had a misunderstanding with someone and didn't get to explain myself. It left a bad taste in my mouth."

"Can't you call them?" Nick asked.

"I don't have their number."

"Huh?" Nick leaned against the lockers, watching him. "Is it a woman?"

Anthony glanced away. "Why does it matter who it is?"

"Because I spill my guts to you regularly." Nick said, studying him intensely. "Why are you being cagey with me?"

Anthony cleared his throat. "Maybe I don't want to talk about it yet?"

"Oh, so this is *big*," Nick said, stroking his chin. "Were you seeing someone and not sharing with the group?"

"No," Anthony said, taking a long drink from his water bottle. "I haven't been out with anyone since the summer."

Nick winced. "The chick that lied about liking camping?"

"Yep."

Nick used one of the white gym towels on his own face, revealing a grin when he lowered it. "Is it about your life as a monk?"

Anthony scowled. "Fuck off. I should have never told you."

"What, that you vowed to stay celibate until you found the one?" Nick asked, fluttering his lashes. "I think that's romantic."

Anthony shut his locker with a snap. "Can we stop talking about this?"

"Sure, but I'm going to wear you down."

"You do what you gotta do," Anthony said, heading for the urinals. "I'm going to take a piss and then hit the bag for a bit."

"Is that your way of trying to get me to shut up? Because I have no qualms about talking to you while we pee." Nick came up alongside Anthony and lowered his voice, "Together."

Anthony snorted. Nick didn't make good on his threat, leaving Anthony in peace. When he'd first decided to give up sex, Nick was the only one he told. He was afraid that he'd end up being a punchline.

Laughter shattered the quiet as more men entered the locker room.

"Damn, did you see the size of her? How does she think coming in here in *that* is okay? I'll never get that image out of my head."

Anthony froze, recognizing Trip Douglas's nasally voice.

"She's pretty, though; if she's trying to lose weight, in about fifty pounds, she'll be bangable. Did you see those tits?"

Anthony was almost surprised to hear Brodie joining in, but he'd been Trip's lapdog since high school. Anthony had played offensive and defensive lines, going shoulder to shoulder with Brodie on more than one occasion. He'd never disliked the guy until this moment.

"The tits are always the first thing to go," Trip said, his voice thick with disgust. "Twenty bucks says she loses weight and looks like a shar-pei."

Anthony crossed the room to the sink, his jaw clenched. This is the type of guy Delilah thought he was? Anthony wanted to throttle these idiots.

"Couple of pricks," Nick muttered, leaning against the sink beside him.

A locker slammed, and Brodie said, "I heard that fat girls are the freakiest in bed, though. They're so happy to fuck someone, they'll do whatever you want."

"Maybe I should ask her out and see if it's true?" Trip responded with a dark laugh.

Today was not the day. He'd wanted something to hit, and these two dick bags would jolly fucking do.

Anthony rounded the corner and spotted them in front of the lockers. Brodie had his back to Anthony, his large frame softer than it had been years ago. Anthony slammed his shoulder into Brodie, sending him catapulting into Trip. Both men hit the lockers, a cursing tangle of limbs, and Brodie stumbled, losing his towel in the process. When they hit the floor, Brodie landed on top of Trip, naked and sprawled out. Neither man moved for several seconds, frozen in place.

"Not in public, boys," Nick deadpanned.

Anthony didn't have to turn around; he could tell by the barely restrained laughter in Nick's voice he was about to lose it.

"Watch where you're fucking going, Russo!" Trip hollered. Anthony glanced back and watched Trip push at Brodie's naked frame.

"Sorry, I didn't see you there."

Nick slapped his back when they exited the locker room, gasping with laughter. "Holy shit, that was the best thing I've seen all day."

Anthony smiled. "I'll admit, I feel a little better now."

"We should probably vamoose unless we want to wait for them outside." Nick shook his head, grinning like a sinner. "By the look on Trip's face, he will be spoiling for a fight."

"Nick! Anthony!" The manager, Frank, called out, heading straight for them. "I heard a crash in the locker room!"

"How?" Anthony asked.

"I was in the women's locker room giving a tour and heard it through the wall."

Anthony saw the dark ponytail before it fully registered Delilah was behind Frank, staring at Anthony with wide eyes. She wore a pink off-the-shoulder top that revealed the strap of her black sports bra and a broad seam of cleavage.

Anthony scanned the room, a sickening feeling settling in his stomach. "You hear anything else before the crash?"

"No, why?" Frank asked.

Anthony's shoulders sagged with relief. Even if Trip and Brodie hadn't been talking about Delilah, he couldn't imagine her wanting to stick around if she'd heard what they were saying.

"I thought maybe you heard arguing or something? The only thing that happened when we were there is I tripped when we were leaving and accidentally bumped into a couple of guys."

"Uh-huh." Frank watched him skeptically before turning to address Delilah. "I need to go in and check on this. I'll be right back, Delilah."

"Not a problem, Frank."

The older man disappeared inside, and Nick clapped Anthony on the shoulder. "You think Trip is going to tell Frank?"

"Tell him what?" Delilah asked.

"Nothing," Anthony said.

"Okay." She dragged out the word before she reached into the pocket of her leggings and pulled out a black earbud case. "See ya."

Delilah hopped onto the nearest treadmill, setting her pink water bottle in the machine's cup holder.

"Anthony!" Frank came out of the locker room with Brodie and Trip behind him, dressed in track pants and T-shirts. "These two gentlemen say you shoved them."

"It was an accident, Frank," Anthony said, innocently. "I came around the corner and didn't know they were there until we collided."

"It's true," Nick said.

Trip and Brodie wore identical scowls, but Anthony almost broke when Trip mouthed, *Fuck you.*

"I'm too old to deal with this shit," Frank said, throwing up his hands. "When you're in this building, act like grown-ups. Otherwise, work your shit out elsewhere."

Frank left them and walked up to the side of Delilah's treadmill to talk to her. Anthony faced Brodie and Trip with a smirk. "You two tattled over a little bump?"

"Why the fuck did you slam me into the locker?" Brodie grumbled.

"If I needed a reason," Anthony said, all amusement erased from his demeanor. "I could have found one in any of the douchey things you said."

"What? You got butt hurt over us talking about banging Delilah Gill?" Trip asked.

Anthony stepped toward him, rumbling in his chest, and Trip's lips tilted into a smirk. "If she's on your radar, Russo, maybe I've been sleeping on her charms."

This motherfucker—

Anthony lunged at Trip, but Nick caught him and dragged him toward the front door. Trip jogged backwards a few steps, calling out "Don't worry, Anthony. I'll keep her warm for ya!"

Anthony nearly escaped Nick's hold, his body pulsating with the need to wipe that smug smile off Trip's stupid fucking face, but Nick tightened his grip and nearly lifted Anthony off his feet.

"Stop fighting me. Fuck!" Nick groaned, getting him through the door and onto the sidewalk before releasing him. He then blocked the door, keeping Anthony from charging back inside.

"Get out of my way, Nick," Anthony panted darkly.

"No! You need to take a walk because this ain't you, man! You don't lose it like this."

Anthony took a breath, closing his eyes. His friend was right. He was the levelheaded one. Not that he wasn't willing to jump into a fight, but he didn't start one over some shit-talking prick he wouldn't wipe his boots on.

"Do me a favor, alright? Go back inside and make sure that dickhead stays away from Delilah?"

Nick nodded. "I can do that, but I gotta know. Are you interested in her?"

He didn't know anymore.

"Pike is interested in her. She's just a friend."

Nick studied him, and Anthony wasn't sure if he believed him. "Get out of here and cool off. I'll keep her safe."

Chapter Nine

"J ust because someone is a bachelor doesn't mean they should be included."

Delilah nodded, agreeing with Merry. They were sitting around the Winters' dining room table in Holly and Merry's parents' home on Wednesday, discussing the details of the bachelor auction. Although they'd already compiled an excellent list, they were still ten bachelors short, and they'd been deliberating for over an hour.

"They are a part of the town and should be included," Holly said, writing Trip's and Brodie's names on the whiteboard she'd brought. It was propped on an easel, and Merry snagged the eraser from the table. She got up slowly, rubbing her stomach, and Delilah wondered if it hurt or it was an instinctual move.

"Are you going to deal with them during the auction and the days leading up to it?" Merry asked, pointing the eraser at Holly. "Because my blood pressure won't be able to take it."

"Lies, you are the picture of health," Holly said, positioning herself in front of the board. "You just don't want to deal with them."

"You're right, I don't." Merry tickled her sister's ribs and Holly moved out of the way, giggling. Merry took the opportunity to erase the names again. "Therefore, we agree. No jerks."

"Delilah, help me out." Holly flopped into the closest chair, clasping her hands in front of her. "Even if we don't like someone, other women in town will fall all over themselves to bid on them."

Delilah shot Merry an apologetic smile. "She isn't wrong."

"Fine, we'll come back to them. Who else do we have?"

"I think we should ask other women of different ages. We're limiting ourselves to men in our age group and above. At the gym . . ."

Delilah's face burned. She tried to think of the right way to word what she wanted to convey, or Holly would be all over her.

"What about the gym?" Holly asked.

Delilah tucked a hair back behind her ear. "I saw some men I didn't recognize that were interesting looking."

"Interesting how?" Holly asked, watching her squirm.

"It should not be this hard to fill a bachelor auction roster," Merry muttered, taking the seat next to Holly.

"I just mean that there were men from their early twenties to their mid-sixties, and we shouldn't just assume that every woman wants what we do. We must broaden our search."

There had been several men at the gym she'd noticed since she started going Monday, but she didn't want to admit to herself there was only one she was looking for. When she'd bumped into Anthony after her explosion at his shop, Delilah had expected him to approach her to talk about it. Instead, he'd left without a word, and she couldn't decipher if she was relieved or disappointed.

"Good point. Maybe we should put it out on social media? It would be a good way to garner interest, and the men can come to us," Holly said, crooking her finger. "Come here, big boy. You know you wanna be auctioned for charity."

Delilah laughed. It had been a long time since she'd hung out with both Winters sisters, but it was lovely to be invited. Even if she wasn't a Christmas enthusiast, this time of year was essential to the town, as were all the events leading up to it. She wanted to do her part.

If only she hadn't noticed Anthony's truck by the tree tent outside. Delilah knew that Anthony and Pike came out to help the Winters family prepare for the rush of townspeople who picked up their trees the day after Thanksgiving. Instead of a family business, they should call the tree farm a family and friends business. She hoped he'd be too busy setting up for the post-Thanksgiving crowds to come to the house and would stay out in the flocking tent.

"On another note, do we want them to come out in casual, evening, or costumes?" Holly asked.

Delilah laughed. "Costumes? Like what, the Village People?"

"I was thinking more along the lines of a lumberjack. Handyman. Cop," Holly drawled out each word seductively, waggling her eyebrows.

"You're getting a little extra there, Hol, and I'm going to need you to dial it back," Merry said.

"I'm a saleswoman and fantasy sells."

The front door opened, and Clark came through with Nick, Pike, Anthony, and Declan trailing behind. Delilah's stomach dropped as she took in Anthony's disheveled appearance before he disappeared into the bathroom. Pike waved at her before he headed into the kitchen. The faucet turned on, and several of the men joined him, presumably to wash their hands.

"You look like you've been rolling on the ground," Merry said, lifting her face for a kiss from Clark. He leaned down to oblige her. He pulled away, holding his hands up. "I'm disgusting, or I'd hug you, too."

Merry's Great Pyrenees, Daisy, got up from the bed in the living room corner and trotted around, greeting each man, starting with Clark.

"Hey, Daisy Mae," he said, his gaze traveling over the room. "Where is Jace?"

"He went with Mom to grab pizzas," Merry said, referring to their son. "With tomorrow being Thanksgiving, she didn't want to cook."

When Anthony returned to the room, Delilah tried to look anywhere but at him. She'd already noticed too much about him, like how the green of his flannel was the same color as his eyes or that his neck was streaked with dirt before he'd headed into the bathroom. Delilah busied herself with reading the list of men who had agreed to participate in the bachelor auction so she wouldn't accidentally catch his gaze. Or Pike's.

After Anthony awkwardly threw her under the bus by mentioning his blanket at the shop, she'd made up a story about locking herself out of her car and Anthony letting her use his blanket to stay warm. Pike hadn't pressed her for more, especially after she ducked out when she spotted Holly, but he had followed her to get her number. It should have thrilled her, but she'd been impatient, itching to escape him.

Delilah wasn't sure how it had happened, but her interest in Pike had fizzled like an antacid in a cup of water.

Ironically, she'd instigated changes in her life meant to catch the attention of sexually confident men, and the one she had wanted for so long was there for the taking, but now she found his interest insulting. Everyone knew how she felt about Pike, and he first noticed her because of a shiny dress like a ferret and a set of keys. Delilah hadn't considered how frustrating it would be if her plan worked on men who had known her for years. Or it could be his overexuberant attention that turned her off? Sex-gods were supposed to be relaxed and commanding.

Like Anthony ordering you to stay in the truck so your feet wouldn't get cold?

Nope, she wasn't thinking about Anthony in that capacity. He'd stopped their kiss last year because he wasn't interested. He'd laughed at her when she admitted the truth about her wardrobe upgrade. Plus, the way he'd disappeared at the gym after seeing her? He was a coward, and she didn't have the patience for his games.

"What are you ladies working on?" Pike asked, coming up behind Delilah's chair and holding on to the back, his fingers grazing her shoulders through her sweater.

"The bachelor auction," Holly said.

"What about it?" Anthony took the seat across from Delilah, and she could have screamed in frustration. He wore a dirty Broncos hat over his dark hair with the brim pushed up, his green eyes on her.

"We're deciding what the bachelors should wear."

Anthony smirked. "Clothes, preferably."

"I don't know; I think I look good in the buff," Pike said.

"No nudity!" Merry said loudly.

"I agree," Holly said, pointing at the board. "Do you guys think we should exclude men because we don't like them?"

"Yes," the men chorused, and Holly threw up her hands.

"Seriously, I thought you would be the voices of reason."

"If you dislike them, something must be wrong," Nick said.

"They wouldn't be dangerous," Holly grumbled, before elaborating, "Just assholes."

Declan walked around the table and rubbed Holly's shoulders. "Do you want to send them off with some unsuspecting woman if you think they're douchebags?"

Pike nodded. "Some women are into jerks."

"I've never understood that," Delilah said, her gaze flicking to Anthony. When he arched an eyebrow, she looked away, her cheeks burning.

"What? Women liking jerks?" Pike asked, taking the seat next to her. "Everyone has a soul mate, even assholes."

Delilah laughed. "You believe in soul mates?"

Pike's expression was incredulous as he reared back in his chair. "Sure, don't you?"

"No," Delilah said flatly.

"What do you believe in?" Anthony asked.

Delilah finally looked at Anthony, who was watching her with a neutral expression, which contrasted with the loaded question he'd lobbed at her. Only his eyes gave away his interest in her answer, the green orbs bright and focused.

"I believe in being in love because you want to be," Delilah said, unable to look away from the intensity in his eyes. "Not because you think the universe planned it out."

"That's where you're wrong, and I'll give you an example," Pike said, clapping his hands and holding them out like a presenter. "My good buddy, Nick—"

"Why am I a part of this conversation?" Nick asked.

"Shush, the grown-ups are talking," Pike said, earning a laugh from the others, while Nick rolled his eyes. "Anyway, Nick went to serve his country, came back, and got dumped. All these things had to align for him to fall in love with his soul mate, Noel."

"Or they happened to be single simultaneously, which allowed them to explore their feelings," Delilah said.

"I'm against being used as the case study for either of your arguments," Nick griped.

"Help me out here, man," Pike said, addressing Anthony and ignoring Nick's protests.

Anthony shrugged. "I don't think I have anything to add to this."

"Why not?" Holly asked, joining the conversation from the comfort of Declan's lap.

Anthony glanced away when he answered, "I've never been in love, so I don't know why it happens."

Delilah's jaw dropped. "Never?"

His cheeks flushed. "Nope."

"What about Yvette?" Pike asked, pointing at his friend. "You dated her for a year after high school."

"Just because I stayed with someone doesn't mean it's love," Anthony scoffed. "Look at Nick. He was with Amber for how many years?"

Nick grabbed the dry eraser from Merry's hand and chucked it at

Anthony. "I would appreciate it if you would stop talking about me and my romantic past, especially since my wife will be here any minute."

Pike made a face. "Is it just me, or is it weird that he calls Noel 'wife' instead of by her name?"

"It's an accurate description," Nick growled.

"Can we get back to the topic at hand?" Merry hollered, retrieving her eraser from the floor and glowering at them.

The group quieted, and Merry burst into tears. Clark hugged her, obviously fighting a smile.

"What did we do?" Holly stage whispered.

"You're all aggravating her," Clark said, glaring at his sister-in-law with mock ferocity, "and I won't tolerate it."

Merry sniffled loudly. "I love you, but you smell."

Clark released her and stepped back. "I do?"

"Someone does." She sniffed the air and gagged. "Yeah, no, you all need to go shower. You smell like moldy sweat."

"Damn, that's harsh," Pike said, lifting his arm. He held it out to Delilah. "Do I smell bad?"

Delilah burst out laughing, leaning away from his pit. "I don't want to find out."

"It's probably me," Nick said, heading toward his sister. "I didn't shower this morning before coming over to help. What do you think, Merry?" He lifted his arm and shoved his pit in his sister's face.

Merry's scream turned into a series of dry heaves, and she pushed him away, dropping the dry eraser in the process. Daisy, who had returned to her bed, jumped to her feet with a ferocious bark. Nick backed off with his hands up as the one hundred and twenty pounds of fluffy white fur rushed toward him.

"Uncle Nick was just playing, Dais!"

"Kill him, baby!" Merry gasped, scrambling toward the first door to the left with Daisy right behind her. Merry shut it before the dog could follow her inside, yelling through the door, "I hate you, Nick Winters!"

"Not cool, man," Clark said, glaring at Nick while Daisy pawed at the door and whined. "She's got a sensitive stomach, and everything sets her off."

"Clark, you know I love you like a brother"—Nick clasped the other man on the shoulder and pointed toward the closed bathroom door— "but that is my sister, and I will torture her even on my deathbed."

Delilah bit back a laugh. She didn't have siblings and watching the antics between the Winters siblings and their in-laws had her second-guessing if she should be thankful or envious.

"It's alright, Clark. I'll get him back later," Holly said, pointing the dry-erase marker her sister had dropped. "Better watch your back, brother dear."

"Whoa, why are you coming for me?" Nick asked Holly. "You should be Switzerland in this!"

Holly laughed mockingly. "Merry is the incubator for my future niece or nephew. Her value has surpassed yours."

"Please don't call your sister an incubator to her face," Clark begged, his gaze shooting toward the bathroom door nervously.

"I won't," Holly said, climbing off Declan's lap to pat Clark on the back, "but only because you're my favorite brother-in-law."

"I'm your only brother-in-law."

"Yeah, lucky for you," she mumbled, going back to being cocooned in Declan's lap.

Clark huffed, addressing Declan. "Run for it, man."

"I can't." He leaned over and kissed the side of her neck. "She knows how I like my coffee."

Holly wrinkled her nose. "You do stink, babe."

Declan chuckled, burying his head into her neck with a growl, and she squealed, grabbing on to the back of his head. Delilah's cheeks burned when her best friend's face contorted, and a little moan escaped her.

"Dude," Nick shouted. "That's my sister."

Holly glared at Nick before flashing Declan a devilish smile. "I think we should go home and get cleaned up."

"Hey, none of that," Delilah protested. "We need to finish this, and there will be no distractions until we do." Delilah flashed the big man an apologetic smile. "Sorry, Declan."

"He's used to you cockblocking him," Holly joked, only to scream when Declan tickled her.

"I don't cockblock him! I'm sure he finished just fine the other morning," Delilah quipped.

The guys erupted into a multitude of groans and laughter. Declan released Holly's shoulders, shaking his head. "Yeah, I am not getting in the middle of this."

The bathroom door opened, and Merry came out with shimmering eyes. She walked past them toward the living room, Daisy trotting by her side. "I'm going to lie down."

"Do you need any water?" Clark asked.

"No," she said, sitting down on the couch. "I just want all of you stinky bastards to go away."

"I'm sorry for making you puke, Sis," Nick said.

Merry held up her hand. "I do not forgive you."

"I'll get him for you, Mer," Holly said, flashing an evil grin. "It will be good."

Merry nodded her head regally. "Thank you."

"What about the bachelor auction?" Delilah asked.

"I'm here listening," Merry said, lying back on the couch with her arm over her eyes. "Holly can write. Find me ten more bachelors." Merry tilted her head up and lifted her arm to glare at all of them. "If you try to sneak Trip onto that list, I will get up and lose my cookies all over both of you."

"I'm going to go home and get cleaned up," Clark said, hovering over her. "Are you sure you don't want to come with me?"

"I'm good here. Take Nick with you, please. He is the smelliest."

Clark kissed her forehead swiftly and headed straight for his brother-in-law. He grabbed Nick around the neck, dragging him toward the door. "You heard her. I'll let you borrow some clothes."

"I'll just go home and get cleaned up," Nick protested.

Holly got up from Declan's lap, crossing to the whiteboard. "Where were we?"

"Finding Merry ten more bachelors," Delilah offered, before adding, "except for the two who are douchebags."

"Trip is who you're talking about excluding?" Anthony said, his voice strained.

"Yeah, and Brodie William." Delilah noticed his dark scowl under the brim of his hat and frowned. "Why?"

"I just think that's a good call," he said, gruffly. "They're pricks."

"I agree," Delilah said, thinking about the times Trip had made comments about her when he'd passed by her in public. Delilah knew he meant for her to hear, otherwise, wouldn't he have waited until she was gone to talk about her?

Anthony frowned at her. "Why do you say that?"

"I can't agree with you about someone's character?" she asked.

Anthony leaned onto the table, his eyes boring into her intensely. "Did they say something to you?"

"Not lately, but I know how they are," Delilah said, her nose scrunched in distaste. "They're dogs."

Anthony glanced over at Nick, who shook his head as Clark ushered him out the door. Delilah watched Anthony's jaw clench at the silent warning and wondered, *What was that about?*

"I'll be back in a bit, Mer," Clark called over his shoulder before the door shut.

"Okay," she said weakly.

"It's an auction, not a popularity contest," Holly muttered, tapping the dry-erase pen against her palm. "I still say we include them."

"Any other suggestions?" Delilah asked, refusing to get into a debate with Holly about this without Merry as backup.

"What about Shane Hill?" Pike offered.

Delilah brightened. "Oh, yeah. The new firefighter. He's nice. We had an issue when the heaters kicked on at school, and a mouse nest caught fire in the vents. They had to call the department, and he came out to tell us we were all good."

"Doing his job makes him nice?" Anthony asked with an obvious 'tude in his tone.

She raised her eyebrow. "He also introduced himself to the teachers. When I told him I was just a sub, he commented about me being a superhero because I can tackle any age or subject."

"At least we know he's got game," Pike joked.

Delilah swatted him playfully. "He wasn't flirting with me."

"Oh, he was. You just didn't appreciate it." Pike's blue eyes sparkled, leaning his elbow on the table and cradling his head in his hand. "Not the way you do me."

"Hey, Romeo, court my bestie on your own time. If you want to stay, then get your head in the game." Holly wrote down his name. "Alright, Shane is on the list. Who else?"

"Let me think about it while I hydrate," Delilah said, getting up and walking around the dining room table to where Merry was lying on the couch. "I'm going to get a glass of water. Are you sure you don't want something to drink or a cool compress?"

"Actually, I'd like both," Merry whispered, flashing her a small smile. "Thanks, Delilah."

"Of course."

"I'm tapping out to use the restroom." Pike got up and headed for the bathroom but suddenly spun around, snapping his fingers. "Ollie Vincent. He worked the road crew with us and is divorced now. Good guy. Carry on."

"I'll be right back," Delilah said, heading into the kitchen. Growing up, she'd been in the Winters home enough times that she knew where everything was. She watched Pike disappear into the bathroom, wondering at his overzealous flirtation. If he asked her out, how would she explain that she was no longer into him?

While Delilah grabbed a glass from the cupboard, she heard Holly ask from the other room, "Do the rest of you have anyone else in your back pocket?"

"If I give up eleven names, can I sit this out?" Anthony asked.

Delilah was surprised that Anthony didn't want to do it. She'd never heard that he was the shy type.

"Absolutely not," Holly snapped.

"Whoa, I was just asking."

"You're like a white whale, Ant," Holly said, and Delilah could tell by the glee in her voice that Holly was grinning. "Especially now that we know you're a love virgin. Every girl is going to be clamoring to be the one to steal your heart."

The image of women rushing the stage, possibly chucking panties at Anthony like he was a rock star, soured her stomach. Delilah reentered the room in time to overhear Anthony grumble, "Hey, I didn't share that for you to use it as public information. I don't like that."

Neither do I. Delilah handed Merry the glass of water and the cool compress she'd collected and went back to her seat.

"Fine," Holly said ruefully, "but your green eyes are too pretty not to exploit."

She resisted the urge to tell her friend they weren't going to exploit anyone. If she defended Anthony, it would bring unwanted speculation as to why. Especially for Holly, who could sniff out a secret better than Sherlock.

Declan wrapped an arm around Holly's waist. "Hey, hey. The only eyes I want you complimenting are mine."

"They're different shades," Delilah said, realizing too late she'd said that aloud. The entire room was staring at her, including Merry, whose eyes had been closed right before she'd spoken. "I just mean that Declan's are light hazel, and Anthony's are a deeper green. Besides, noticing someone's eyes doesn't mean you're interested in them."

"Thank you for pointing that out, Del," Holly said, her brown eyes watching her intensely. Holly wasn't the only one in the room studying her and Delilah squirmed in her seat when she caught Anthony smirking.

The front door opened, and Mrs. Winters entered with Jace. "Soup's on!"

Saved by the pizza.

Chapter Ten

The Winters family living room had been turned into a stock trader floor, only eligible men were the commodity.

They'd moved the easel out of the dining room when Mr. and Mrs. Winters had joined the fray, and they had over fifty bachelors on the list. Delilah and Holly had been on the phone for over an hour, calling potential bachelors and asking them to participate for charity. Delilah was giddy with exhilaration at the enthusiasm most of the men had exhibited.

"Thank you so much for participating, Ryan! We'll email you the details Monday." Delilah ended the call and cheered, "We got another one!"

The room whooped and hollered, except for Jace, who was curled up in the corner with noise-canceling headphones, playing a game on his Nintendo Switch. Daisy lay next to his feet, her brown eyes darting around as Merry wrote Ryan's name in the plus column on the whiteboard.

Pike and Anthony were seated on the couch next to Nick, who'd returned with his wife, Noel. The willowy brunette was cradled on his lap, her arm wrapped around his shoulder as she watched the group. Most of the men, including Clark, had gone home to shower and change before returning, so as not to upset Merry's stomach anymore. Anthony and Pike had gotten cleaned up at Anthony's place, leaving Delilah with a few minutes to breathe. If Mr. and Mrs. Winters hadn't returned, she might have tried escaping during the men's absence, but she'd missed her window.

Mr. Winters was in his chair while Mrs. Winters and Declan were on the couch. Clark stood next to Merry with a dry eraser in his hand.

Merry replaced the cap on her pen with a yawn. "I think it's about time I called it a night."

Her mother chuckled. "I remember being pregnant with Nick. I could never make it past eight o'clock at night without wanting to curl up in bed."

"Plus, Jace needs to detox from that thing before bed," Clark said, pointing to the handheld.

Merry slapped his arm playfully. "Please, you just want to put him to bed so you can play it."

As the two of them started a debate on video games, Delilah checked the time and slipped her phone into the pocket of her workout leggings, trying to figure out a way to leave without drawing attention. So far, she'd been able to avoid being alone with Pike, but every time she turned around, he was watching her. He'd sent her several texts since Monday, asking when Delilah was available to hang out. Although she'd answered them, suggesting they wait until she got back from her parents' place after Thanksgiving, she should be honest about her change of heart.

But that interaction could wait another day.

Delilah cleared her throat before climbing to her feet. "I hate to cut this short, but I gotta get up early tomorrow."

"What are you doing?" Anthony asked from his perch next to Pike.

"I'm driving to my parents' place in Boise for the weekend." Just because she was angry with him didn't mean she couldn't be polite. She turned to her hosts with a wide smile. "Mr. and Mrs. Winters, thank you for feeding me. Now, I must feed my dog before she thinks I've abandoned her."

"Delilah, you are allowed to call us by our first names." Victoria Winters got up from the couch and hugged her. "Pike and Anthony have been calling me Victoria since they were seniors, and I like you better than them."

"That hurts me!" Pike gasped, clutching his chest and falling back against Anthony, who pushed him off with a grunt.

Victoria shook her finger in their direction. "She doesn't come and eat all my food."

"It's a compliment to your culinary skills," Pike protested.

Victoria shook her head, but Delilah caught the small smile on her lips. The Winters were a warm, welcoming brood who loved to tease one another and their guests. Delilah was just happy to be included.

"Thank you, Victoria," she said, before addressing everyone else with a wave. "Good night, everyone. Holly, I'll text you when I make it home."

Holly got up and ran over to her, hugging her tight. "Thank you for your help."

"Of course. That's what besties do."

A chorus of "Bye, Delilah" resounded from the room, and she gave another little wave.

"I'll walk you out," Pike said, getting to his feet.

"Oh–okay." She caught Anthony's gaze accidentally, but he wasn't smiling. He watched Pike round the couch and reach her side with what could only be described as a resigned expression.

Pike grabbed the front door and held it for her, calling back over his shoulder. "I'll be back in a minute."

Holly caught her gaze, eyes wide, and she mouthed something that looked like, *Oh my God.*

Holly probably thought she was jumping out of her skin at Pike's interest instead of her stomach twisting with uneasy stress. If Pike asked her out again, and she told him no outside the Winters' home, would he walk back inside, vocalizing his disappointment to everyone?

She did not want to be responsible for a scene like that.

Delilah stepped over the threshold and down the steps, slowing down for him to catch up. "What's up?"

"I just wanted a chance to talk before you took off. It was crowded in there."

"It always is when the family gets together."

He chuckled. "Fair enough." Pike suddenly got ahead of her, stopping in her path. "I know you've got places to go, but I need to get this out there. I want to make plans with you before another man beats me to the punch."

That sounded like spending time with her was a game he wanted to win, and her irritation boiled to the surface. "Why are you suddenly interested in me, Pike? I mean, why now? I wasn't exactly subtle in my adoration all these years."

His mouth flopped open for several seconds before he started stammering. "I mean, it's hard to pinpoint the exact moment—"

"Come on, be honest."

"I am! You've always been an attractive woman, but I guess if I had to give you a reason, you caught my attention that night at Brews. You walked in, and it was like seeing you for the first time."

Delilah laughed bitterly. "Do you understand how insulting that is? I mooned after you for years. I've been the same size for at least ten of them, so it's not that I lost weight or something. All this pursuit is because of a dress?"

Pike's eyes widened, as if this was the last reaction he'd expected, but how could he not have thought through every scenario after waiting so long?

"I'm confused," he said, running a hand over his beard. "Did you not wear that dress because you wanted attention?"

"Technically, yes—"

"Then why are you mad at me for giving you what you wanted?" Pike interjected.

"Because it's superficial!" She exploded, her emotions outpouring like lava from a volcano. "You don't know anything about me. You liked how I looked Saturday night, but can you tell me a single fact about myself that makes you think, 'Wow, I want to pursue that girl?'"

"I–you're a good dancer."

"I took dance classes until seventh grade, so fantastic observation," Delilah said, refusing to dial back her sarcasm. "Anything else?"

Pike seemed befuddled and finally said, "I need a minute."

"You take all the time you need," Delilah said, wondering why she was so angry at Pike. He liked the way she looked. That was what she wanted, right? "I've had men who weren't interested in me romantically, but they didn't disregard me as a person. You barely spoke to me in all the years that you've known me. You wrote me off until you liked the way I looked."

"No, I just thought of you as a kid!" He glanced at the house, lowering his voice when he continued, "You were the best friend of Nick's little sister. I was graduating high school when you were just starting. You went away to college for four years and came back when I was with someone. It took me a long time to get over my first love, and now I am ready to find something real. There hasn't been a time for us until now."

"Except I'm not feeling it, Pike," Delilah whispered, sadness twisting in her chest. She couldn't believe she was saying this. This was everything she'd dreamed of since she was twelve!

"Are you sure?" Pike stepped into her and brought his hand up above their heads, holding a sprig of mistletoe. "Should we put this to the test to be sure?"

Delilah laughed. "Why do you have mistletoe in your pocket?"

Pike grinned. "Victoria always hangs a few sprigs around the farm during the holidays, and I thought it might be useful." His smiled dissolved and he watched her with earnest blue eyes. "What do you say?"

Maybe Delilah was avoiding Pike because she was fascinated with Anthony. Even though nothing would happen between Anthony and Delilah, kissing his best friend seemed skeezy.

Why are you worried about Anthony's feelings when he laughed at you and didn't even apologize?

The little voice in her head wasn't wrong, and Delilah barely finished her nod before his mouth dropped to hers, the whiskers of his beard tickling the skin around her mouth and chin. He delved into her mouth with confident expertise, and it was evident from his skill level that he'd had all the practice needed to become a glorified sex-god.

Yet she silently evaluated his kiss like a sardonic judge on a competition show. There was no warm, fluttering sensation in her lower stomach as his lips moved over hers, no desire to draw him closer and lose herself in his touch.

Not the way she'd felt while kissing Anthony.

Delilah broke the kiss, pressing her lips together thoughtfully.

"You still not feeling it?" he murmured.

Before she could respond, the front door closed with a thwack. Delilah gasped in surprise, whirling around.

"Don't let me interrupt," Anthony's deep voice said. Her gaze flicked to the man in question coming down the front porch steps. He stared straight ahead from beneath the brim of that ball cap, his jaw clenched, and her stomach dropped. How much had he seen and heard?

"You've got some timing there, bro," Pike muttered.

"Like I said, carry on. It's not my fault you picked the only exit to make a move."

He passed by, and Delilah fought the urge to turn and watch him leave, especially since Pike's eager blue-eyed gaze had returned to her face.

Delilah forced herself not to watch Anthony's retreating back and focus on the man in front of her. "Sorry, what did you say?"

"I asked if you were still not feeling it," Pike said.

"I—" she cleared her throat when Anthony's truck roared to life and heard the crunch of gravel under tires. "I'm sorry, Pike. I think we missed our boat."

"Wow," he said, his hand running through his hair like he hadn't seen this coming. "I thought the mistletoe was charming."

"It toed the line between charming and corny," she said lightly, hoping to ease the sting of her rejection. "I think it would work wonders with the right girl."

"But that's not you, huh?" he asked.

"It's not. I'm sorry."

Pike shrugged. "Well, nothing ventured, nothing gained, right?"

"Yeah." Delilah stood awkwardly, trying to figure out the best way to make a graceful exit. Instead, Pike gave her an out as he took a step back with a small smile. "I'm gonna head inside and grab another slice for the road."

"Good night, Pike."

"You, too. Safe travel tomorrow."

"Thanks."

Chapter Eleven

Anthony didn't head straight home like he said. He took a detour into town, stopping by Mistletoe Market for a case of beer, a bottle of whiskey, and some easy fixings for Thanksgiving. Although he'd planned on stopping by the Winters' for dinner, he wasn't in the mood for company. Not after seeing Pike making out with Delilah on the sidewalk in front of their house.

He'd expected to see them talking, maybe flirting, but he'd had a perfect view of Delilah's closed eyes and flushed cheeks imprinted on his brain like it had been seared there with a hot iron. They'd closed Adventures for Thursday, Friday, and Saturday so he could hole up in his trailer and avoid polite society until Monday. Hopefully, by then, he'd have some perspective.

He set a container of microwavable mashed potatoes in his cart next to his thirty-pack of Keystone and his bottle of Kessler. The market was quiet since it was half an hour before closing the night before a holiday, and Anthony was glad for it. All he needed was one of the older women in town to get a look at his cart and start praying for the lonely alcoholic Anthony Russo.

Anthony's cell phone rang, and it was Pike. He debated sending it to voicemail, uninterested in listening to his best friend regale him with how he'd nailed down Delilah for a date, but it wasn't Pike's fault that Anthony was struggling with his vow of celibacy. Or that he coveted his best friend's love interest.

"Hello?" Anthony said, turning onto the cereal aisle.

"Hey, where you at?" Pike asked, the sound of the radio playing quietly in the background. "I swung by your trailer, but you weren't there."

"I went to the store." Great, Pike was looking to really celebrate with him. "I think I'm going to stay home tomorrow. Relax without having to be social."

"I hear ya," Pike said, his voice sad. "I'm not in the mood to sit around and smile either."

"What do you mean?" Anthony asked.

"I went for it with Delilah, and she told me I missed my chance."

Anthony hit the corner display of tortillas, taking a turn too sharp, and exhaled, "Shit!"

"I know." Pike sighed. "I pulled out all the stops, too."

Anthony shoved his cart off to the side of the next aisle, lowering his voice. "She really said that you missed your chance?"

"That and a lot more. Which is why I need a drink if I'm going to talk about it. Want to meet me at Brews?"

Even though his best friend hadn't gotten the girl, Anthony didn't want to listen to a forlorn Pike mourn his chance with Delilah either. Still, if the roles had been reversed, Pike would have been there for him.

"Sure, but it will be a bit," Antony said, pushing his cart again. "I've got to finish shopping and put it away."

"That's fine, I'll head on over and get started without you."

"Alright, see you soon." Anthony slipped the phone into his pocket, a wide grin splitting over his face. He should not be this happy about his best friend getting rejected, but Pike would get over it. The real question Anthony had circling his brain was why had Delilah said no? After carrying a torch for Pike for years, what had changed?

Hope blossomed in his chest as he thought about everything that had happened between the two of them. Had Delilah told Pike no because she had feelings for Anthony?

First thing to do was comfort his friend and then fix things with Delilah. Once Anthony told her that she'd misunderstood him and ask her to forgive him, she'd tell him the truth, right?

He found the last honey ham at the bottom of one of the refrigerator bins and tossed it in the air with a grin, catching it effortlessly. A flash of pink came around the corner, and Anthony looked up to meet Delilah's deer-in-the-headlights expression and his chest seized.

"Hey," he said.

She scoffed in response, turning her cart around and disappearing out of sight. What the hell had he done now?

Anthony chased after her down the aisle, riding the cart until he was almost on her heels, and hopped off before he crashed into her. "What, I don't even get a greeting? Is this about me interrupting your make-out session with Pike?"

"We weren't making out," she hissed.

"That's not how it looked from my angle."

"Well, it wasn't like that. Pike pulled a piece of mistletoe from his pocket and suggested we kiss." She tossed a bag of Dot's pretzels into her cart and turned onto the next aisle, with Anthony following behind. "He wanted to test out whether we had chemistry or not."

"Did he really pull out mistletoe?" he asked.

Delilah nodded. "Yes, he freaking did."

"Was he walking around all day, every day, with mistletoe in his pocket?" Anthony chuckled.

"I asked the same thing." She was facing away from him so that he couldn't tell for sure, but he thought she was laughing. "But he said no. He took it from the Winters' house just in case."

"I don't know whether that is genius or creepy."

"It was a little creepy." This time, he heard the giggle.

Anthony swallowed back another laugh. He shouldn't be standing in the middle of the store with her, laughing at his friend's antics. He didn't want to tell her that Pike had told him everything in case it gave her another reason to get angry with him.

"You were looking for someone good in bed," Anthony said, soberly. "Rumor has it Pike fits the bill."

Delilah flushed. "I'm not talking about this in the middle of the soda aisle."

"Good with me," he said, calling after her when she tried to take off. "Could we talk about that bullshit hissy fit you threw on Monday?"

Real smooth, Russo.

Delilah gasped, whirling on him. "Hissy fit? You laughed at me!"

"I was surprised! You said there were certain characteristics of someone good in bed, which struck me as funny!"

Delilah glanced around, but they were the only ones in the vicinity. "I told you I don't want to discuss this here."

"I can wait until you're done with your shopping," Anthony said, pulling up alongside her. "I just need to get rolls and a package of gravy mix. What else are you buying?"

"It doesn't matter. Go away."

Anthony shook his head. "I can't. I'm invested now and need to know the details. Watch my cart while I grab my last few things, will you?"

"No, I will not!" she yelled, but he ignored her. Anthony jogged two aisles over to grab a packet of gravy mix, snapping up a package of Hawaiian rolls from an endcap on his way back to his abandoned cart. Anthony knew Delilah wouldn't stay with it, but there was no way she'd already left.

He saw Delilah in the checkout line, snagged his cart, and rolled up behind her. "I can't believe you left my cart there." Anthony started putting his items on the belt behind the separator, continuing, "A teenager could have come by and smuggled that bottle of whiskey out the door."

Delilah stared at the clerk while addressing Anthony. "Then maybe you should attend to your own grocery shopping and stop bugging me."

"Do what, Delilah?" Wally Feldman, the clerk, asked, clearly puzzled.

"Sorry, Wally, I was talking to him," Delilah said, motioning to Anthony with her head.

"Hi, Anthony," Wally said, ringing up the last of Delilah's items. He was a few years older than Anthony, with thick glasses and a receding hairline.

"Hey, Wally, how's the family?"

"Doing well. Ready for tomorrow."

"Me, too." He turned his attention back to Delilah, squeezing in next to her. "I'm done shopping, so I can bug you all I want."

"Lucky me." The clerk told Delilah her total, and she put her card into the machine.

While Wally turned to address his manager, Anthony stepped closer, whispering in Delilah's ear, "I found what you said interesting; most guys just want someone to have sex with, regardless of skill level, and I'd never heard a woman talk about it so plainly, which is why I laughed. I didn't have a chance to correct you when you believed the worst of me."

"Oh ho, you had plenty of chances to correct my assumption in the two days since it happened." She pulled out her card and smiled at Wally as he handed her the receipt. "Have a happy holiday."

Wally nodded. "You, too, Delilah."

Anthony's face burned because she wasn't wrong. He should have hunted her down to fix their misunderstanding, but the nagging thought at the back of his mind considered that the two of them might be better off not speaking. Especially if she was going to date Pike.

Now that the possibility of the two of them being more was over, Anthony didn't want anything else to fester between them.

She picked up her bags as Wally ran Anthony's items over the scanner. Outrage shot through Anthony like a missile when she headed for the exit.

"Delilah Gill, don't you dare walk out that door! We aren't finished," he called after her.

She danced backward with her bags in fists. "I am, so I guess if you want to talk to me, you'll have to catch me."

Delilah walked out the door without a backward glance, clearly not heeding his warning.

"Fuck." Anthony tapped his foot impatiently as Wally rang up his items, asking for his ID when he scanned the alcohol. Anthony handed it to him with a grumble.

"Cash is faster if you want to chase after her," Wally said. "Just don't forget to put in your club card."

Anthony punched in his number aggressively, looked at the total and thumbed through his wallet, pulling out a hundred-dollar bill. "Keep the change." Anthony gathered up his bags and hustled toward the exit.

"Happy Thanksgiving, Anthony!"

"You, too, Wally," he called over his shoulder. Anthony made it out to the parking lot as Delilah was pulling out of her parking space. He dropped his groceries next to his truck and ran up alongside her. "Stop the car or I'm jumping on the hood."

Delilah rolled her window down but didn't stop the car. "Have you lost your mind?"

"No, I'm just not afraid to finish our conversation."

"Ha! You're a few days too late to be so brave."

"When could I talk to you about it, Delilah?" He asked, grabbing her back passenger door and climbing inside. She slammed on the brakes and he grabbed on to the seat as to not pitch forward.

"Get out," she ground out.

Anthony ignored her, continuing on topic until he got it all out. "After my best friend walked in and started mooning all over you? Would that have been a good time to discuss our misunderstanding? Or how about at the gym? I guess I could have asked you to go outside and talk, but I didn't want to cause a scene if you refused. Or better yet, should I have interrupted your kissing situation with Pike to tell you that I definitely think you should seek out dynamite men in bed because, of course, you deserve good sex? Would that have sealed the deal with him?"

Delilah turned around to glare at him. "This has nothing to do with Pike and everything to do with you!"

Anthony had enough. "Stop the car, Delilah, and have an adult discussion."

Delilah whipped the car into a circle and ended up next to his truck. They both got out and while he bent over to pick up his dropped groceries, she let him have it.

"You want to have an adult conversation?" She slammed her hands on her hips, and he could feel her eyes burning a hole into his back as he put the groceries away. "How about apologizing to people immediately when your actions could be misconstrued as hurtful? Who cares if it was in front of Pike? At least I wouldn't have sat with the idea of you being the biggest asshole in the world."

"Oh, sugar, I'm not even close to the top ten." He'd hoped to break the tension with the joke, but it seemed to set her off more.

"Fine. Well, I guess there's nothing else to discuss," Delilah said, making a move to get back in her car. "Clearly, you're not really interested in working through this."

Before she got far, Anthony picked her up by the waist and tossed her over his shoulder.

"What are you doing? Put me down," she hollered, pounding her fists against his back.

"Not until we get a few things straight." Anthony unlocked his truck and opened the passenger side door, keeping his arm locked around Delilah's calves to hold her in place. He deposited her onto the seat and followed her inside, forcing her to scoot across the bench seat to make room. He closed the door behind him, leaning over her.

"What are you doing," she snapped, shoving his shoulder.

"I want to know why Pike didn't fit the bill for your 'sexually experienced man,'" he said, his voice low and warm, like a caress across her skin, but she would not be seduced by him.

"Why does it matter?" she asked.

Anthony grinned. "Call it overwhelming curiosity."

"I answer this question, and you'll drop it?"

"Yes."

Delilah sighed. "Part of what makes someone good in bed is being attracted to them. It's why I didn't press the issue with you after last year."

Anthony reeled back. "What is that supposed to mean?"

She looked away, refusing to reveal how much his disinterest affected her. "I know that you don't find me attractive."

Anthony took her chin in his hand and turned her toward him. "How did you figure that?"

Delilah swallowed hard as his eyes bored into hers. "You stopped our kiss and walked out of the room."

Are you fucking kidding me? That's what she's believed for the better part of a year?

"You thought I stopped kissing you because I didn't want you?"

Her gaze swept his face, her voice rushing out breathlessly. "You didn't, did you?"

"I did." Anthony's pulse quickened as he admitted out loud what he'd been holding in since the first time he'd kissed her, tasting whiskey and heat on her lush mouth. Anthony crowded Delilah, his hands cradling her jawline, stroking her soft skin with his thumb. "Stopping that kiss was the most painful experience of my life. Do you have any idea the thoughts running through my head when you climbed onto my lap?"

"What?" she whispered.

Fuck, he wanted to show her, but he needed to get it out. To give her a chance to run. He brought his mouth against the shell of her ear and told her the truth. "I wanted to lift you onto that bed, rip off your pants, and bury myself in your pussy."

Anthony felt her shiver. "You . . . you did?

"Fuck yes, I did." His mouth grazed her skin along her cheek, just above his fingertips. "I still do."

Delilah moaned, swaying toward him, and his hands left her cheeks to thread through her hair, her mouth hovering mere inches from his.

"Then do it."

Chapter Twelve

Well, she'd asked for it.

Anthony's mouth covered Delilah's at a slant, the pressure hard and intense from the very beginning. She opened hers, allowing him access inside, and he took her invitation, sweeping his tongue along hers, his fingers tightening in her hair. Delilah was mush, letting him take control, his ministrations passionate and hungry, and suddenly, she craved more. She gripped his sides and scooted closer, her breast flattening against the wall of his chest, and he nipped at her bottom lip, drawing a little gasp from Delilah when Anthony released his hold on the right side of her head and slipped his hand underneath her sweatshirt.

His fingertips glided over her skin softly, grazing the band of her sports bra, distracting her from his kiss. Anthony's thumb gained entrance underneath the elastic, and she arched her back, wanting his hand over her breast, cupping her, and kneading her flesh. She lifted her sweatshirt from the bottom, breaking their contact to yank the heavy pink cotton over her head. The tinted windows kept them hidden from the outside world, and Delilah climbed onto Anthony's lap in the passenger seat, straddling him. He lifted the tight spandex of her sports bra over her breasts, releasing them from the confines, and she raised her arms, signaling him to dispose of the constricting bra. He whipped it over her head and flung it across the truck's cab.

When Anthony's hands covered her flesh, giving her exactly what she wanted and more, Delilah leaned into his touch. He turned his hat backward, the brim no longer shadowing his eyes, and they glittered in the low lighting. Delilah wanted to feel his mouth under hers, every part of them connected from their lips down. She wrapped her arms around Anthony's shoulders when he caressed her, his fingers molding her shape before they gripped her in the most exquisite grasp. She ripped her mouth from his, their noses touching as she chanted, "Yes, yes."

"Fuck, Lila," he murmured against her lips, and the new nickname sent a tingle down her spine. "You're so fucking beautiful. You like it hard, don't you, baby?" Anthony's teeth grazed the sensitive skin of her neck, and her pussy spasmed.

When she felt the push of his palm against her abdomen, she leaned back, and he took full advantage of the access she'd given him to cover her right nipple with his mouth, tonguing her until it peaked. Anthony tormented the erect, sensitive nub while his other hand squeezed her left breast, rolling the taut nipple between his thumb and forefinger. Liquid heat pooled between her legs, and she rocked against him in an attempt to ease the throbbing ache. She could feel her panties saturating with her arousal, her center pulsating with intense need, and she wanted more.

Anthony suddenly deposited her off his lap, and she landed across the bench seat on her back, gasping when he stayed on the passenger side and slipped his finger into the top of her leggings, then tugged them down her body until they got caught on the top of her tennis shoes. As he untied her laces, she realized he hadn't removed a single piece of clothing, not even his hat, and vulnerability settled in the pit of her stomach. Her hands came up to cover her body, but he grabbed her hands, pinning them to the seat.

"Why are you hiding from me?" he asked.

"You're dressed, and I'm naked."

Anthony grinned, his hooded gaze traveling over her slowly. "And?"

"Are you going to take your clothes off?"

Anthony lifted her hands and placed them up above her head, her breasts rising with the motion, and his eyes lingered there. When he finally met her gaze again, the shadows across his face disappeared as lights flashed across the windshield, but he didn't move. Anthony stared down at her, his lips parted into a feral smile.

"I'm not fucking you tonight, Lila, so I'm not taking off a damn thing. I'm going to strip you down until there's nothing between my mouth and your skin." He licked along the column of her neck, and she moaned, arching her back as tingles gathered in the muscles above her tailbone. "Your glorious tits." She flexed her hands, but Anthony held them tight as he licked and sucked each nipple, circling them with his tongue, his mouth opened wide as he dragged the entire width of it over her, and Delilah cried out, squeezing her legs together as her pussy bucked.

Anthony kissed his way back up through the valley between her breasts, and when he brushed his mouth over hers, his words rushed over her lips in a hot, guttural growl. "I know what you want." He circled her wrists with his one hand and trailed his fingers down her body slowly, over her breasts and her stomach, settling just above the juncture of her thighs until she was gritting her teeth with frustration. Anthony gave her a sweet kiss against her jawline as his hand plunged between her legs. Delilah released a breathy "Oh" when his finger slid up her seam, teasing her labia. When he bit down on her bottom lip, she thrust her hips against his hand in desperate need.

"Please," she groaned, and Anthony chuckled, his chest vibrating against her.

"Tell me, baby. Tell me what you want."

"Finger me," she begged.

"Mmm, that might be what you want, but what I want is much better."

His finger lifted from her sensitive folds, and she gasped, struggling to reach for him.

"Lila." His voice was low, warning, and she stilled. "I'm going to release your hands, but I want you to keep them right where I put them. If you need to grab on to something, I'd say the seat cushion will allow you the most give." Anthony's thumb stroked the inside of her wrist, and she wondered if he could feel her pulse fluttering there. "Are you going to be a good girl?"

Delilah nodded.

"Mmm mmm, I wanna hear it. Are you going to be my very—" Anthony's hand was back, one finger slipping inside her, and she sucked in a breath. "Very—" Another finger joined the first, curling up and sending a sizzle of joy lancing through her. "Good girl?" This last was a rumble in his chest as his thumb pressed into her folds and found her swollen clit, rubbing it in firm, fast strokes.

"God, yes, yes, I'll be a good girl. I swear."

"That's what I like to hear."

Anthony released her hands and Delilah swiftly untied her shoes and dropped them onto the floorboard of his truck with a loud thump, followed immediately by her socks and leggings, her cheeky panties tangled up somewhere inside.

Delilah heard a buzz but didn't move, afraid Anthony wouldn't follow through on what she hoped was about to happen. The spring of a lever got the best of her curiosity when the seat shifted beneath her, and she lifted her head to see he'd lowered the seat on the passenger side until it nearly lay flat. He kneeled in the expanse of the floorboard, and her body vibrated with anticipation of what was coming next.

"Alright, baby, we'll change things up a bit. Come here."

Delilah sat up, and he grabbed her, lifting her onto the passenger seat as he kneeled between her legs on the floorboard.

"Grab the headrest and slide as far up on the seat as possible."

She did what he asked, aware of him kneeling in front of her, especially when he took his hands and slipped them between her legs, widening her. He took first one leg and then the other, resting them over his shoulders, and Delilah was dizzily aware of his hot breath on the short hair of her pussy.

"Enjoy the ride, beautiful," he murmured seconds before his mouth fused over her, his tongue gliding between her pussy lips. She let out a strangled rasp as he found her clit and licked her rapidly, the tip of his tongue playing with her until she was writhing against his mouth.

Delilah couldn't remember the last time any man had gone down on her, let alone brought her to the edge. Every time she thought she would come, he slowed down his rhythm, torturing her with his soft sweeps and gentle touches.

"Anthony, please, I need . . . more."

"More what, baby? This?" He slid two fingers inside her again, curling until she shivered.

"Your mouth. I want your mouth back."

"Fuck yes," he said, spreading her lips and diving in. The whiskers on his face rubbed against her sensitive flesh, and she held on to the headrest hard, her hips bucking against his face. His mouth latched on to her clit, sucking it hard, and Delilah screamed with ecstasy, her body trembling with the force of her orgasm. Bone-liquifying heat rushed through her, turning her limbs to jelly, and she lost her grip on the headrest.

Anthony slid her legs off his shoulders, and her bare butt touched his chilly leather seats, and she yelped, "Cold!"

Anthony hovered over her, and even in the dark, she could see the self-satisfied grin spread across his face. His hands slid under her, cupping her cheeks. "Better?"

"Yes, but I can't . . . move. Not yet, anyway," Delilah laughed softly.

"I don't want you to move. I want you to lie there so I can watch you."

Delilah leaned forward and kissed him, and his fingers dug into the globes of her ass. Her lips traveled along his jawline and down his neck, whispering, "I know you said we wouldn't go further than this, but if you want to come back to my place, I can at least return the favor."

Anthony groaned and retook her mouth hard and fast. When he pulled away, he rested his forehead against hers. "You have no idea how badly I want to say yes, but—"

Anthony's phone rang and he swore. "Shit, I forgot about Pike."

Delilah stiffened. "What about him?"

Anthony held a finger to his lips and answered the call. "Hey, I'll be right there."

Delilah could hear the loud thump of music and then Pike said, "alright, man, don't leave me hanging. I'm a sad sack who needs his wingman."

"See ya." Anthony ended the call with a deep sigh. "I was supposed to take my groceries home and meet Pike at Brews and Chews, but I got distracted."

A sick feeling settled in the pit of her stomach. "Did you know I'd told Pike I wasn't interested?"

Anthony frowned. "Yes, but I didn't know the details."

Delilah pushed Anthony away and searched in the dark for her sweatshirt and found it hanging on his emergency brake. She scooted out from under him, grabbed the pink hoodie, and pulled it over her head. "Was this some kind of competition with the two of you? Go after the same girl and see who can nail her first?"

"Of course not!" Anthony reached for her, but she shied away. "You really think I'm that type of guy?"

"I don't know, Anthony. You ignored me for days, and when Pike struck out with me, you wanted to talk. You insisted on it, and then you—"

Delilah couldn't even say it out loud. He'd been incredible, made her lose herself like no one ever had, and he'd done that knowing he was supposed to be meeting Pike any minute.

"Delilah, I didn't plan on what happened between us, but I don't regret it either. It had nothing to do with Pike and everything to do with wanting you."

Delilah wanted to believe that so badly, but his phone rang again, Pike's face flashing across the screen.

"Can you hand me my clothes so I can get dressed? Then you can be on your way."

Anthony picked up her leggings and held them out to her, ignoring the call and setting his phone in the cup holder. It beeped with a text seconds later from Pike. Before he could check, Delilah looked at the phone and whatever she saw made her face fall. Anthony picked up the phone and read the text.

I was just going to tell you, I'm sitting at a table with these two beautiful women seeking a holiday adventure.

Delilah shook out her underwear; her jaw clenched as she slipped her feet through the holes and wiggled them up her calves and thighs. "It sounds like your friend Pike bounced back from my little rejection and has a fun-filled plan for you. The good news is, you didn't clear the pipes, so you should be good to go."

"Stop it!" he snapped, taking her leggings from her and turning them right side out. "I'm going to help you get dressed, and while I'm doing that, I need you to understand he is my best friend. This is something I've never done before and I feel guilty as hell, so I'm going to go out with him and try to find the right way to tell him. I'm not going for the girls." He gathered the left leg and rolled it over her ankle, doing the same thing to the other side. "This is what Pike does when he's unhappy."

"Finds gorgeous women to drink with? I'm pretty sure that's every time you go out." Delilah yanked up her leggings, and Anthony passed along her socks and tennis shoes.

"Pike hasn't been happy in a really long time, so when he was interested in you, I backed off. I knew you'd had a crush on him for years, and he has a big heart. He deserves someone who will treat him well."

What about you? Don't you deserve someone?

"And where does that leave us? Is this going to be another interlude we don't talk about?" Delilah knew she sounded like a bitter woman, but they'd had an incredible moment and he was running.

"Absolutely not," he said firmly, cupping her face in his hands. "I need to go now, but I'd like to continue this conversation later."

"Tonight?" she asked.

"I was thinking tomorrow? I'm not sure when Pike will finish tying one on."

Disappointment swept through her and Delilah turned her head and he released her face. She could feel him watching her as she put on her socks and shoes. "I'm headed to Boise in the morning, remember? I'll be gone all weekend."

"What if I drive you?"

Delilah laughed, then realized he was serious. "That's crazy. You'd drive me to my parents', turn around, and head home?"

"No, I'd visit my dad. He lives in Boise and invited me for Thanksgiving, but I didn't want to make the drive."

Delilah thought about the night at Brews and Chews, when Anthony talked about his family estrangement. He'd had no plans to see them, and yet suddenly, he was headed to his dad's and could drive her?

The fact that he was willing to do something so uncomfortable just to be near her made her anger dissolve slightly. Especially when Anthony took her hands and brought them to his mouth, kissing her knuckles. "But, if it means I get to spend two hours in the car with you and two hours driving home Sunday, that will give us plenty of time to hash all of this out."

Delilah wasn't stupid; rarely did anyone get one over on her, but despite her initial suspicion, she wanted to give Anthony a chance to tell her everything. If she didn't like his answers, it would be a long drive to Boise, but her dad could always drive her back on Sunday.

She tied her shoes and nodded. "I want to be on the road by eight a.m. Meet at my house?"

Anthony flashed a smile. "Sounds good."

Delilah opened the door on his driver's side and slowly climbed out, dropping gingerly. "Also, we're taking my car. Better gas mileage, and I don't feel like I will fall to my death getting in and out of it."

Anthony hopped out of the passenger's side and came around the front of the truck, catching her against the hood. He pressed his pelvis into her, and she could feel the telltale signs of his unsatisfied arousal against her.

"I know you don't fully trust me yet, but I'm not interested in hooking up with anyone. I'm going to the bar to ensure that Pike doesn't get himself into trouble, and then I'm going straight home."

"You're a free agent," she said. "You don't owe me a thing."

"Can I see your phone, please?" he asked. She pulled it out of her leggings and handed it to him. "I'm putting my number in and texting myself so I'll have yours. Let me know when you get home, and I'll do the same."

Delilah took her phone back, fighting a smile when she saw the text he'd sent himself.

Anthony is a sexy AF.

"You need to go before he starts calling again or comes looking for you."

"I know." His thumb smoothed over her bottom lip before he kissed her, a hard, fast kiss. "Text me."

"I will."

Chapter Thirteen

I'm not a terrible person, am I?

Anthony climbed out of his truck the following morning at seven fifty-five with a drink containers in one hand and a bag in the other. He'd stopped at Kiss My Donut to get them breakfast and caffeine, although despite getting very little sleep, he was wired and ready to get on the road. Unfortunately, he'd failed to tell Pike he was traveling to Boise with Delilah. The guilt was eating him alive. He hated lying, knew the consequences and how even small lies could turn someone's world upside down, and yet he'd omitted the truth from his best friend.

It wasn't that Anthony thought Pike was broken up about Delilah's rejection, but Anthony didn't want to start anything with Delilah until after he'd had time to talk to his friend. Although, watching Pike pound back drinks and bemoan his single circumstances had been severely less fun than everything he could have been doing with Delilah last night. Only sex with Delilah wouldn't solve his more significant issue and the reason he'd taken the vow of celibacy in the first place.

He'd never been in love at this point in his life. He was worried that he wasn't capable of it. Nick and Noel had both been in multiple relationships before they realized their feelings for each other, and Pike had engaged his fair share of partners as well. They'd all experienced some degree of love multiple times. Anthony loved his mom and friends, but he'd never burned for anyone romantically, never experienced the overwhelming need to tell them he loved them. Even Yvette, whom he'd dated the longest, hadn't moved him. There wasn't a hole in his life when she broke up with him. He'd just gone on living.

Much like his father had after leaving his mother.

Just the thought of the man who'd sired him sent Anthony into a rage and he was going to the man's house all day? Anthony tried not to think about what he'd agreed to, knowing that although he'd been invited to dinner, his reception would most likely be less than cordial. His other brothers weren't exactly warm and fuzzy types. Part of him was curious as to why his father extended an invite now, but mostly, visiting his estranged family was a necessary evil to spend time with Delilah. After last night though, how could he tell her they needed to pump the brakes?

On top of the raw nerves about seeing his family, Anthony was nervous to tell Delilah about his vow. Would she believe him? Laugh at him?

He cradled the food in his other arm and used his free hand to ring the doorbell and heard Leia's high-pitched barking inside. Delilah wore a maroon sweater dress that showed off her creamy shoulders when she opened the door. He noticed her legs were bare above the knee-high black boots she wore, and he swore, "Fuck me, woman, you've lived in Idaho your whole life, and you're out here dressed like you're from California. Why aren't you wearing pants?"

Delilah scowled. "Good morning to you, too! To answer your question, I will sit in my nice warm car for the two hours and twenty-seven minutes of our drive." Delilah's dark look dissolved when she pointed to his hands. "I'll be fine! Is that coffee and breakfast for the both of us?"

"Yes." He should have left them in the car and just come up to see what she was doing first. "I think we should take the truck. I keep a blanket, a case of water, an emergency food kit, and other essentials in my back seat. I'm prepared for everything."

"Well, aren't you a Boy Scout?" she said dryly. "It would take three times more gas to get there in that tank than mine. I'll make you a deal, though. I'll let you hang on to my car, so if you need to duck out of your dad's place, you aren't trapped. Or paying insane Uber holiday prices."

"Except I don't feel comfortable taking your car to my dad's and leaving you stranded." Especially if things go south and he needed to head back to Mistletoe.

Delilah shrugged. "If I want to go somewhere, my mom will let me use her car. Seriously, I'm fine."

"Alright, if you're sure," Anthony said, lifting his full hands up in surrender, "I'll put these in the car and my duffle in the trunk."

"Let me get my bag and Leia and I'll meet you at the car." Delilah turned and Anthony stepped over the threshold, checking out her house. The cream walls had photo collages and bookish art on the wall from what he could see. Delilah bent over to unlock Leia's cage and the fabric of her dress stretched, drawing Anthony's attention to the round, thick ass.

Realizing he was staring at her like a creep, Anthony cleared his throat and looked away. "Don't you want to change into something warmer?"

"No," Delilah said, the cage springing open with a metal twang. Leia bounded out of the cage and ran circles around him, stopping to sniff his boots. "All my sweaters are vacuum sealed in my suitcase, and if I open them up, I won't be able to close them, and I'll have to repack."

Anthony looked to the sky, calling on a higher power to give him strength, when Delilah returned with a large roller luggage, a tote bag, and a backpack slung over one shoulder. Leia gave up her inspection of his footwear and wiggled her fuzzy butt by Delilah's side but didn't cross over the threshold when her mom paused in front of Anthony.

"Why would you need to pack so much?" Anthony grumbled. "Aren't you only going for the weekend?"

"I like to have choices," she said, releasing the handles to point to each bag. "My mom usually packs in half a dozen fun-filled activities, and the tote is Leia's food, dog bowls, and toys."

"What about the backpack?" he asked.

"That has my laptop for work, my iPad, my headphones, chargers, knitting—"

Anthony held up a hand. "Did you say knitting?"

"Yeah, it relaxes me." She stepped onto the porch and closed the door on her dog. "I'll put this in the car, come back for Leia, and lock it."

"If you want to leave them by the trunk, I can put them in after I load mine. I just need to set these down." Anthony held up the pastry bag with a sheepish grin. "I don't know why I thought we'd have time to eat before we hit the road."

Delilah rolled her eyes with a huff. "I told you I wanted to be gone by eight."

"So you did." Anthony followed Delilah down the walkway toward her car. Despite his protests on the ridiculous dress, he enjoyed the view. He set the bag and the coffee cups on the driver's seat and shut the door. When he looked at the back of the car, Delilah was trying to lift the massive suitcase into the trunk. "What are you doing? I told you I'd get it."

"Maybe I don't like being bossed around?" she grunted, setting the suitcase back down.

"That's funny," he said, passing her to grab his duffle from his truck. When he returned to her side, Anthony dropped his bag into the space and took the handle of her suitcase from her, lifting it into the trunk easily. "The night I took you home wrapped in my blanket, you liked it fine. You disobeyed me and came running back to me so that I'd carry you inside again."

Her cheeks flushed. "Yeah, well, that was before."

Anthony shut the trunk and leaned against it, crossing his arms over his chest as he grinned down at her. "I also remember you doing exactly what I said last night."

"That is in a completely different capacity and has nothing to do with right now," she said, setting the tote bag in the back seat. "Can you start the car while I get my dog?"

"Someone woke up feisty today."

"I'm just trying to stick to a schedule," she said, pulling out her phone and tapping the screen. "I had us leaving five minutes ago, and in an hour or so, we'll stop for a bathroom break and continue to Boise."

Anthony ate up the distance between them and plucked her phone out of her hand, studying the detailed chart. "This is very type A of you. I would have never figured that."

"Only because my parents expect me at a certain time," Delilah said, hopping up to grab her phone, but Anthony held it just out of reach, "and they start calling if I don't arrive within a ten-minute window." Finally, she gave up her ridiculous retrieval mission and asked, "Can I please have my phone?"

"Of course, you just needed to ask," he teased, ignoring her fuming. "Better get your little dog so we can get back on track."

Anthony heard her grumble something about impossible men, but he didn't take offense. He'd rather have Delilah griping and sarcastic than ignoring him any day of the week. He moved the food bag and coffee onto the passenger seat and tried climbing into the driver's seat, but his knees wouldn't fit under the wheel. His head hit the ceiling and he scrambled for the seat adjustments on the side when his leg got stuck. The seat was so close to the steering wheel that he couldn't climb back out and kept pressing the seat adjustment frantically, taking deep, calming breaths as he was able to adjust slowly.

When Delilah came into view holding Leia's leash, Anthony continued holding the button. "Jeez, I didn't realize how short you were."

"Excuse me?" Delilah said, placing one hand on her hip.

"I'm just saying, I'm not sure if this seat goes back far enough for me." Anthony pressed down on the other button and the seat dropped slowly. Finally, he could sit up straight instead of keeping his head at a painful angle.

"If you need me to drive, I will," Delilah said sweetly.

"Nope, I think I've got it." He tilted his seat back a tad and when he was finally comfortable, he moved the coffees into her cup holders and placed the pastry bag on the middle console. Delilah opened the back door and pulled a folded cube out of the pocket on the passenger chair. She hooked the two straps on the cube into the back seat before picking up Leia and setting her inside, attaching a short leash in the cube's center to her harness.

"Is that a car seat for your dog?"

"Yes, why? She needs to be safe, too," Delilah said.

Anthony didn't comment, as she already seemed to be on guard with him. He'd hoped that texting her to say he'd made it home safe and adding the number of hours before Anthony would see her again would soften her to the fact that he was being genuine, but apparently not.

When she climbed into the passenger seat, Anthony cleared his throat. "Delilah, do you not want me to drive you? Because I can take off now if you want nothing to do with me."

Delilah ran a hand over her head with a small laugh. "I'm not angry with you. I'm nervous. I will be stuck in a car with you for two and a half hours, and I have no idea what you'll say."

"Do you want me to go through the highlights, and you can decide if I'm worth the drive?" he asked, turning in the seat to face her. "Your mom and dad will understand if you're a few minutes late."

"You're probably right." Delilah reached for the coffee closest to her and twisted so she could watch him. "Go ahead. Lay it on me."

No point in pussyfooting around it. "I haven't had sex with you because I've been celibate for almost two years." Delilah's mouth opened, most likely in shock, and he chuckled. "You probably weren't expecting that, huh?"

"No, I wasn't," she said, studying him. "Why are you celibate?"

"As I mentioned yesterday, I've never been in love. I got tired of dating women, having sex, and having it lead nowhere." Anthony rubbed his hand over his hair with a sigh, flustered. He'd only ever talked to Nick and Pike about this, and Pike had teased him about it. "I guess I agree with you to a point about how sex is only good when you're attracted to each other, but I'm going to take it one step further. Sex is truly amazing when you're in love with someone."

Anthony braced himself for laughter or even mockery, but she simply took a sip of her coffee, cradling the cup between her hands.

"If you've never been in love, how do you know?" she asked.

"I can imagine it."

Delilah took another sip, as if contemplating her next response. Finally, she said, "So you're not having sex until you're in love, which you've never experienced, but you're sure you'll know what it feels like when it happens?"

"That is the plan."

Delilah's smile stretched across her face. "You are an extremely romantic man."

Anthony chuckled. "I don't know about that, but I want something special. I just don't want to rush in or force it. I am looking for something natural, without any complications and drama, so I wanted to drive you to Boise and get to know you better. I'm incredibly attracted to you. You're smart. Funny. Unique. Gorgeous."

"Thank you. I—I feel the same way about you."

Anthony leaned across the console toward her. "You don't sound so sure."

Delilah scoffed. "Well, it's true." Delilah reached out, her hand trailing over the skin of his cheek. "Thank you for telling me all that."

"Of course," he murmured, turning his head to kiss her palm. Her warm flesh trembled against his mouth and he resisted to urge to nibble her skin, or they might never get out of there. "Do you think we can get on the road now, or do we need to lay everything bare right before we leave?"

Delilah smiled softly, booping him on the nose before she settled back into the seat and put on her seat belt. "I think unless you tell me you have a clown kink, we're good."

"Clown kink, huh?" he said, pressing the button to start the engine. "I'm afraid to ask why that's your deal-breaker."

"The title isn't self-explanatory?"

"Good point." Anthony backed out of her driveway and spun the wheel to the right, heading for the main road out of town. "Wanna grab your pastry out of the bag?"

"What about you?"

"I'll wait until I'm on the main highway." Anthony kept his eyes on the road, listening to the bag's rustle as he passed all the shops on Main Street. "When was the last time you visited your parents?"

"The weekend before Halloween. I try to go down at least once a month, depending on what I can afford."

"You're a substitute teacher, right?" he asked. "Are you still writing?"

Anthony saw Delilah turn toward him out of the corner of his eye. "You remember that?"

"Why not? I've never met anyone who writes magazine articles. I always think of those kinds of writers living in a loft in New York, using a typewriter by an open window, hearing the sound of car horns, listening to their music of choice."

"I'm impressed you've given this so much thought," she laughed. "I prefer writing in bed on my laptop or iPad, the sound of instrumental pop music in my ears."

"Yours sounds less stressful." Anthony took in the scenery around them, watching the pine trees give way to sage brush and meadow. "I've always loved reading, but I'm not into classic literature. I need a decoder ring to figure out what they're saying."

"Let me guess, not a Shakespeare fan?" she teased.

"Not if I can help it. I like modern books that are action-packed. If I'm going to read, it will be for entertainment."

Anthony heard a crunch and Delilah's moan as she took her first bite of breakfast. "I did not realize how hungry I was. Do you like audiobooks?"

"I've never listened to one before," he said.

"The narration has to be enthralling, or I'll lose interest, but I've found it's an amazing way to keep up my reading goals."

"Maybe we can find one to listen to together if we run out of things to discuss." Anthony didn't think that would happen, mainly because there were open-ended issues they needed to discuss from last night.

"I'd like that."

The fact that she didn't reject him driving her home, too, gave him hope. But not far from Anthony's mind was what he would tell Pike if things went well this weekend.

When Anthony arrived at the bar last night, Pike was lit and sitting at a table with two women, regaling them with stories about all the snow activities in Mistletoe. Anthony sat down with them, conversing politely, until it was apparent Pike wasn't making it home without a ride. Anthony said goodbye to them and helped Pike to his feet. When he swayed, Anthony held on to him by his waist and assisted him to his truck. When Anthony opened the passenger door, he spotted Delilah's sports bra on the floorboard of the driver's side so he kept Pike distracted until he could close the door and extinguish the light again. When Anthony climbed in the driver's side, he picked up the bra and shoved it into his back seat. Anthony didn't want to get into a discussion with drunk Pike about how Anthony had a right to Delilah before Pike because he noticed her first. That wasn't rational or mature, but it was like an invisible claim had occurred, and he didn't want anyone, least of all Pike, pining for her.

I kissed her so she's mine.

After dropping Pike at his apartment, Anthony went home and texted Delilah but she didn't answer. Sleep eluded him and he only got a few hours before he had to be up but he wasn't tired. Energy coursed through him like electrical currents just being near Delilah. He could still remember tasting her, and he wanted to do it again. He just wasn't sure that Delilah would be satisfied without sex since that was her current mission. Could he break his celibacy and give her everything he had? Yes, but he wanted his next sexual experience to mean something. Even his first time had been lacking because he'd just wanted to see what the fuss was about. Did it feel good? Yes? Was it mind-blowing? No.

Now, going down on Delilah last night and making her lose it all over his tongue? That had been epic, and he hadn't even come.

"You're awfully quiet over there. Not falling asleep on me, are you?" Delilah teased.

"I'm just thinking about what a beautiful morning it is and how that bear claw is calling my name."

Delilah laughed and he heard the bag rustle before the pastry was placed on his thigh. "I'd feed it to you, but I've always thought people feeding each other was a weird fetish."

"Kinks and fetishes are awfully similar creatures. Are you trying to segue so you can share yours with me?"

"I'd say exhibitionist after last night, but that was a one-time thing."

Anthony's stomach bottomed out. "You don't want a repeat of last night?"

"No! I would love to do it again. Just not in a truck, even if it does have tinted windows. I think it would be nice to try a couch or a bed." Delilah laughed. "I know, I'm so vanilla."

"You say that like it's bad," he murmured. "Vanilla is my favorite flavor."

Chapter Fourteen

How could the women of Mistletoe have been sleeping on Anthony Russo all these years? The man was a riot. There was a point outside Mountain Home when Delilah thought she would pee her pants before she made it to a restroom. On top of his perfect comedic timing, while she'd gone away to college, he'd taken online classes to finish his business degree and worked full-time. He'd saved up and bought a piece of land, slowly getting it prepared to build his dream home. Hardworking, motivated, and responsible with money . . . he even offered to take Leia out to pee when they stopped, so he liked animals. He was what every woman was looking for.

Except he couldn't fall in love.

Although she hadn't asked any more about his predicament or his vow, it hadn't been far from her mind. Besides her infatuation with Pike, Delilah had loved one man she'd met her sophomore year of college. They'd dated for a few months, and she thought he could be the one. Then he'd dumped her for another girl, and instead of staying in Boise for the summer to be with him, Delilah headed back to Mistletoe to hang with Holly and mend her broken heart. Although it had been brief, and she'd been more emotionally involved than he was, Delilah knew what love felt like.

Didn't she?

"Boise on the horizon," Anthony said as they crested the hill and saw the suburban outskirts and outlet mall that signaled the start of the biggest city in Idaho. "And twenty minutes to your parents' place."

Delilah had set up the GPS when they'd stopped because she'd been too flustered this morning and forgot.

"I know you probably need to get to your dad's, but will you come inside and meet my parents? Not because we . . . I mean . . . no pressure to meet the parents, but with you driving me home, they wanted to thank you."

Anthony patted her thigh with a laugh. "You don't have to get squirrely about it. Of course, I'll come meet them."

Before he pulled away, she covered his hand with hers, resting it on her thigh.

"Thank you. I should warn you that my dad looks like an accountant but is a total gearhead. He has an old Impala in the garage, and he's always fiddling with her on his days off. Her name is Marie."

"Beautiful name."

"My mother picked it. She said if she had to deal with her, then she was going to name her. It's my mother's middle name."

"What are your parents' names?" Anthony asked.

"Bernard and Natalia."

"You don't hear those names often." He paused a moment before adding, "My mom's name was Rose."

"I'm sorry for your loss."

"She'd had cancer before and beat it. They caught it too late this time, but at least she didn't suffer long."

"Do you mind me asking why you and your dad aren't close?"

Anthony's hand flexed against her thigh, and she wondered if it was a stress reaction. She opened her mouth to take it back, but he started talking.

"I can't remember spending time with him when I was young. As I got older, I realized that he avoided me on purpose. I overheard my parents arguing once when I was around six, and my dad admitted I was a mistake. That he didn't want me." Delilah sucked in a breath, and Anthony shot her a little smile. "Don't feel bad about that. You can't miss what you didn't have. When my mom got sick the first time, he left, and Grant went with him. He didn't give me the option, but I wouldn't have gone anyway."

"He sounds like a jerk," Delilah said, then realized this was his dad. "I shouldn't have said that."

"No, you're right. He is. Grant was closest to me in age, but I had a better relationship with my brother Bradley. He'd moved out the year before and still came home to see us. Cam and Paul were already married and living out of state when my parents divorced. They were much older because my mom had Cam when she was sixteen and Paul at eighteen." Anthony obeyed the GPS's instructions to make a right, and Delilah remained silent, waiting for him to continue. "I don't know why my brothers are this way, but she was an amazing mom to me."

"That's all that matters. I've been a substitute teacher for three years and taught multiple grades. I've seen siblings come from the same house with night and day personalities. Just because you all grew up in the same house doesn't mean you had the same childhood. That's not a criticism of your parents by any means."

"I get that. Anyway, I'd see my dad when he went to family events my mom and I were invited to, like Bradley's wedding and his kids' birthdays. Bradley wasn't a fan of Dad either. I think the first real conversation we actually had after the divorce, though, was at Mom's funeral when he asked what I was going to do with *his* house." His fingers flexed again, and Delilah rubbed the back of his hand with her palm. "I snapped, and we got into a fight. Grant and Nick pulled us apart, and he left. I hadn't heard from him again until Grant showed up with a message from him that I should come to Thanksgiving."

"Why would you go, though? If he was so horrible?"

Anthony hesitated. "I guess I thought maybe he'd had a change of heart."

Delilah's chest squeezed, and she threaded her fingers through his. "I hope you're right."

His phone rang in the cup holder, and she saw Pike's name and face flash across the screen. Anthony grabbed it and slid his finger over the screen, sending it to voicemail.

"I'll call him after I drop you home."

"I can't believe I didn't think about this, but . . . you parked your truck in front of my place. What if he sees it and has questions?"

"I guess I'll have to answer them."

"What are you going to say?"

"What do you want me to say?"

Delilah wasn't sure what to tell Anthony, especially since they hadn't talked about last night or where they stood. She hadn't wanted to broach the subject for many reasons and figured they were holding hands, touching, flirting . . . that was indication enough that he liked her, right? There is no need to examine it at this point.

"That we carpooled together since we were heading to the same place?"

Anthony snorted. "I'm not telling him that."

"Why not?"

"Because I hate lies. I already feel like an asshole for not telling him about last night."

"What stopped you?"

"I don't know. I've never been in a position where Pike and I have been interested in the same woman. It's new territory, and I'm unsure how to navigate it, especially since I want to keep seeing you."

"You do?" she asked.

Anthony rubbed his thumb over her skin lightly in a gentle caress. "I thought I made that pretty clear last night. And today."

"I'm sorry. When did you say that you wanted to keep seeing me?"

Anthony held up their clasped hands. "Do I really have to say it?"

"Every girl likes clear, articulated intentions, so we're on the same page."

Anthony took a hard right into a gas station parking lot, and Delilah squealed in surprise. He pulled around back and put the car in park. He released her hand and cradled her face in both of his hands. "I want to date you, Delilah Gill. Is that clear enough for you?"

Delilah's heart took off like a shot when he kissed her, the rapid pounding drowning out the cars passing by on the roadway, lost in Anthony's touch, in the taste of his mouth as he opened his lips over hers, his tongue delving inside to play with hers. It was deep and possessive, things she'd never thought to experience with any man, and it sent a shiver of excitement up her spine. She wanted this man like she'd never desired anything else, and he wanted her, too, which was a heady feeling.

Anthony pulled away slowly, giving her one more soft peck on the lips. She opened her eyes in time to catch his smile as he put her car in reverse and started backing up.

"We don't want to keep your parents waiting."

Delilah laughed breathlessly. "They're probably watching me on our location app."

"Damn, they still track your phone?"

"Don't stress about it. They'll think we pulled off to get something to drink." Delilah turned in her seat, watching him drive the last few minutes to her parent's house. They lived in a quiet neighborhood with mostly retired people their age and the street was tranquil this time of morning.

"This is a nice area. I prefer the mountains, but your parents chose a great location."

"My aunt bought a house here a few years before my parents moved. I think they thought I'd eventually settle down here close to them, but writing jobs in Boise aren't abundant."

"I thought you had a job?"

"My writing is all freelance. I sub to supplement my income, but I've been applying for permanent writing jobs. Some have been remote, but most want you to live locally."

"So, you're thinking about leaving Mistletoe?" he asked softly.

The navigation announced they'd reached their destination, and Delilah unbuckled her seat belt once Anthony put the car into park. "I'm not ruling it out. My rent is going up again in January and substitute teachers make less than a kid working at Taco Bell. I have a call next week that I hope will bring some good news, but I'm not holding my breath."

Leia barked rapidly, and Delilah turned, noticing she was staring out the window. Delilah saw her parents coming out the door waving, and she smiled. "There they are."

"We better get out and say hi," Anthony said, exiting the vehicle. Delilah was surprised by his brisk tone but didn't have time to analyze it before someone pulled open her door.

"Hi, Mom," Delilah said, climbing out of the car. She was immediately enveloped in her mom's warm embrace and returned it with enthusiasm. She really did miss her parents.

Her mom pulled away, holding Delilah's shoulders in her hands. Natalia Gill was a few inches taller than her daughter, with dark hair and blue eyes, although hers were a shade lighter than Delilah's.

"I was getting worried!"

"We're not that late. Besides, I know you were stalking my location."

"Guilty."

She saw her dad hold out his hand to Anthony from the corner of her eye. "Bernard Gill."

"Anthony Russo. It's a pleasure to meet you."

"I remember you. Your mom was a good woman. I was sorry to hear about her passing."

"Thank you."

"Mom," Delilah said, linking her arm through her mother's and leading her to the two men. "This is Anthony Russo. Anthony, meet my mom, Natalia."

"It's very nice to meet you."

Natalia held her arms open. "We don't need to be so formal."

Anthony chuckled and hugged her mom.

"My, you are tall!"

"How was the drive, Pip?" Her dad walked around her mom and Anthony to hug her, using his nickname for her affectionately.

"It was great since I got to sit in the passenger seat." Her dad's mustache tickled her cheek when he kissed it.

"The traffic shouldn't have been bad today," he stated, giving her a once-over. His blue-gray eyes missed nothing, and she wondered if her lipstick was smeared.

Leia's insistent barking gave her an excuse to turn away and check in the window as she opened the back door to release her excited dog. The minute she did, Leia sprang from the car and started running in circles around her parents.

"Oh, there is my favorite grand-puppy! I made you some pumpkin dog biscuits," her mom said, earning a happy yap from Leia. "Why don't we go inside and get one?"

"Let me get my bags," Delilah said.

"I've got them," Anthony said firmly, popping the trunk. He nodded toward the house. "Go enjoy your time with your mom."

"Thanks." Delilah smiled, and he returned it weakly, but she turned away from him and her dad before either of them saw her frown. Was he really upset she was open to leaving Mistletoe? Or had she said something else to irritate him?

"Come on, Delilah! I can't wait to show you the new quilt I made."

Delilah followed her mom into the house, trailing behind her through the entryway to the living room. When she spotted one of the pictures of her on the wall, she rushed over to it. "Mom! I thought I told you to burn this?"

"What? It's one of my only sixth grade pictures of you!"

"And there is a reason for that! I was hideous."

"Oh, you were not. Everyone was awkward at eleven."

Delilah doubted Anthony was and took the picture down, slipping it into the top drawer of the entertainment center. "There. Any more embarrassing pictures you've got on display?"

"Sweetheart, why are you worried if he sees your childhood pictures? He knows what you look like now and must like what he sees if he drove down here."

"I think he does," Delilah said, smiling.

"And how do you feel about him?"

"It's early still," Delilah said cagily.

"Well, I just want to say one thing."

"What's that?"

"If you marry that man, my grandbabies will be beautiful."

"Mom!"

Chapter Fifteen

Anthony carried Delilah's bags in through the second door on the left that Bernard had indicated was the spare room. He lined up her roller, tote, and backpack in the corner and left the room to join them in the kitchen, where Delilah groaned loudly.

"Seriously, I've been here five minutes."

"I am just throwing it out there that teachers in Boise get paid better than anywhere in Idaho," Natalia said.

"I don't want to be a teacher. I want to write. I teach because I have to, but the goal is to make enough money writing to support myself eventually."

"I understand, honey, but very few writers make—"

"Why can't you just support me?"

Anthony stepped into the kitchen, and both women stopped talking. "Hey, I don't want to interrupt, but I should probably head out to my family's holiday."

Natalia smiled. "Well, thank you for bringing her home."

"Yeah, no problem. I appreciate that she saved me a ton of money in gas. My truck takes over a hundred to fill up and does not get great gas mileage."

"You should switch it out for a hybrid SUV," Bernard said, adjusting his glasses. "Best thing I ever did."

"Unfortunately, I need the truck for my business."

"What kind of business are you in?" Bernard asked.

"I run a sports equipment and experience shop called Adventures in Mistletoe with my business partner. We take tourists out hiking, snowmobiling, and quad-riding on trails. We're working on buying a boat for water sports, but we've only been operational for nine months."

"I bet that does well up there," Natalia said.

"So far, so good."

"I'll walk you out," Delilah said.

"It was nice to meet you both." Anthony held out his hand to Bernard and accepted another hug from Natalia. Leia trotted after Delilah and him as they headed for the door, so Anthony squatted down. Leia placed her paws on his knee, standing up on her back legs. She stopped panting as he rubbed her ears. "See you later, Leia."

She dropped her feet as he stood, and they exited the house side by side, silent for several steps.

"Sorry you had to hear that," Delilah said.

"Hey, you know all about my family drama. Seems only fair I should get a glimpse of yours."

"My mom doesn't see writing as a real job, even though I can pay my bills every month. In her mind, it's a hobby if you aren't leaving the house for a certain length of time." Delilah laughed. "I'd love her to tell that to someone like Stephen King."

"I'm making it sound simple when I say this, but it's not her life. Just because she doesn't think it's a job doesn't mean she's right. You just have to prove her wrong."

"That's the goal." Delilah gave him a saucy grin before adding, "If I were taller, I'd kiss your cheek."

Anthony leaned down to give her access, whispering in her ear, "If your dad weren't watching, I'd give you a lot more than that."

She pressed her lips to his cheek, her mouth trembling with suppressed laughter. "I think you're going to be a bad influence on me."

"I don't know what you're talking about," he said, whistling as he rounded the front of her car.

"Let me know when you make it there, okay?"

"I will. See you Sunday?" Anthony asked, leaning on the top of her car, watching her.

"I hope so, since you have my car."

Anthony chuckled as he climbed into the Subaru. He set up the GPS and connected his phone to her car so he could make hands-free calls. Then Anthony pulled away from the curb, watching her in the mirror until he turned the corner. His first call would be to Pike because he'd called and texted Anthony several times that morning. Guilt ate at him for not telling Pike last night about what had happened between Delilah and himself, but he'd already been tipsy when Anthony arrived at the bar.

Anthony couldn't imagine Pike being receptive to his friend wanting to date Delilah when he was sober, let alone three drinks in.

If Anthony had known she wasn't interested in Pike anymore, he would have told Pike days ago that he had a thing for her, and Pike would have backed off, but Anthony had thought she was still carrying a torch.

But wanting to clear things up wasn't the only reason he wanted to talk to his best friend. Anthony was afraid if he was left alone with his thoughts too long, he might chicken out and skip his father's house for whatever diner was open holidays.

The call went out with rapid beeps, then rang twice.

"Finally. Where have you been?"

"Driving to Boise."

"Why?" Pike asked.

"I decided to take my old man up on his offer and join them for Thanksgiving."

"You mean I gotta go to the Winters' Thanksgiving hungover and alone? Do you know how depressing it is to be the only single guy in a room full of happy couples?"

"Actually, I do, but you won't be alone. I'm sure Clark's brother, Sam, will be there."

"Sam is way too cool for me. I can't carry on a conversation with that guy."

"I don't know what to tell you, bud. I left early this morning. I'm about fifteen minutes from his house."

"You could have brought me as backup! Someone is going to have to drag your ass out of there if he starts running his mouth again."

"I hope this is a peace offering, but if not, I'll leave."

"We could have gotten a hotel downtown and gone barhopping! Why didn't you tell me you'd changed your mind?" Pike asked.

"It was a last-minute decision, and I figured you needed to sleep."

"I did, but I would have been there for you. I know how hard it is seeing your dad." Pike's support was like dumping rocks on top of the pile of guilt situated in the pit of his stomach. "Besides my mom called to tell me they were bringing back my sister's Christmas present to me tomorrow. I have no idea why she needed to wake me up at seven thirty in the morning to tell me that, but she sounded excited about it, which scares me."

"Why?" Anthony asked.

"My sister is evil, and my mom thinks it's hilarious."

"I like your sister."

"Because the two of you enjoy giving me rations of shit!"

"That's true. Still, I think you're worrying over nothing."

"We'll see. So, will you be back tonight?" Pike's voice sounded helpful and Anthony cleared his throat, trying to dislodge the lump of guilt.

"I'm not sure. I might get a hotel for the night and drive back tomorrow."

"Let me know what you decide, or I'll come looking for you. I can't run this business without you."

"I will."

"It's funny. Delilah is in Boise this weekend, too. If you see her, talk me up."

Anthony hated lying to Pike, even by omission, but he didn't want to have this conversation over the phone.

"Sure thing, man."

The GPS ordered him to make a left, stating, "You have arrived at your destination." Anthony drove past the line of cars in front of the large brick house and parallel parked at the corner.

"Sounds like you're there. Have fun with your brothers, at least. I might stay home and drown myself in pie and whiskey."

"You'll have fun with the Winters. Don't be a sad sack. When you meet the right woman, everything will fall into place."

"How do you know?" Pike asked.

"Because, like you said, even assholes have soul mates."

"Fuck you, bro," Pike laughed. "Later."

"Later."

Anthony ended the call and exited the car, hesitating outside the door. He'd texted Grant that he would stop by, but the knot in his stomach grew heavier the closer he got to the front door. It was almost eleven thirty, and the invitation said appetizers started at eleven. He hadn't wanted to arrive too early and be stuck with his dad and his wife to talk to, but from the look of the street, everyone was already there. He recognized Bradley's Suburban and was glad this visit would have one bright spot.

Anthony knocked on the door and waited with his hands in his jacket pockets. When the door swung open, Bradley stood in the doorway, grinning.

"Is that my baby bro?"

Anthony held out his arms with a laugh. "The black sheep has arrived."

"None of that, you boob." Bradley enveloped Anthony in a tight, backslapping hug. "I miss you, kid."

"I miss you, too." Anthony knew he should make more effort to travel north to see Bradley and his family, especially with their mom gone.

"I'm so glad you're here," Bradley whispered, pulling back. "Audrey insisted we come down and make an appearance but if you're the black sheep, I'm the odd duck."

"Maybe that's why we get along so well."

"Probably," Bradley said, throwing his arm around Anthony's shoulders. He let his brother lead him out of the entryway and into the large recessed living room where Cam, Grant, and Paul sat on a large gray sectional, hollering at the TV. Gregory Russo sat clutching a beer in an oversized recliner, his sour expression glued to the screen. His gray hair was cut short, and although his shoulders were still broad, the round paunch of a beer gut stretched the confines of his gray T-shirt. It was like walking back into one of his childhood memories, only the people were older, and the setting differed.

"Look who decided to join us?" Bradley said, shaking Anthony by the shoulders.

The four men looked his way, but only Grant got up to greet him. "Glad you changed your mind."

"Thanks," he said.

"Unca Antney!" a small voice screamed, followed by shoes running across wood floors. Anthony turned in time to catch his five-year-old niece as she launched herself at him.

"Whoa, lil' bit! You almost took out your uncle's throat," Bradley laughed.

"She still might," Anthony rasped as skinny arms squeezed his neck tight. "Lillianne, Unca can't breathe."

She loosened her hold but kept her arms around his neck. "You wanna see my new doll? She looks like me but Mama says I have to take care of her cause she is super 'spensive! She is in with Mama helping cook dinner."

"Wow, your doll sounds awesome, Lills."

"She is! You wanna play with her? I didn't bring another one but Mama says—"

"Bradley, can't you shush that girl up? We're trying to watch the game."

Anthony felt his niece curl into him and he splayed his hand over her protectively. "Come on, Lills, let's go see this doll of yours."

Lillianne buried her face in his neck and wailed as he carried her down the hall. Anthony heard Bradley snap, "Real nice, Grandpa."

Audrey appeared in the hallway with a dark-haired toddler on her hip. Audrey was a tall, full-figured woman with curly blond hair and light brown eyes. She and Bradley had met in college and married shortly after graduation. She was an amazing woman with a kind heart. Even though they only visited a couple of times a year, Audrey had always been good to his mom, and Anthony would always adore her for that alone.

"What happened?" she asked.

"She was telling me about her new doll; some people said she was too loud."

Audrey's mouth pinched together. "Do you want me to take her?"

Lillianne's arms tightened around his neck, and Anthony shook his head. "Nah, I've got her. Just point me in the direction of this awesome doll. I heard it can cook."

"It's in the kitchen. Come on." Audrey shot a disgruntled look over Anthony's shoulder, presumably at her husband.

"Hey, don't look at me that way. I wasn't the one who suggested we come."

Audrey shook her head, leading the way into a spacious kitchen where Anthony's brothers' wives sat at the table, scrolling through their phones. Evelyn Russo, his father's second wife, stood before the oven, pressing buttons. She'd put on some weight since he'd last seen her, and when she turned around and saw him, Anthony noticed her eyes were puffy, and her shoulders were stooped, as if she was carrying the weight of the world.

"Hey, Evelyn," Anthony said.

Evelyn gave Anthony a tight smile. "Hello, Anthony. I'm glad you could make it."

Funny, because you don't sound glad.

"We're looking for Lill's doll. Have you seen it?"

Paul's wife, Melissa, looked up from her phone absently. "I think Celia has it."

"Why does your daughter have Lillianne's doll?" Audrey asked.

"I don't know, because it was left lying around?" The pointy-nosed woman snapped.

Like his older brothers, who were carbon copies of his dad, Anthony wasn't a fan of his eldest brothers' wives or their children. Cam and his wife, Whitney, had two boys, seventeen and fifteen, while Paul and Melissa had three children: Max, Ryan, and Celia. If he had to guess, the boys were probably in the back playing on whatever gaming consoles they had packed.

"Maybe you should teach your child not to touch things that don't belong to her?" Audrey shot back.

"Oh my God, it's just a doll. She isn't going to hurt it. Celia," Melissa hollered.

Celia came back into the room, dragging the doll by the hair. The nine-year-old had her mother's features, except the smirk on her lips was unsettling.

"Give Lillianne back her doll."

"Okay." The girl held the doll up, and Anthony noticed half the hair on the doll's head was missing. When Lillianne started to turn, Anthony tried to move her out of the room, but when she saw the doll, she let out a bloodcurdling scream. Not only was the doll missing hair, but she was sporting a black mustache, and her eyes were sunk back in the sockets as if someone had shoved their fingers into them.

Audrey gasped and handed her son to Bradley before she marched over and snatched the doll away from the girl. "How could you do this to someone else's toy?"

"I was playing beauty shop," Celia said, her chin jutting out.

"What the hell is going on in there?" a booming voice hollered from the other room.

"She was just being a kid," Melissa said.

"I think she's old enough to know better," Bradley said.

"It's just a doll! Here." She started tapping on her phone. "I'll Venmo you. How much?"

"A hundred and twenty-five dollars," Audrey said.

"For a flipping doll?" Melissa scoffed.

"It's an American Girl doll," Audrey gritted out.

Melissa shook her head. "I'm not paying that. Maybe you shouldn't have brought such an expensive toy if you didn't want it to get broken."

"Or we shouldn't come around people without any consideration for others." Audrey held her arms out to Lillianne, who forgot all about her favorite uncle for the comfort of her mother's arms.

"Oh, because you're so perfect?" Melissa drawled sarcastically.

"I have two toddlers, and yet I was in this kitchen from the moment I arrived, trying to help Evelyn while you two sat on your asses at the table on your phones."

Evelyn stood helplessly by the stove, hands ringing as Audrey rushed out of the room with her crying daughter.

"At least I don't have a fat ass!" Whitney yelled after her.

Bradley snarled, "Watch how you talk about my wife." When his son started crying, he left the room and Anthony started to follow.

"I don't know why they even come," Melissa said.

Whitney crossed her arms over her chest, nodding. "I know. No one wants them here."

Anthony turned slowly and saw Celia playing with a small hand-held game. He crossed the room and snatched it out of her hands. "How much was this?"

"Hey, that's mine!" Celia cried.

"Looks like it's worth about a hundred bucks."

"That is her Nintendo Switch," Melissa screeched. "It is more than a hundred dollars!"

"Seems like a fair trade for Lillianne's doll and emotional damages."

Anthony ignored mother's and daughter's protests and walked out of the kitchen, disappointed when he saw Bradley and his family putting on their coats by the front door.

He approached them and held out the gaming console. "Melissa wanted you to have this with her apologies."

Bradley took it with a grin. "You sure that's what happened?"

"Where are you going?" Gregory Russo finally looked up from the game to ask.

"We're not staying for dinner," Bradley said.

Their father got up from the chair and climbed the stairs. "Why the hell not? You drove eight hours to get here."

"And that was a mistake."

Suddenly, Evelyn marched out of the kitchen and past them, grabbing her purse and coat off the hooks by the door.

"Now, where are you going?" Gregory asked.

"I'm leaving."

"What are you talking about?"

Evelyn swirled on her heels and blasted him with a voice full of bitterness. "I've wasted thirty years of my life, and I'm not sacrificing another moment. Turkey needs to come out at two. Potatoes must be drained and smashed, and all casseroles are in the fridge with cooking instructions on the top."

"Evelyn," their dad shouted, but she was already slamming the door on him.

The rest of their brothers had gathered at the bottom of the living room steps, exchanging wide-eyed expressions.

"That was a twist," Bradley said.

"What did she mean?" Anthony asked softly, facing his father for the first time since he arrived. "When she said she'd wasted thirty years of her life on you?"

Everyone stood silently while Anthony stared at his father, puzzle pieces snapping into place.

"You son of a bitch."

Before he realized what he was about to do, he threw a punch that knocked his father backward into Cam and Paul, all three of them ending up on the floor. He shook out his hand, glaring down at Gregory Russo.

"I think that's our cue to leave," Bradley said, taking his arm. "Come on, little brother."

Chapter Sixteen

Delilah stood at the kitchen sink, scrubbing the remainder of the dinner dishes and humming along to a Sam Hunt song playing on her parents' Alexa. Her dad was in the garage tinkering with Marie, while her mom sat at the table, dishing out dessert. So far, they'd avoided the topic of her writing and living several hours away from them, but Delilah could feel the moment coming.

"So, I haven't wanted to annoy you," her mom prodded, drumming her nails on the tabletop, "but I am curious about Anthony."

Delilah paused in her scrubbing but didn't turn around. "What about him?"

"I've just never heard you mention him before. Last time you talked about anyone, it was that red-haired loudmouth."

Delilah snorted. "You mean Pike?"

"Yes!" her mother said, a tinge of disgust in her tone, "Good-looking man but kind of obnoxious from what I remember."

"He's really not, but it doesn't matter." Delilah returned to her scrubbing as she added, casually, "I'm not interested in him anymore."

"Because of Anthony?" her mom asked.

Delilah didn't want her parents latching on to this relationship before it became something. It was still too early. "Partly, but also because I decided that I deserved more. I deserve to have my dreams come true, to be someone's first choice and not just a convenient one. I've decided to stop hiding and figure out who I want to be."

"And who is that?"

"I'm not sure," Delilah said, scrubbing the last dish and putting it into the drying rack. She turned around to face her mother, who was watching her with keen interest, hanging on her every word, and that was both wonderful and terrifying. "But I'm trying new things to see what I like. I wore a dress out to a bar last week and multiple men hit on me. It was flattering."

Her mom flashed a sly smile. "Was Anthony one of those men?"

"No, he just made sure I got home okay."

"See, I knew I liked him," her mom crowed.

Delilah rolled her eyes. "Yeah, yeah. I also started going to the gym. I want to get in better shape to try some new things."

"Like what?" her mom asked.

Delilah felt like an idiot even saying the word out loud. Her mom was going to see right through that. "Snowboarding?"

Her mom laughed. "You hate being cold!"

Delilah shrugged. "I still want to say I tried. I haven't done anything except play it safe." She took a seat across from her mom with a sigh. "Even my writing."

Her mom frowned. "I thought you had an agent taking out your stuff?"

"She is, but no one wanted my manuscript." Saying it out loud was a struggle past the lump in her throat. Before her mom could catch on to her emotional meltdown, she cleared her throat and continued, "But one of the editors is interested in working with me on another project. I think I will take the series they rejected and self-publish it. See if I can find an audience for it."

"How will that help you get in with a publisher?" Her mom asked.

"If the book does well in the indie space, those sales make me more marketable with a built-in audience."

Her mom nodded, although the expression on her face still had an air of confusion. "Well, I hope it works out that way for you."

"Why do you say it like that?" Delilah asked.

"Like what?"

"Like it isn't going to happen?"

Her mom snapped the lids back on the pies with a huff. "I swear, Delilah, I don't know what you want me to say. If I tell you my concerns, you get angry with me for not supporting you, and then if I wish you luck, I've got some kind of hidden message. Either way, I'm the bad guy."

"No, it's just that I already know how you feel about my writing, which is why I don't like to talk about it." Delilah wiped her hands on the towel and headed for the door. "I'm going for a walk."

"Delilah! What about your pie?"

"I'll eat it when I get back. I just need some air."

Delilah hooked up Leia to her leash and stepped out the front door, closing it behind her. Her breath fogged in front of her face as she walked down the walkway and onto the driveway. When she hit the sidewalk, Delilah turned right and listened to the evening sounds of the suburbs. She could hear music coming from a house down the street. Cars passing out on the main road. Laughter erupted from someone's backyard.

She passed by a parked gray Subaru and suddenly stopped when Leia barked excitedly and started jumping on the passenger door. Delilah checked the license plate. It was her car.

Delilah returned to the passenger side window and bent over, peeking inside the car. Anthony was in the front seat, hat pulled low over his face. He appeared asleep, and she knocked on the window, noticing him jump a foot in the air. She waved at him, and he rubbed at his face before rolling down the window.

"Hi," he said.

"What are you doing out here?"

"Sleeping."

"Why? I thought you would be at your dad's and getting a hotel for the night?"

"I was going to do that, but there was a bunch of family drama. My brother and I left and went out to eat at the closest place that was open. Afterward, I tried to get a hotel room, but they were all booked unless I wanted to spend almost five hundred bucks and I wasn't going to crash in my brother's hotel room with his family. I figured I'd sleep in the car and head home tomorrow. Even if I come back Sunday to grab you, it would be cheaper than that hotel room."

"Why didn't you text me?"

"I didn't want to intrude on your family's Thanksgiving."

"That is ridiculous. Get out of the car and come inside."

"Delilah, I'm okay—"

"You are not sleeping in the car, Anthony. I forbid it."

He laughed. "Forbid, huh?"

"Absolutely. Grab your bag and let's go inside."

Anthony climbed out of the car and headed for the trunk. "Why are you out here?"

"You aren't the only one who gets aggravated with your parents."

"I bet my aggravation trumps yours."

"It probably does, since I planned on going back inside. Wanna talk about it?"

"Not at the moment. I'm still processing it." He slung his bag over his shoulder and wrapped an arm around her, his warm embrace making her nipples peak. "What happened with your parents?"

"Same old thing. My mother wants me to get a real job, preferably close to them."

"Are your parents pretty good overall?"

"Yeah, they are. You were going to say I should suck it up and humor them?"

"I would never presume to give you any advice about family. I do think that your mom is coming from a place of love."

"I know that. I just want to stop having the same argument repeatedly."

"The only way you're going to stop the argument is by not engaging."

"Hey, Russo, stop making sense. Nobody likes that!"

Anthony chuckled and pressed his lips against the top of her head. "Sorry, beautiful. Won't happen again."

They reentered the house and Delilah stopped in the doorway of the kitchen. Her mom and dad were at the table with their pie untouched.

"So, I went for a walk and found a stray. Can I keep him?"

Her mom spotted Anthony first and smiled. "Anthony! Did your family's dinner end already?"

"It did. Unfortunately, my hotel plans fell through and I planned on bedding down in the car, but Delilah isn't having it. I just want to be clear that I don't want to impose or cause a problem."

"It's no problem at all," her dad said. "We've got a couch that folds into a bed downstairs in the basement. I've slept on it a time or two when I've said the wrong thing."

"Really? We're going to make a guest sleep in the basement when the guest room bed is a queen?" Delilah asked.

"Are you suggesting I sign off on you two sleeping together under my roof?"

"Dad, you realize I'm an adult, right?"

"The couch is fine, sir. I want to assure you that I would never disrespect you or your wife's hospitality in any way."

"I appreciate that," her dad said.

"Honey," her mom said, putting a hand on his arm. "Anthony and Delilah can share the guest room."

"Really, ma'am. I'll be fine downstairs."

Delilah scowled at him, but her mom just shrugged. "It's up to you. If it gets too cold or the couch isn't comfortable, you have the option."

"The man said he's fine, Natalia," her dad said. "Are you going to stay through the weekend?"

"I'd planned on heading back to Mistletoe tomorrow morning and coming back for Delilah on Sunday."

"Well, that seems like a waste of gas! If you don't have anything that requires your attention, you should stay the weekend."

"I've got to talk to my business partner. We're planning the Mistletoe Winter Games and the committee wants us to pitch activities tomorrow."

"What kind of a winter games?"

Bernard sat forward. "We've thrown around a couple of ideas. Snowmobiling. Skiing."

"What about keeping it simpler?" Bernard asked. "Igloo building. Snowball fighting. Sledding or tubing. You don't need fancy equipment to make things exciting."

"That's true," Delilah said. "Plus, if you make it simple, even people who aren't necessarily big winter sports enthusiasts can enter and kick butt."

"Sounds like a plan," Anthony said. "I'll shoot Pike a text and discuss it with him."

"Wait, your business partner is Pike?" her mom asked, shooting Delilah a heavy look. Delilah figured her mom was wondering why she was interested in Pike's partner, but she couldn't exactly explain to her mom in front of Anthony that it was a happy accident.

"Yeah, he is. We've been best friends our whole lives and decided to go into business together."

"I think that's great," she said. "Do you want some pie?"

"No, I'm okay. My niece fed me most of hers and mine."

"How old is she?" Delilah asked.

"She's five and her little brother is two. They're my brother Bradley's kids."

"I will never know what it is like to have nieces or nephews because my parents refused to have any more children," Delilah said, shooting her folks a sour expression.

"Why bother when we got it right the first time?" her dad teased.

"Besides, you can have them if you marry someone who has siblings."

Delilah's face burned. "Touché."

"Should we play a game before bed?" her mom asked.

Her father groaned. "Why is it anytime we're sitting around relaxing, you insist we play a game?"

"Oh, wah wah! Anthony? Have you ever played Hot Words?"

"No, ma'am, I haven't."

"It's actually really fun," Delilah said, getting up from the table. "Anthony's my teammate."

"Rude!" her father called after her.

Delilah grabbed the game from the closet, keeping one ear on their conversation.

"Usually we invite Delilah's aunt and uncle over to play, but they traveled to Salt Lake City to visit their son for the holiday. You showing up worked out perfectly."

"Glad I could help," he said.

She sat back down and let her dad help her set up the board while her mom explained the rules. After one round, it was obvious that Delilah and Anthony made a really good team, but it was after round two that her mom called foul.

"Alright, you two need to be separated! You are too good together."

Delilah blushed, avoiding Anthony's gaze as she set up for one more round. Anthony looked down at his phone and after a moment's hesitation said, "I'm sorry, I need to take this."

"No problem, I'm getting tired anyway," her mom said.

When the front door opened and closed behind Anthony, her mother leaned across the table and whispered, "You didn't tell me that Pike and Anthony were business partners."

"It's not relevant."

"So you really aren't interested in Pike and using his friend to get his attention?"

"No, Mom. If I'd wanted to date Pike, I could have. He asked me out yesterday and I told him no."

"Why?"

"Because I realized that Pike was an infatuation and Anthony is someone that I could have real feelings for."

Her mother sat quietly for several moments, watching her thoughtfully before nodding. "Well, he seems quite taken with you. I notice that when you speak, he watches you like he wants to truly absorb everything you say."

"Mom, that's weird."

"I think it's romantic."

"Him staring at me and trying to absorb my words sounds creepy."

"He seems like a good egg to me, although I've been fooled before," her dad said.

"Stop!"

The door opened again and Anthony walked into the room and sat down. "Everything okay?" Delilah asked.

"It's fine," Anthony said, but Delilah could tell he was distracted.

Her mom seemed to pick up on the tension and yawned dramatically. "We were just saying it's probably time to call it a night."

"Yeah, we can't keep up with you kids," Delilah's dad said.

They both got up from the table and her mom kissed her on top of the head. "Good night, sweetheart. Sleep well, Anthony."

"Thanks, you, too."

Her dad held his hand out to Anthony. "Good night."

"Good night, sir."

When it was just the two of them, Delilah watched him, noticing the knitted forehead.

"Are you going to tell me what's wrong or do I need to beat it out of you?"

Anthony shared a weak smile with her and it made her heart ache for him. "Maybe in the morning? I don't have the energy for anything but sleep tonight."

"As you wish," Delilah said. "I'll show you to the basement. Unless you changed your mind?"

Anthony chuckled as he climbed to his feet. "I don't think your dad was thrilled with the thought of us sharing a bed."

Delilah pushed in her chair with a huff and led the way out of the kitchen and through the living room to a carpeted staircase. "The guest room is the first door on the right, if you change your mind."

"Duly noted."

Delilah sighed and descended the stairs in front of him, opening up the door at the bottom. Delilah flipped on the light and pointed to the left. "Bathroom is over there."

"Thanks."

"I'll grab the sheets and help you make up the bed."

"I appreciate that. I think I'll take a shower after. I don't like crawling into bed dirty."

She took out a sheet set and a couple of blankets from the linen closet, trying not to think about Anthony naked and wet. Ever since last night she'd had a hard time not imagining him in some form of undress, but not only had he vowed not to have sex, he'd also promised her dad he wouldn't even touch her!

Anthony had the bed pulled out by the time she returned and they stood on either side of it, tucking in the sheets and spreading out the blankets. When they finished, Delilah hesitated. They'd had the chance to share a bed and he was choosing to honor his vow instead?

Celibacy was for the birds.

"Well, good night." She took a step toward the exit and Anthony caught her at the door.

"Were you really going to leave me without a proper good night?"

"What would that be?"

Anthony lifted her off the floor and pinned her to the wall. "A kiss, at least."

His mouth covered hers and Delilah's arms and legs circled his shoulders and hips, returning his kiss enthusiastically. Her hands tangled in the short strands of his hair as his body plastered against her, pressing her into the wall. Delilah rolled her hips, rubbing her center against the hard bulge in the front of his pants.

He broke the kiss, his breath coming out hard and fast. His hands gripped her waist as he lowered her to the ground, kissing the top of her head.

"Night, beautiful."

Delilah's eyes narrowed as he pushed away from her and picked up his bag, disappearing into the bathroom with a click of the door.

Frustration coursed through her and she bit her lip, a plan formulating as she climbed the stairs. While she understood Anthony's reasons for taking his vow, Delilah had set out to attract a sex-god and she wanted Anthony, all of him. She'd do whatever it took to win him, but first, she wanted to make him as crazy as he was making her.

By the time she was done with him this weekend, Anthony's iron control was going to snap.

Chapter Seventeen

Not even a cold shower helped the raging hard-on that had popped up at the thought of sleeping next to Delilah. Why the hell had Anthony told her parents he would be respectful? All he wanted to do was climb those stairs and join her in the guest room, stripping her down to skin.

Anthony returned to the large basement room in his pajama pants and a T-shirt. Even though he slept naked at home, he took an overnight bag that included a change of clothes, toiletries, and pajamas everywhere he went in case he ever got stuck somewhere. Delilah wasn't wrong when she'd called him a Boy Scout. He liked to be prepared.

Although, nothing had prepared Anthony for walking into the basement bedroom and seeing Delilah leaning over his bed in a pair of indecently skimpy plaid shorts, her lush cheeks hanging out the bottom.

"What are you doing to my bed?"

Delilah straightened and turned. Anthony sucked in a breath when he saw the deep V of her shirt, her tits threatening to spill out. Her gaze flicked his way, her eyebrow arched innocently.

"I was just giving you an extra blanket, in case you got chilly."

Was she messing with him? She had to know those shorts were gloriously hot and enticing, daring him to sneak his hands around and slide them up the back of her thighs until his hands gripped the globes of her ass. Was she even wearing underwear?

Fuck, stop, think about anything else but what she's got under there.

"I'm going to go to bed," he said, his voice coming out raspier than normal.

"Sweet dreams," she murmured, her hips rolling all the way to the stairs and he couldn't tear his gaze away from that gorgeous ass. "I guess I'll go take care of myself."

Anthony's cock jerked as she shut the door, leaving him with that torturous picture.

Think of something other than Delilah and her pretty pussy.

His father sprawled across his older brothers flashed through his mind and worked like a bucket of cold water.

Thirty years. Before Anthony was even born, his father had been seeing Evelyn. Bradley had filled in the blanks once they left the house, but it was all so unreal. He'd planned on leaving their mom for Evelyn but her pregnancy changed all that. He couldn't abandon his pregnant wife for a younger woman. What would people think?

Unfortunately, Evelyn grew impatient after ten years and threw out an ultimatum. Either he left his wife or she was done. He'd made the choice but never imagined Rose would fight him on everything. She'd gotten alimony, child support, and the house. Gregory angrily raged against his ex-wife, claiming she'd financially crippled him. When his new wife wanted children, Gregory had to tell her about the vasectomy he'd had after Anthony was born. She'd been furious but hadn't left.

Until today.

The phone call he'd received from Evelyn tonight had opened his eyes to everything. She'd resented his mother not just for holding on to his Dad, but that she'd had Anthony. Rose had the child Evelyn wanted and instead, she'd gotten Dad, his obnoxious older sons, and their lazy wives. Bradley and Audrey were the only ones who ever treated her as anything more than a cook or maid and they didn't visit often. The life she imagined had never happened and instead, she'd ended up childless with a bitter old man for a husband.

Anthony wanted to say he could sympathize with her but karma had delivered her just deserts. While Anthony was a firm believer that it took two to tango, Evelyn knew his dad was a married father of four and she still thought he was going to leave his wife and what? Treat her like a pampered princess and give her six more strapping kids?

She'd either been oblivious or in denial to not know what a selfish prick Gregory Russo was.

Anthony lifted the comforter and climbed inside, thanking the painfulness of family drama, the surefire cure to make a man go limp.

He opened his message center and sent Pike a text.

Been thinking about the winter games. Let's keep it simple. Snowball fights. Sledding or tubing. Activities the average person could do. What do you think?

Anthony sent the text and tapped on his Instagram feed, spotting a picture of Pike holding up the phone in order to get the entire Winters clan in the picture. Seeing his friend's smiling face made him sick with guilt. He should go home tomorrow and talk to Pike. At least if he faced him like a man and explained everything, Pike might be pissed at first, but he'd get over it. Dragging this out was only going to make it worse.

A text popped up from Delilah and he clicked on it, staring at the picture of her shiny pink labia.

She misses you.

Fuck me.

He texted her back with shaking fingers. Hasn't anyone told you it isn't nice to tease?

Three little dots popped up and she responded with Look who's talking.

I'm not the one sending naughty pics.

No, you're the one putting the brakes on something we both want.

Oh yeah? What's that?

Anthony knew he was wading into dangerous territory taunting her but she wasn't wrong. He was the one denying them both, but Anthony was tired of meaningless sex. He wanted more.

Are you sure sex with Delilah wouldn't be exactly what you've been looking for? You went down on her and it was the most incredible experience you've ever had doing that to a woman.

He heard the faint squeak of feet on the stairs and tensed, watching the door open. A sliver of light illuminated the dark room and Delilah, who shut the door with a click, entered, plunging the room into the dark again.

Anthony fumbled with the lamp on the stand next to him and it clicked on in time for him to watch her pull the ponytail holder from her hair and run her fingers through the dark strands. The action raised her large breasts and he noticed her nipples were pebbled under the thin cotton of her tee.

Shit, his dick hardened with a vengeance as she wasted no time climbing onto the edge of the bed between his legs, crawling up the comforter toward him.

"What are you doing?" he whispered.

Delilah's sexy smile made him swallow audibly. "You asked what we both wanted. I'm showing you."

His heart thundered in his chest as she straddled him, her lips pressed against the pulse of his neck, and her warm breath rushed across his skin when she murmured, "Also, I'm testing your resolve."

"Shit," he said, earning a giggle from Delilah. Her hand cradled the back of his neck as she kissed her way along his jawline, finally brushing his mouth with hers. Delilah's other hand slipped between them, under the comforter and cupped him in her palm.

"Hmmm, what have we here?"

Anthony took her shoulders and rolled her from on top of him, kicking off the comforter to follow her. Anthony pressed her into the mattress, throwing his leg over her thighs to hold her there.

He slid his hand over the backs of her thighs and glided it over her skin until he touched the bottom of her flannel shorts.

"Oh," she gasped as his fingers explored past the hem, discovering that Delilah was indeed naked underneath. His palm cupped the globe of her ass and she wriggled against his touch.

"You're a very bad girl, Lila." He removed his hand from her shorts and gave her a soft swat on her posterior. She gasped softly and he brushed the hair from the back of her neck. "Did that hurt?"

Delilah shook her head and Anthony pushed up onto his hands and positioned his knees on either side of hers, leaning over to nip at the back of her neck. Delilah jerked in response, arching her back and he did it again, following it up with a flick of his tongue. Her skin tasted clean and carried a subtle floral scent that he couldn't place.

"I promised that I wouldn't disrespect your parents." Anthony rubbed his hard length against the curve of her ass and she whimpered, pushing back against him. Delilah was incredibly responsive, just one more thing that made her nearly irresistible. It took everything in him not to give in, to pull those adorable shorts down and bare her to him. It wouldn't take much to have her writhing under him, wet and ready for his cock, but there would be no stopping once he started. Delilah tempted him to throw his vow to the wayside, to forget about her parents upstairs, to let the rest of the world fall away and bury himself in her.

"What about me?" she whispered. "Shouldn't you be more worried about disrespecting me?"

"And how am I doing that, baby?"

"By holding back, you're telling me I'm nothing more to you than all the others."

Anthony jerked back like he'd been shot, her words cutting deep. He turned her over so he could see her face, and he saw the tears clinging to her lashes. His heart squeezed, and he brushed the tear away. "Don't manipulate me."

She opened her eyes, blinking at him. "I'm not."

Realizing he'd come off harsher than he meant, Anthony softened his tone. "Holding back is about me and has nothing to do with you. I feel a great deal about you."

"I get it." Delilah relaxed into him, smiling softly. "You don't want to have sex until you fall in love. That doesn't mean we can't do other things, right?"

"What did you have in mind, Lilah?" he asked, brushing his mouth over hers. "Do you want me to go down on you again and play with your sweet pussy until you come all over my tongue?" Anthony untied her shorts and slipped his hand inside, cupping her with his palm. "Or maybe you want to get on your knees and suck on my cock? Hmmm, so many possibilities."

Anthony grabbed the top of her shorts and dragged them down her legs, exposing her to the light. His cock throbbed, flexing as he slipped a finger between her lips and rubbed along the wet folds, his excitement reaching explosive heights as he slipped from the bed. He fully removed her shorts and met her gaze, holding it as he stripped off his T-shirt and pajama pants.

"Close your eyes, baby."

"Why? I like watching you."

Anthony smiled. "Trust me. You're going to love this more."

Delilah closed her eyes, feeling exposed in the light, but too turned on to truly care. The bed shifted under Anthony's weight as he climbed back onto the mattress and she held her breath, waiting, expecting to feel his mouth and tongue probing her already soaking wet center.

Something rubbed against her seam, dragging along in an upward motion until it connected with her clit. It circled her, warm and soft, the texture creating electric currents of pleasure and she gasped.

"Feel good?"

Delilah realized as he pressed between the lips of her labia and rubbed against her opening that it was his cock. Anthony was using his cock to tease and torment her. He pushed against her slightly, and she cried out, "Yes."

Anthony's hips moved, the length of him sliding against her sensitive flesh and Delilah opened her eyes. He held himself over her, watching her face as he ground into her. Delilah's back bowed when his tip connected with her clit, whimpering.

"God, you feel so fucking good. Wet and hot." He picked up speed and that heavy ache built inside. Delilah bit her lip to keep from crying out and waking her parents. When the tip of him slipped inside, Delilah gasped, hips arching to take more, but he was already pulling back.

"No," she begged.

Anthony lowered himself between her legs and devoured her like a starving man, his tongue pressing her clit in hard circles. His whiskers rubbed against her labia and the skin of her thighs, the pressure building until she couldn't climb any higher. Delilah grabbed a pillow and screamed into it as she came writhing against his mouth, her body shuddering with release. She pulled the pillow from her face and took a deep breath, languid with pleasure.

He crawled up the bed until his stiff cock rested against her. His mouth brushed hers, trailing soft kisses across her cheek. "Is that what you wanted?"

Delilah chuckled. "It will do for now."

"Oh, yeah?"

Delilah's eyes fluttered open and met his as her hand pushed between them to wrap around him. He sucked in a breath as she pumped him slowly. "This is what I really want."

Anthony bucked against her. "Oh, yeah?"

"Hmmm, all of it. First in my mouth and then inside me, as deep as you can go."

"Fuck yes."

Power surged through her as she pushed him off her and he was flat on his back, watching her with hooded eyes as she tied her hair in a knot on top of her head.

"Jesus, no one has ever looked at me like that before."

"How am I looking at you?" she whispered.

"Like you're a kid at Christmas and Santa brought you exactly what you wanted."

"That's incredibly accurate." Delilah kissed his abs, making her way down to where his hard-on bobbed and flexed, the round head glistening. She kissed the tip and then swept her tongue along the underside, listening to his breathing hitch. Blow jobs weren't her thing and she had never thought of herself as good at them, but with Anthony, she wanted to learn everything about him. The different textures of his dick, the salty taste of him as she sucked him down her throat. That breathy sound he made when she circled his tip rapidly. Delilah didn't just want to do it because he'd done it for her. Everything with Anthony had been unlike the intimacy with anyone else and she wanted to know if it was the same for this.

His cock flexed against her tongue and his hips jerked.

"Lila, shit, baby, if you keep that up I'm going to come."

Delilah bore down on him, intensifying her ministrations. His fingers slipped into her messy bun and tightened, thrusting against her mouth until he stiffened and she swallowed down the warm evidence of his orgasm.

Delilah released him after one last brush of her tongue over him, smiling when he shivered. "That was fun."

Anthony chuckled, taking her by the arms and dragging her up his body until she was snuggled against his side. "I'm glad you liked it."

"Didn't you?"

"I fucking loved it. I'm pretty sure that counts as breaking my celibacy, though."

"Hmmm, do you regret it?"

Anthony pressed a kiss against her forehead. "No. I haven't regretted a single moment with you."

Delilah's heart raced, scared that he only felt that way because they were away from all the stress and complications in Mistletoe, but once they returned, his guilt about Pike would overwhelm him.

"I guess I should go back to the guest bedroom," Delilah said.

"Not yet. I'll set an alarm. What time do your parents wake up?"

"Six?"

He grabbed his phone and tapped the screen for a few moments before he returned it to the side table. "There." Anthony grabbed the blankets and sheet and pulled the covers over both of them. "I'm not ready to let you go."

Delilah closed her eyes, listening as Anthony's breathing deepened, a disturbing thought lingering at the back of her mind.

What happened when Anthony *was* ready? How could she protect her heart from him when she was afraid it was already too late for that?

Chapter Eighteen

"Is it weird that I wish we weren't heading back today?"

Anthony glanced over at Delilah from the driver's seat, his hand clasped between both of hers in the center of her lap. She wore a blue sweater dress that perfectly matched her eyes over leggings, her dark hair braided over her shoulder. He understood what she meant; they'd been in this little bubble of bliss far away from the complications that waited for them back in Mistletoe, and now they were headed back to reality. Anthony had spent the weekend going over his speech for Pike and every scenario ended with his best friend either punching him out or calling him everything under the sun.

Still, they had another half an hour until they pulled into town and he wanted to stay in this space with her for a few more miles. To enjoy her company and who they were together before he had to think about what happened next.

"Honestly, I was getting kinda concerned about the way your dad was looking at me."

Delilah laughed. "And how was that?"

"Like he knew I was doing ungodly things to his daughter in their basement."

"I wouldn't say ungodly."

He caught her telltale blush out of the corner of his eye and grinned. Since Thursday night, they'd kept things conservative in front of her parents while they went shopping at the mall or out to dinner and driving around to look at Christmas lights, but the minute they went to bed, Delilah would sneak downstairs to be with him. The way she'd smile at him, like a cat ready to lick every last drop of cream, was irresistible and it was all he could do to keep from forgetting why he'd decided to stay celibate and bury himself in her.

The hardest part about staying strong was the aftermath, when she'd curl up against him and they'd talk. Her hand would stroke his chest hair as she told him about some mischief Holly dragged her into and he'd laugh, running his palm over the silky skin of her hip. Talking to Delilah about anything and everything was the most intimate experience of his life. When he'd been with women before, he'd found snuggling with them uncomfortable and couldn't wait until they fell asleep.

Delilah just fit. The curve of her body. Her warm, breathless laugh. How she didn't mind being the big spoon when his arm fell asleep and he needed to reposition.

"You're right," he said, bringing her hands up to kiss the knuckles of the closest one. "Nothing that feels so good could be wrong."

Anthony felt Delilah turn in the seat and her intense gaze made him look away from the road for a second and at her serious expression. "What?"

"I'm feeling a little guilty."

"Why's that?"

"I haven't been respecting your feelings about sex. I've been so focused on how much I want to be close to you, when I should have let you take the lead."

"If you'll remember, I'm the one who started all the closeness," he teased.

"So, no regrets?"

"I already told you I could never regret what's between us."

"And when we get back home?"

Anthony swallowed, debating on how best to say what he was thinking without sending her reeling. "There's no question I want to see where you and I go, but I need to talk to Pike before we go public. I know you two never dated, but when he asked if I was interested in you, I told him no."

"Why did you tell him that?" she asked softly.

Anthony could feel her grip on his hand slacken and he pulled the car off the road at the next turnout, putting it into park. "Hey, no, don't do that. Remember, I thought the two of you were into each other. There was no point in saying anything if he was your first choice."

Delilah leaned across the middle console and he met her halfway, their kiss sweet and insistent. When she tried deepening it, Anthony pulled back with a laugh.

"I can't have you distracting me. It's time to go home and face the music."

Delilah pouted. "Fine. Since we're pulled over, let me grab my water bottle from the back."

"Alright," he said, leaning back against the seat. A red car in the distance crested the hill and caught his attention. It drew closer and Anthony's stomach bottomed out.

Shit, fuck, no, it's not—

As the car passed by, Anthony watched the driver do a double take and flip around farther up the road, tearing back toward them. Delilah climbed back inside and asked, "Jeez, what's that guy's problem?"

"It's Pike," Anthony said, gripping the steering wheel.

"Oh, no," Delilah put her hand on his arm, a comforting gesture, but Anthony was too busy watching his best friend whip his car into the space in front of him and open his door. Pike, in a black jacket with a beanie pulled over his head, climbed out and marched toward their car. He stopped in front of the hood and pointed his finger at Anthony.

"I fucking knew it!"

Anthony checked for cars and hopped out, shutting the door as he jogged after Pike, who was already headed back to his car.

"Pike, hold up. It's not what you think."

"I'll bet," Pike scoffed, twisting around and shoving Anthony backward. Caught off guard, he stumbled a bit but caught himself. "I asked you, point blank, if you were interested and you said no."

"I can explain everything but I don't want to do this on the side of the highway."

"I don't want to do this at all. I just had to make sure it was you because I thought I was making myself crazy. Telling myself it was a weird coincidence that you changed your mind about visiting your dad."

"That was all true!"

"When did it start? How long were the two of you fucking around and laughing at me?" Pike asked, his eyes blazing.

There was no use trying to tell Pike that wasn't what they'd been doing. "Wednesday night."

"After she rejected me? So, while I was waiting at the bar for you to show up, you were together?"

"It wasn't like that—"

"Then explain it to me, man, because I knew you liked to razz me, but I always thought you respected me."

"I do respect you, which is why I didn't tell you about us over the phone. It's why I said I wasn't interested when you asked, even though I've been into her for almost a year."

"The fuck are you talking about?" Pike asked.

"We kissed last year at Merry and Clark's party. I knew she liked you so I stopped it, but I didn't forget."

"Why didn't you tell me that when I was going on and on about dating her?"

"Because I thought she wanted you, too!"

Pike scoffed. "And the minute you found out she'd turned me down, you made your move."

Anthony wanted to deny it, but that was exactly what happened. "I honestly didn't expect you to be so invested, man. It had only been a couple of days."

Pike laughed. "I can't believe you're trying to turn this around on me. Forget the fact that you made a move on her behind my back, you're my business partner. My brother. And you fucking lied to me. That's what I can't get over."

Anthony let Pike return to his car, at a loss for what to say. Pike wasn't wrong. He'd lied. He hated liars and yet he'd become one because he wanted Delilah.

Her door opened and closed and he heard the crunch of her shoes on gravel before her hands covered his arms, lips pressing into his back. "He'll get over it. We weren't dating, so it's not like we cheated."

"I did worse. I lied to him, repeatedly."

"Anthony, you're both blowing this up way bigger than it needs to be. When he calms down, he'll call and the two of you will patch this up."

Anthony couldn't take her cheerful optimism, not right now. "Let's get you and Leia home."

He started to walk back to the car but something hard connected with his butt. Anthony whirled around, his jaw hanging open. "Did you kick me?"

"Yes, and I almost fell over trying to reach your freakishly tall ass cheeks, but you needed it! The two of you are acting like children fighting over the same toy and it's partly my fault. I should have told Pike when I turned him down it was because of you, but I didn't know you cared until you tracked me down at the store that night. We can't go back and fix our mistakes, but we can move forward. We've already let the horse out of the barn. Just"—her voice shook with emotion as she continued—"please don't toss us aside because you think it will fix things."

"I'm not tossing anything aside."

"Really? So, you're not thinking of cooling this off while you fix things with Pike?"

It had been at the back of his mind but hadn't fully formed yet. "Not necessarily."

Delilah laughed bitterly. "Wow. Just like that?"

"No, I just—my whole life, it's been Nick, Noel, and Pike. Always the four of us, having each other's backs. I fucked that up and I gotta fix it."

"But why do you need to give me up to do that?"

Anthony didn't have a good answer and Delilah shook her head. "You know what? I figured out why you've never been in love. There's no room left to let anyone else in."

"Delilah, stop." He reached for her but she shook him off.

"You're a coward, Anthony Russo. You chased me. You made me think this was going to be something amazing and now, you're running scared." Delilah dashed at her eyes and he wanted to hold her, to tell her he was sorry, but she didn't want that from him. "Give me my keys."

"They're in the ignition."

"Good." Delilah rounded the car and climbed inside. Anthony barely got the passenger door closed behind him before she took off, gunning it for home.

Anthony buckled his seat belt, his mind racing. Normally he was the voice of reason in their friend group, but he'd messed up big-time, not just with Pike, but Delilah, too. While he was normally good under pressure, he'd never experienced anything like this and had no way of knowing how to navigate it.

"Lila," he tried, but she cut him off.

"Don't call me that. That's over now."

"Come on. Now who's blowing things out of proportion?"

"You don't get it. You are this tall, gorgeous, perfect specimen of manhood. You probably got picked first for every sport, girls fell all over themselves to go out with you. I have only ever been two people's first choice. Holly's and then yours. At least, I thought I was, but it turns out I'm not."

The catch in her voice made Anthony sick to his stomach because he was the cause of her pain.

"Delilah, I'm not picking him over you. I just don't want to throw away almost thirty years of friendship."

She didn't respond, just took the left onto the main road into Mistletoe and Anthony grabbed the oh-shit handle in response.

"Can you slow down a bit?" he asked.

"No, because as soon as I get home, I can get the hell away from you."

Anthony didn't know what to say to make any of this better, so he kept his mouth shut until she pulled into her driveway.

"Delilah, can we please talk about this?"

"What's there to say?" Delilah got out of the car and went around to release Leia from the back seat. "Be sure to lock it after you get your stuff out."

Anthony opened the door and stood up, calling after her, "I don't want this to be the end."

"I guess we don't always get what we want."

Chapter Nineteen

"Miss Gill, are you alright?"

Delilah looked up from her sub notes and caught several of the kids watching her. "What do you mean?"

"You seem cranky?" Megan said.

"If I do, I apologize. I'm still recovering from the holiday weekend."

This launched the kids into a rapid discussion about how it went by too fast and they couldn't wait until Christmas break. Normally, Delilah would be in the thick of their conversation, laughing at their stories and cracking jokes, but Megan wasn't wrong about her being cranky. She wanted to go home and crawl into bed, but at least being in the classroom distracted her from thinking about Anthony.

The bell rang and she dismissed them, wishing them a nice day. It was the last period and Delilah packed up her notes for the day, stapling them together before sliding them into the pocket at the front of the sub binder. She turned off the lights and closed the door, went into the hallway and weaved her way through the sea of middle schoolers. The smell of too much cologne and perfume combined with the sour stench of body odor made her stomach turn. While she loved teaching this age, Delilah wished their parents paid attention to their hygiene.

She dropped the binder at the front office and exited the side door toward her car. A few students called out to her and she waved, but she wasn't going to stop for anyone. The minute she climbed into her car, she pressed the button and the ignition came to life. Delilah's car connected to her phone and it started going off, alerting her to multiple phone messages. She pulled her phone out of her purse and checked her messages. The first several were texts from Holly and she tapped her name, scrolling through.

You and Merry were wrong!

The mayor says we can't exclude anyone from the auction.

Brodie and Trip caused a stink.

They are back in.

Are we ever going to talk about this weekend?

Delilah grimaced. Holly had spotted Anthony's truck over the week-end and called her Saturday, hammering her with questions about their relationship. When Holly swung by her place yesterday and surprised her, Delilah didn't want to let her bestie in. She'd faked a migraine and Holly told Delilah to call her when she woke up. Instead, she'd been avoiding her anxious text messages and behaving exactly like Anthony.

A coward.

Maybe she could have handled his reaction to the fight with Pike with understanding and grace, but it was all so ridiculous. While she'd never had any conflict with Holly over liking the same guy, Deli-lah couldn't imagine them ever blowing up their friendship over one. Whether Anthony had made a move on Delilah without telling Pike or not, she'd already told Pike there was no chance. Thus, his betrayal was an imagined, childish reaction and Delilah couldn't believe Anthony was buying into it.

Maybe he is looking for a reason to run.

While the little voice is mean, ultimately it made sense. The fact that Anthony's first inclination was to take a step back from her hurt like a gutshot, and she didn't like how easily she'd let him past her defenses, believing he was the real thing. So what if he hadn't fallen in love before? In her idiotic, romantic mind, she'd imagined that it was because he was waiting for her.

So stupid.

Her phone rang and the number that flashed across her car screen was a Colorado area code. She almost didn't answer but finally pressed the accept button. "This is Delilah."

"Delilah Gill?"

"Yes?"

"This is Tabitha Newton with Outside Publications. How are you doing?"

"I'm good, thanks. How are you?"

"I'm doing well. I'm calling because a few weeks ago you submitted an article that really resonated with us. I know it was a freelance job, but are you looking for anything more permanent?"

"In Colorado?"

"Preferably, yes. Some of our writers have worked out of state but we do a lot of team building and in-person collaboration, so it's nice to have everyone in a single place."

"What is the job?"

"We're looking for a plus-size outdoor enthusiast. Your realistic portrayal of hiking while plus size was funny and engaging. The way you described the serenity of the woods makes me want to move there."

"Thank you."

"If you're alright with it, I'd love to send you the standard contract and starting salary. Hopefully you find the compensation reasonable. We also provide a small stipend for moving expenses if you're coming from out of state."

"Sure, I'll take a look at it. You have my email, right?"

"Yes. We are looking to fill the position before the first of the year, so if you could let us know as soon as possible."

"I'll look this over when I get home. Thank you again."

"We'll talk soon."

Delilah ended the call, making the turn off the main road. She'd already made up her mind not to take the job, especially because they thought she was a plus-size outdoor enthusiast. She'd written the piece after a walk in the woods with Holly and although it had ended with her stepping on a hornet's nest and being stung several times, she'd used it as inspiration to write the article.

She pulled into the driveway and once she parked, headed inside to let Leia out. Delilah was halfway up the sidewalk before she heard someone calling her name. She spotted Holly coming from the other side of the street, where she'd parked kitty-corner. She probably thought that Delilah was avoiding her, which she was, but no way would she admit it.

"Hi, what are you doing here? Shouldn't you be selling Christmas ornaments?"

"Erica is closing up for me so I could hunt you down. What's going on with you?"

"Nothing!"

"Lies!" Holly marched after her when Delilah turned away, unlocking the door while Holly railed, "There is mischief afoot! Pike and Anthony aren't speaking and you're avoiding everyone. You didn't even get coffee this morning."

"I made it at home."

"You never make it at home!"

Delilah pushed the door open and set her purse on the side table before releasing Leia from her kennel. The little dog zoomed around, saying hello to Holly before running to the back doggie door and outside.

"I felt like it today," Delilah grumbled.

"Alright, I feel like I need to introduce myself again because I feel like you forgot who you're talking to. Hi." Holly held out her hand. "I'm Holly, your best friend. The one you share all your troubles with. There are no judgments, no recriminations. Just love and support from someone who loves you."

Delilah sank onto her couch, staring out the window at the gray sky. "Pike kissed me on Wednesday."

Holly flopped next to her. "Which you don't sound thrilled about?"

"I thought he was what I wanted for so long, but when he kissed me, I felt nothing."

"So, what happened after?"

"I told him that I wasn't interested in him."

"Sounds like you were honest."

"I was, but when I went to grab road-trip snacks that night, Anthony was there, too. He wanted to talk about the blowup on Monday—"

"When you thought he laughed at you for wanting good sex."

"Who is telling this story?"

"Hey, I'm just clarifying!"

"Yes, because we had a misunderstanding. So he followed me out to the parking lot. He told me to get into the truck and one thing led to another . . . "

"Oh my God! You had sex with Anthony?"

"Not . . . quite."

Holly squealed, grabbing one of the throw pillows and hitting her with it. "You evil wench, you've been holding out on me since Wednesday!"

"We've both been a little busy!"

"There is no excuse! So how was the not-quite sex?"

Delilah's chest seized, remembering Anthony's eyes on her while he touched her. "It was glorious."

"Oh, good Lord. Okay, so you have an encounter on Wednesday and then . . . "

"He left to go to the bar to meet Pike but asked if he could drive me to Boise on Thanksgiving. I said sure. I had so much fun with him." Delilah's voice broke on the words. "He was funny and sweet and then he kissed me before we got to my parents and told me he wanted me."

"This is all good stuff!"

"Just wait." Delilah grabbed the other pillow and hugged it. "He ended up back at my parents' house for the weekend and it was all practically perfect. We were talking about what would happen when we got back to Mistletoe, after Anthony talked to Pike—"

"Wait, back up, Pike didn't know that Anthony stayed the weekend with you."

"No, he didn't want to tell him over the phone."

"I see. So, when did he find out?"

"We were parked off of Highway 20 so I could get my water bottle and he saw us. He flipped the car around and the two of them got into it on the side of the road. I tried to talk to Anthony, to reassure him Pike would get over it, but I could tell he wanted to run."

"Oh, honey." Holly reached for her and Delilah laid her head in her best friend's lap, sobbing. "How did you leave it?"

"I told him that he was a coward and I was done."

"Are you sure that's what you want?" Holly asked.

"No, but the whole thing is stupid! Pike and I weren't dating, so why does Anthony have to ask permission?"

Holly shrugged. "I don't think that's what this is about, love."

"What do you mean?" Delilah asked, sitting up.

"I talked to Pike a bit on Thanksgiving. I'm not saying you aren't a catch, but I think Pike has a lot of insecurities when it comes to women and friendships. I think the problem is that Anthony wasn't up front and hid it from him and it reminded him of his past relationships."

Guilt twisted in her stomach. "We weren't trying to hurt anyone."

"Hey, you were both single and into each other," Holly said reassuringly, squeezing her hand. "You didn't do anything wrong. This is between the two of them and if Anthony needs a little time to mend his friendship with Pike, maybe you should give him grace. Pike not speaking to him would be like the two of us beefing."

"Ugh." Delilah buried her face in her hands and groaned. "Am I the selfish a-hole?"

"No," Holly said, scooting closer to wrap Delilah into her arms. "You're human and you've got your own relationship scars. I think that might have contributed to how you reacted to Anthony."

"Maybe this whole thing was a sign," Delilah said.

"What do you mean?" Holly asked, cocking her head to the side.

"I got a call today with a job offer." She glanced away swiftly when she noticed the narrowing of her friend's eyes. "This magazine I submitted an article to liked my writing and wants me to come write for them as their plus-size outdoor enthusiast."

"You hate the outdoors," Holly scoffed. "Besides, I thought you were waiting to talk to that editor. When is that happening?"

"Tomorrow." Delilah's heart sped up thinking about the talk and the possibility of leaving Mistletoe. She didn't want to go anywhere, but writing opportunities were few and far between. "I just figured I'd keep this in my back pocket. I can fake it until I make it."

"So, you want to take it?" Holly asked, her tone neutral.

Delilah shrugged. "I don't know. They sent a contract and salary, but I haven't looked."

"What are you waiting for?" Holly said, waving her hand impatiently. "Pull out your phone and let's see."

Delilah got up and removed her phone from her purse, tapping on the Gmail app. Delilah clicked on the email and whistled. "Well, it's more than I make subbing and writing combined."

"Let me see." Holly frowned. "Why is there a moving allowance?"

"The position is in Colorado."

"Nope, no! Not a fan."

"I need to at least consider it, Holly." She took her best friend's hands. "I love you more than anything, but I'm spinning my wheels right now. I feel like I'm in the limbo of waiting on good things to come to me. The whole point of my tirade and trip to Brews and Chews was to start my own inferno, but it turned into a dumpster fire. I'm just keeping my options open in regards to the job. I do have a favor though."

"What's that?" Holly asked.

"Will you teach me to snowboard?"

Holly arched a brow. "Is it for this potential job offer?"

"Yes."

"Then nope, sorry, I'm busy that day."

Delilah released her hands with an exasperated huff. "You don't even know what day."

"Doesn't matter. I'm not going to let you run away."

"Even if it ends up being what's best for me?" Delilah asked.

"I'll make you a deal. See how the conversation with that editor plays out and if you really feel like this would be a good change for you, I'll drive the U-Haul."

Chapter Twenty

"Flipping Holly," Delilah grumbled as she grabbed bags of chocolate and dropped them into her cart. She'd gotten the text from her bestie, asking Delilah if she would be willing to host book club since the traffic around Evergreen Circle, where Holly lived, was ridiculous this time of year. Still, why had Delilah been her first choice to have a bunch of local women over to eat, drink, and talk about smut?

Holly could have asked her parents or even Merry, but no, Delilah was going to get stuck with fifty million people eating and drinking in her tiny duplex because she couldn't say no.

Suddenly, someone rounded the corner, and nearly crashed into Delilah's cart.

"Sorry about that," Pike said, stiffening when his eyes met hers.

Well, this isn't awkward at all.

"My fault." Delilah stared up at him, nodding. "I wasn't looking where I was going."

Pike's gaze traveled over the contents of her cart. "Looks like you're having a party."

"Book club," Delilah said, rolling her eyes. "Don't ask me how I got roped into hosting. It was supposed to be Holly's bag, but with the light displays on Evergreen, she was afraid no one would be able to get in."

"Makes sense," he said, glancing behind her. "I should let you finish. Enjoy your night."

Pike started to step around her cart, but she couldn't let him just walk away. Not when she knew that Anthony and Pike were still at odds.

"Pike," she called out, and he stopped a few feet from her and turned, waiting. "I am sorry for coming between you and Anthony. You should know that we aren't . . . seeing each other anymore."

Pike shook his head. "When did that happen?"

"About five minutes after your fight on the side of the road." She cleared her throat. "He loves you, you know? We had a moment, a long time ago, but he didn't want to get in the way of you and me."

"So, he said," running a hand over his beard thoughtfully. "Exactly what did he do to drive you away?"

"He wanted to take a step back with me and fix things with you. I told him that he was trying to fix the barn after the animals got out, but you're important to him." Delilah walked over to the cold section and picked up a tub of cookie dough. "You should think about that before you throw away your friendship."

"Anthony lied to me," Pike said, his voice tight. "Just because he regrets it now, doesn't change the fact—"

"Oh, jeez, do you hold yourself to those standards as well?" Delilah said, tossing the tub aggressively into her cart. "Did you ever make a mistake or hurt someone and regret it after the fact? When you tried to make it better, did they forgive you or drop you? Because I seem to remember you saying something idiotic to one of your ex-girlfriends and she never forgave you."

"Damn, people in this town cannot keep their mouths shut."

"Pike, I've heard you complain about it more than once when you've had a few. At first, I felt bad, but right now, you are doing the same thing to Anthony. We have—had feelings for each other and he still chose you. Maybe consider how you would feel if the roles were reversed and Anthony wouldn't forgive you."

"If you're so angry at him, why are you defending him?" Pike asked.

"Because I can't turn off my feelings as well as you, apparently," she said, pushing her cart away from him and disappearing down the candy aisle with her heart beating fast.

Why had she stepped in and gone so hard for Anthony? Was it because if Delilah ever lost her best friend over something like that, she'd hope someone would stick their neck out for her.

And maybe, you're hoping if the two of them patch things up, there might still be a chance for the two of you?

Delilah ignored the voice, grabbing the soda with a grunt. She was not going to hold out hope any longer. It had been almost a year of back and forth, waiting and wondering. She was done hoping that Anthony Russo was the real deal.

* * *

Anthony stood by the shop window on Tuesday, watching the flurries fall to the ground and cover the sidewalk. It was almost closing time and any minute, Nick would pull up so they could head to the gym together, just like yesterday; then Anthony would head home, make dinner, and go to bed. Pike hadn't been in all day, staying out with clients and answering Anthony's texts with shorthand responses. He missed his friend.

He ran a hand over his face, wondering how he'd let things spin so far out of control. There were so many moments he could have handled differently, and instead, he'd acted like a self-centered ass.

Like father, like son.

Anthony wasn't sure why Gregory Russo had been occupying his mind so much. Maybe because he had a better understanding, now, of how incredibly flawed his family truly was. Delilah was right that he was afraid to let new people in, but she was wrong that there wasn't any room for her.

If he told her how miserable he was without her, would she feel the same?

The front door opened and Holly stepped inside, shaking the thin layer of white snow from her hair and shoulders. Her brown eyes narrowed on him and she pointed. "You!"

Anthony held his hands up and slowly backed away. "Whoa, what's up?"

"If she comes in here asking for snowboard lessons, you tell her no. You got me?"

"Who, Delilah? Why would she want to learn to snowboard?"

"Because some magazine in Colorado wants her to take a job at their magazine as their plus-size outdoor enthusiast and she's thinking about taking it."

"Delilah wants to move to Colorado?"

"No, but she is convinced this is some kind of sign. That all the drama with you and Pike proved that she doesn't belong here." Holly crossed her arms over her chest. "I can't lose my best friend, Ant."

"What am I supposed to do? I guarantee you that she's not going to come ask *me* for lessons. She made it pretty clear that she didn't want anything to do with me."

"What about you?"

Anthony shot her a disgruntled look. "I'm not discussing my personal feelings with you, Holly."

"Why not?"

"Because we're not that close." *And you're best friends with the woman I can't stop thinking about.*

"Fine, but if it's any consolation, I know my bestie. She misses you."

"I didn't end things, Holly. She did."

Holly threw up her hands. "You are both pigheaded turds! Don't forget about the bachelor meeting after the Festival of Trees on Saturday."

"I don't want to do that anymore, Holly."

"Too bad! It's for charity! You don't want to be a Scrooge, do you?"

She walked out the door before he could respond. Anthony pulled his phone out of his pocket and texted Pike. Getting ready to close up.

K.

His jaw clenched at the short response. He hated where they were at but had no idea how to fix it.

Nick came in and waved at Anthony, releasing an exaggerated shiver. "It is freezing, dude. Maybe we skip the gym and head to Brews for a drink or two."

Anthony shook his head. "I need to work off some of this energy or I'm going to lose my mind."

"Pike still not talking to you?"

"No. I know I messed up, man, but you'd think he'd at least hear me out."

"I agree. I think we're going to have to pull out the big guns for this one," Nick said, grinning wickedly.

"I'm afraid to ask what that means."

"A lot of groveling, maybe even some bribery, and possibly, a grand gesture."

"He's not my girlfriend."

"No, he's Pike. He isn't like us." Nick arched a brow. "Speaking of girlfriend, what is going on with the woman in question?"

"She's not speaking to me either."

"It is so weird after all these years to realize you're human and not a man-droid," Nick deadpanned.

"Dick."

"It's Nick, actually. Come on. Let's go to the gym and see if we can't track down our wayward friend and make amends."

Anthony flipped off the lights and grabbed his gym bag from behind the counter. He followed Nick out the door and locked up, carrying his stuff over his shoulder as they headed down the street to the gym.

Nick opened the door and went in ahead of Anthony, whose gaze immediately locked on Brodie and Delilah talking and smiling. When she glanced over and caught him watching, she held out her hand to Brodie, who took it with a smarmy grin. Anthony's hackles went up and Nick glanced over his shoulder.

"Bro, did you just growl?"

Delilah took the long way around the gym edge and exited the front door. Anthony handed Nick his bag. "I'll be right back."

Anthony followed Delilah out the door, calling out her name. She didn't turn around but he caught up in half a dozen strides, pulling her into the alleyway between buildings.

"What are you doing?" she snapped.

"I want to know what you were talking to Brodie about."

"None of your business."

"Maybe not, but I still want to know." Anthony caged her in with his arms against the building, bending down to catch her eye, but she wouldn't look at him. "Delilah . . . " he dragged out her name and her chin rose, her blue eyes flashing defiantly.

"What?"

"Why were you talking to Brodie?"

She huffed. "Not that it's any of your business, but I asked him for snowboarding lessons."

"The fuck you did."

"I asked around about snowboarding and he said he'd teach me."

"Why didn't you ask me? I do this for a living."

"You're joking, right? I'm giving you what you wanted. You wanted time to fix things with Pike and I'm giving you that."

"Except this feels more like a punishment." Anthony bent low, his lips resting against her ear. "Don't you miss me, Lila?"

"Don't," she whispered.

"I've laid awake the last two nights missing you. Your scent. Your laugh. Your body pressed against mine."

Her breath hitched when his mouth traveled along her jaw, hovering over her mouth. "Tell me."

"What?"

"That you don't think about us."

Delilah grabbed the front of his sweatshirt in her fists, but instead of pulling him in, Delilah pushed him away. "Stop. Don't make me want you because we both know I can't have you."

"Delilah—"

"No, Anthony. It's been almost two weeks of this push and pull between us. I may have overreacted on Sunday about Pike, but the truth is, you don't know what you want. You've got me in this alley, making my knees weak and every part of my body wants to give in, but I'm not your dirty little secret. You had me screaming your name in your truck and far away from your friends in Boise, and now I'm starting to wonder if you didn't tell Pike because I was right all along. You're ashamed to want me."

Horror flashed through him. "Absolutely the fuck not."

"Prove it. Stop hiding, Anthony. I've been waiting on you to wake up and realize I'm yours for the taking, but I'm not waiting around forever."

Delilah dropped his sweatshirt and exited the alleyway, disappearing out of sight.

Anthony's emotions raged, warring between frustration, desire, and disbelief. He'd never imagined how his actions would have been interpreted by Delilah, making her think he was hiding her, that he was embarrassed of her.

Anthony headed back to the gym and searched for Nick, spotting him in the back by the weights. "You still up for blowing this off and getting a drink?"

Nick nodded. "You alright?"

"No, I'm a fucking idiot."

"Hey, Russo," Brodie called, crossing the room to stop in front of him. "Guess who I'm taking out this weekend?"

"Your mom?" Nick quipped, earning a glare from Brodie.

"Delilah Gill. Wants to learn how to snowboard."

"And?"

"I find it interesting she didn't hire you. I heard a rumor the two of you were hanging out. Wanna give a guy a heads up what I'm getting into?"

"It's not a date," Anthony said. "She asked you for lessons."

"Yeah, but I figure that's just a cover. The girl's got good taste and wants to get in a warm-up before the real workout begins."

Anthony grabbed Brodie by the shirt, bringing him nose to nose. "You touch her and I'll fuck you up."

"Whoa, Anthony!" Nick said.

"Get the fuck off me," Brodie hollered, drawing attention from the other patrons.

"I mean it. You try anything with my girl and I'll—"

"Whoa, cowboy," a familiar voice said, grabbing Anthony's arm. "Let the Neanderthal go before you catch a case."

Anthony looked down into Pike's amused blue eyes and was so thrown by his jovial tone, he dropped Brodie's shirt. The minute he was free, Brodie shoved Anthony, who stumbled into Nick.

"Next time you come at me, Russo, we're going to finish this outside."

"Brodie, Brodie," Pike tsked. "You don't want to bite off more than you can chew."

"What the fuck are you talking about, Pike?"

"I can't have you putting hands on my boy or his girl. You understand? Delilah Gill is off-limits to you and anyone else in this town."

"I think that's up to her, don't you?"

"You can think that, but then again, I still have a certain photo you probably wouldn't want going viral on social media."

Brodie's face paled and Pike slapped his shoulder. "Glad we understand each other."

Pike turned to face Nick and Anthony, cocking his head to the side. "I thought we were going to get a drink?"

"We are," Nick said.

"Great, let's vamoose." Pike pointed at Anthony. "You're buying every round."

Pike walked out the door, with Nick and Anthony trailing behind, Anthony still blown away by the change in Pike from Sunday morning to now.

"What is going on?" Anthony asked. "I thought you were pissed at me."

Pike stopped next to Anthony's truck and shrugged. "I took some time to sit with the situation and reflect."

Nick cleared his throat.

"And listened to the advice someone close to the situation. Here is what I realized. You said that even though you wanted her, you took a step back when you thought that she and I were feeling each other. That's what makes you an amazing friend. Just because I had you up on this pedestal, thinking you were this paragon of virtue, doesn't mean you can't ever fuck up. She wasn't my girlfriend—hell, she'd been pretty clear that she wasn't interested in me at all. I pulled out some moves, too."

Anthony held up a hand. "I don't want to hear about it, thanks."

Pike chuckled. "Fair enough. Besides, it's obvious you love the girl. I can't stay mad at you when you're in love for the first time and already fucking up. You need me."

"I don't—" Anthony paused, considering. "How do you know?"

"That you need my help?"

"No, that I—"

"Can't get it out yet? It's always hardest the first time. As to how I know, you were about to tear Brodie apart for just talking about her. You've either lost your mind or you're in love." Pike opened the passenger side door and waved a hand. "Now, get in the truck. Considering how pissed off Delilah looked when I passed by her on my way to the gym, this will require several mixed drinks and careful planning if you're going to win her back."

"You saw her?"

"Oh, yes. That is one angry woman."

"Speaking of, why were you at the gym?"

"Nick texted that something was about to go down and I'd want to see it, so I raced over here from the store to check it out. Watching you lose your cool? Priceless."

"You're both a couple of meddlesome fuckers."

"I think the word you're looking for is friends." Pike pulled himself up and pounded the top of his truck. "Now move! Times a wastin'!"

Chapter Twenty-one

"Y ou should send her flowers. Classic show of remorse."

The men at the table booed Clark's suggestion and Anthony sunk back against the chair. They'd been at this for hours, drinking copious amounts of alcohol and batting ideas back and forth about the best way to apologize.

"You can boo me all you want," Clark said, popping his collar with a smirk, "but I am a happily married man and you are the ones stumped at how to please a woman."

"Whoa now, choose your words wisely, little brother," Sam Griffin said, holding up his tumbler in a salute, the tattoo sleeves on his arms colorful and intricate. "I am the master at woman pleasing."

"And yet, you're still single," Pike said.

"By choice, leprechaun."

Pike spluttered. "That's just rude."

Anthony chuckled, the tension of the last few days eased by the jovial heckling of the men around him. He'd been surprised by Sam's presence, as he usually worked too late to join them, and Anthony forgot how much he liked the elder Griffin.

Declan tipped back a pink shot and wheezed, "I decorated Holly's house."

"I made Noel a mixed CD," Nick said, flipping a quarter into a shot glass.

"That's so nineties," Pike joked.

"Maybe," Nick said, pointing a thumb at his chest. "But it worked."

"What does Delilah like?" Clark asked.

"Her corgi, Leia," Anthony blurted.

Pike grinned. "We could kidnap it and make her think it's lost."

Sam chucked a balled-up napkin at Pike. "You are a sick man."

Anthony shook his head, the world spinning a bit. "I'm not doing that."

"Fine, no dognapping." Pike threw the paper ball at Anthony. "What else do you got?"

"What about a favorite song?" Nick chimed in.

"Oh! Her name. That song that has her name . . . " It took Anthony a moment to remember it through the cloud of alcohol and then he belted out, "Hey there Delilah—"

"That's better than a boom box!" Pike exclaimed, shooting to his feet with his glass held high. "We shall march to her house and romance her with the power of song."

"How do you ever get laid, Fish?" Noel asked, leaning over to give her husband a kiss.

"Hey, what are you doing here?" Nick asked.

"Picking up Ricki up for book club." She stood up straight, pulling her phone from her pocket to glance at the screen. "She gets done with her bartending shift at six."

"Since when are you in a book club?" Anthony asked.

"As of today." Noel placed her hand on the back of Nick's chair and grinned wickedly. "I figured with you boys out plotting and scheming, I'd join the girls and see what kind of trouble we can get into."

Pike scoffed. "Trouble at a book club? Book clubs are for sipping wine and gossiping."

"How do you know?" Sam asked.

"My mom used to host one every Tuesday. I snuck out of my room and listened in once. I was traumatized."

"Sounds like fun," Noel said, giving Ricki a hug when she joined her. "See you later, boys. Behave."

"Never," Pike crowed, and the other men echoed him, except Anthony who stared at the screen of his phone. He'd changed his background to a picture of Delilah with her head on his shoulder, laughing at something he'd said.

"Ah hell," Pike said.

"What?"

"Trip, Brodie, and the goon squad just walked through the door."

Anthony looked up and saw Brodie making a beeline toward him. "Russo, I heard you and Pike are in charge of the winter games?"

"Yeah? What about it?"

"I just wanted to tell you that I'm going to enjoy kicking your ass."

"Ha," Pike said, pointing at the group of men. "You couldn't kick a can if it was right in front of you."

"You want to wager on that?" Trip asked.

If Anthony wasn't hammered, he would have recognized the alarm bells going off in his head, but instead, he said, "Absolutely."

"If we win, you're going to buy each of us a snow mobile."

"And if we win, we want your boat."

"Deal."

The other men walked away, laughing.

"That was a little too cocky," Nick said.

"I'm not worried about those clowns." Pike stood up, grabbing Anthony by his arm. "It is time!"

"How did you talk me into hosting a book club?"

Delilah was putting out the plastic cups Holly had brought onto her dining room table, the sound of excited feminine chatter surrounding her. Holly had proposed the idea of starting a monthly book club for their friend group as they'd gotten busier with their lives, but it had spread beyond the original six women. There were several women that Delilah didn't recognize who had come as guests.

"Because you love me and know my place is a mess to get to during the holidays."

She agreed with Holly. Cars lined up and down the block to see the Christmas displays in Evergreen Circle during the holiday season and there was no way of getting into the place unless people parked down the road and trekked in. Unfortunately, it had started snowing earlier and hadn't let up yet, which would have made that situation even worse.

Holly wrapped an arm around Delilah's shoulder and squeezed. "It will be fun. I promise."

Delilah hoped so because she could use a little fun. After her interlude with Anthony in the alley, she'd wanted to come home and cry. Delilah had heard of chubby chasers, men who were attracted to plus-size women and didn't want to go public, but she'd never imagined Anthony would be one of them. She hadn't realized the thought had been at the back of her mind until she'd said it out loud, but once it was out there, she couldn't take it back.

How can you think that? He told Pike he'd liked you for a year.

Only that confession had come after he'd been caught with her. No one had known about the two of them and the first thing he does today is pull her out of sight?

You didn't tell Holly about the two of you. Maybe you're doing what you accused him of. Making excuses to run.

"That makes no sense," she grumbled.

"What do you mean?" Holly asked with a frown.

Delilah hadn't meant to say anything and laughed. "Nothing! I'm just talking to myself."

"Want to go mingle before we get started?"

What she wanted to tell her best friend was no. She didn't have the desire to do anything but hide in her room with Leia, but instead, she nodded. "Let me get a drink first and I'll join you."

"Okay, pumpkin."

Delilah watched Holly as she approached Officer Wren, Noel, Ricki, and another woman she didn't recognize.

"You're Delilah, right?"

Delilah jumped, spilling a little wine onto the tablecloth as the woman approached her out of nowhere. "Shit."

"Sorry, didn't mean to sneak up on you. I'm Ryler Colby. I'm the personal assistant to Alia Cole." The woman extended her hand and Delilah took it.

"Nice to meet you." Delilah had no idea who Alia Cole was but Ryler was adorable, with a genuinely friendly smile and a smattering of freckles across her nose and cheeks. Her dark brown eyes were lined with thick lashes that Delilah would have killed for and her sandy brown hair hung to her shoulders in loose waves. She was midsize and her green cropped sweater and high-waisted jeans were casual but chic.

"Your outfit is so cute," Delilah said.

"Thank you. I'm a huge thrifter, so these jeans I snagged for six bucks and the sweater was five. Still had tags on it."

"That's awesome. Unfortunately, most clothes I find thrifting look like something my grandma would wear."

"Not where I shop. You ever want to take a road trip, I'll show you some hidden gems with fantastic finds. Can I get a glass of that?"

Delilah poured her a cup and passed it to her. "So, I apologize, but who is Alia Cole?"

"Ah, Instagram travel blogger Alia Cole? She's the gorgeous blonde over there. She's my cousin and boss."

"Is that weird?"

"Sometimes." Ryler leaned over, lowering her voice. "Full disclosure?"

"Um, sure."

"I was in the car with Pike on Sunday. When he saw you with . . . what's his name? Anthony?"

"Oh, yeah. That was—"

"None of my business. We were on our way to meet Alia when he saw you."

"I didn't get out of the car until you were gone. How did you know it was me?"

"I heard your name and put two and two together. He was on a pretty good tirade on Sunday."

Delilah's face burned. She could only imagine what he'd said about her to this stranger. "Just to be clear, I'm not in the habit of causing issues between friends. I try to avoid drama."

"Are you kidding? You were not the issue. He had nothing negative to say about you at all. Anthony, on the other hand, was getting a lot of heat, but I think they made up."

"Well, I hope they make up soon. They've been friends a long time." Delilah studied Ryler with a smile. "Sounds like you've been spending a lot of time with Pike."

"Yeah, he's taking me around Mistletoe so I can do research . . . for Alia, I mean."

"And how do you like Mistletoe so far?"

"It's beautiful. I've heard all about your holiday festivities and I'm excited to hang around and join in."

"Where are you from?" Delilah asked.

"Boise originally, but I think I'll be traveling quite a bit after this."

"Well, if there's one thing Mistletoe goes all out for, it's Christmas."

"Not a fan?" Ryler asked before taking a sip of her wine.

"It's not about being a fan. I'm just not as diehard as my best friend."

"Which is an amazing Christmas movie, by the way."

Delilah laughed. "Don't say that too loud or you'll start a rumble. That is a hot-button topic."

"Gotcha. I love your shirt, by the way."

Delilah glanced down at the electric blue off-the-shoulder sheath she'd pulled from the back of her closet, a new purchase she'd snagged over the weekend. It made her feel fancy and feminine, and she'd bought it to wear out with Anthony.

So much for that.

"Thank you. It made me feel pretty." She shared a small smile with Ryler.

"You're gorgeous."

"I appreciate that. You're not trying to butter me up and sell me something, are you?"

Ryler laughed. "No, I just call it like I see it. And I'm trying this new thing where I don't hold back. Everything I think, I'm saying it."

"That could be dangerous."

"Maybe, but I've spent a lot of time keeping everything close to the breast, afraid of offending someone or embarrassing others. I've finally decided I don't give a shit. If someone doesn't like me, warts and all, I'm fine on my own," Ryler said, shrugging.

"Damn, girl. I need that energy in my life." Delilah grinned, waving her cup around the room. "I got persuaded to play hostess at the last minute when I really wanted to escape into my room."

"Hey, if you want to do that, I'll totally cover for you." Ryler wrinkled her brow. "Oh, you're looking for Delilah? I think she's in the kitchen. Not there? Oh, you know what, I think she had to pee."

"You're good."

"That's why Alia keeps me around. I'm the best."

A steady rise of male voices registered and Delilah looked around the room. "Do you hear that?"

"What am I hearing?"

"It sounds like singing."

Ryler frowned, standing perfectly still.

Suddenly, there was a pounding at the door.

"Delilah!"

She covered her mouth with her hand at Anthony's bellow. The entire house of women quieted, gathering in the dining room doorway to watch.

"I think that's for you," Ryler said.

Delilah crossed the room to answer the door. Holly joined her, whispering, "What's going on?"

"I don't know." Delilah opened the door and stared at the group of men standing in her yard. Anthony was front and center, looking sheepish.

"What are you doing here?" she hissed at them.

"We have come courtin'," Pike said.

"No, we're not," Sam said.

Delilah grabbed her coat from the hook and stepped onto the porch, wrapping her arms around herself as the cold hit her. "Again, why are you all gathered on my lawn?"

"I'm getting to that," Anthony said, clearing his throat. "Nick?"

Nick held his phone up, and the first notes of "Hey There Delilah" sounded and suddenly, Anthony was singing at the top of his lungs, the men behind him humming along with him.

"Oh, it's what you do to me!" Anthony belted. He wasn't bad, but he was slightly offbeat, and obviously a little drunk.

"Oh my God," Holly said behind her. Delilah realized all the women were filing out onto the porch or watching from the window as he serenaded her.

He threw his hands out to his side as he sang, "And you're to blame!"

Delilah fought a smile as the men chorused, "Oooooooh," but her gaze remained on the disheveled man who hadn't looked away from her once. Her neighbors had all stepped out into their yards to watch, some of them laughing. Others shaking their heads.

The song ended and Delilah didn't move as Anthony took a few steps toward her, grinning.

"Aren't carolers supposed to sing Christmas songs?" she asked.

"Not when they're trying to win back their girl."

Delilah's stomach flipped and an eruption of feminine "aws" echoed on the porch.

Anthony blinked, as if realizing for the first time that they had a rather large audience.

"I didn't know you were having a party."

"It's book club."

He climbed up on the first step, swaying. "What book are you reading?" he asked, smiling at her.

"Stay focused, man! I am freezing my balls off!" Declan said.

"Right, sorry." He cleared his throat. "Delilah Gill. I like you and want to take you out on a date. 'Cause I like you."

"You already said that," she whispered.

Even on the step below, he still towered over her and leaned in. "I thought it bore repeating. I like the hell out of you, and I will shout it to the world any time you doubt me."

"Would you kiss him already?" Holly hissed.

"I swear, if you don't, I will!" another woman called from inside the house.

"Will you date me, Delilah?"

Delilah laughed. "You are very drunk."

"That is a statement of fact but not what I'm looking for."

"And you'll get an answer when you're sober."

"Booo," the men on her front yard hollered.

"Sloshed or not, that was pretty epic," Ryler said, leaning against the railing. "Although the redhead was pitchy."

Pike glowered at her. "Witch, I have the voice of an angel."

"A fallen angel."

Suddenly, Pike bent over and gathered up a handful of snow, letting it fly. It missed Ryler and hit Holly on the side of her face. Delilah's mouth dropped open as Holly dived off the porch.

"You're a dead man, Pike!"

"I wasn't aiming at you!" he protested, hiding behind one man after another. "Declan, control your woman!"

"I don't know, man. I kinda wanna see what she does when she gets you."

Wives and girlfriends passed Delilah to join in the fray, while the bystanders whooped and cheered. Snow exploded against the side of her house and the window and women dived back inside, slamming the door closed.

"We're going to get the cops called on us if we don't simmer down," Wren said, making a motion to quiet down with her hands.

"Officer Wren, is that you?" Sam called. "I didn't think you knew what fun was."

"Smug son of a bitch," she muttered, hopping off the porch. Her blond hair was up in a high ponytail that swung as she bent over to get a handful of snow. "You've been asking for this for weeks."

"Well come on, hot stuff! Catch me if you can!"

"Delilah?" Anthony said, the deep rumble drawing her attention away from the chaos around them.

"Yeah?"

"Pike and I aren't fighting anymore."

"I can see that. And I'm glad."

"You said when I fixed it with Pike to tell you. That you were mine but you weren't going to wait forever. I may be inebriated, but I remember everything. I know what I'm saying." Anthony stepped up next to her and cradled her face in his hands. "But if you want to hear it when I sober up tomorrow, I'll tell you then. And the next day. And the day after that."

"I get the picture," she laughed softly.

Suddenly Anthony turned sheet white and before she could fully get out of the way, he bent over and puked on her front porch. Vomit splashed onto her shoes and pants.

"Seriously, again?!" she said.

"I think I'm feeling better now," Anthony said.

Chapter Twenty-two

Anthony blinked a couple times against the harsh sunlight pouring in through the window and realized that he wasn't in his own bed. His mouth tasted rancid and he grimaced at the nausea twisting his gut into knots.

He lifted his head and a flash of pain ripped through his skull, reminding him of the three mixed drinks Pike ordered for him that had been sweet and tasty on the way down. He normally stuck to beer or whiskey, but he'd let his guilt guide him, swallowing everything Pike put in front of him.

They were more than even for everything. He might not survive this.

He rolled over and opened his eyes again, staring at a watercolor painting of a corgi dog running through a field.

Delilah.

He was in Delilah's house. They'd walked there from Brews and Chews, freezing their asses off. He'd sung to her and then . . .

"Oh, no," he groaned.

Anthony rolled off the bed, shirtless and barefoot, and slunk away. He heard her voice down the hall and followed it, watching her from the doorway. She sat on the couch with her phone in front of her, hair tucked behind her ear to reveal a white ear bud. Leia hopped off the couch to greet him, hopping around his legs. He bent over to pet the dog, but the motion made his head ache.

"Yes, I understand. So, you don't like the character or the way they speak?"

Anthony backed out of the room to find a bathroom, Leia trotting along next to him, until he crossed into the small room and shut the door. He relieved himself and after he washed his hands, he opened the top drawer searching for toothpaste. Even if he put some on his finger and scrubbed it over his teeth, it would be better than the funk he had going on in there now.

When he exited the bathroom, Leia was sitting outside waiting for him.

"You're a stalker, you know that?"

She wiggled and bounced and took off down the hallway.

Anthony went back into the room he'd woken up in, searching for his phone. It was sitting on the side table plugged in and he disconnected it. When he opened it up, the first thing he noticed was the time. He still had a couple hours before he had to open the store, so at least he could go home and get cleaned up.

Then he saw was the dozens of texts on his phone.

There was a group text with the guys and as he scrolled through them, he realized his fuzzy memory wasn't just a nightmare.

Congratulations go out to Anthony! I think that was the first time any man in history puked on his girl while executing a romantic gesture.

There was a slow clap GIF below it from Sam, and Declan had texted Leonardo DiCaprio raising a glass of champagne.

I hate you all. Anthony texted.

His phone chimed several times and he read the replies with only mild irritation.

Hey, he's alive!

At least she let you stay after that. Noel would have kicked my ass off that porch.

The sound of panting got his attention and Anthony saw Leia in the doorway, a rubber pacifier in her mouth.

Anthony tossed his phone onto the bed and climbed to his feet. "You wanna play, huh?" He ignored the pain in his head as he took the toy and tossed it down the hall. She tore after it, her short legs pumping rapidly. She grabbed the toy, squeaking it between her teeth as she disappeared into the living room to find Delilah. When Anthony padded back out to the living room, Delilah was sitting in the same spot but her ear bud was gone and Leia was settled across her lap.

"Good morning."

Delilah turned away from the window and smiled. "Well, hello, sunshine. How are we feeling this morning?"

"Shhh, not so loud," he said, lifting her feet to sit on the couch next to her and placing them on his lap. "Please tell me that I did not puke last night?"

"Oh, you did. Several times."

"On you?"

"Just the once and most of it ended up on your shirt. After that, you were pretty good about making it to the toilet."

"I am so sorry," he said, scrubbing his face with his hands. "Not exactly a perfect rom-com moment."

"I don't know. It was pretty good up until that point. I think I just have that effect on drunk men. Best to avoid them and places they frequent."

"I normally stick to beer, but Pike kept bringing me drinks and I didn't want to tell him no more."

"Ah, well, I guess he got his revenge, huh?"

"And then some." Anthony leaned his head back against the couch, staring at her. "You look upset."

"I had a call with an editor this morning. She read my manuscript and wasn't a fan of the story but allegedly liked my writing."

"It didn't go well?"

"I guess I got mixed signals. She told my agent she loved my voice but then proceeded to tell me everything wrong with it. She gave me a couple of authors and books to read to improve my writing and I don't know . . . " Delilah looked away. "Maybe this isn't going to happen for me."

"Hey," he said, lifting her feet so he could scoot closer, and Leia jumped down out of the way as he wrapped her in his arms. "It was one person."

"But she was the only one who spoke to me. The others rejected me outright," Delilah told him, sounding like she was about to cry.

"So?" he said, rubbing a hand along her back. "That's a handful of people. It's not the entire publishing industry."

"Holly told me I should just self-pub it."

"Why don't you?" he asked.

"I've looked into it, but it's expensive. Thousands of dollars in editing, plus paying an artist for cover art. There's formatting, unless I buy the software myself. And there's no guarantee I'll make my money back."

"What if you do, though?"

She looked up at him, blue eyes shimmering with unshed tears. "You don't think that a bunch of editors from major publishers have their thumb on what's good?"

"I think what's mainstream isn't always what stands out. Look at how many indie films hit it big because they found their audience." He ran a thumb over her cheek, wiping away her tears. "If this is your dream, Delilah, go for it. It's better than never trying."

"I just don't know how much longer I can survive on my income here. That job in Colorado is a lot of money."

Anthony nodded. "I get that. My road crew job was good money, too. I wouldn't have been able to achieve my goals without it. So, if you have to take it, I get it. I just don't want you to settle and accept this job because you think there isn't anything better out there for you. You're better than that." He kissed the top of her head. "You're extraordinary, Delilah Gill."

"You're just saying that so I'll go out with you," she teased.

"On that note, you left me hanging last night," he said, cupping her chin and tilting her face up. "Are you going to put me out of my misery and say yes?"

"Depends on where you're taking me."

"I was thinking we could go get Lord of the Fries before I have to open up the store to start. Are you hungry?"

"Starved." Her hand covered his, peeling it away from her face. "I do think we should take things slow, though. We kind of rushed into this before. At least until things settle down and get sorted."

Anthony knew she was talking about whether or not she took that job and nodded. "I can do slow."

Delilah smirked, her brow cocking skeptically. "Really?"

Anthony chuckled. "Yeah," He got up from the couch, holding his hands out to her. "I think I better take a shower first. I smell like a bar."

"Your shirt is in the dryer. I'll grab it," she told him, as she got up from the couch. She headed toward the laundry room. "Towels are in the hallway closet. Everything you need should be in there," she yelled out.

It was on the tip of his tongue to ask her to join him, but he didn't want to make the same mistakes he had before. Dating meant taking the girl out, planning activities. As much as he enjoyed being intimate with Delilah and missed it, he could wait.

"Thanks, I'll see you in a bit."

Anthony felt a bit skeevy putting on the same underwear he'd worn yesterday, but there was nothing he could do until he ran home. He shot Pike a text, asking him if he could open the store and hold down the fort so he could go home and change. Pike sent him a thumbs-up and a GIF of Shaq puckering up and kissing the air.

He would have stayed under the burning stream forever if he wasn't keenly aware of Delilah waiting on him. He came out of the bathroom drying his wet hair with a towel to find her standing in the hallway, holding his shirt at the end of her finger.

"Thanks," he said, kissing her cheek.

"You're welcome. While I don't mind washing your clothes, I'd prefer it happens under different circumstances."

"Me, too," he chuckled. He pulled his shirt over his head. "Now, socks, boots, and phone and we'll be off."

"I'll go out and warm up the car. I'm assuming your truck is at Brews?"

"Yeah. I wasn't planning on drinking."

"We can grab it after breakfast." She looked at the screen of her phone. "Do we need to hurry?"

"Pike is covering the store. One of the perks of owning a business. You're the boss, so you can't get fired."

"Still, we probably shouldn't make a habit of being late. I don't want to cause any more problems between you and Pike."

Anthony snaked an arm around her waist and brought her against him. "You know it was me, not you, right? Everything is good now."

"Okay, I believe you. Let me go get the car warmed up."

Anthony let her go reluctantly and tracked down his shoes and socks in the spare bedroom. He had a missed call from Bradley and checked for a voicemail. He pressed the button and hit speakerphone.

"Hey, little bro, call me back when you get this. I've got big news."

Anthony's mind raced and he itched to return the call but Delilah was waiting on him. He left the spare room and spotted her putting Leia in her crate. "Why do you lock her up if she has a doggie door?"

"She likes to dig if I leave her out. Can't have her escaping when I'm in school with my phone off."

"Ah, that makes sense."

"Were you on the phone?" she asked.

"Yeah, my brother Bradley called and left a message to call him back. He said he has big news."

"So call him!"

"I can do it later."

"Don't be ridiculous. I'm driving anyway, passenger princess. Call your brother."

"Thanks." He followed her out the door, then took her hand in his, and followed her around to the driver's side to open her door.

"You don't have to do all that."

"This is still a date, even if I make a phone call."

"Whatever you say."

They climbed inside and Anthony pressed the call button, listening to it ring. It was almost eight thirty, but he wasn't sure if his brother was already at work.

"Hello?"

"Hey, it's Anthony."

"Hey, bro! Guess who's coming back to town?"

"You mean to visit?"

"Nope. We're putting our house on the market and going to head down there for Christmas to start looking at houses."

"Are you serious? That's amazing, man!"

"We're going to rent an Airbnb while we're there, so you can come spend Christmas with us. I know you're still living in that tin can in the woods."

"Hey, that tin can has been my saving grace. Show her respect."

"I'll try, but hey, I'm at work and I gotta get loose ends tied up before I leave, so we'll talk later. Audrey and the kids are excited."

"Give 'em a hug for me and tell them I can't wait."

"Bye."

Anthony ended the call and let out a whoop.

"Whoa, I guess it was a good call?" she laughed, coming to a stop at the four-way.

Anthony leaned across the seat and cupped the back of her head, bringing her in for a smacking kiss. "My brother Bradley and his family are moving back to Mistletoe."

"I'm so happy for you."

"Me, too. We talked about it a bit when we ducked out of Thanksgiving, but I never thought he'd pull the trigger."

"Looks like you were wrong." Delilah made a left onto the main road and followed the fork in the road to the right, claiming a parking spot in front of Lord of the Fries. "Look at that."

"Things are really looking up for both of us, I think." He grabbed her hand and squeezed it. "Let's eat."

They got out of the car and went into Lord of the Fries, a popular café in town. Pages of the classic book were placed under glass to form tables, along with other forms of book-related art and memorabilia on the walls. The owner, Harold Flanagan, said it was one of his favorite books growing up and he identified with the way the children had turned on one another during the course of the novel's events.

The waitress brought over menus, and Delilah opened hers while Anthony left his at the end of the table. He turned his attention away for a minute to speak to the waitress and caught Delilah's pained expression. He followed her gaze to a woman across the room who was watching them with a smile. The blonde got up and left her group of friends behind.

"Hi there, I am Aimee," the blonde said, holding out her hand to Delilah. Then she transferred her attention to Anthony and gave him a dazzling smile. "It's a pleasure."

"I am Anthony and this is Delilah," he said.

Delilah made a face. "Yeah, we went to middle school together," Delilah mumbled and Anthony realized that the two of them had history.

"Ah, Delilah. I remember you," she said looking her up and down briefly before turning to Anthony, "You are someone I'm unfamiliar with her."

"Well, I've lived here my whole life," he said, already annoyed with her.

"I just got back. I left in high school and went away to college on the East Coast." Aimee pointed between Anthony and Delilah, "I'm just here visiting my parents during the holidays. "If you ever want to give me a private tour of the changes around here, I could give you my number."

"I hope that you enjoy your stay," Anthony said, reaching across for Delilah's hand. "But we're a little busy right now."

Aimee's eyes widened. "Are you two together?"

"You didn't catch that from the hand holding?" Anthony's sarcasm came through like molasses, thick and unmistakable.

Aimee's lips tightened and she nodded at Delilah. "You are a very lucky girl."

"I know." Delilah gave the woman a pleasant smile.

"See ya," Anthony said, giving her a little wave with his free hand.

Aimee walked away and Delilah pulled her hand away and went back to her menu, making a clicking noise with her tongue. "Well, I think it's safe to say that she likes you."

Anthony snorted, aware that her mild tone was anything but. If a man had come in and flirted like that with her, Anthony would have been livid.

"She's just a flirt," he said, leaning forward on the table so she would look up at him from the menu. When she finally did, he added, "And not anyone I would be interested in even if I wasn't with you."

"Really?" she drawled, closing her menu and setting it aside. "Tall, leggy blondes aren't your thing?"

Anthony shook his head. "I'm not interested in any woman who's going to take five hours to get ready and pick matching outfits for us just to go on a hike."

"Why do you assume she's like that?" Delilah asked.

"Did you see her nails?" Anthony said, making a clawing motion. "Those things look expensive and deadly. I don't want her anywhere near me."

"I wonder why she approached us like that?" Delilah asked.

"Who knows?" Anthony picked up both menus and stacked them on the end of the table, shooting her a saucy smirk. "I don't really care, and I'm not interested in talking about her."

Delilah picked up her napkin and started fraying the edges. "I guess I should be flattered that you are ignoring a girl like that for me."

"Hey," Anthony said, getting up and sitting next to her in the booth. "She doesn't even compare to you." Anthony cupped her face and gave her a soft, sweet peck. "She's Chardonnay. You're a bottle of ninety proof."

"I make you sick and give you a headache?" she joked softly.

"No," he said, kissing her a little harder this time, "you taste better than anything else on the shelf."

"I feel like that's a weird compliment," Delilah said breathlessly, a smile teasing over her lips, "but I'm going to accept it because it's you."

The waitress appeared at the table, giving them a brief, knowing look before tapping her pen onto her pad. "Are you ready to order?"

"Yeah, I want a breakfast sandwich, hash browns, and black coffee," Anthony said, sliding his arm around the back of the booth.

The waitress scribbled it down and asked, "How about you, Delilah?"

"I would like a short stack, fresh fruit, and a coffee with room for cream." Delilah picked up the menus and handed them to her. "Thanks, Pam."

"You got it!"

Once the waitress disappeared, Anthony leaned into her, running his finger over her cheek "Are you going to cancel your snowboarding lesson with Brodie?" Anthony asked.

"I had forgotten about it, actually, but I probably should." Delilah scooted closer with a flirtatious smile. "I wouldn't want him to get the wrong impression. Does your offer for snowboarding lessons still stand?"

Anthony stroked his chin, eyes narrowed playfully. "That depends on if you're going to use the skills I teach you for good or evil."

"How would I use them for evil?" she laughed.

"By using them to write another article and move to Colorado far away from me."

"First of all, not everything is about you," she said, nudging him. "And second of all, you were right and so is Holly. I don't really want to take a job that has nothing to do with what I like to write, but I do want to at least try snowboarding and maybe submit another freelance article, because it does pay well."

Anthony dipped his head to kiss her. "Then I'm happy to teach you the power of snowboarding."

"You're such a dork," she said, accepting his kiss with a sweet little sigh that he could listen to for the rest of his life.

Oh damn, where did that come from?

Chapter Twenty-three

Delilah stood off to the side with her clipboard, taking notes as Holly and Merry addressed the room full of bachelors, who were acting like middle schoolers instead of grown men. Several were shoving each other, half of them had their phones out, listening to Merry's instructions with half an ear, and Delilah was pretty sure Paulie the bouncer was nodding off in the back row. It was almost seven thirty at night and Friday to boot; Delilah understood they were probably anxious to head out and tie one on or sleep off the work week like her.

Delilah had grabbed another latte on her way there to wake up, but she was ready to go home and crawl into bed. It had been a long day researching what and who she needed to self-pub her books and the information out there was overwhelming. There were hundreds of freelance editors, all with great references on their websites, but some of the price quotes were daunting. She didn't have thousands of dollars in disposable income. Add in the cost of website hosts, formatting software, and cover artists and she had no idea how to justify the cost if she couldn't at least break even.

If Delilah could cut costs on some of the other items, she might be able to pay for a copy editor at least. She needed to talk to Holly about marketing strategies, but she might have to corner her tomorrow. Tonight, she looked ready to knock a couple heads together and Delilah didn't want to aggravate her more by making her think. Holly had owned her shop for more than five years and had helped Merry launch her online craft business two years ago. She was a social media genius.

Delilah would bring it up while they set up for the Festival of Trees in the morning. It was an all-day event that didn't end until seven in the evening, and then it would take several hours to get the place cleaned up and the trees loaded up with each buyer. Plenty of time to pick her brain.

The sensation of someone watching her tickled the back of her neck and Delilah looked up, catching Anthony's gaze. He sat a few rows back on the end next to Pike and Sam, and that little smile playing across those full lips made her heart race with anticipation. Since their breakfast Wednesday morning, they'd struggled to find time to be alone. Wednesday, she'd been with Holly, helping her organize everything for tonight's orientation and Thursday, he'd been with Pike and Merry, going over the final details for the winter games. She'd hoped they'd get out of here early enough to go out for dinner, but at the rate it was going, they might have to snag a bag of tacos and head back to her place.

Although that came with its own form of issues. If they were sleeping together, it wouldn't be a problem for him to spend the night, but they were taking things slow. They both needed that at this point, but when they were together, Delilah forgot that in the overwhelming urge to kiss him senseless and rip his clothes off.

Delilah caught his eye again and the smoldering look on his face made her face burn. God, had he guessed what she was thinking about?

She turned her attention back to Merry, who was trying to bring the rowdy group under control.

"Guys, can we hurry up and get through this so we can go home?" Merry asked, her tone exasperated.

Holly wasn't so subtle. Putting her fingers into her mouth, she released a high-pitched whistle and the room quieted.

"Listen up!" Holly shouted.

Merry nodded toward her sister, addressing the crowd with a strained smile. "Thank you. Next week after the Parade of Lights, you'll come straight here and get ready backstage. Please dress appropriately in a coat and tie. We'll call your name alphabetically and when you cross the stage, smile, dance, show off, whatever you want to do." Merry pointed to the elevated stage behind her before continuing, "You'll see on stage we have a backdrop and a camera set up because we want to get everyone's picture for the program including a brief bio. Delilah, Holly, and I are going to call your names and gather that information while you're waiting for your picture. Once you are finished with your picture and bio, you're welcome to leave and enjoy the rest of your evening. I want to thank you again for being here. Your participation is going to make a world of difference for our school extracurriculars this year." The room erupted in applause and Merry's smile became a genuine one. "Let's get started. Trip!"

"Pike!" Holly hollered.

"Brodie," Delilah called, watching as he stood up from the back row and headed her way. She was glad he'd ended up on her list so she wouldn't have to track him down to cancel her snowboarding lesson. While she'd been sincere previously about not wanting to ask Anthony, it didn't make sense now. The lesson gave them the excuse to spend time together, which was something she'd been dreaming about for days.

Brodie ambled over and flashed a wide smile. "Hi, there."

"Hey." She tapped her pen against her clipboard nervously, rattling off, "I need full name, age, occupation, height, hobbies, and your idea of the perfect date."

"Easy enough," he said, shoving his hands into the pockets of his workman's jacket. "Brodie Williams. Thirty. Roofer. Six foot. I like camping, fishing, hunting, snowboarding. My idea of the perfect date is one where we are enjoying each other's company."

"Great," she said, finishing the last of his bio before she gave him an apologetic smile. "Speaking of snowboarding, I know we were supposed to go on Sunday, but I actually need to cancel."

Brodie's face fell. "Oh, man, really?"

"Yeah."

"Damn," he said, suddenly flashing a grin that bordered on smarmy. "I was looking forward to teaching you a thing or two."

How had she ever found his attention flattering? The way he leered at her now made her skin crawl. "I appreciate that but I started seeing someone exclusively and he really wants to teach me." Delilah's gaze flicked to Anthony, who was standing with a few other men, his attention fixated on Brodie and her.

Brodie turned around to see who she was looking at and let out a snort before facing her again. "Would that be Anthony Russo?"

Why did he have to say it so snidely? "Yeah, it is."

"Oh, man, yeah." He nodded, seeming to lose the attitude. He frowned, his expression clearly crestfallen, but Delilah had a sneaking suspicion it was all an act. For whatever reason, Anthony and Brodie did not like each other and Delilah couldn't believe it had taken her this long to see it.

"So, you get why I need to cancel."

"I understand. I'd never want to make things uncomfortable for you."

"Thank you for understanding."

"One thing, though." Brodie took her arm gently and led her farther away from the group.

Delilah looked back over her shoulder and saw Anthony watching them and she smiled at him, before whispering to Brodie, "What are you doing?"

"I just wanted to talk to you without anyone overhearing," he said, stopping in the corner of the room and releasing her. "I don't mean to overstep, but are you sure that he's the guy for you? I heard he's kind of a player. Never stays with the same girl for long. In fact, I thought I saw him out with Pike and two girls that looked like a double date recently." He put his hands up in the air, his expression earnest. "I just don't want to see you get hurt."

A painful doubt settled in her stomach, but Delilah waved it off, along with his words. "I appreciate the concern, but I'm walking into this with my eyes open. We are still getting to know each other and I'm not worried about a potential date."

Brodie held his hands up. "Sorry, I shouldn't have said anything."

"It's fine," Delilah lied, irritated with Brodie for dampening her mood. Although she tried to see the best in people, she knew this little show of his was about driving a wedge between her and Anthony. If only she'd realized how petty he was before she ever gave him a chance. "I need to get back and finish these interviews."

"Delilah, one last thing—" He looked up and Delilah realized somehow they'd ended up under one of the sprigs of mistletoe they'd been dispersing through the building for the event. "You don't mess with tradition, right?"

Delilah had the sneaking suspicion that Brodie had set her up but couldn't prove it. "Oh, no, we wouldn't want that."

He'd either been oblivious to or ignored her sarcasm because he dropped his head and went for it. Delilah turned her cheek and stood still to let him kiss her there but, in a blur, someone wrapped an arm around her waist and lifted her off her feet, spinning her away from Brodie's seeking lips.

Delilah's squeal of surprise turned into peals of laughter when she realized it was Anthony holding her off the ground. "Anthony! How did you get over here so fast?"

Anthony dropped her to her feet, keeping an arm around her waist and his body between her and Brodie. "Didn't you know? I'm Superman."

"No, I guess I missed that."

"I freaking hate mistletoe," Anthony said, gruffly. "Too many people using it as an excuse to kiss you."

Delilah bit back a laugh when she noticed Brodie's glare and was afraid if she looked toward the crowd that they'd all be staring their way. She squirmed against Anthony, her back wriggling against his front. "Can you put me down now?"

"Not quite. Did you get everything you needed from Brodie?"

"Yes."

"You heard her, pal. Walk away."

Delilah couldn't see the other man's expression anymore but heard his stream of curses.

Delilah giggled. "You're ridiculous."

"Hey now," he said, pressing his mouth against her ear. "How would you feel if a girl backed me under some mistletoe and tried to kiss me?"

The rush of his warm breath against her skin sent a shiver down her spine. "Point taken."

"See," Anthony said, dropping her to her feet and spinning her around. "What's good for the gander is good for the goose."

"What does that mean?"

"It means"—Anthony cradled her chin in his hand, stroking his thumb over her bottom lip and wreaking havoc on her libido—"these lips are for me only. I don't care if he's got a tree of that green weed in his hand and offers you a million dollars."

"First of all, I turned my head, so it was going to be a kiss on the cheek. Secondly, a million dollars is a lot of money—eep!"

Anthony's mouth covered hers, cutting off the rest of her teasing as he kissed her roughly, making her knees weak. He broke the kiss abruptly, keeping his mouth hovered over hers. "Mine."

That one word rocked her world and she wished that there weren't eighteen more names on her stupid list to interview because she wanted this man alone so he could kiss her just like that and more.

"Hey, hey, break it up!" Holly hollered at them. "Some of us got places to be! Anthony! Get over here. You're with me."

Anthony let her go, skipping backward. "Wanna grab something to eat after this?"

"I do."

He spun around and sauntered over to Holly, who was shaking her head at his antics, but Delilah couldn't stop smiling.

Chapter Twenty-four

Although Anthony presented Holly with a winning smile, he was still seething on the inside at Brodie's audacity. How dare that asshole try to kiss Delilah. Didn't she cancel the snowboarding date? Could the idiot not take a hint? It had taken everything in him just to move her out of the line of lip-lock and not deck the guy.

"Alright, Romeo," Holly said, breaking into his thoughts with her sharp tone. She tapped her pen rapidly against the clipboard, watching him with piercing dark eyes. "What is going on with you and my bestie?"

"We're dating. Didn't she tell you?"

"She did but I wanted to hear from you what your intentions are."

Kiss every inch of her body before I make her scream my name?

Not that he would ever say that to Holly. She'd be liable to kick him in his family jewels.

"My intentions are to date her and see how things go. Nothing more or less than that."

"Oh, yeah?" Holly crossed her arms, the clipboard tucked beneath them against her chest. "Then what's with the jealous display of affection I just witnessed? If this was casual, you wouldn't have sprinted across the room like the Flash to take her away from another man."

"Lila is not a toy," he grumbled.

Holly's eyes widened. "Did you just call her Lila?"

"So?"

"Nothing," she said, smirking, "the plot just thickens."

"No, it doesn't. We're dating. Ergo, I don't want her kissing anyone else."

Holly arched a brow. "I'm sorry, did you just 'ergo' me?"

"Er—" Anthony said slowly, snapping his fingers with each syllable. "Go, no kissing other guys."

Holly uncrossed her arms with a huff. "I assume the rule applies to you, too?"

"Of course."

"Good," she said, grinning. "Then we won't have a problem. Now, I need your full name, age, occupation, height, hobbies, and your idea of the perfect date."

Anthony scoffed. "Really?"

Holly scowled. "What? It's basic dating profile fodder."

"I just got through telling you I'm dating your best friend and you still want me to go through with this farce?"

Holly burst out laughing. "I can't believe you still do that thing."

"What thing?" he asked.

"Where you use fancy language when you get frustrated," she said, shaking her head. "You did it a lot when I'd annoy you as a lowly freshman in high school."

Anthony crossed his arm. "And a decade later, you haven't learned not to irritate me?"

"Please, it will only get worse now that you are dating my girl." She tapped that pen twice on the wooden clipboard and Anthony fought the urge to take it away from her. "Now, name."

"Anthony Russo."

"Age?"

"Thirty-one."

"Wunderbar. Occupation?"

Her rapid-fire questions were making his head ache. "You're really going to go through this like you don't know the answers?"

"I've got all night, Ant."

"Business owner."

"Three more. Height, hobbies, and perfect date?"

Anthony caught sight of Delilah laughing at something her interviewee said and his fingers flexed. "Six foot three. I like fishing, camping, hiking, anything outdoors." She was still talking to the guy and his jaw tightened. "Punching idiots who think they're funny."

Holly looked over her shoulder and rolled her eyes. "Would you get a grip on your alpha maleness? Delilah is crazy about you and has no interest in anyone else. Now, perfect date?"

Anthony continued to watch Delilah give the funny guy she'd interviewed a little wave and the next man stepped up. She was a ray of sunshine whose smile exuded warmth and he wanted to be the one basking in it, instead of sharing her with a roomful of people.

Suddenly, something hard smacked against his bicep and he realized that Holly hit him with a clipboard. "Ow! What?"

"Perfect. Date! I'd like to go home some time tonight."

"Fine, you wanna know what my perfect date looks like? Just me and my girl, eating a meal, and spending time together. Alone."

"Was that so hard?" Holly asked, scribbling rapidly with her pen across the paper. Finally, she pressed the top with an aggressive click. "Now, go away! I have twenty more people on this list and you took forever. Next!"

Anthony turned and headed to the back of the room where Pike waited for him. He pulled up next to his friend, shaking his head. "Has Holly always been mean?"

"She once added glitter glue to my body wash when I spent the night at Nick's house. Yeah, she's mean as fuck," Pike said.

Anthony chuckled. "I guess dating her best friend makes her extra mean."

"Could be. I've never been in your position, so I have no idea. Or maybe she's afraid that you're going to drop out of the bachelor auction now that you've got a girlfriend."

Girlfriend. It was a foreign word that he hadn't used for anyone in a long time but Delilah could definitely do justice to that moniker. Since their first kiss, there had been a lot of doubt and misunderstanding between them. Maybe this was the time to put all that to rest and show her how special she is.

"I'll be right back," Anthony said, heading back toward Holly.

"Dude, where are you going? I'm starving!" Pike called after him but Anthony ignored him. He reached Holly before her next victim and she rolled her eyes.

"What do you want now?"

"I want to change my answer."

"To what?" she asked.

Anthony grinned. "My perfect date."

The rest of the interviews went smoothly, and when Delilah finished her last one a little over an hour later, she was ready to collapse. She walked over to Holly and Merry, who were stacking up their bios in a neat pile on the front table. Delilah set her own pile next to theirs with a smile.

"All interviews complete and accounted for."

"Perfect," Merry said, picking up Delilah's papers and adding them to the stack. She leaned a palm over them, facing Delilah with a sweet smile. "Will you type them up and send them to Holly in a Google form? She's going to make the brochure and it will be easier for her to copy and paste the info under the pictures."

"Absolutely. When do you need them by?"

"Would Sunday morning be alright?" Merry asked. "No need to dive into them tonight. With the Festival of Trees tomorrow, I doubt Holly will have time to look at them until then."

"Sounds good." Delilah picked up the papers and clutched them to her chest, anticipation making her antsy. Anthony had texted her several times, asking when she was going to be finished and Delilah couldn't wait to get some quality time with him. "If you don't need anything else, I'm going to head out."

"Oh, yeah?" Holly said, appearing beside her with a sly grin. "Doing anything special? Or should I say, doing anyone?"

Delilah's face burned and she elbowed Holly in the ribs. "Shut up. We're just going to dinner."

"Before he has you for dessert?" Holly teased.

"You're a monster."

"If I'm lying then why are you blushing?"

"If you want to hit her, by all means, go right ahead," Merry said, rubbing a hand over her stomach. "I'd help you hold her down, but I have precious cargo."

"Delilah loves me," Holly said.

"Do I?" Delilah responded, feigning surprise.

Merry chuckled. "I'll leave you two to hash out your friendship status. Thanks for your help, Delilah. I'm going to find my husband, put my feet up, and hopefully convince him to rub them. I'm beat."

"'Night, sis."

"Good night, Merry," Delilah called, watching Merry waddle away. When they were alone, Holly grinned in the most unsettling way at Delilah.

"What?" she asked suspiciously.

"Nothing," Holly singsonged. "I just love how he is with you."

"Who? Anthony?"

Holly snorted. "No, Santa Claus!" She hopped up to sit on the table, that smile widening. "I've never seen him with a girlfriend—at least, not that I can remember—but he is like a kid. Less serious. And you look happy."

"It's early still," Delilah said, hesitantly. The last thing she wanted to do was jinx this, especially since they really hadn't been dating long in the scheme of things.

"Why are you so afraid of being happy?" Holly asked.

"I'm not afraid." Delilah gripped the stack of papers against her chest like a defensive shield. "I'm just cautious. I'm afraid if I'm too excited, he'll dip."

"I just watched that man rush across the room like a bus was headed straight for you to keep another guy from kissing you. That should make you jump up and down like a kangaroo."

"With all the stress I've got going on, I'm living in the moment. No pressure, no hype."

"You sound like that car dealership ad they play every commercial break," Holly said, reaching for her hand. "Talk to me. I know things didn't go well with that editor and you think your only option is to move to Colorado or find another job elsewhere, but what about self-pubbing your book? Have you thought any more about it?"

Delilah sighed, setting the papers down next to Holly and leaning her hip against the table. "I've been researching, but it's a lot of money up front. It would demolish my savings and the editors I've contacted are months out."

"You said your agent read through it and already pointed out major plot holes, right?" Holly asked.

"Yes?"

"That should work as your main content editing. What about one of the teachers you work with? Could they read it and just look for grammatical errors?" Holly shrugged. "That's one way to cut down on costs. Or an online editing program? Something you can use for each book."

"How do you know about this stuff?" Delilah asked.

Holly shrugged, reaching out to take Delilah's hand. "I don't want my best friend to leave me so I've been doing my own research."

Delilah tugged Holly off the table and hugged her, grateful that this sweet, wonderful woman was her person. "Thank you."

"Like I said, I'm selfish and can't live without you." Holly pulled back, squeezing Delilah's shoulders. "We will figure something out. You'll see."

"Hey!" Delilah's heart lurched, recognizing Anthony's voice. She turned and watched him cross the community center, dressed in a button down with his hair wet and swept back off his forehead. He must have gone home to take a shower while she finished and the fact that he cleaned up for her kicked her pulse into high gear. Was he ready to forgo his vow and take the next step with her?

She almost scoffed aloud at her wishful thinking. They'd agreed to slow, yet here she was rushing him in her mind.

Holly stepped back when Anthony reached them, allowing him to slip an arm around Delilah's waist and kiss her cheek. "Ready to go?"

"Yep." She smiled at her bestie, hoping Holly recognized how much her support meant to Delilah. "Thanks again, Hol."

"Always, babe. You two have fun."

Anthony squeezed her against him. "I hope so."

"Oh, girl," Holly laughed, backing away from them. "Enjoy."

Delilah shook her head. "She is so transparent."

"No," Anthony said, leaning over to kiss her neck. A sizzle of heat zigzagged down her spine in response to the warm brush of his lip and her eyes closed. "She just understands that I'm anxious to get you alone."

Chapter Twenty-five

"When you said that you wanted to get me alone, this wasn't exactly what I pictured."

Anthony grinned as he opened up the driver's side door, the dome light coming on to illuminate Delilah's skeptical expression. "Have you ever been axe throwing before?"

"No," Delilah drawled, her gaze fluctuating between the target and Anthony, "but that's only because I prefer all my extremities attached."

"I promise, you won't lose so much as a baby toe and you'll have fun." He opened the door to the stall and added, "Trust me," before closing the door. He was still full and happy from the bag of tacos they'd shared after leaving the community center. The converted equestrian center had been remodeled and renamed Ax's and O's. It had opened over the summer and become a favorite activity for his friend group. The owners had built up the walls of the horse stalls and turned them into the target areas. Anthony didn't trust himself to be alone with her and figured this would be a tension relieving activity, with the added benefit for laughter and getting to know each other better.

Delilah walked to the edge of the stall with a limp and Anthony frowned. "Are you okay?"

"Yeah, I just landed wrong when I jumped out of the truck," she said, rubbing her hip.

Anthony chuckled. "Aw, man. I might have to get a shorter truck."

"Hey now, don't you start making fun of my height!" she protested, giving him a playful push.

"Hell, no, I like you just the way you are."

Delilah's bright smile flashed. "I feel the same about you."

Anthony took her hand, lacing his fingers between hers, and lifted it to his mouth to kiss it.

"Since you haven't done this before, do you want me to demonstrate?" he asked, releasing her hand to pick up the closest axe, which sported a red handle.

"Sure," she said, releasing him to lean against the wall. "Show me your skills, Viking warrior."

Anthony chuckled. "Are you trying to turn me on?"

"Being called a Viking gets you hot?" She giggled, an incredulous expression on her face. "Weird, but okay."

Anthony cupped the back of her neck and leaned down, hovering his mouth over hers. "Everything you do makes me hot, Lilah."

"Then why are we here instead of back at my place?" Delilah whispered, her hands gripping his waist.

Because I want to be sure.

Before Anthony gave up his vow of celibacy and took that step, he wanted some without-a-doubt sign that what he was experiencing with Delilah was love. He knew it was strong and something he'd never experienced before, but he couldn't be wrong. There was too much riding on this for him to make a misstep and risk Delilah getting hurt. Or worse, leaving town.

Losing people had become old hat for him. His father, whom he never really had. His brothers, with the exception of Bradley, and then his mom. The only constants remained Pike, Nick, and Noel. Anthony couldn't lose them.

"I thought we should have a few dates outside the house where we're less likely to give into temptation," he said.

"Yeah," Delilah drawled sarcastically, dropping her voice as another couple walked by, "because that first time in your truck was so secluded."

"Hey," he protested, holding the axe against his side as he leaned over, nose to nose with her, "I could channel my sexual frustration into sarcasm, too, but I'm choosing to use it to perfect the sacred art of axe throwing."

Delilah released him and waved her hand with flourish, shooting him a sheepish grin. "I apologize. Please continue the lesson."

"Very good, now"—Anthony stepped back and positioned himself behind the throwing line—"the key is to keep your elbow in and your arm straight. It doesn't require much force, so when you bring it back like this—" He let the axe head drop back behind his shoulder before smoothly launching it forward. It turned over twice before the blade impaled the wall. "See?" He turned to her, pointing to the axe with the blue handle. "Now, you try."

Anthony stood back as Delilah grabbed the axe and took a similar stance to his, letting the head of the axe fall back and then throwing it with delicate force. It struck the center of the target and Anthony narrowed his eyes.

"Lila?" he drawled.

She turned around with wide, innocent eyes. "Yes?"

"You've done this before, haven't you?"

Her lips twitched. "Maybe."

"Then why did you let me think you hadn't?"

Delilah approached him, placing her hands on his chest. "Because I've had this fantasy about a big, strong man teaching me how to do something." Her palms slid down, settling on the waistband of his jeans. "Unfortunately, I thought the lesson would be a little more hands on."

Anthony groaned, covering her hands with his and bringing them back up to press against the front of his shirt. "You're killing me, love."

Delilah took a step closer, licking her lips. "I like that."

"What? That you're killing me?"

"No. I like it when you call me love."

He reached up to cradle her face in his hands. "What are you doing to me, love?"

Delilah leaned into him, stretching to meet his mouth as he dipped down to take her lips with his. She was sweet and soft, and he wanted to get lost in her. To enjoy her with his hands and mouth, but tonight was about talking. Taking the steps to converse and make sure what was brewing between them was more than raging hormones.

Anthony broke the kiss, brushing his lips against the tip of her nose. "Now that I know you're not a beginner, I don't have to hold back."

"Oh, was that your plan?" she laughed playfully, walking down the length of the stall to the target and yanking her axe from the board. "To teach me how to throw an axe and go easy on me as if I'm too delicate for a little competition?"

Anthony's lips twitched as he pulled up next to her to retrieve his own axe. "Something like that."

"Then how about this? For every time I hit the bull's-eye, you have to agree to one of my demands." Anthony started to protest, sure she was going to finagle sex out of him, but she held up her hand. "Not that. More along the lines of information."

"Why do I feel like a perp on a cop show about to get the screws?" he asked.

"Are you nervous?" Delilah asked, jutting out her hip with an exaggerated pout. "If you want, I could go easy on you."

Anthony took a step back against the wall and waved a hand. "Give it your best shot, love."

Delilah chucked the axe toward the target and hit it dead center. She turned to Anthony, smiling like a proud cat who'd caught a parakeet. "Tell me about the first time you had sex."

Anthony choked in surprise. "Way to just ease on into things."

"I'm the type to jump in with both feet," she said, stepping back to let him take his stance.

"Fine. It was my senior year with my girlfriend of six months. We had sex in a tent on a group camping trip. She cried and a few of her friends came to the tent to check on her, so we didn't finish." Anthony threw the axe, which hit just above hers. "Not exactly my finest moment. What about yours?"

"Mine was college with a guy I had been dating a few months." They walked alongside each other to retrieve their axes, their hands brushing. "I tried to pull out all the stops to make it perfect. Rose petals. Champagne."

"Was it perfect?" Anthony asked, yanking both of their axes from the target.

"Not at all. He didn't understand what foreplay was and brought a jar of Vaseline because it was cheaper than lube. I ended up getting a bladder infection. It sucked," she said, taking her axe from him.

"I'm not supposed to laugh, right?" he said, his lips twitching.

"Shut up," she giggled, bumping him with her hip.

They continued to take turns throwing, asking personal questions, and laughing so hard their stomachs hurt.

Delilah threw the axe again and asked her fifteenth question. "Do you want to have kids?"

Anthony paused, watching her expression for any tell about what the right answer would be. Finally, he said, "I want kids, but there is always that fear I'm going to be a shitty dad. I didn't exactly have the best example."

"But you had your mom, right? She was pretty great."

Anthony smiled, stepping up to the line. "Oh, yeah. She was awesome. On December first, she'd pull out the advent calendar and fill it with See's Candy, which is really expensive. I held on to the calendar when she passed, thinking that maybe I'd have kids one day if I ever met someone." Anthony threw the axe and it hit the edge of the target, but he didn't care. Facing Delilah, he asked, "What about you? Kids?"

Delilah smiled warmly. "I'd like a few kids running around. Of course, I'm not sure how I'll do during the toddler stage, but once they hit middle school, I've got it handled."

"Oh, yeah? Because you're a substitute?"

"Because I am the cool sub," Delilah said, taking his hand this time as they walked across the sawdust.

"I have a feeling that I'll be okay with littles," Anthony said. "I'm not sure about diapers though."

"What if we have kids and you take them for the first nine years, I take them for the last nine years, and we find someone to change their diapers?" Delilah teased.

Anthony didn't freak out at the thought of having kids with Delilah. In fact, spending all his time with her, for the rest of his life, sounded pretty damn good.

"I think that's the perfect compromise," he said, kissing her softly. She stretched into him, deepening the kiss and murmured, "If we're done playing twenty questions, wanna go make out somewhere?"

"Hell, yes."

Chapter Twenty-six

Delilah stood at the top of the hill, staring down at the white expanse below and the tiny moving dots that represented people. The lump of fear that had been climbing up the back of her throat since she and Anthony had climbed onto the ski lift threatened to choke her and she leaned back slightly. The entire drive up, she'd been wavering between anticipation and apprehension, but now that she was standing there, all the excitement disappeared.

"I don't think I can do this," she said, swallowing hard but the lump didn't go away.

Anthony chuckled, placing his hands on her shoulders and giving them a squeeze. "Yes, you can."

Delilah took a breath, inching her board closer to the edge. "It's so high."

"This is the bunny hill, Lila."

"I don't care if it is the mouse hill, the ant hill, or a microbe hill! It looks huge, okay?" Delilah was aware of people around her stepping up and heading down the hill on skis and snowboards. When a little girl who couldn't be more than five and her mom went down together, Delilah glanced up at Anthony and groaned. "You think I'm a wuss."

"I didn't say that," he said, kissing her forehead. "We could catch a lift down and practice falling some more."

Delilah shot him a dark look. "You're so funny."

"I'm serious, if you don't think you're ready, we can keep practicing until you feel comfortable." He wrapped his arm around her and hugged her to him. "I've got all day."

Delilah leaned into him for several moments, staring down the hill. Finally, she took a deep, shaky breath, and said, "No, I'm good. I can balance. I rode that horrid lift up here. I'm good."

"Attagirl!" Anthony released her and came up alongside her, his dark goggles hiding his green eyes, but his comforting smile eased her tension slightly. "Just remember that if you feel like you're going too fast, dip the front of your board into the snow and bend your heel slightly. If that doesn't work and you're scared, just sit down on your butt."

Delilah nodded. "I can do that."

"I know you can." He took her hand and gave it a gentle press. "I'm going to stay right next to you. You got this."

"I got this," she said weakly, clearing her throat to try again. "I got this."

"Yeah, you do," he said.

"Here I go." Delilah released his hand but she didn't move.

"Do you want me to go down a few feet so you just have to get to me?" he asked, scooting forward.

"No," she shrieked, wishing she didn't wear her panic like a scarf, slowly choking her. The last thing she wanted was to be left up here all alone, where some rogue boarder might bump into her, sending her careening down the hill.

Delilah realized her rapid breathing was making her lightheaded. "This is . . . it's a lot. Maybe snowboarding was too advanced for me and I should give something less adventurous a try. Like snowshoeing!"

"You want to go snowshoeing in the woods?" Anthony chuckled. "We can do that, but wolves are hungry this time of year. We might need to practice running in the shoes, in case we get in a hairy situation."

Delilah glared at him. "It is not nice to terrorize the girl you are dating when she is standing on top of a mountain, balancing on a toothpick."

"You aren't giving the snowboard enough credit. It's perfectly formed to keep you upright. The rest is up to you."

"What about snowmobiling?" she asked.

"Avalanches. Lilah?" She looked away from the steep hill and focused on his face. "People snowboard all the time and survive. It's the ones who do stupid shit like try a flip in the air or jump giant mounds that break their necks. You are simply going down the bunny hill and if you get scared, just drop right onto your butt for a full stop."

"Makes sense. Most of my weight is in my butt," she joked.

"No self-deprecating humor," Anthony said, his hand coming up to squeeze her. "I like this butt."

"I feel like any second now, you're going to shove me down the hill by a tap on my cheeks!"

"I would never do that. Now, deep breath." Delilah sucked in air with him and let it out slowly. "Are you ready?"

She nodded vigorously, although she still wasn't sure. However, Delilah had asked for this lesson and it was unacceptable to back out now.

Shifting her weight forward, Delilah's stomach dropped as her snowboard dipped and she took off, screaming, "Oh, shit!"

The snowcapped trees whizzed by and it wasn't until Delilah was halfway down the hill that she realized she'd managed to stay on her feet. She heard Anthony call out from somewhere nearby, "Use your edge! Delilah! Look at you go! Yeah, baby!"

She turned slightly, slowing herself down and screamed with excitement, "Oh my gosh, I'm doing it. I'm doing it!"

Delilah turned to smile at Anthony, who was several feet over from her. Suddenly, Anthony looked up and yelled, "Look out!"

Delilah didn't have a chance to react to his warning before she hit a mound of snow and tumbled over it, rolling several times down the remainder of the hill. When she finally stopped, Delilah lay on her back, staring up at the blue, cloudless sky and figured little cartoon birds were going to appear at any second.

She heard rushing movement and Anthony's worried green eyes came into view, his hands all over her face. "Delilah? Baby, are you okay?"

"I think so, but someone should probably get the license and registration of that snowbank," she joked.

"I'm such an idiot," he said, smoothing a hand over her forehead; she noted he'd ditched his ski gloves, his warm skin gliding over hers. "We went too far left and I didn't see the pile until it was too late."

Delilah smiled at him, still a little dazed. "No self-deprecating, remember? Up until I went ass over tea kettle, I was doing pretty good, right?"

Anthony chuckled. "You were great."

"Is she alright?" Pike asked, wearing a yellow vest and hovering over Anthony's shoulder, peering down at her with a frown. "That was quite a tumble."

"One out of ten, would not recommend," she murmured.

"Think you can stand up?" Anthony asked, his eyes full of concern.

Delilah nodded and held her hands out, each man taking one and hauling her to her feet. She stumbled and Anthony caught her, his arm locked around her waist. "I think that's enough snowboarding for one day."

"Probably for the best," Delilah groaned, rubbing her head. "Next time I might end up on the roof."

"You should take her to infirmary and have her checked out for a concussion," Pike said, studying her. "And keep her conscious until you know for sure."

"Thanks, I will."

"Oh my God, Delilah!" someone called out.

Delilah squinted as a woman glided over to them on a snowboard, stopping next to Pike. Delilah recognized Ryler, the travel blogger's assistant she'd met the other night, and gave her a reassuring smile.

"I'm alright." Delilah rapped her knuckles on the side of her helmet. "Anthony made sure I was wearing noggin protection."

"Can you help me get her to that chair?" Anthony asked, pointing to some chairs in front of the hot cocoa hut. "I'm going to run back and get my equipment. I kind of threw it in a panic."

"We've got her," Pike said, taking her hands from Anthony's and gliding her over the snow to the closest chair.

"First time snowboarding?" he asked as she plopped into the seat.

"How'd you guess?" she laughed.

He chuckled.

Ryler put a hand on her shoulder. "Do you want something to drink? Chocolate always makes me feel better."

"A water, please?" Delilah said.

"You got it."

"Not gonna ask me, kitten?" Pike called out as Ryler got in line.

"I already know what you want," she shot back.

Pike chuckled again, only it was darker, like the two of them shared a secret.

A hot secret from the way she was looking at him.

Delilah quirked a brow when Pike met her gaze and she nearly gasped when she spotted the blush staining his cheeks. Pike kneeled down in the snow and unbuckled her board, clearing his throat. "Seemed like you were having fun up until your forward flip."

"I was. How about you, Pike? Are *you* having fun?"

Pike glanced up at her and smirked. "You pumping me for information about my love life, Delilah?"

"Nope, I just noticed some sparkage, but if you don't want to share . . . "

Pike set her snowboard to the side of her chair with a sigh and stood, dropping into the chair next to her. "Not to sound cliché, but it's complicated."

"It always is." Delilah caught sight of Anthony making his way back and sat forward, watching him maneuver with grace and precision.

"You like my guy a lot, huh?" Pike asked.

Delilah sat back. "I do."

"Good. He deserves someone great." He leaned closer to her and she turned his way as he added, "Not to sound melodramatic, but don't hurt him, okay? This is the first time I've ever seen him in love and I don't want him becoming Thanos and destroying the world if it doesn't work out."

Delilah almost choked when he said love. Did it look like love from other people's perspectives? Was that what Anthony was feeling?

Furthermore, was that the warm, loopy feeling that settled in her stomach every time she thought about him love, too?

"Water for you," Ryler said, handing her a clear cup with a bright pink straw. She sat on the edge of Pike's chair with a white cup in her hand, sipping from the top of the black lid. "What did I miss?"

Laughter drew her attention and she saw Brodie and Trip approaching them from a few feet away with a group of men. Brodie was at the front and stopped a foot away from her. Delilah arched her neck to look up at him, noting the twisted sneer on his mouth and knew this was going to be as fun as a trip to the dentist.

"Guess you should have stuck with me, huh, Delilah? Not crashing at the bottom of the bunny hill is lesson number one."

Before she could respond, Anthony snarled, "I've got a lesson for you, motherfucker." He was rapidly approaching the group and Delilah's eyes widened as he dropped his gear, looking like he was ready to swing.

"You better uncork my boy soon," Pike said with a shake of his head. He flashed a small smile at her as he climbed to his feet. "I think everything being pent up is what's making his fuse so short."

"Anthony," Delilah called softly, trying to climb to her feet but a sharp explosion of pain at the back of her head made her woozy.

"Pike's got him," Ryler said, patting her knee with her free hand.

Delilah took in the scene of Pike standing between Brodie and Anthony, who were calling each other every name in the book, when Pike finally hollered, "You two wanna keep slinging insults or settle this like men?"

"What are you going on about?" Brodie asked.

"You two stop this pissing contest until the winter games. No more making moves on his girl," Pike said, poking Brodie in the chest before pressing Anthony back with both hands, "and you stop trying to get yourself thrown in jail for assault."

Watching the much smaller man try to move an irate Anthony would almost have made Delilah giggle, if she wasn't worried about an all-out brawl erupting.

"What happens after the games?" Trip asked.

"Same bet we made at Brews and Chews," Pike said, keeping a hand on Anthony as he addressed the other men. "Either we have a new boat or you have new snowmobiles. Somebody's going to be happy."

"I want one more thing if I win," Brodie said, smirking, and Delilah could see the evil hamster wheel turning in his head.

"No, we agreed," Pike said.

Brodie pointed past Pike's shoulder at Anthony. "That was before this prick humiliated me."

"It's really that easy?" Anthony scoffed, slapping Brodie's hand from his face.

"Stop it," Delilah said softly.

"What did you say?" Ryler asked Delilah.

Delilah opened her mouth to repeat herself but was cut off by the next words out of Brodie's mouth.

"If I win, your girlfriend is going to give me a victory kiss," Brodie said, puckering up at Delilah. Trip and the rest of his crowd laughed and jeered while Anthony tried to get over Pike.

"Over my dead body," Anthony snarled.

Pike wrapped his arms around Anthony's middle, hauling him back with a grunt, and Delilah wished she had enough strength to pick up the snowboard and bonk them all on the head.

"Hey, you heard him, Pike," Trip laughed. "Your boy's got a death wish. You should let him go!"

"Um, hello! This isn't the eleven hundreds!" Ryler said loudly. "Consent is sexy and we don't use women as bargaining chips."

"Whatever, I don't even need a prize," Brodie said, cracking his knuckles like a bully from an eighties movie. "I'm going to enjoy kicking your ass on principle."

"Stop it," Delilah said, getting to her feet unsteadily. She hobbled over the group of men, her entire body starting to feel the full impact of her snowboarding gymnastics and she glared at them. "Whatever you guys have going on, grow up and leave me out of it."

Brodie's dark expression dissolved into one of malice. "Hey, no worries. I just wanted to see what it was like to fuck a fat girl."

Delilah reeled back like he'd slapped her. "Sorry to disappoint."

"As soon as Anthony's done with you, he'll share with the class if you were worth the effort."

Anthony took her shoulders and moved her out of the way, telling Pike, "Take care of her for me, would ya?"

"Anthony, don't—" Delilah told him, but it was too late. Pike wrapped his arms around her and hauled her backward seconds before Anthony threw the first punch. Brodie recoiled, blood spewing out the side of his mouth, and Trip caught Anthony with a swift uppercut to the stomach.

"Ah, hell, no!" Pike yelled, dropping her out of harm's way and jumping into the fray. "No tag teams!"

Pike grabbed Trip and flipped him onto his back. Another of Brodie's crew went after Pike, but Pike cracked him across the jaw, sending him spinning away. Pike grinned at the remaining men and made a come-on motion with both hands. "Step up, kiddies. I've got plenty to go around."

Delilah groaned in disgust as Pike seemed to be having fun with the fight, meanwhile Anthony had Brodie in a headlock, kicking at another goon.

Ryler put her arms around Delilah's shoulders. "How about we go to urgent care while they sort this out?"

Delilah nodded, letting Ryler lead her away.

"Why are men such idiots?" Delilah asked.

"If I had that kind of information, do you think I'd be an assistant? Girl, I'd be president, saving the idiots of the world from themselves."

Chapter Twenty-seven

Anthony and Pike stayed in the cell inside Mistletoe police station and waited for Nick to come bail them out. Brodie, Trip, and the rest of their crew sat in the second cell next to them, bitching and moaning every few moments, which made Anthony feel better. Although it had been two to five in the fight, Anthony and Pike had come out better than the others. Pike's eye was swelled shut and turning an ugly shade of purple and Anthony's lip and cheek were swollen and bruised, but security at the resort had busted things up before they went too far.

Anthony sat down on the bench next to Pike, thinking about all the crap they'd been through the last few weeks, all the times he'd wanted to take his friend to task for being impulsive and overextending them, and, yet, when Anthony was the one to lose his cool, Pike had jumped in without a single question or thought for himself.

"Hey, man," Anthony said, clearing his throat. "Thanks for jumping in."

"Sure, what are friends for but to have your back when you start a fight with six guys?" Pike's sarcasm with a hefty dose of condemnation wasn't lost on Anthony and he turned toward his friend. Pike rested the back of his head against the wall with his eyes closed and Anthony gave him a hard nudge with his shoulder.

"Hey. What's your problem?"

Pike opened his eye to glare at him. "You're supposed to be the smart, levelheaded guy in this friendship. Instead, you're betting our equipment and getting into fights that lead to us sitting in a jail cell facing possible charges. It's like you've been replaced by a pod person!"

Fury shot through Anthony and he snapped, "So because you have me to curb your spending, you think volunteering us for everything is fine because I'll create a budget? News flash, sometimes the budget is too much."

"Uh oh. I think the lovers next door are fighting," Trip said, earning a chuckle from a few of their friends.

"Will you shut the fuck up?" Pike hollered.

"Why don't you make me, Lucky the Leprechaun?"

"I thought I already did," Pike said, pointing to his mouth. "Nice lip, Trip. Looks like it split open again."

Trip touched his fat lip, which had started oozing blood. "You'll pay for that later."

"Stop your whining, you big boobs!" Officer Wren barked from the other room, the stomp of her boots growing louder before she cleared the hallway and stood with her hands on her hips, glaring at them. Her dark hair was pulled back in that severe bun that reminded Anthony of a woman in a marine movie.

"If you weren't fighting like a bunch of middle schoolers," she said, her tone resembling a teacher disappointed in her students' antics, "you wouldn't be hurting so damn bad."

Pike laughed. "You tell them, Wren."

"I'm talking to you, too, ya idjit," she snapped, approaching their cell and piercing Anthony with dark eyes. "You are supposed to be leaders in this community. Leaders control their damn tempers."

Pike shrugged. "We tried to take the high road, but he started talking shit about Anthony's lady."

"They're just words," Officer Wren said, lowering her voice to add, "and he's dimwitted anyway."

Brodie hollered, "Hey!"

"Hey yourself," she said without turning Brodie's way. Her entire focus was on Anthony, who shuffled his feet under her disapproving gaze. "Why would you care what he thinks? Do you like the guy? Respect his opinion?"

"No," Anthony said.

"He's a douchebag," Pike added.

Brodie smacked the bars with his hands. "I am sitting right here!"

"Yeah, we can see you." Pike grinned at Wren, his left eye purple and swollen. "Admit it. The shiner makes me look tough, huh?"

"Idjit," Wren muttered, turning her back on him and disappearing down the hall.

"I think Officer Wren likes me," Pike said.

Anthony shook his head. "I think Officer Wren wants to take us all out back and tase us. Can't really blame her."

"What are you talking about? We are the victims here. Innocently making sure your girlfriend was okay and then, blam! They walk up on us and start talking shit."

"It was stupid of me to let that dick get to me," Anthony said.

"So, why did you?" Pike asked.

Anthony closed his eyes. "I guess I've just been on edge. Stressed out."

"I'm sure you have been," Pike said, groaning as he sat down on a bench. "And sounds like I've made things worse. But I think you went off on Brodie because he was saying hurtful things to Delilah."

"Maybe," Anthony grumbled.

"Obviously," Pike countered. "Any man would have reacted to a woman being verbally attacked, but only a man in love would have pummeled the idiot the way you did."

Anthony stiffened, Pike's words sinking in as Brodie muttered, "I think I'm going to puke."

Pike snapped back at Brodie, but Anthony tuned the argument out. Love. It was something he'd wanted, had been waiting for it to hit him, but it had never happened.

Until now.

Here he was, stuck in a cell, when he should have been the one taking his girl to the hospital. Wren was right, Anthony was an idiot. What must Delilah be thinking about him, especially after he got hauled away in a squad car. What the hell was wrong with him? He never used to start fights. If someone tried something, he was more than happy to finish it, but he didn't get into brawls, and he certainly didn't get arrested.

Maybe Pike had a point about him being wound too tight. He'd taken that vow when he hadn't wanted to have sex with anyone, when he hadn't even been tempted. Now he was making himself crazy not having sex with Delilah when all he wanted to do was be near her. Pike was right: Anthony wasn't being honest about his feelings. Pike knew the truth. Hell, he'd said it out loud and Anthony couldn't even bring himself to admit it.

This was love. It was so far removed from anything he'd ever experienced that he'd almost blown it. After his behavior today, would she even speak to him again?

Anthony wiped a hand over his face. He needed to get out of this cell and go to her. Beg her to forgive him and if she slammed the door in his face, he'd camp there until she did.

Now that he knew what love felt like, there was no way he was ever letting it go.

"I hope Nick gets here soon," Anthony said.

Pike nodded. "I am ready to blow this Popsicle stand." He sat forward, his forearms resting on his legs. "I'm sorry, man. I know I can be moronic, and I need to learn to slow down and ask you before I agree to things for the business. I just get excited and I'm still getting used to having a partner."

Anthony smirked. "Me, too. I did a ton of research before we got into this and there were a lot of people saying that going into business ruined friendships for them. I don't want that for us."

"Agreed." Pike got up, holding out a hand to him. "Forgive me?"

Anthony took his hand and pulled him in for a hard hug. "Always."

"Someone get these assholes out of here before I lose my cookies?" Trip hollered, with Brodie and the rest of their friends shouting in agreement.

Wren appeared through the hallway again, jingling a set of keys. "Your wish is my command." Wren unlocked Anthony and Pike's cell. "It's your lucky day, boys. You've been sprung."

"What about us?" Brodie asked.

"Can I call my father again?" Trip bellowed.

"I'm sure it will be any minute now," Wren said, smirking. Anthony and Pike picked their jackets up from the bench and followed her. Once they passed through the hall, she whispered, "You've got a ten-minute head start before I release the goon squad."

"Thanks, Wren," Anthony said.

Wren pointed at each of them in turn. "You can thank me by staying out of trouble. You're lucky no one wanted to press charges."

Anthony's smile disappeared when he saw Delilah and Ryler standing next to Officer Wren's desk, wearing identical frowns. Despite the less-than-warm welcome, Anthony's chest tightened at the sight of her, but then her lips spread into a relieved smile and his tension eased. She wouldn't be here bailing him out if she couldn't stand the sight of him, right?

"Hey, you don't get to give me that look," Pike said, pointing at Ryler. "You ain't my girlfriend."

"Thank God for that," she laughed. "No man of mine would get into a fight wearing snow pants." Ryler shot Delilah an apologetic smile. "No offense."

"None taken." Delilah took a step closer to Anthony and reached up, her hand hovering over what he was sure was a massive bruise on his cheek. "You look terrible."

"I know, but really, you should see the other guys."

Delilah shook her head, but he could have sworn he caught a glimpse of a smile. "I have your truck outside."

"You're all good to go," Wren said. "And I wouldn't worry too much about those idiots changing their minds about pressing charges. I think they're too ashamed that the two of you kicked all six of their asses."

"You're good people, Wren," Anthony said with a wink. "Don't let anyone tell you differently."

Wren's cheeks flushed unexpectedly and she scoffed. "Get them out of here."

Anthony stepped ahead to get the door, tossing his jacket into the back seat, and asked, "On a scale of one to ten, with one being not angry and ten being, 'I'm going to kick your ass, too,' how pissed are you at me?"

Delilah glanced his way, arching a brow. "I'm at a two." Her smile disappeared as she quickly added, "But that's only because you going all agro on a jerk like Brodie isn't the worst thing that's happened today."

"Uh oh, hey," Anthony said, taking her arm gently and slowing her to a stop to face him. "What else happened after we got picked up?"

"It doesn't matter." Delilah extracted her arm from his grasp and handed him the keys. Delilah called over her shoulder to Ryler, "Do you have Pike?"

"Yeah, I'll take him home," Ryler said, rolling her eyes. "He's so tore back, I'm afraid he might pass out if I made him walk."

Pike snorted, rounding to the passenger side of the rental car. "Don't act like I'm a chore to be around, when we both know I'm a fucking delight."

"You're more like a de-blegh," she said, making a gagging sound.

"That's mature," Pike deadpanned.

"Says the man who looks like he went five rounds with a badger." Ryler waved at Delilah and Anthony before climbing inside, cutting off the rest of their argument. Delilah walked toward the passenger door and Anthony got ahead of her, opening her door.

"I'm sorry," he said softly.

"I figured you might be after the fact. I would have been here sooner, but urgent care was backed up."

"Another thing I feel bad about," Anthony said, stroking his fingers over her cheek, elated when she didn't pull away. "I should have been taking care of you."

"It's over now, so no use rehashing it. Besides, a mild concussion and a few bumps and bruises isn't too bad. I should be okay in a couple of days."

Delilah climbed up into the truck and Anthony took her waist, helping her inside. "No taking advantage of you then, huh?"

"Not for a bit." She clicked her seat belt into place and added, "Besides, you could probably use a few days to heal, too."

"I'm fine," he said casually, closing her door and heading around the front to the driver's side. In all honestly, he was trying not to walk like his body ached, but it did. His ribs, back, arms, face. Taking a few pain meds and a nap sounded like heaven at this point.

Anthony climbed up into the truck and winced when something in his ribs pulled.

"You're really hurt," Delilah said. "We should take you to the hospital."

"I'm fine. A couple of bumps and bruises." Anthony turned in the seat, watching her. "As far as making today up to you, what are we talking? Chocolates for a week?"

"You don't have anything to make up to me," she said, staring at her hands. "I'm the guilty one."

Anthony leaned back in surprise. "Why are you feeling guilty?"

"Because every time you get into trouble, it's because of me. Someone says something about me, and you come to my rescue. You and Pike got into a huge blowup because of me." Delilah sighed, leaning her head back against the seat. "Maybe we just aren't meant to do this."

Her words knocked the wind out of his chest. "Don't say that."

"Anthony—"

"Please." He reached out and picked up her hand up, squeezing it. "I know it's been a lot but . . . I'd like to show you something. Would you come with me?"

"To where?" she asked.

Anthony didn't answer right away. He took his hand back and started the car, pulling out on to Main Street.

"Where are you going?" Delilah asked.

"There's something you need to see, and then I want you to stop saying we're not meant to be together."

Delilah didn't say anything else for several moments and he couldn't take the silence, so he started rambling. "I think I'm feeling insecure, and maybe that's why I keep acting like a jealous lout."

"Lout?" she said, her voice soft and amused. "That's very medieval of you."

"Hey, I read. I'm educated."

"I know that," she said, placing her hand on his arm. "I'm only teasing."

"Yeah, I know. I'm just sensitive about it. People assume because I played football and worked road construction that I'm some uneducated slacker, but I paid my own way through school to earn my degree."

"I know all of this, Anthony," she said, squeezing his bicep until he glanced her way. "Why do you sound like you're trying to convince me?"

"Because I've never felt this way about anyone." He took a right past the Winters' farm and up a dirt road, snow piled up on either side of the one lane.

"And that's why you're taking me up into the forest?"

"My home, actually," Anthony said, his voice shaking with the bumps of the road or maybe that was nerves. "Or, my home site. I know I told you I live in a trailer right now and even though I fixed it up and put in new flooring and appliances, it is still just a trailer." Anthony stopped the truck in front of the camper and pointed out the window. "But the view is beautiful."

Anthony watched Delilah take in the scenery for several seconds before she opened the car door. They both got out of the truck and Anthony studied Delilah across the hood of the truck, her gaze focused on the view of rolling mountains, acres of pine trees, and imposing, craggy mountains in the distance. Did it take her breath away, the way it did his? Was that why she wasn't saying anything?

He'd fallen in love with this view the first time he saw it and as he watched her take it in, he only prayed she loved it, too.

"This is heaven," she whispered, and his breath rushed out in relief, an eager grin plastering his face.

"I think so, too, which is why I placed the trailer in the exact spot I'm having the house built." Anthony knew that the 1990s camper didn't look like much, but he'd done a lot to the inside to make it a home. Hopefully, she would see that. "The home will have a wrap-around porch. Do you want to come inside and I'll show you the plans?"

"I'd love to see your place," Delilah said.

Anthony held the door open for her and she walked past him up the metal stairs and into the trailer. He knew it wasn't much, but it had everything he needed to live. "I pulled out the linoleum floor and put in LVP when I gutted it." He climbed the steps behind her, watching her face as her gaze trailed over his temporary home, or so he'd been saying the last ten years. He'd installed his bed to the right of the entrance and ordered a new table booth to replace the broken one the trailer had come with. He'd also updated the couch to a leather one and put in small but modern cabinetry in the kitchen. He'd taken out the bunk beds in the back and expanded the bathroom to put in a shower big enough for him.

"I did most of the work myself watching videos on YouTube and hiring out for what I couldn't do myself," he said, following her as Delilah peeked into the bathroom.

"Anthony this—" She turned around in the doorway of his bathroom, a bright smile on her face. "This is beautiful. When you said that you lived in a trailer, I was expecting a messy bachelor pad at best or something out of a *Wrong Turn* movie at worst."

"Hey," he laughed, giving her hip a little pinch.

Delilah giggled. "I'm just saying, this is a lovely place on the inside. I can't wait to see what you do with your next house."

"I'll show you my plans," Anthony said, grabbing a book off the back of the couch, waving his hand toward the booth and table. "Have a seat." She sat across from him as he slid into the booth, opening the book. Anthony removed the plans from inside, spreading them over the kitchen table. "This is the main floor where there will be the master and a guest room, with the master bath, guest bath, and half bath. Upstairs are two bedrooms with a Jack and Jill bathroom in between them and a loft slash playroom."

"Playroom?" Delilah asked, her finger trailing over the upstairs floorplan, almost caressing it. "You mean for kids?"

"Yeah, of course I mean for kids. My playroom will be in the garage."

Delilah laughed. "I'm just surprised they get a whole room dedicated to their toys."

"Our playroom when I was growing up was in the basement," he said, remembering the afternoons spent watching his brothers play video games together. "It kept us out of our parents hair."

"Being an only child, our house was pretty quiet unless I had friends over."

Delilah studied the rectangle on the plans and tapped one side with her fingertip. "You should put in built-in cubbies for toy storage."

"That's a great idea."

Relief swept through him and he brought her hand up to his lips, kissing the back of it. Energized, he continued explaining the layout. "The kitchen has a smuggler's pantry and a large island where I can prep food."

"You cook?"

"I dabble," he said, playing at modesty. He wanted her to be shocked and delighted the first time he cooked for her. "If I had a real kitchen, I could get better. Let's see. The main living room will have a fireplace and this"—he indicated a square next to the large rectangle labeled living room—"will be an office."

"Oh, yeah? You're going to need a whole room to update your appointment books and spreadsheets?"

Delilah's voice was light, a teasing smile on her face, but he needed her to know that this wasn't just a passing notion. He'd been thinking about what his home would look like with her in it for a while now.

"I'll use it, too, but I also thought you could use it to write. A quiet space where you could stare at the mountains and we could put a bed in the corner for Leia to sleep in."

"You want to share your office with me?" she asked breathlessly.

"I want to share a lot of things with you." Anthony used his other hand to cup her one hand between both of his. "My trailer, for starters. You and Leia are welcome anytime."

Delilah climbed up on her knees and leaned across the table, brushing her lips over his. "We'd like that," she said, settling back into the bench seat. "Although I'm a little concerned that I'll take her out one morning and there will be a bear just waiting to go chomp."

Anthony laughed. "I've never seen a bear anywhere near the trailer."

"And yet, this is the mountains, where there are bears."

"Then I'll take her out for you, and I promise," he said, taking back a hand to make a cross over his heart, "I will protect her with my life."

"So you're offering to get up at all hours and take my dog out to go potty? To wrestle bears to keep her safe?" Her brilliant smile made him feel like a superhero. "You're doing a lot."

"I'd do more than that to make you happy."

Delilah pulled her hands free and got up, coming around to sit beside him on the other bench seat. She gently wrapped her arm around his waist and laid her head on his shoulder. "That is the nicest thing I've ever heard."

"Well, then, I'm about to do you one better," he said, turning a bit so he could face her. Anthony wanted her to see his face when he told her the truth, "because I've got more to say."

"What's that?" she asked, gazing up at him with those deep blue eyes and he drew in a breath. This was the moment and he rubbed his palms against his snow pants.

"I'm absolutely, beyond a doubt, in love with you."

Delilah gasped and let him go, covering her mouth with both hands. He released a nervous laugh at her reaction.

"Are you horrified or just surprised?" he asked.

"Are you sure?" Delilah whispered.

"Yes." Anthony tucked a hair behind her ear, his gaze never leaving hers. "I've been all over the place the last few weeks because I have never felt this way about anyone, and I didn't know what to do with myself. My emotions were everywhere. Up, down, angry, delighted, aroused. Always aroused." Delilah smacked his arm and he yelped, "Gentle! I am injured."

"I'm sorry," she said, leaning over to drop a kiss on his arm.

"It's okay," he murmured, watching her straighten up. "See, that is what loving someone is all about. Forgiving them and moving on. Plus, you know, make-up sex."

"Which neither one of us can have at the moment," she laughed.

Anthony pouted. "Even if I am gentle?"

"What if I don't want you to be gentle?" she said, scooting closer, their bodies several inches apart, and it was still too far. The need to pull her in close, to consummate their feelings was overwhelming, but when he reached out for her, a sharp pain exploded in his side and he gasped.

"Anthony?" Her hands reached for him, hovering, as if she was afraid to touch him and cause him more pain. "Maybe we should go to the doctor?"

"No, Doc Hutchinson stopped by and checked us out. My ribs are bruised, not broken." He leaned over, kissing her forehead. "We better wait a few days just the same. I want our first time to be so incredible that neither one of us can move for at least an hour. Not because we further injured ourselves."

"I hate to break it to you, but even if my knees are like jelly, I will be getting up right after we're done."

"Why?" he asked.

"Women have to pee after sex or they get bladder infections? Don't you know this?"

Anthony groaned, straightening his posture to face the table again before sliding an arm around her shoulders. "I tell you I love you and all the mystery goes out of our relationship?"

"Did that really bother you?" she huffed.

"No. I spent half my life over at Nick's and Pike's houses. Their sisters had no qualms sharing all the gross details about what happens to their bodies every month, and on top of that, I learned that girls actually fart."

Delilah laughed. "Poor Anthony. Holly and Merry destroyed the mystery of women for you."

"Not fully," he said, squeezing her to him gently. "I figure I'm still going to mess up and do the wrong thing when it comes to us."

"To err is to be human," Delilah said, resting her cheek against his chest.

"Hey, don't act holier than thou," he scolded, tilting her chin up with his hand so he could see her face. "You're going to mess up, too. But I'm going to be the best boyfriend and forgive you."

"Magnanimous of you." Her eyes were suddenly shuttered and he wondered what shifted her mood.

"Anthony?" she said, licking her lips.

"Yeah?"

Whatever she'd been about to say, she shook it off with a smile. "Nothing." She wrapped her arms around him again and kissed his chest. "I love you, too."

Chapter Twenty-eight

Delilah sat at her computer Wednesday afternoon and stared at the certified letter in her hands. She'd opened it hours ago, but the contents of the very formal correspondence hadn't sunk in yet.

> Dear Ms. Gill,
>
> Due to the rising costs of maintaining rental properties in Idaho while the owner is living out of state, they have decided to put the property you currently rent on the market for sale. Therefore, you have thirty days from the postmark of this letter to find another residence and vacate the premises. We appreciate your attention to this matter and apologize for any inconvenience.
>
> Regards,
> H.G. Yearly
> Snow Cap Property Management

How could this be happening now? Things were starting to look up. She'd sent her manuscript to her friend Erica, who worked at Holly's shop and was an English major. She'd bought a program for her computer that would format the book for publication. She'd even paid for a gorgeous premade cover she'd discovered on Etsy, which fit the story to a T.

And then there was Anthony.

But after the accident and the altercation on Saturday, she'd been sitting in urgent care waiting to be seen when she'd gotten a text from her friend at the middle school and discovered substitute teachers were losing two dollars in pay starting January 1. The school district had some surplus incentive pay to get more subs, but the money would run out in the new year. It was one more sign the universe was against her staying in Mistletoe, and Delilah had been prepared to accept the truth, no matter how much it hurt.

When Anthony told Delilah how he felt, it was like a light had gone on inside. All her doubts and frustrations over the last few weeks disappeared. Delilah stopped looking at the problems as signs and decided that if she wanted a future with Anthony, if she wanted to help him build that house and fill those kids' rooms, she needed to stop being such a defeatist and fight for what she wanted.

The first thing she'd done Saturday after Anthony dropped her off, after a much needed nap, was to finish the snowboarding article and send it to *Outside Magazine*. She attached an email thanking them for their job offer but informing them that she couldn't accept it.

Maybe Delilah was crazy to turn down an opportunity that would keep her afloat, but being without Holly, her town, and the man he loved? It just didn't make any sense.

Anthony had stopped by every night after work to hold her and kiss her while they both healed, telling her about all the things they could do to make his house theirs. They'd argued over plates and couches until she'd slipped her hand into his pants and caressed him, making him close his eyes as he arched into her hand.

"This is unfair."

"When you want something, I'll let you torture me with your tongue."

"Mmm, fine. We can get the floral plates."

Delilah hadn't left him hanging, bringing him to paradise slow and gentle with her mouth. They'd already been anticipating their first official time together happening after the bachelor auction on Friday night and Delilah had ordered a special surprise to wear under her dress.

She stared down at the letter and crumpled it into a ball, tossing it against the wall with a feral yell. Leia hopped off the couch with her ears back, staring from the ball of paper to her mama in terrified confusion.

"I'm sorry, baby. Mom's having a bad day."

Leia turned around and trotted outside, obviously afraid Delilah might lose her shit again.

Delilah had been utilizing the power of positivity in order to make herself believe that she could stay here, but this? She had nowhere to go. She'd been checking for months, looking for a cheaper place to rent but the prices kept going up, not down. The only way she could afford to stay in Mistletoe was to ask Holly if she could move in with her and

Declan for a bit, and she couldn't imagine her bestie's boyfriend loving that idea.

And while Anthony had looped Delilah into his dream home, it was so early in their relationship, she couldn't ask that of him. She shouldn't want to. Moving in with a man after three weeks was something that she would have never considered. His home was at least six months away from being built, so that would mean staying in his tiny trailer with him and her dog. He'd boot them out in a week.

Maybe you should at least ask his opinion. He could be excited about it.

Or he'd think she was a desperate mooch trying to sponge off him.

Delilah got off the couch and slipped on her Hey Dudes. She put Leia into her kennel before she left. Delilah couldn't stay in the house and stew for another minute, or she would lose her mind.

Once she climbed into her car, Delilah dialed her mom, who picked up on the first ring. "Hello, Delilah?"

"Hi, Mom." She couldn't stop her voice from catching on a sob and prayed that her mom hadn't heard it.

"What's wrong?" her mom questioned, knowing something was off just like all moms do.

"Why does something have to be wrong?" Delilah sniffed, starting her car and waiting for the call to switch over to her Bluetooth. When it finally did, Delilah put her phone in the cup holder and added, "Can't I just call you to say hi?"

"I know when there is something wrong; I've been your mother for many years."

"And not just my whole life? Weird." Delilah wasn't sure where she was headed, but a drive might help her clear her head. That, and a little vent session with her mom.

"Spill it, child. You called me for a reason."

Delilah sighed, struggling with how to start. "I don't know, Mom. I just—" Delilah paused, realizing she should set some ground rules before her mother went off on a tangent that would put her in a worse mood than she was in before. "Can I preface this conversation by asking that you not use this as an opportunity to tell me I should move to Boise or that I should get a more reliable job?"

"Delilah, I won't do that. I hope you know that I only want you closer to me because I miss you."

The sadness in her mother's voice twisted the knot of guilt tighter. "I know that, and I miss you, too, but I am really heartbroken right now and I just need to vent."

"Vent away, my love. I'll just listen," her mother said, her voice warm and understanding.

Delilah took a deep breath at the stoplight to center herself before beginning. "So, I got rejected by all of the publishers for the fantasy book series my agent took out, but I've been trying to see the silver lining, like Holly always tells me to do. As a result, I researched self-publishing and got the ball rolling on getting my book edited and formatted, but in the meantime, I got this job offer from a magazine in Colorado—"

"Colorado!" her mother cried, already gearing up to naysay it, but Delilah cut her off.

"You promised."

Delilah's mother cleared her throat. "You're right, please continue."

"They offered me a really great opportunity, in a well-compensated position, but it was for an outdoor magazine and I am not outdoorsy at all. That should have been the end of it, because even though I considered taking it, Anthony told me on Sunday that he loves me."

"He did?" her mother squealed. "Oh my goodness! What did you say?"

Delilah smiled, relishing this bright spot in the sad news. "That I love him, too, of course. Mom, he is so great. I mean, he got into a fight Sunday"—her mom gasped, but Delilah plowed through without allowing her to ask questions—"which was really stupid, but it was in defense of me. How can I get mad at that?"

"How was it in defense of you?" she asked. "What happened? Did someone hurt you? Are you okay?"

"Yeah, I'm fine, I mean, I got a concussion, but I'm better now!"

"Someone gave you a concussion?" she shrieked. "I'll kill them."

Delilah realized that she'd forgotten to tell her mom about her snowboarding accident a moment too late. "Oh, no, I got the concussion while snowboarding. The guy Anthony fought with was just calling me nasty names and Anthony lost it."

"Does he lose it with you?" her mom asked quietly, her voice laced with concern.

"No, never. He is so sweet." Delilah drove past Adventures in Mistletoe but didn't see Anthony's truck. "He's been saving for ten years to build his dream house and he finally has all his ducks in a row and he wants me to be a part of it. He's got his business, the land, all the utilities in place . . . "

"Delilah, I don't mean to rush you, but with the exception of the fight and concussion, I haven't heard an end-of-the-world problem yet."

"I'm getting to it." Delilah took a deep breath as she took a side street back onto the highway. "All of this really good stuff with Anthony has been overriding all the badness, but then I got a letter today that they're selling my duplex. I have thirty days to move out and find a new place, but I can't afford anywhere else in this area. I can't live with Holly because it's not fair for her and her boyfriend to have me third-wheeling them for who knows how long. Anthony keeps talking about how he wants my opinion on his house, but I can't ask him if I can stay with him. It's too soon, right?"

"I don't know. I knew I loved your father pretty soon after meeting him."

"But you didn't just say, 'Hey, I know we just started dating and we're in the honeymoon stage, but do you want to move in together?'"

There was a heavy beat of silence before my mother agreed, "You're right, I did not say that. However, he did ask me to marry him a few months after we started dating."

"That's my point." Delilah stopped at the three-way stop sign, looking to the left at the curvy road that led to the Winters' farm and Anthony's place, but he wasn't home or out with tourists so . . .

Wednesday. It was set-up day for the Mistletoe Winter Games.

"Delilah? Did I lose you?"

"No, sorry, I lost my train of thought," Delilah said, making the right toward the town center. "What was I saying?"

"You were talking about it being too soon to move in with Anthony."

"Right. I have no idea if he is serious or not about this house stuff or if he is going to freak when he realizes I'm a stray puppy looking at him like he's got a doggy door I want to crawl into."

"That is a unique analogy," her mother said dryly.

"I just . . . I feel like the universe is trying to tell me that this is it and I should just bite the bullet and leave Mistletoe. Take the job in Colorado"—her mom make a loud clearing throat noise and Delilah rolled her eyes—"or some other equally well-paying position and settle in somewhere else."

"What about Anthony?" her mom asked.

"I don't know. This is where I need your sound, motherly advice."

"Oh, you want my advice now, huh?"

Delilah rolled her eyes. "Alright, any more of that and I'm going to lose service."

Her mother laughed. "I would be honest with him, honey. If he isn't ready, then you two know you are in different places. That way you know if you have to leave Mistletoe, you either need to make it work long distance or let it go and see if you get a second chance with him down the road. Sometimes relationships are all about timing."

"Our timing has been awful, but I thought things were finally coming together."

"Can I give you my unbiased opinion? No ulterior motives?" she asked.

"Sure."

"I think that you are afraid to tell him everything because you don't think he can handle it, which means you're holding back because you're unsure you can trust him."

"I trust him."

"Not as a person, sweetheart, but with your heart. You love him, but if you give him all your troubles and ask him to be your partner, you think he's going to run."

Delilah parked the car along the edge of Mistletoe Community Park, closing her eyes against the truth. How many times had she told Holly she thought he was going to panic? That he was a coward?

Maybe he wasn't the only one.

"Thank you," Delilah said.

"For what?"

"For listening."

"Anytime, my darling," her mother said, and Delilah could hear the smile in her voice. It made her miss seeing that smile in person.

"I've been thinking that maybe I could come see you guys this weekend?" Delilah said abruptly. "Maybe stay the night?"

"Of course, but aren't there a bunch of Mistletoe Christmas events going on?"

"Yeah," Delilah said, watching the garland that the town had stretched along the play structure sway in the wind, "but you know I'm not really into that stuff."

"Well, if you want to come down here and hang, I will not argue. I miss being able to see my girl anytime I want."

"You know, you guys could always sell your house and move back up here."

"Now, you told me I couldn't do that to you," her mother scolded.

Delilah grinned. "I know, but you left yourself wide open."

"As beautiful as it is up there, I can't do more than a few inches of snow and neither can your father." There was a brief pause before her mother came back with a wheedling tone. "You know what might get us back up that way someday?"

Delilah realized what her mother was about to say and shouted, "I love you, hanging up now."

"Grandbabies! Lots of cute grandbabies. I love you, too!"

Delilah ended the call, her body shaking with laughter. Her mom was amazing, the best person in the whole world.

But she always had to find some way to be a giant pain in the ass.

Delilah climbed out of the car and headed toward the crowd of people setting up tents. The roar of a chainsaw buzzed to life and Delilah was a little afraid of the kind of winter games Adventures in Mistletoe had in store for them.

As she drew closer to where the games would take place, she noticed several men on the outdoor skating rink in full hockey gear running drills.

"Delilah!"

She turned at the sound of Anthony's voice and spotted him jogging toward her across the snow-covered lawn, his unbuttoned flannel flapping behind him like a cape. With all the work he and Pike had put into this event, she could believe he was a superhero.

"Hi," she said, lifting her face up for his kiss.

Anthony started to lean down and winced, clutching the back of his neck. "I can't wait until you are healed so I can pick you up. All this bending over is giving me a crick in the neck."

"Shut up," she said, laughing. He grinned before leaning down and finally giving her a hello kiss, fast and sweet.

"How are your ribs?" she asked.

"Better. You should see Pike's eye though. It's more green than purple."

"That sounds gross," she said, watching several mean waving chainsaws in the air over his shoulder. "Can I ask what the chainsaws are for?"

"We're filming a horror film. *Mistletoe Christmas Chainsaw Massacre*," he deadpanned.

"That isn't even clever. It's too long and wordy."

"It's a working title," he quipped. "We can workshop better ones later." He slung an arm over her shoulder, leading her toward the noise. "No, the chainsaws are for the ice sculpture contest."

"You're going to have people carve ice sculptures using chainsaws?" Even out loud it sounded insane. "Did you make sure the ambulance would be on sight or are we to watch people bleed out in the snow?"

"You have a gruesome imagination, but no. We are taking precautions and the people signing up are professionals. It's the relay race where all bets are off."

"What are you doing for the relay race?" she asked.

"The players are going to start by the elementary school," he said, pointing at the hill in the distance that blocked the view of Mistletoe Elementary, "and work their way to the park, gathering their snowmen supplies using a set of clues."

"Like a scavenger hunt?"

"Yes, I was inspired by the night we officially met."

Delilah snorted. "We've known each other for years."

"Not really," he said, leaning down to nuzzle her ear. "We knew *of* each other, acknowledged the other's existence, but didn't *know*-know each other until that night."

"You have a point. Continue."

"So, the track will run from the elementary school to the hill, where the first person will sled down. The sledder tags in the skier at the bottom of the hill, who will cruise down Main Street, finally tapping in our reindeer—"

"Reindeer?" she questioned.

"Yeah, the person who runs the final leg will have to put on a reindeer costume and gather up the rest of the scavenger hunt supplies while dodging snowballs."

Delilah shook her head. "I feel like you're doing too much here."

"I disagree, but I will let you have your opinion. The third player will build an epic snowman using only what they gathered. First to finish wins the race."

"It sounds like chaos," she laughed, scanning the people and tent, her attention returning to the men skating in full hockey gear. "What are the hockey guys doing on the outdoor rink?"

"Oh, we're going to have a hockey game as the finale."

"Um, are you playing?" she asked, her heart thundering in her chest. "Yeah, why?"

"Because I like your teeth right where they are?"

Anthony kissed her forehead. "I'll be fine."

"Hmmm, those skates are also super sharp. They could easily slice your balls and then that would be all she wrote."

"Okay, I think someone has been watching too many Christmas horror films and not enough *Rudolph the Red-Nosed Reindeer*."

"Rudolph is a horror movie," she argued. "Rudolph was bullied and his friend was eaten by a yeti."

Anthony burst out laughing, wrapping her in a hug. "Man, what is with you? You have a bit of the Grinch in you today. What do I need to do to make your heart grow ten times bigger?"

Delilah sighed. "Sorry, I just got some bad news is all."

"You want to talk about it?" he asked.

"No," she said, returning his hug. "I want to spend time with you and hear more about these wild winter games."

"Oh, I like that. Remind me next year to use that."

Delilah's chest tightened, hoping that there would be a next year for not just the games, but the two of them together.

Chapter Twenty-nine

Anthony parked his truck against the curb in front of his brother's Airbnb, throwing it into park. It would be nice to have his brother and his family visit during the holidays, especially as he hoped to share all future festivities with the woman sitting beside him.

"This is a nice place," Delilah said from the passenger seat, staring out the window at the beautiful three-bedroom house in one of the newer neighborhoods. They were built just outside of town to accommodate the one-acre parcels that went along with them.

"My brother has good taste."

"Are you sure I should be here? He invited you to dinner and I don't want to impose."

"How could introducing my brother to the woman I'm in love with be an imposition?" Anthony leaned across the seat and kissed her, sensing an unease in her that had been hovering beneath the surface since yesterday. Anthony didn't have any doubts that she loved him, but maybe all his house talk made her feel rushed or uncomfortable and she didn't know how to tell him.

"I don't know. I'm just nervous. I've never been brought home to meet a guy's family."

"Technically this isn't home. It's like a glorified hotel."

"Whew," Delilah breathed, pretending to wipe sweat off her brow, "pressure off then."

"If you'll recall, I spent an entire weekend with your parents."

"We weren't technically together then."

"Are you saying it doesn't count?" He placed his hand over his heart, feigning affront. "I think it counts, especially since I lost nine years off my life each night you snuck into that basement, worrying that your dad was going to hear you when you came."

Delilah covered his mouth with her hand, giggling. "Stop. I am not that loud."

"Oh, baby, even with your face buried in a pillow, I guarantee they heard you. The looks your dad gave me the next day chilled me to the bone. I kept waiting to wake up and find him hovering over me with a socket wrench in hand, ready to beat me to death."

"You know," Delilah said, stroking her chin thoughtfully, "I used to wonder how you and Pike were such good friends because you seemed so different, but I see it now."

"What's that?" he asked.

Delilah leaned in and gave him a quick, hard kiss. "You're both drama queens."

"I resent that! I prefer to be called theatrical." Anthony climbed out and rounded the front of the truck, but she had already exited before he could open her door. "You're getting faster at climbing out of the truck. I'm going to have to step up my game to be a good boyfriend."

"I don't care if you get my door. Just don't leave me alone tonight. Your brother is probably going to take one look at me and wonder what you're doing with me."

Anthony glanced down at her in a light blue sweater and jeans and had no clue what she was talking about. He circled her neck with his arm and bent down to kiss the top of her head. "No, he is going to think I tricked you into coming with me tonight."

Delilah snorted and when they reached the other side of the street, Anthony leaned over, cupping her chin to make sure she was paying attention. "Hey. I love you and they will, too."

Delilah nodded and he kissed her like they had all the time in the world.

Suddenly, the door flew open and Lillianne came running out. Anthony had seconds to release Delilah and catch his niece on the fly, holding her in the air with a laugh.

"You better be careful, Lil! You keep trying to catch me off guard and one of these days you're going to get dropped."

"You won't drop me," she said, her young voice sure. Lillianne looked over at Delilah, her voice sweetly curious. "Who are you?"

"I'm Delilah."

Lillianne looked at Anthony, her forehead furrowed and her tiny pink lips pursed thoughtfully. "Is this your girlfriend?"

"She is," Anthony said, balancing his niece on his hip. "I thought it was time for my two favorite girls to meet."

Lillianne seemed to consider this with her head cocked to the side and finally broke the silence by asking, "Do you like dolls?"

Delilah smiled. "I love dolls, although it's been a while since I've played with them."

"Mom got me a new one because my mean cousin broke my first one, but Unca Antney got her back. He stole her game."

Anthony burst out laughing at Delilah's horrified look. "Stole is such a strong word."

"My little brother is like Robin Hood," Bradley called from the doorway. "Only he steals from the naughty and gives to the nice."

Anthony took her hand with his free one, leading her up the walkway. "Har har."

"So, he's Santa Hood?" Delilah quipped, squeezing his hand.

Bradley chuckled. "Exactly. My wife is going to love you. You two have the same sense of humor." Bradley leaned inside, calling, "Audrey! Anthony is here with his guest."

Bradley stepped back and let Anthony and Delilah pass by. Lillianne squirmed out of her uncle's arms and took off for the back room. "I'm going to get my doll."

Audrey leaned out of a door down the hall, calling after her in a stage whisper, "Don't wake your brother!"

"I won't," the little girl responded loudly.

Audrey shook her head and padded down the hallway in bare feet, holding out a hand to Delilah as she drew nearer. "Hi, I'm Bradley's wife, Audrey. You're Delilah?"

"Yes. It's very nice to meet you."

"Likewise." Audrey shot Anthony a wicked smile, her eyebrow arched. "Not sure I've ever met one of Anthony's girlfriends before."

"That's because he hasn't brought one around," Bradley said, grinning. "You must be pretty special."

"She is," Anthony said, pulling her closer to his side.

"Well, come on in and sit down," Audrey said, leading the way into an open living room to the left of the entrance way. "I want to hear all about how you two met."

"Oh, boy, that's a weird one," Delilah said.

"I wouldn't say that," Anthony argued. "The first time we met was at Holly's . . . sixth birthday?" Anthony took a seat on the couch, pulling her down with him. "Pike and I were spending the night with Nick and his mom told us to leave you girls alone."

"You remember that?" she whispered.

"Well, you were wearing that fluffy blue dress with the different color bows on the skirt. It was such an eyesore, it was hard to forget."

Delilah pinched him and he playfully whimpered, "Ow, be gentle! I'm injured."

"I noticed the bruise, although it looks like it's almost healed," Bradley said, pointing to his cheek. "What happened?"

Anthony shrugged. "Some guy thought he was clever and I needed to set him straight."

"Okay, stop," Delilah laughed, shaking her head at him, "you sound 'cringey' as my students would say. You are not the tough guy you pretend to be."

"That's not what you said when I was defending your honor against six ruffians—"

"Preppy snowboarders, you mean."

"Lila, you're supposed to support my exaggerations," he groaned.

"Whoops, sorry"—she cleared her throat playfully—"it was actually two giants, an ogre, a Skin-walker, and two ruffians."

"That's what I'm talking about," he said, hugging her to him.

"Stop manhandling her, brother," Bradley said, leaning back in the recliner chair. "Or I'm going to get a squirt bottle."

"Oh, quit it," Audrey said, grinning. "They're adorable."

"Nauseatingly so," Bradley said, dryly.

Anthony pointed a finger at his brother, "Watch it!"

Audrey ignored them both, focusing on Delilah. "So, I take it you're a teacher, Delilah?"

"Not quite. I sub at the middle school a couple times a week and I work as a freelance writer at the moment. I'm looking for a position that's remote, so I can stay in town, but those are hard to come by."

"Really?" Bradley said.

Lillianne returned with her pretty new doll and climbed into Delilah's lap. "This is Lilli Two."

Anthony watched Delilah ooh and aah over the doll. "Hello, Lilli
Two. I'm Delilah One. It is a pleasure. That dress you are wearing is
simply divine."

"Thank you so much. I like your sweater," Lillianne pretended to
speak for Lilli Two in a high-pitched voice.

"Thank you!" Delilah caught him watching her and winked, "What
do you think of Uncle Anthony?"

"He needs a haircut," Lilli Two responded solemnly.

"Why am I getting picked on by everyone?" Anthony grumbled.

Lillianne giggled and hopped down. "Mom, can I play my game?"

"Yes, go ahead."

The little girl scurried from the room, dragging her doll behind her.
When the doll's face bounced against the step, Anthony winced. "You're
going to break Lilli Two's nose if you don't pick her up!"

"Okay!"

Audrey shook her head. "I wonder if there is a limit on how many
times a doll can be replaced."

Delilah giggled. "I'd have a closet full of them until she outgrows
them, just in case."

"Good plan," Bradley said, grinning. "Back to what we were talking
about before our daughter came in and stole the show, if you're looking
to settle down and stop freelancing, there is a copywriter position opening with my company after the New Year. And it's a remote position,
great benefits."

Anthony watched Delilah's cheek flush, her gaze flicking between
him and Bradley. "I . . . sorry, but wouldn't that be weird? Working for
you while dating your brother."

Bradley shrugged. "Not for me. You wouldn't be working directly
for me anyway, but for a branch of my company out of Coeur d'Alene.
I'd have nothing to do with whether you got the job or not, but I know
they are always looking for good writers, so I could get you the information for where to apply."

Anthony didn't say anything to urge or discourage her, afraid he'd
spook her if he seemed too eager. He hadn't wanted to talk about the
Colorado job, but it had been hanging over his head like an axe waiting
to strike a chopping block. She hadn't talked about it, so he assumed
she'd turned it down, but if she hadn't, that could be why she seemed
stressed.

"Thank you, I'd appreciate that," Delilah said, and Anthony almost sighed in relief. Not that she had agreed to take the information, but that she was open to options besides moving out of town and leaving him. They were just getting started.

"Anthony said you are looking to move back here?" Delilah asked.

"Yes, we're putting our house on the market up there," Bradley said.

"We want at least a three bedroom," Audrey added to the conversation, reaching out to take her husband's hand. "With a little land to give us space from our neighbors. We're not flashy people, but it's nice to get what you want."

"I'd say the duplex I'm renting is coming up for sale, but it's only a two bedroom."

Anthony frowned. "Your rental is being sold? When?"

"Uh, I got a letter yesterday. I have thirty days to find a place."

His surprise melted into frustration that she'd been holding on to this for over a day and she didn't want to tell him. Why? Because she was still considering leaving and didn't want him to talk her out of it?

"Why didn't you say anything?" Anthony asked.

"I'm still in shock, I guess," she murmured. "I've been there since I moved back after college, but I've got options."

Anthony wanted to ask what her options were, but he felt his brother and sister-in-law watching them closely. He didn't want his questions to sound like an interrogation.

"It's good to be open to new opportunities," Audrey said, releasing Bradley's hand. "When I graduated from college, I was living with four roommates in a three-bedroom house. Bradley was my next-door neighbor and got sick of not being invited to our awesome parties."

"First of all, I got tired of the loud music when I was trying to sleep."

"Tomato, potato," she shot back with a grin. "You were just jelly because you wanted to be one of the cool kids, you nerd."

"Seems like it worked out for you," Delilah said.

What about us, Lila? Is everything going to work out for us?

"Yes, I was coming home from work one night and my car broke down." Audrey turned her attention to her husband, her expression softening. "Bradley stopped and offered me a ride. And that was all she wrote."

"I think there was a little more to it than that." Bradley smirked. "I remember begging you to go out with me and you said I was too uptight."

"You were uptight," she laughed, getting up out of her chair and leaning over to give him a lingering kiss. "That's why I knew you needed me. I loosened you up."

"That's true."

Audrey straightened, transferring her attention to Anthony and Delilah. "Anyone want something to drink while I'm up?"

"Water, please," Delilah said.

"A Coke if you have it."

"I'll be right back," Audrey said, trailing her fingers over her husband's hand as she left the room.

That was what he wanted with Delilah. A future with a home, kids, and reassuring touches. Talking about their past and how they first met with fondness.

Anthony reached for Delilah's hand and squeezed it, giving her a warm smile. She returned it with a hesitant one and Anthony hated not knowing what was going on in her mind. Suddenly, he couldn't wait to get her alone and find out how he could help.

"Your brother and his wife are really nice," Delilah said several hours later as they left the Airbnb.

"They are." Anthony and Delilah followed the walkway out to the sidewalk, where Anthony took her hand and twirled her into his side. "I'm glad you and Audrey hit it off. I know Bradley and I talking about the Broncos and the Seahawks got a little heated, but we were just goofing."

"Honestly, I expected another brawl to break out." She shook her head. "I will never understand getting so aggressive about a sport."

Anthony shook his head in disbelief. "It's the Broncos. This is important," he said, opening her door and holding out a hand to assist her. "Just wait. Next year I can't wait to see you in a Broncos jersey, screaming your head off every Sunday. I will make a fan out of you yet."

"Hmmm," Delilah said, making a face in the truck dome light, "blue and orange are not my colors."

Anthony stuck his tongue out at her and closed the door on her laughter, going over the conversation he'd been practicing for hours in his head as he walked around the truck bed. He was going to ask her if she really had a plan for a new place to live or if she was putting on a brave face, because either way, he wanted to be a part of her decision. To let her know he was here to support her because he had plans.

Anthony hopped into the driver's seat and started the truck up, rubbing his hands together as the heater kicked on with cold air. "That temperature really dropped, huh?"

"It sure did." Delilah didn't offer up anything else, staring out the window at the darkened street.

He put the truck in drive, heading toward her home, which was only a few streets over. There wasn't much time to have the conversation he'd been dreading for hours, afraid he was going to say the wrong thing and piss her off.

It's now or never, man.

"Delilah," he said, clearing his throat nervously, "I need to ask you something and I want you to be honest."

"Okay," she drawled, turning in the passenger seat. "Shoot."

"Are you in trouble?" Anthony asked.

"You're going to need to be more specific, since trouble is a euphemism for any number of issues, including unplanned pregnancy, which I am not since we haven't—"

"I mean are you in a tight spot?" There. Not as tactful as he'd planned to be, but the Band-Aid was ripped off. "You've been on edge the last couple days and then you bring up losing your rental tonight out of blue."

"I didn't want to put a damper on the evening."

"I appreciate that, but I hope you know that if you need help, you just have to ask."

"What do you mean by help?" she asked slowly, a wary edge in her voice.

"I mean, if you need to borrow some money to get by—"

"I am not going to take money from you," she said curtly.

Anthony looked away from the road at her stiff posture and set jaw, cursing himself for not saying the right thing. "Lila, I love you. I'm not trying to insult you. I just want to help you."

"I don't need you to take care of me, Anthony." Her tone was sharp and precise, leaving him with the impression that he had definitely crossed a line he hadn't known existed. "Like I said, I have options. They might not be great options, but if it means not owing anyone or taking advantage of my friends, then that's what I'll have to do."

"What do you mean, taking advantage of your friends?" he asked.

"Holly already offered to let me stay with them, but I'm not going to do that."

"That seems like a temporary solution that works perfectly for now, so why not?"

"Because they deserve to have their privacy without me invading their space."

You can invade my space.

It was on the edge of Anthony's tongue to tell Delilah that his trailer was hers, but if she reacted so heatedly to him offering to loan her money, he was afraid asking her to move in would send her over the edge.

Proceeding cautiously, he queried, "What are your options then?"

"I could always stay with my parents for a little while. Just until I got back on my feet."

"In Boise? You would rather move two hours away from your friends and me than accept help when it's offered?" Throwing caution to the wind, he continued, "What about my place?"

Delilah sucked in a breath. "You want me to stay with you?"

"Why not?" he said, warming up to the idea. "I've been including you in plans for my house and you're into that."

"Anthony, deciding to move in together because we want to is different than doing it because we're afraid our relationship can't survive a little distance."

"It's not that it can't survive, but why do you need to leave if I'm offering you a place to stay?"

Anthony pulled up to her duplex and put the truck in park and waited for her to respond. Finally, Delilah turned to face him, reaching for his hand and he let her take it.

"There is a difference between us talking about building a life with each other in a home six months from now rather than you offering your trailer up like a sacrifice." He opened his mouth to argue, but she help up her hand, silently asking to finish and he let her. "I don't want either one of us to feel pressured into moving too fast or making a decision that could put an unequal strain on our relationship."

The weight of her words crushed him and he whispered, "Are you saying you're afraid I would hold it against you if you moved in with me?"

"No," she protested, her voice coming out high and squeaky.

"Are you sure? Because that's what I took from that."

"I think you could grow to resent me for invading your space."

"Why do you think that?" he asked, dumbfounded that this conversation had taken a complete left turn off a cliff.

"You've never lived with anyone except your parents, right? We'd be tripping over each other in that trailer and you'd start resenting my hair everywhere or Leia waking you up at five in the morning to go to the bathroom."

"And you've lived with so many people that you know this for sure?" Anthony hated the cutting edge to his voice, but he'd been talking with her about the house he was building for weeks, inviting her into his life. Yet she was writing him off as a bachelor so set in his ways he couldn't share his space with her? Did she think he was blowing smoke up her ass when he'd told her that he would take Leia out at night to go to the bathroom? What did he have to do to convince her that he wanted her in every aspect of his world?

"No, but it's a safe bet and I don't want to take the chance that I'm right." Delilah unbuckled her seat belt and crawled across the console to straddle his lap, and he moved the seat back to give them more space. "Can we just stick to our original plan and take this slow? I want to enjoy being with you and not worry about anything when we're together. You know?" She kissed him softly and he let her, his mouth parting as she teased his lips with hers. "Be my happy place."

Anthony didn't say anything more, but her words resonated in him, because she was that for him. Not because she was an escape, but because she'd been the missing piece of a puzzle he'd been searching for. There was no way he was going to lose her now, but she wasn't ready to believe that he was in this. That he wasn't going to tuck tale.

Anthony had less than a month to convince her and he would do everything in his power to do it.

Chapter Thirty

Women poured through the double doors of the community center in droves, wearing sparkling formals and short, tight cocktail dresses and everything in between. The Parade of Lights had ended almost an hour ago, but they were still waiting on several bachelors to finish getting ready. Delilah and Holly stood by the doors, handing out programs and directing women inside to Merry, who had their numbers and table assignments. For being such a crunch-time event, it had come together well.

Knock on wood.

The committee had really outdone themselves with the decorations. One side of the community center had dozens of tables with white linen tablecloth and floral centerpieces. Twinkling fairy lights were looped across the ceilings, and the lights had been dimmed to give the room an almost starry night effect. Everyone seemed happy with the results. Mostly everyone.

A blond woman in her thirties took a program and flipped it open in front of her. "I'm just disappointed they waited until now to host one of these." She looked up, meeting Delilah's gaze, but speaking to her brunette friend with the pointy red nails. "There are several men not on this list I would have happily dumped money into."

"I think he's cute," her friend said, stopping on a page and holding it out to her.

"Hmmm, definitely tempting. Let's go find our seats and browse the merchandise."

This really is like a meat market, Delilah thought, her stomach lurching at the thought of these women talking about Anthony like a rack of lamb. Of ogling him. Betting on him.

Oh, God, what if I didn't bring enough money?

"Hey," Holly stage whispered, breaking through her panic. She pointed to her mouth and gave Delilah a wide, garish grin. "Smile. That dress is stunning, but your face . . . "

"What's the matter with my face?" Delilah asked

"You look like you're judging them."

"I do not." Although, she absolutely was, she couldn't admit that out loud. "I've just got a lot on my mind."

"You mean besides the fact that you may not have brought enough cash to buy Anthony?"

Delilah gasped. "How did you know I was thinking that?"

"I've seen several women flashing their wads and marking pages. Trust me, if Declan was on that stage, I'd be having a panic attack."

Delilah scowled. "I thought boyfriends were off-limits."

"Long-term boyfriends. Recently developed relationships are fair game."

"I'm not worried. I can always pull more." After all, what did she need rent money for if she didn't have a place to live?

Her conversation with Anthony haunted her, not because she thought that she'd made the wrong decision, but because she'd wanted so badly to say yes. He'd done exactly what she'd expected him to do, except him offering her money had been quite jarring. When he'd asked her stay with him, she had to bite her tongue to stop herself from saying yes. It wouldn't be fair to accept such a big gesture from him so early. What if they moved in together and it destroyed them?

"If it isn't the potential outbidding for your man, why are you a mopey ma?"

There was no use trying to downplay her circumstances, but Delilah didn't want Holly to fly into a dramatic fit. "Besides losing my place? Nothing, I'm grand."

Before Holly could respond, another swarm of women crowded the door.

"Hi," Delilah said, greeting a lady in her sixties. The silver-haired woman opened the pamphlet and disturbingly murmured, "Hubba-hubba."

Delilah did a double take. And some of these women complain about what men say.

"I told you our door and spare bedroom are open to you."

"I'm sorry, but doesn't Declan live there, too? Shouldn't you ask your boyfriend how he feels about your best friend coming to stay for an extended length of time? He already thinks I cock—er—cognitive block him." Her second grade teacher, Mrs. Wilton, gave her a look so terrifying, Delilah remembered why she still avoided the old bat.

"Of course, I'll clear it with Declan, but you are my bestie and you are without a safe, comfortable roof over your head. I am sure he will agree that we need to help you."

"I am not a lost puppy. I have an adorable dog, but I am not helpless."

"Oh, I forgot about Leia! Bonus puppy! Leo loves her."

"Debatable, but I'm not going to come stay with you and have Declan hate me more than he already does. That would be one more flip on my roller coaster of shh—taki mushroom," Delilah said, smiling at the reverend's wife as she passed.

"Declan doesn't hate you."

"Maybe not, but he wants time alone with you, which he will not get if I'm there."

"Where are you going to live then?" Holly asked.

"I don't know, I haven't figured it out yet."

"The offer stands."

"There is no offer until I hear it from the man you share a bed with." There was a gasp from Margaret Ulner, the cashier at the corner gas station and Delilah huffed. "Prude."

Holly giggled. "Maybe you should switch and take your butt behind the curtain. You're in no mood to cater to the masses."

"No, I absolutely am not." Delilah waved Nick over, who gave her a befuddled look. "What?"

"Here. Hand these out."

She held the programs out to him and he recoiled. "I'm a waiter tonight."

"I need to be the server for a minute," Delilah said waspishly, but when he didn't move, she gave him her best tearful gaze. "Please, Nick? Just a short break."

Nick sighed, taking the programs from her. "Fine. But if they start asking me how much I'm worth, I am out."

Delilah winked at Holly, silently thanking her bestie for sharing the weaknesses of all the men in her life. She passed by the dining room and entered the backstage area through the curtain. She weaved her way between gray, black, navy, and white suit jackets, looking for Anthony's broad shoulders. She spotted Pike first and snorted at his powder blue jacket and matching top hat.

"What's up, my fair laddie?" she joked, imitating a dreadful Irish accent.

"I'm not wearing a kilt, so your joke makes no sense."

Delilah ignored him as she got a real up close inspection of Anthony looking dapper as hell in a gray suit and white shirt. The bright blue tie he wore popped against the shirt. His hair was brushed back, drawing attention to those lush lips, high cheekbones, and those green, arresting eyes.

Anthony smiled at her, holding his arms out to the side. "What do you think?"

"Um, no."

Anthony laughed, the discoloration from the bruise on his cheek nearly faded. "What do you mean no?"

"You are not going out there looking like a snack in front of a roomful of horny women. My pockets are not deep enough to fight off the rabid hordes."

"It's just a suit," Anthony said, snaking his arm around her waist, his mouth grazing the shell of her ear. "Meanwhile, I can't stop thinking about getting you out of that little black dress later tonight."

Delilah shivered because she was just as eager to get him home and have him all to herself. They'd been good this week, allowing each other to rest and heal, but it was well past time for her to get the full effect of Anthony Russo's unrestrained passion, especially if their time together was running out. She wanted to have the memory of him giving her every last part of him to keep her warm in her sad, lonely years.

"Ten minutes to curtain," Merry yelled, making her way through the throngs of bachelors. When she spotted Delilah, she pointed. "You are supposed to be by the door!"

"I actually traded with Nick," Delilah said unabashedly. "I should be serving food or something."

"Then get out of here and do that!" Merry roared, pointing at Anthony. "No canoodling with the merchandise until he is bought and paid for!"

"Way to dehumanize me, Merry," Anthony called after her, earning a finger for his cheek.

Delilah sighed. "I better go before she comes back and boots me altogether."

"I love you," he said. Those three little words sounded like the sweetest melody and she wanted to hear them again.

"I love you."

"And I'd love it if the two of you weren't quite so nauseating," Pike said, grabbing his tie and pulling it over his head. "Please go before I hang myself."

"That's rude," Delilah said, making a face at Pike, "but I will go because I need to hit the ATM again. I want to be ready when they call your name."

"Good luck," Anthony said, green eyes sparkling and beautiful. If she were a man, or at the very least, a woman who lifted, Delilah would have thrown him over her shoulder and carried him out of there. As it was, she would just have to contend with the swarms of pick me's thinking he was up for grabs.

Delilah pushed through the sea of people, almost snickering when she spotted Brodie's face wasn't quite as healed as Anthony's or Pike's wounds. Although it wasn't the first time a man had targeted her looks after she'd turned him down, it was such a low blow that she didn't feel the least bit bad for him. He deserved the puffy lip and bruised ego.

Delilah relieved Nick from door duty once more, although he gave her plenty of side-eye as he retreated toward the kitchen. Luckily, the flow of traffic had become slower and less dense, as it was a few minutes to nine.

"Ladies and gentlemen," Merry greeted the room from onstage, a black wireless mic in her hand. She wore a long black dress that hid her adorable baby bump until she turned to the side. "Please find a seat and get ready for an evening of charity, conversation, and Mistletoe's finest bachelors!" The room erupted with excited screams and Delilah shot Holly a "what the heck did we agree to" look.

The lights flickered and music exploded from the speakers, signaling the start of the show, and everyone who was still standing started moving at once, scrambling to find their seats. Merry came back on the mic, waving at the crowd. "Thank you, everyone. This evening, I have the pleasure of introducing you to some of Mistletoe's finest specimens of the male species. Handsome. Hardworking. Intelligent. Athletic?" The last was said with a playfully suggestive tone and the crowd woo-hooed, only quieting down when Merry continued. "Remember that every bachelor is a prize and that we are raising money for our children and our community so dig deep and bid hard. Are you ready?"

The crowd erupted with wild hoots and hollers, until Merry read the first name. "Sam Griffin, come on out. Sam is a thirty-eight-year-old tattoo artist with ambitions to own a shop of his own again. He is over six feet with dreamy eyes and tattoos in all the right places. Shall we start the bidding at twenty-five dollars?"

"Twenty-five."

"Thirty!"

"Forty!"

The rapid fire of the bids were too fast to keep up with who was bidding what. Several more paddles flew into the air and Delilah watched the exchange nervously. She did not want to walk out of here tonight without Anthony, but these women were like ravenous wolves.

Maybe it was just Sam. He was a bad-boy commodity with a reputation and a huge fan base in Mistletoe. This type of bidding could be reserved for him and guys like him.

Holly came up alongside her and bumped her with a hip. "You're looking nervous again."

"I'm fine."

"Does Anthony know you're losing your place?" Holly asked, distracting her from the flurry of paddles.

"Yes, I mentioned it last night."

Holly poked her again. "And?"

"And nothing. He asked me to stay with him and I said no."

"Why did you say no?" Holly asked incredulously.

"Because I didn't want him to ask me to stay with him and then regret it. Or worse, we fall apart because it's way too early in our relationship for such a big step."

"I thought you were picking out drapes and shit for his house?"

"Yes, but that's fantasy," Delilah said, noticing the paddles were slowing now that they were closer to the eight hundred mark. "Moving into someone's studio trailer with your dog and fully formed adult habits is terrifying."

"Interesting. I thought it was building a life together and making plans."

"Are you trying to make me feel worse about my situation?" Delilah asked, turning to face her best friend.

"No, of course not. I just want to clarify and work through your decision so that you make it reasonably and not because you're terrified of the unknown. Maybe it's not Anthony you're worried about having a meltdown when previously formed habits are discovered."

Delilah set the programs down on the nearest table and crossed her arms. "You aren't suggesting that I would be the one to freak out over Anthony snoring or not putting the seat down?"

Holly shrugged. "You are an only child who has never lived with anyone, except me for a short time. Do you remember sandwich gate? You didn't talk to me for two weeks."

"Sandwich gate was about boundary issues! You took a bite of my sandwich without asking."

"Whatever you need to tell yourself, bestie. You better get ready," Holly said, pointing at the stage. "Your boy's up next."

Delilah glared at Holly's retreating back, only to straighten up when Merry called Anthony to the stage. He held his arms out and did a little turn, sauntering to the edge, and when a few women made as if they were going to reach for him, he jogged back.

Don't make too big a show, pal, or I'm going to need more cash.

"Anthony is a thirty-one-year-old local business owner who stands six foot three in his bare feet. In his spare time, he likes to partake in outdoor activities like quad-riding, snowmobiling, or waterskiing, and spending time with his beautiful girlfriend, Delilah."

Her mouth dropped, picking up one of the programs and flipping to Anthony's page. There it was, plain as day.

He'd included it in his profile, told the entire town they belonged together.

"As Anthony is in a serious relationship, he does not feel comfortable being auctioned off." The crowd of women started booing and hissing, some of them even shooting her angry looks. "However, his company, Adventures in Mistletoe, has agreed to donate generously. Not to mention his bachelor replacement is a young, virile firefighter whom you all might remember for running a car up the flagpole his senior year, give it up for Bladen Moon!"

Anthony took the stairs down into the crowd and she lost sight of him for several moments, or maybe it was the tears blurring her vision that made it hard to track him. The women in the crowd had forgotten about Anthony and Delilah as the blond man wearing a red suit and black button-down took the stage, dancing to elated cheers.

When Anthony stepped out from the crowd and made a beeline for her, Delilah's heart pounded rapidly with anticipation as his expression intensified the closer he got.

Hunger. Anthony looked ready to eat her up and she couldn't wait.

"Come on, baby, time to go. I got plans for you."

Chapter Thirty-one

The moment her front door closed behind them, Anthony reached for Delilah, his control snapping with the knowledge that this was it. No holding back or pumping the breaks tonight. He was going to make love to Delilah, although he wasn't sure how gentle he'd be this time. The pressure had been building up too long and too strong for him to go slow. He needed to make her his, to show her that there was nowhere else, no other man, nothing in this world that could make her feel the way he did.

At least, that was the goal.

Leia whined and Delilah murmured against his mouth, "I need to let her out."

"Hurry," he said, following behind her as she bent over to lift the cage door and release her dog. Leia bounded around them for a few seconds before she raced for the back door. Meanwhile, Anthony's hands gripped her hips, grinding his aching erection against her ass and she gasped, "Bedroom."

Anthony picked her up and dumped her over his shoulder, carrying her down the hall like a conquering Viking, ready to claim his prize. He dropped her onto the bed and reached for her feet, staring into her eyes as he removed first one black ankle boot, then the other.

"You and these dresses are going to be the death of me," he growled, gathering the hem of the black fabric and rolling it up over her thighs. Delilah leaned back on her elbows, her eyes heavy lidded, her lips wet and parted. When he had the skirt bunched at her waist, Anthony took the top of her tights and dragged them down her legs, the sheer black fabric ripping under his rough hands, but he didn't care. Anthony wanted inside her and any garment that got in his way wouldn't survive.

"I liked those tights," she murmured.

"I'll buy you new ones." He flung them across the room, staring down at the sliver of black fabric covering her pussy. "Is that a thong?"

"Yes?"

"Fuck, you're going to break me, love." Anthony took her thighs in his hands and flipped her onto her stomach, staring at the gorgeous globes of her ass exposed, that thin strip of fabric creating a little arrow pointing down and he wanted to follow it.

"Get on your knees." Anthony lifted her off the mattress and she balanced herself on her hands and knees like he asked.

"Such a good fucking girl," he murmured, tracing a finger from that little black triangle down between those sweet, lush cheeks. Anthony felt her shiver as he bent over and pressed a kiss against the small of her back, skimming the slim barrier of her thong until he found the soaked strip covering her pussy. Anthony rubbed his fingers against her, playing with her wet folds. She sucked in a breath as he slipped a finger underneath and inside, teasing her seam with slow, steady strokes.

"You're so wet for me." Anthony dipped his finger between her labia, circling her opening before pressing inside her. He curled his fingers, rubbing against the rough patch of her G-spot and listening to the hitch of her breathing with every swipe.

Anthony dropped to his knees on the floor behind her, and fisted his hand into her thong, yanking it to the side so hard it snapped. Without anything between them, Anthony added a finger inside her, his voice rough as he ordered, "Place your cheek against the mattress and hold on to something."

"What do you mean—oh God," she moaned sharply when he dragged his tongue over her pussy as he rubbed her G-spot in harsh circles. He sucked her labia into his mouth, tonguing her as she pushed back against him, giving him better access. Anthony loved her pussy, her arousal musky and sweet against his tongue, and when he felt the first spasm under his mouth, he nipped her flesh.

"Fuck, Anthony," she cried out, bucking against his mouth and fingers. "I I'm coming."

He didn't let up until he tasted her orgasm, lapping at her as her trembles subsided. When she collapsed on the bed, he climbed to his feet and shrugged out of his suit jacket.

"Roll over, Lila," he growled, staring down at the contrast of her black dress bunched at her waist, highlighting the gorgeous pale globes of her ass, the curve of her thighs, and the dip of her calves. She was amazing, but he was growing impatient. He needed to possess her, to feel her surrounding his cock, sucking him into her sweetness.

"Now, love. I want you to see what you do to me."

Delilah rolled over slowly and as he watched her sit up, leaning back against her hands watching him, he jerked his tie loose, a frenzy taking over him at the anticipation lighting up those gorgeous blue eyes. Delilah climbed to her feet, standing in the middle of the bed, a teasing smile curling the corner of her lips and his heart slammed rapidly in his chest when her hands gripped the bottom of the dress, pulling it over head. The black and satin bustier underneath had delicate pink flowers over the cups, her soft breasts spilling over the tops, and with the taste of her still lingering on his lips, he ripped open his shirt, crazed with the need to be inside her.

Delilah stepped across the bed and slid to the end, shyly reaching for his belt with her eyes lowered. Anthony wasn't fooled by her pretense, but he let her tease him, stroke him through his suit pants with one hand as she loosened his belt buckle. He grit his teeth, loving and hating the delicious torture her hands delivered until she finally pushed his pants down, revealing his dick stiff and pulsing.

"I remember thinking that it should be criminal to look that hot in a simple shirt and tie, but like this? You're put the fucking sin in sinew."

Anthony chuckled, slipping off the remainder of his shirt and dropping it to the floor. "Was that a line you just came up with?"

"Mmm, maybe." Delilah wrapped her hand around his cock, swiping her finger along the head. "I want you, Anthony. All of you. Inside me. Now."

"Fuck, Lila," he groaned, threading his fingers in her hair and gripping the strands in his fist. He bent over, taking her mouth in a hard, deep kiss, sweeping his tongue inside the way he did her pussy. Delilah pumped him, her hands sliding to the base, grazing his balls, and repeating the action until his balls tightened, pulsating with the need to come.

Anthony jerked his mouth away, sucking in air. "Delilah, I fucking love you, but if you don't stop touching my cock and let me get the rest of my clothes off, we're both going to be disappointed."

"Impossible," Delilah said, but she released him, stepping back toward the bed. To his surprise, she laid back on the comforter, and spread her legs, her hand traveling over the curve of her stomach. When it reached the juncture of her thighs, Delilah lifted her heels onto the bed, baring her to his eyes as her fingers sought between the folds of her labia. A sweet gasp escaped her and he was mesmerized by the circular motion of her fingers on her clit.

"Are you going to strip or am I finishing alone?"

One of his shoes hit the floor with a thump and Delilah released a breathy laugh. He couldn't take his eyes off her, which made getting out of his clothes more difficult, but he was enjoying the show too much to look away.

Finally naked and painfully hard, Anthony climbed onto the bed and crawled next to her, crushing his mouth against hers. His fingers gripped her hips, dragging her over his body until she sat above him, her wet heat taunting his turgid flesh.

"Are you on birth control?"

"Yes," she said breathlessly.

Without being told, she opened her legs and he didn't give her time to catch her breath. Anthony adjusted the tip of his cock between her pussy lips and thrust upward. Delilah held on tight to his shoulders as he rolled his hips, working his way inside her. Anthony watched her lashes flutter until she was completely seated, fingers curled against the wall of his chest.

"Holy shit, Lila. I should have fucked you that night in my truck. You're so incredibly perfect."

"See? Now, don't you feel dumb for holding ou—oh!"

No more short and slow. Anthony gave her three hard, fast thrusts, and paused, listening to her panting. "You were saying?"

"Don't fucking stop!"

Anthony took her demand to heart and picked up speed. The sound of their bodies slapping together and their harsh breathing filled the room and he lifted her higher, heard the sharp inhale and knew he'd found her spot.

"Be my good girl and come for me, love. I wanna feel your pussy clench around my dick."

Delilah cried out, the muscles of her channel clamping down around him and he held on tight, keeping up the rapid-fire thrusts until her shaking became soft trembles and she sagged against his shoulder, her lips pressing tiny kisses against his skin.

"Mmm, sex-god."

Anthony chuckled, his cock aching. "You're gonna have to hang on a little longer, baby. I'm not there yet."

Reaching behind her, she deftly unhooked her bustier clasps and slipped it down her arms until her breasts sprang free. Fuck, he wanted those babies in his mouth, but that meant pulling out of her and there was no way that was happening.

Anthony's hips flexed in hard, jerky motions, the soft brush of Delilah's lips against his neck, passionate murmurs and a rush of breath against his skin as she told him how amazing he was. How good he felt inside her.

And then she completely broke the dam by gasping, "I love you, Anthony. Forever and always, I'm yours."

Anthony, unable to hold back anymore, pumped into her, head thrown back, his body trembling.

"Yes, yes, yes," she whimpered, and the sound of her pleasure took him out completely.

"Delilah, fuck!" he shouted, his balls tightening almost painfully as he came hard, his dick flexing as he released everything into her, giving her all that he had.

When Anthony fell back onto the bed, he kept his arms around Delilah, who sprawled across him like a blanket.

Delilah lifted up and over him, and when he realized she was getting up, he grabbed her thighs, holding her against him. "Where are you going?"

"Bathroom to clean up."

"Now?"

"I told you! Women need to take care of things after."

Instead of letting her go, he cupped the back of her neck and brought her mouth down to his, kissing her roughly, far from ready to let her go.

When he finally broke the kiss, he rubbed his nose against hers. "You're never getting rid of me now."

Delilah laughed, a full-throated, contented sound.

"You think I'm joking, but I'm addicted to you, Lila."

She cradled his face in her hands and kissed him again. "I'm laughing because the thought never crossed my mind." Suddenly, she rolled off him and when he protested, she giggled. "Calm down. I'll be back in a few minutes."

Anthony grunted. "You've got one before I'm coming in after you."

"Weirdo," she teased before shutting the door.

Anthony stared up at the celling as he waited for her to return, thinking about what his next move was going to be. He'd been making a list of all the reasons that Delilah should stay with him, but he didn't want to scare her off. He was trying to go slow and live in the moment with her, but this was his first time being in love and while he planned on it being his last, Anthony wanted to enjoy every moment without holding back.

When Delilah came back into the room and climbed into the bed, Anthony settled her in along his body, his hand stroking over the soft skin of her back.

"Mmm, you're so warm," she murmured.

"I'm actually freezing," he admitted, and she sat up. Anthony maneuvered to the side so he could grab the blanket at the foot of the bed and cover them. "I've been thinking about tomorrow. When I kick Brodie's ass in the games, we should come back here afterward and have our own victory celebration."

"Hmmm, it would have to be a quickie. I told my parents I'd be coming for a short visit."

Anthony froze, thinking about the timing. Was she going to ask her parents if she could stay with them? Now, after they finally made love and made promises?

"Is there something wrong?" Anthony asked.

"No, why?"

"I don't know. I guess I thought you'd head down there closer to Christmas or they'd come up here for a visit."

"I've just been under a lot of stress this week and I thought a short visit with my mom might help me clear my head and put things in perspective."

Anthony bit his tongue, afraid to ask what she needed perspective on. Her mom already wanted her to move closer to them and now that the only things tying her to Mistletoe were Holly and Anthony, would her argument make sense? They were her parents, after all. She wasn't ready to live with him because she was afraid that they wouldn't survive taking such a huge step too soon, but living with her parents was doable.

"Ow, Anthony. You're holding me kind of tight."

"Sorry," he whispered, loosening his hold on her.

"Anyway," she said, snuggling against him, her leg slipping between his. "I'll be back Sunday or Monday."

"I'll be here waiting."

"I know," she whispered, sleepily. "This is your home."

What about you, Lila? Will you be my home?

She'd become so dear to him that the thought of her not being here, even temporarily, made his chest ache.

Whatever Anthony was going to do to convince her to stay, he needed to work fast.

Chapter Thirty-two

Delilah stood on the sidelines with Holly, Erica, and Ryler, waiting for the winter games to start. The park was packed with people there to watch, curious about this new event. Anthony told her to wait at the finish line for him, so that's where they set up their cheering section. The snow that had fallen over the last week had coated the trees and ground with a sparkling white blanket, and the large food and vendor tents were attracting a crowd. Many people were congregating around the outdoor heat lamps that were scattered around the park.

"I find it fascinating that someone picked up a chainsaw one day and thought, 'This is the perfect tool to make ice sculptures,'" Holly said.

"I don't give a fuck about any of this other stuff," Erica said, looking up from her phone in a huff. "I just want to see these guys play hockey. Hmmm, love hockey."

"I know. The only time I get a decent day of work out of you is in the off-season," Holly teased.

Erica scoffed. "Please, I know that ain't true because hockey isn't on while I'm working at the shop."

Delilah laughed, only partially listening to them talk. Delilah wanted to be here for Anthony since this was his baby. He'd put it together and planned everything with Pike, but a storm was going to roll through tonight and she didn't want to get caught in it on her way to her parents.

"What's got your knickers in a twist?" Holly asked, elbowing Delilah gently.

"Just thinking."

"About?" Holly prodded.

"Anthony's offer to stay with him."

"The gall."

"I'm serious, Holly."

"I thought that was a no go. Why are we rehashing it?" Holly asked.

Erica looked away from the stretching hockey players, frowning. "What are you two going on about now?"

"Delilah's boyfriend told her she could live with him but she's afraid it's too early."

"Huh?" Erica shot Delilah a wide-eyed look. "That makes no sense! What's wrong with the man who loves you offering to help?"

"I don't want him asking me to live with him out of obligation or pity. And I especially don't want him to offer me money because he thinks I can't take care of myself."

"Maybe he offered it because he knows you're in a tight spot and he, I don't know, *loves you*?" Holly said, giving her an exasperated look.

Erica shook her head. "For a woman who can write the hell out of a fantasy romance, you sure know how to complicate your own damn life. Just move in with the man and then maybe next time, you can pay me to edit your books."

Delilah laughed because Erica's edits had been line edits, mostly sentence structure and grammar. She'd even commented about how light the book was on issues, and now, she simply needed to polish the last-minute changes and format it. Once all that was done, she could publish it. Market it.

Have a mental breakdown if and when someone hated it.

Between being so close to having her dream realized and wavering between living with Anthony or not, she was a cauldron of emotions swirling and bubbling without an end in sight.

The crackling of a speaker preluded the cheerful announcement of Merry's voice. "We're ready for the first annual Mistletoe Winter Games. We'd like to thank our sponsors and organizers, Adventures in Mistletoe, for putting together this exciting, delightful event. Please be sure to visit our local vendors today for fun-filled crafts, holiday food and drinks, and more."

"Brings a new meaning to the eat, drink, and be merry part of the holiday," Erica mumbled, showing her empty wallet. "Events like this are put on to make us broke college girls feel worse."

Delilah pulled out a ten and held it out to her. "If I buy you a corn dog, will you feel better?"

Erica snatched up the money with a sniffle. "I may need a churro, too. I am very, very sad."

"Get out of here," Holly laughed.

Erica danced away with the last of her cash, but she didn't mind. The woman was helping her out when she didn't owe her a thing. The least Delilah could do was buy her a meal.

"We're almost ready to kick off the first annual Mistletoe scavenger race. All racers on your mark!"

"Scavenger?" Holly asked.

"Yeah, the participants in the first two legs of the race have to find all the pieces for the snowman that the people competing in the third leg build." Delilah was trying to get a glimpse of Pike because she very vaguely spotted Nick in the distance, waiting at the bottom of the sled hill, and Anthony hopping from foot to foot next to the large food tent. He looked so cute in his inflatable reindeer costume, she wanted to run over to him and throw herself into his arms.

"Huh," Holly said. "Well, that's weird. Declan and Sam are hanging out by the chainsaw tent. I'll be right back, okay?"

"Sure, I'll be here. I think this is the best spot to watch."

"Sounds great." Delilah figured Holly hadn't really been listening to her and watched her cross the park to greet her boyfriend and friend. Although Sam and Holly had electric banter that drove Declan crazy, Delilah knew that Holly considered Sam her other bestie.

Ryler walked up to Delilah with a white coffee cup in her hand and stopped alongside her. "Hmmm, this better not be boring or I'm going to chuck a snowball at Pike's head."

Delilah laughed. "I guess if it is, they won't have another one next year."

"Ooof, don't put that out into the universe. I actually want them to do well."

Delilah shot Ryler a curious glance. "I do, too, but I'm surprised you feel that way. I thought you and Pike hated each other."

"'Hate' is such a strong word," Ryler said, taking a sip of her coffee. "I prefer to think of it as mild dislike with a friendly dose of animosity."

Delilah shook her head. "Whatever you say."

"Everyone, get ready to cheer on your favorite holiday trio. The first team to complete the final task wins! On your mark. Get set." A loud bang sounded in the distance and Delilah kept her eyes peeled on the crest of the hill, watching for a flurry of motion.

"If he comes in last, I'm never letting him live it down," Ryler said.

"Look!" Delilah pointed to a redhead on a blue sled zipping down the hill. She bumped Ryler with her hip. "I guess you can't torment him now, huh?"

"Don't think that doesn't piss me off," Ryler said with no real heat.

Holly came back with Declan and Sam in tow, asking, "How are they doing?"

"Pike just handed off the bag of goods to Nick, who has to put on skis."

"Who came up with this idiocy?" Sam asked. A snowball caught him on the side of the head and he frowned at Ryler. "Did you just nail me with snowball, girl I don't know?"

"Why would I hit a stranger with a snowball? That would be really odd."

"Go Nick!" Delilah yelled.

Erica returned with a corn dog in one hand and a churro in the other, all smiles until Sam tried to take a bite.

"Hey now, get your own! You ain't pretty enough to share my food with."

Delilah was ready to scream at all of them to shut up as she watched Nick ski down the road, stopping every ten feet or so and picking something up. Someone in an orange parka was gaining on him.

"You can see them?" Erica asked.

"Barely," Delilah said, pointing. "I'm watching between a couple trees."

"Go, go, go!" Holly cheered, her voice fading as she squinted. "Wait, is that Anthony in an inflatable reindeer costume?"

"That had to be Pike's idea," Delilah said.

"I think it's genius," Ryler said, making Delilah grin. Ryler and Pike had been spending a lot of time together, always bickering and one upping each other. Maybe all that tension was turning into something more.

Delilah whooped when she saw Nick ski around the corner and hop up onto the lawn toward Anthony. Once Nick was within arm's reach, Anthony grabbed the bag and took off running toward the pile of snow just before the finish line in the inflatable suit that was several inches too short on him. Another reindeer was bouncing up and down like a frog behind him and when they hit the snow-covered lawn of the park, they were neck and floppy neck. Anthony was close enough that she could see the flush of his cheeks as he rolled each ball of his snowman into position and started removing items from bags. The inflatable suit looked awkward, and by the sound of his curses it was making the situation more difficult.

Delilah recognized the second reindeer as Brodie when he skidded across the snow-covered ground. He started picking up the snowballs to set them one on top of the other, but they kept rolling off. Finally, he looked over at Anthony and seemed to realize he needed to pack snow around each section to keep them in place, because he followed Anthony's lead. Brodie started gaining ground on Anthony and Delilah found herself jumping up and down anxiously.

"Come on, Anthony," she whispered, right before he stood up with his hands in the air and yelled, "Finished."

The last man hadn't even made it to the snowman section yet when he heard Anthony, and he waddled off in a huff.

Delilah could hear Brodie bitching and hollering about how Anthony must have practiced the course and had an unfair advantage since he created it. Anthony said something about Brodie being a sore loser and Brodie stood up and stomped away, yelling over his shoulder, "I'll see you on the ice."

"I know! I set up the match!" Anthony called after him.

"Anthony!" Delilah called, and the rest of the people around her, even Sam who wasn't exactly an enthusiastic guy, started cheering and hollering. Anthony spun their way in the blow-up costume and spotted them, waving back with a grin.

"I wonder how he pulled the short straw," Sam asked.

Anthony jogged over to them, the material of the reindeer suit creating a high-pitched noise, and Delilah giggled when he wrapped his arm around her, burying her in the material until she felt Anthony underneath.

He released her and fiddled around with something inside the suit until the low hum of the fan stopped. The material deflated around him, creating a brown, wrinkled mess, and he turned around, giving her his back. "Could you get me out of this thing before Sam and Declan start slinging zingers my way?"

"Wouldn't dream of it, buddy," Declan said, coughing to cover a laugh.

Delilah pulled down the zipper and held it open while he stepped out. He was wearing a blue thermal shirt and jeans, his hair damp and plastered in every direction. He looked like an adorable mess, and she reached up, waving him down so she could fix his dark hair.

Anthony obliged her, their noses nearly touching as she ran her fingers through his hair and tried to create some semblance of style.

"I'm going to be playing hockey in an hour, love. No sense in wasting your time when I'm going to just mess it up again."

Delilah gave up with a sigh. "Fine, but the mussed hair is supposed to be for my eyes only when you first wake up."

"This is different hair," he said, pointing at his crown. "This is 'I just got done running in an inflatable reindeer suit' hair versus 'waking up next to my beautiful woman' hair."

"My God, are they always like this?" Sam asked.

"Worse," Holly joked.

"Gross," he said, walking away from them without another word.

"See, if that had been you," Holly said, addressing Declan, "I would have chased you down for being rude, but that is only because I love you and care about what other people think about you."

"So, Sam can be an ass and get away with it, but I can't because you love me?" Declan asked.

"Exactly."

Declan shrugged. "Makes sense."

"I'm going to hike my butt across the park and settle up with the redhead," Ryler grumbled.

"Settle up?" Delilah called after her retreating back.

Ryler turned to face her, walking backward. "I may have bet against him and now I have to pay the piper."

"I'll see you when I get back," Delilah said, and Ryler waved in response. Delilah glanced up at Anthony and caught him hiding a frown a second before he forced a smile. She knew that her leaving for the weekend made him nervous, but she was running out of time to figure things out. She had to go now.

"So, what did you think about the games?" Anthony asked.

"Strange but entertaining."

"I'll take it," he said, kissing her. "I'm going to get changed for the hockey game."

"Okay. There is a storm coming in, so if I have to leave early, I hope you kick ass."

A shadow crossed Anthony's face but he nodded. "Drive safe. I love you." He pulled her in for a tight hug before kissing the top of her head and walking away.

Delilah's chest tightened at his reaction. "I love you, too."

Holly placed a hand on her arm, drawing her attention away from his retreating back.

"Do you really have to go to your parents' tonight?" Holly asked. "I feel like you're causing yourself more drama and stress by fighting the people who care about you instead of accepting help."

"My parents care, too. I just want to talk to them before I make any decisions."

Holly sighed. "Alright, but if you call me tomorrow and tell me you aren't coming back from Boise, I'm going to kick your ass."

Delilah hugged her. "I'm hoping to come up with a solution that makes everyone happy."

"Good luck with that."

Delilah glanced up at the sky, the darkening clouds making her nervous. "I should get on the road, but I don't want to miss his game."

Holly snorted. "It's just a small-town hockey game, not the NHL Championship. He'll be fine."

"Are you sure—"

"I'm sure he'd rather you go down there and get back early than leave late and get stuck in some storm system, scaring the daylights out of all of us." Holly gave her a gentle shove. "Be safe."

"I will."

Delilah crossed the snow-covered park to her car. Once she climbed into the driver's seat, Delilah called her mom, letting her know that she was on her way. She wasn't lying when she told Holly the entire point of this trip was so everyone could be happy.

She just hoped that this trip didn't mean disappointing Anthony twice.

Chapter Thirty-three

Anthony stood in the middle of the ice with his stick in hand, watching Brodie and Nick go head-to-head for the puck. It had been a few years since he'd played a game, but he was ready to dive in and take out his aggression on some of these guys. Again.

He scanned the crowd again, searching for Delilah, but there was no sign of her in the small metal bleachers with Holly and Merry. Anthony knew it was just a stilly scrimmage game, but he hated her making that two-hour trek alone, especially with a storm coming.

I should have offered to go with her.

Only would she have even said yes? The point of this impromptu trip was to talk to her parents. She probably didn't want her anxious boyfriend tagging along.

"Anthony, look alive!" Pike's loud order brought Anthony back to the present, where they stood on opposite sides of the makeshift center, waiting for Clark to release the puck into play. They were teams of five on five, although Declan had been a last-minute addition as goalie when Mr. Franklin had to bow out because his wife said he was quote, "out of his mind." Declan had played in a junior hockey league growing up, so he wasn't completely useless.

Anthony couldn't afford to be distracted, not when they had two snowmobiles on the line. Losing them would cut them down financially and Anthony wanted to kick himself for leveraging them to begin with.

Waiting for the puck were Nick and Brodie, staring each other down mildly. Anthony had wanted to be the one at center ice, but Pike was afraid one word from Brodie and they'd never get the game started.

The minute the little black disk hit the ice, Nick's and Brodie's sticks were all over it, knocking it across the ice where Pike snatched it up, carrying it down the ice toward the other team's goal, passing it back and forth between him and Paulie, their other teammate. Paulie lost his balance and pitched forward, leaving Pike alone. Anthony raced to help but Trip plowed into Pike from the side, knocking him off his feet and snatching the puck up, heading the opposite way. Nick caught him on the edge and checked him into the foam walls they'd set up around the perimeter of the outdoor rink, but Trip kept coming, winding back, and letting the puck fly into their goal past Declan's glove.

One–zero.

"Shit," Anthony said, collecting the puck and putting it back in the play. They were all out of shape and practice, whereas Brodie and his team had been playing in a rec league out of Boise for years. How had he forgotten that detail?

Anthony didn't know why he suggested hockey as a winter game, except that it has been a popular request among the people of Mistletoe when he'd sent out the email survey for activities. Like the Romans who watched the gladiators fight to the death, the townspeople were blood-thirsty and enjoyed the violence of the game.

Nick had the puck in his control and was racing down the make-shift rink with Brodie hot on his heels. Nick wound up his stick and hit the puck at the goal. The shot went wide and bounced off the metal pole of the net. Brodie picked it up, taking it back down toward their goal. Pike chased after him with Anthony too far behind to do anything and could only watch helplessly as they scored another goal.

"Declan, you are a giant!" Pike hollered. "Do something!"

Declan flipped Pike the bird and Anthony took a deep breath. Pike was losing his mind thinking about those snowmobiles, same as Anthony, but they couldn't start turning on their friends. It was his fault they were in this mess, not theirs.

"Declan, switch," Anthony hollered, skating toward the goal. He smacked the bigger man on the shoulder. "Thanks for doing this."

"You sure you want me out on the ice? If Pike mouths off again, I might trip him."

"As long as you wait until the game is finished." Anthony swallowed, hard. "We've got those two snowmobiles riding on this. We can't afford to lose."

"Shit, man," Declan said.

"What do you say, fellas?" Brodie said, grinning behind his mask as he skated by the net. "Should we say first team to three and stop this torture?"

"Whatever, I can do this all day, son!" Pike said behind Brodie, huffing and puffing with exertion.

I can't, Anthony thought.

"Anthony, look out."

Anthony realized too late he'd been so in his head that he hadn't seen Brodie racing straight for the goal. He braced for impact as Brodie launched him off his feet and onto his back, knocking the wind out of him. Brodie hovered over him and asked, "Are you okay, man?"

Anthony nodded, dazed.

"Yeah, I'm good," he wheezed.

To Anthony's surprise, Brodie held out a hand to him. Anthony took it and Brodie helped him to his feet. "Thanks, man. I appreciate it."

"No worries." Brodie took a step as if he was going to skate away but stalled. "Look, I know I haven't exactly been your biggest fan and vice versa lately. I don't even really know how it started, but I don't hate you."

"I don't hate you either. I just didn't like the way you talked about my girlfriend, even before she was my girlfriend. The way you discuss women in general, man."

Brodie shook his head. "You mean that thing with me and Trip in the locker room?"

"Yeah, that's what I'm talking about."

"You never just talk shit with your boys and don't mean it?" Brodie asked.

"You seemed to mean it when you told Delilah to her face you were just trying to fuck her because of her size."

"Alright, so I'm a jerk sometimes," Brodie admitted, "I fully admit it. I thought she was cute and when I tried to shoot my shot, you were always in my way." Brodie shrugged. "I guess I took it a little too far when she picked you and not me. I'm not exactly the guy women chase."

"Well," Anthony said, unsure if Brodie was extending an olive branch or if this was another trick. "A good way to get them to run in the opposite direction is to keep doing what you're doing."

"You're right," Brodie said, holding out his hand to Anthony. "I'll apologize to Delilah for my behavior. Are we cool?"

Anthony took it. "We're cool."

"And about our bet—"

"Hey," Pike yelled, "are we gonna braid each other's hair? Or are we gonna play hockey?"

Anthony would have choked Pike if there weren't so many witnesses. What had Brodie been about to say?

"Doesn't that guy ever get on your nerves?" Brodie asked.

"Yeah, but he's my brother." Anthony cleared his throat. "You were saying about—"

The other players started hollering at them to get on with the game. "After," Brodie said, tossing him the puck. Anthony dropped it, launching it back into play.

After twenty more minutes of chasing their tails, Anthony, Pike, and Nick admitted defeat, and Brodie and his team were crowned Mistletoe hockey champions. Anthony and Pike presented Brodie's team with a makeshift championship belt they'd ordered online. Brodie and Trip shook first Pike's hand, then Anthony's.

"We'll drop off the snowmobiles tomorrow," Anthony said.

"Yeah." Pike grimaced. "A bet's a bet."

"Actually, I have a proposition for you," Brodie said, grinning.

"You do?" Trip asked.

"I do. You obviously need a boat and I have one. How would you guys feel about a partnership? We can iron out the details, but you can rent my boat for a fee."

Anthony couldn't believe it. It had taken everything in him not to cry as he said they'd deliver the snowmobiles, and after everything, Brodie was standing here offering him another option? One that would grow their business instead of cripple it?

"I think—"

Anthony cut Pike off before he could fuck up and say something stupid. "We'd love to sit down and draft something up with you sometime next week."

"Great," Brodie said, nodding at Pike as they walked away, lifting the belt in the air.

"Why are you entertaining that asshole's proposal, after you've spent the last month wanting to pummel him?"

"Because renting his boat puts us in a better position than losing two snowmobiles, don't you think?"

Pike grinned, slapping him on the shoulder. "That's why you're the brains of this operation."

Anthony laughed, bringing Pike into a headlock. "Don't forget it."

While Anthony was changing out of his gear in the contestant tent fifteen minutes later, Holly barged into the room and approached him with her arms crossed over her chest. Her red hair was up in a high ponytail that swayed as she walked and Anthony couldn't help wondering how hair could be angry.

"I think she's going to do something stupid," Holly said.

Anthony waited for her to elaborate, and when she didn't, he prodded her.

"I'm going to need more than that."

"I think she is going to tell her parents she'll move in with them just so she doesn't have to inconvenience us."

Anthony's stomach twisted into a knot, but his voice gave nothing away. "Then that's her choice."

Holly glared at him. "I'm sorry, can I please speak with Anthony Russo, the guy who is desperately in love with my best friend and does not want her to move away?"

"What would you like me to do about it?" he asked. "I tried to give her options, and she brushed off every single one."

"Go after her? Make her see reason," Holly said, pointing toward the outside of the tent. "I have been doing my best to show her she belongs here but I need help."

Anthony's frustration mounted with every flailing hand gesture and he finally said, "I did help."

"Well try again."

Anthony sighed, dragging his hands over his face. "I don't know what else to do, Holly. I told her I loved her and I asked her to move in with me. I offered to help her find a new place and pay for it until she got back on her feet and she said absolutely not."

"But you didn't tell her that she was the one."

"Have you not been listening? That's exactly what I did." What was he missing? Anthony had offered her everything he had and somehow it wasn't enough to make her want to stay.

"You're coming to her like a white knight instead of like a boy-friend. What are you willing to do if she leaves? Do you want to be driving back and forth and not spending every night with her? Is what you have here more important than what you could have with her?"

"She's never been anyone's first choice," he whispered to himself, the realization hitting him like a ton of bricks.

"Wait, what?" Holly asked.

"I'm going after my girl."

Chapter Thirty-four

Delilah sat back and stared at the computer screen. She'd signed in to check the analytics of her book, even though she'd told herself to wait a few more hours, but she couldn't stand it anymore. Two thousand downloads was not a bad start when she'd only been posting about the book for the last few days on TikTok. Holly had helped her pick certain sounds and trends to hop onto and garner more views. As a result, her first book had gone viral after three videos.

Delilah switched over to the spreadsheet she had worked out with her parents, when someone knocked at the door. Her dad was in the garage and her mom was napping, so Delilah got up from the table and went to answer it. When she pulled open the door, Anthony was on the other side standing on her parents' front porch. His hair was mussed like he'd had it under a hat all day and he stared at her with big, pleading eyes.

"Anthony, what are you doing here?" she asked.

"I've been thinking a lot, and I know that you think it's too early for us to live together. So, if you want to take that job in Colorado or live in Boise to see what opportunities you have here, I fully support you and understand."

Delilah smiled at him, warmth spreading throughout her body. "You drove two hours to tell me that?"

"That, and if you decide that coming back to Mistletoe isn't in the cards for you, I will sell my property and follow you anywhere."

He finished, his breathing ragged, and her mouth hung open in shock. "What? Anthony, no, it's not—"

Anthony cut her off, clearly having more to say. "Delilah, I have never had this before and I don't know how else to show you that this is it for me. You are it for me."

"Your property is your dream," she protested, stepping out onto the porch with him. "You can't give up on building your house and running Adventures in Mistletoe for me."

"Delilah, of course, I can," he said, taking her hands in his. "From the moment we fell in love, you became my dream. Everything else just doesn't matter if I can't have you to share it with."

Delilah's eyes shone with tears. "You are such an idiot."

"Well, that's not very nice after he drove all this way and gave you such a romantic speech," her mom said, stepping into the doorway.

"Mom, can you please give us a little privacy," Delilah asked, giving Anthony a wide-eyed expression.

"Sorry, sorry." Her mom went back to the kitchen.

"What I was trying to tell you," Delilah continued, "is that I drove down here to talk to my parents about an opportunity I have on a fixer-upper property. The owner of the duplex I'm living in now said he would give me a discount on the rent if I agree to make improvements to the property. I didn't want to get scammed, so my dad was just telling me to get everything in writing. I thought it would be a good compromise instead of moving into your space. I would have my own space while we spend time together, building a solid relationship. And if you really want me to be a part of your home and future, then it won't be a situation where we *have* to live together; it will be because we *want* to live together. That's all I was ever trying to do. I didn't expect you to come and give up everything that you've worked so hard for me," she said, tears running down her face.

"I'm happy to hear that," Anthony said, bringing her into his arms. "I just want you to know that when it comes to you, everything else is a no-brainer."

"Even Pike," she teased.

"Oh, yeah, fuck that guy. Oops, sorry Natalia," Anthony called out to her mother, realizing the door was open and she could hear everything he said.

"That's okay, carry on."

Anthony laughed, his arms still looped around her waist. "So, does this earn me a check mark in the romantic column or the crazy-and-insecure column?"

"I'm going to put this in the one-of-the-million-reasons-why-I-love-him column."

"Hmmm, does that mean I can come inside now?"

"You may, but first, I want to show you something." Delilah whipped out her phone and signed into her sales tracking app, pointing at the screen. "Two thousand downloads of my book in just a day."

"I'm so proud of you," he told her with a beaming smile. "My girlfriend is famous."

"Thank you." Delilah stepped back, allowing him to pass inside. Anthony entered the kitchen where Natalia and Bernard were both sitting at the table waiting for them.

"Bernard, look who decided to join us."

"Anthony, good to see you."

Anthony swallowed hard, and Delilah bit back a laugh at his nervous expression. "It's good to see you, too, sir."

"Just to let you know," Bernard said, his tone pleasant and nonchalant, "I fixed the lock on the basement door, so if you're staying with us, you can lock it now to stop Delilah from sneaking down to the basement to have her way with you."

Anthony banged his forehead on the table. "I told you he knew."

"Well, if he didn't before, he definitely does now!" Delilah cried, nudging him with her shoulder.

"I'm sorry about that, sir. I tried to tell her no, but she insisted."

"So you're saying"—Bernard leaned forward, steepling his fingers—"you are the innocent victim and you did not defile my daughter under my roof? That she took advantage of you?"

Anthony looked at Delilah and mouthed, *Help me.*

Delilah laughed. "Oh no, no, no, no. you're trying to throw me under the bus! Now it's your turn and you must suffer."

"Just so we're clear, sir, I didn't defile her. I am in love with her. I even asked her to live with me when she got the letter saying she was gonna lose her rental."

"So not only did you defile her, but then you wanted her to live in sin with you?" Bernard thundered, launching himself to his feet. "You, sir, are a villain."

"Dad, stop." Delilah was laughing so hard she had tears rolling down her face.

"Anthony, he's messing with you," Natalia assured him, shooting a disapproving look at her husband. "Right, Bernard?"

"Am I? I don't know." He walked away from the table, calling over his shoulder, "I'll be in the garage if you want to find out, Anthony."

Anthony looked at Delilah and said, "For such a skinny, kind of nondescript guy, your dad's a little scary."

"You haven't seen her mom when Delilah's had her heart broken," Natalia said.

Anthony took Delilah's hand and squeezed it. "As I don't have any plans to ever break your daughter's heart, I hope I never do."

Epilogue

On Christmas day, Delilah and Anthony were visiting Anthony's brother Bradley and his family at their Airbnb. Delilah and Audrey were in the kitchen cooking while Bradley and Anthony were busy installing batteries into various toys and appliances. Delilah looked beautiful in a green off-the-shoulder sweater and Anthony couldn't stop staring at her, thankful that she was his.

Bradley raised a glass to Delilah. "To Delilah. May my little brother be good to you and I hope that joining my company will be a place you can call home."

Delilah had applied for the copywriting position and Anthony knew she was excited that the salaried position would give her more time to write.

Bradley's phone rang, and he looked at the caller ID, holding it up for Anthony's inspection. "It's Dad."

"Are you going to answer it?" Anthony asked.

Bradley pressed the answer button and set up with the phone to his ear. "Hey, Dad, yeah, I have. Merry Christmas to you. Just sitting in my living room talking to Anthony. Yeah, he's here, too. That's good, yeah, we're here in Mistletoe renting an Airbnb and spending time with him and his girlfriend. Well, I like it here. Cam and Paul and Grant are there, right? What about Evelyn? Divorced? Wow, I'm really sorry, Dad. No, I am. I think that's really sad. You guys were together a really long time. Maybe you can talk to her and work it out after the holidays. Do you want to talk to Anthony?" Bradley frowned, shooting Anthony an apologetic look, but he was okay. He'd never had a dad before, and sometimes people weren't supposed to be a part of your life.

Even if they were blood.

"Merry Christmas."

Bradley ended the call and Anthony laughed bitterly. "He didn't want to talk to me, huh?"

"I don't think he knows what to say to you. He doesn't even know what to say to his wife."

"Yeah, well, it is what it is, right? He wasn't there for me most of my life, so why would I expect to have a relationship with him now?"

"Honestly, man," Bradley said, putting his arm around Anthony's shoulder, "out of all of our siblings, we are the only two who have functional relationships with other people and aren't completely miserable human beings. That's because of Mom."

Anthony raised his whiskey glass in the air and smiled. "To Mom!"

Bradley clinked his glass with his brother's and smiled back at him. "You remember how every Christmas she would fill up the stockings and put them in front of the fireplace and tell us that if we came out before six she'd throw them in the fire?"

Anthony chuckled. "Yeah, I don't think she wanted a repeat of the year Grant and I woke her up at four o'clock in the morning when she'd just gotten in the bed at three."

"It's funny, I saw a meme the other day that the magic of Christmas is really just the love of a good mom."

Anthony looked around the Airbnb, which wasn't even technically their home, and yet there was a tree in the corner decorated with gorgeous bulbs and homemade ornaments with a light-up angel on the top of the tree. There were twinkling lights and garland on tabletops along with some other fun holiday trinkets that Delilah and Audrey had picked up while shopping in town. There was a sign on the counter that said Hot Cocoa Bar and little containers of marshmallows, sprinkles, and chocolate chips that Lillianne had been excited to drop on top of her hot cocoa. Audrey had done all these things to turn a rental house into a holiday wonderland for her family to enjoy.

"Is that how you feel about Audrey?" Anthony asked.

"Well, she's not my mom," Bradley teased.

"No, I mean do you think that the holidays have been more magical since you got together with her?"

"Yeah, I think so. Before I was just a lonely kid trying to get a degree and that made me a bitter old man like Dad. She brought something alive in me," Bradley said, smiling at his wife.

"I know what you mean," Anthony said. As he stared at Delilah, he couldn't help thinking how much he wanted this with her.

Delilah looked up from the potatoes she was mashing and sent him a sunny smile that he returned by blowing her a kiss.

Bradley laughed and told him that they were nauseating.

The sound of singing came from outside, and Anthony stood up and went to the door. A group of Christmas carolers were out in the front yard singing "Jingle Bells." Delilah, Audrey, and Bradley joined him as they watched the carolers.

Delilah gave Anthony a hug. "They're no Anthony and the Drunken Carolers but they're alright."

"That wasn't our group's name," he said, smiling down at her. "We also had a better song selection."

"Hopefully this group doesn't puke on me."

"You are never gonna let me live that down, are you?" Anthony asked her, holding the door for her to head back inside.

"Maybe in fifteen years or so, unless I do something equally embarrassing before then."

Anthony rubbed his hands together. "I'm sure eventually I'm going to catch you doing something wacky."

"It's not nice to hope for someone's downfall."

"I am not hoping for your downfall per se. I just want us to be on equal grounds."

"Well, you can just keep waiting, sweetheart, because I know how to hold my liquor, unlike all the men in Mistletoe."

Anthony's phone blared to life and he checked the caller ID. "It's Pike."

Delilah laughed. "Answer it, goofy."

"We already said Merry Christmas though!"

Delilah and Audrey were already heading back to the kitchen and Bradley was still watching out the window. When Pike called again, Anthony picked up the call.

"Shouldn't you be celebrating with your parents?"

"Listen, I need your help. I know you're with your brother, and normally I wouldn't ask, but I'm in fucking love and she's about to leave the country."

"I'll be out the door in twenty."

About the Author

Codi Hall is the pen name of Codi Gary, author of more than thirty contemporary and paranormal romance titles like the bestsellers *Things Good Girls Don't Do* and *Hot Winter Nights* and the laugh-out-loud Mistletoes series. She loves writing about flawed characters finding their happily-ever-afters because everyone, however imperfect, deserves an HEA.

A Northern California native, Gary now lives with her husband and their two children in southern Idaho, where she enjoys kayaking, unpredictable weather, and spending time with her family, including her array of adorable fur babies. When she isn't glued to her computer making characters smooch, you can find her posting sunset and pet pics on Instagram, making incredibly cringey videos for TikTok, reading the next book on her never-ending TBR list, or knitting away while rewatching *Supernatural* for the thousandth time. To keep up with all her hijinks, subscribe to her newsletter at codigarysbooks.com.

DISCOVER
STORIES UNBOUND

PodiumAudio.com